CW00358102

Return items to **any** Swindon libr
time on or before the date stamp~~e~~
and Audio Books can be renewe~~d - phone you~~
library or visit our website.
www.swindon.gov.uk/libraries

10/08/17

CEN

~~ob~~/14

HG ⇒ cen
5/7/116

26/08/14

02/09/14

22/09/14

⇒ CEN
16·5·16

08/18
Central Library

01793 463238

Copying recordings is illegal. All recorded items
are hired entirely at hirer's own risk

MUSIC 780·92

SwinDon
BOROUGH COUNCIL

ABRSM
6 803 523 000

First published in 2009
by ABRSM (Publishing) Ltd, a wholly owned subsidiary of ABRSM
24 Portland Place, London W1B 1LU, United Kingdom

© 2009 by The Associated Board of the Royal Schools of Music

ISBN-13: 978 1 86096 298 1

AB 2849

A CIP catalogue for this book is available from The British Library.
Design and formatting by www.9thplanetdesign.com
Typeset by Hope Services, Abingdon.
Printed in England by Page Bros., Norwich

Acknowledgements

Music extracts

Now does the glorious day appear, Purcell Society Edition, vol. 11 (1993), p. 24. By permission of Novello & Company Limited.

Dido and Aeneas, No. 6, Purcell Society Edition, vol. 3 (1979) pp. 13–14. By permission of Novello & Company Limited.

We are grateful to the following for the permission to reproduce photographs:

Front cover
"The British Orpheus": portrait of Henry Purcell, engraved by Robert White, after John Closterman. Frontispiece of *Orpheus Britannicus*, Book 1 (1698). By permission of the British Library, London.

Westminster Abbey from the River Thames. London, Westminster Abbey by Wenceslaus Hollar (c.1637–43). © The Trustees of the British Museum.

Inside pages
1. Map of Westminster in about 1680, drawn by William Morgan. Image © 2003 Motco Enterprises Ltd.

2. Bird's-eye view of Whitehall, St James's Park, Arlington House, and St James's Palace drawn by Leonard Knyff. © The Trustees of the British Museum.

3. "The English Amphion": portrait of John Blow drawn and engraved by Robert White. Frontispiece of *Amphion Anglicus* (1700). By permission of the British Library, London.

4. Interior of Whitehall Chapel, 1623. Illustration of His Majesty in England signing the Spanish Marriage treaty (1623). © The Trustees of the British Museum.

5. Westminster Abbey from the River Thames. London, Westminster Abbey by Wenceslaus Hollar (c.1637–43). © The Trustees of the British Museum.

6. Dorset Garden theatre: engraving by William Sherman. Frontispiece to Elkanah Settle, *The Empress of Morocco* (London, 1673). By permission of the Bodleian Library, Oxford.

7. Cross-section of Dorset Garden Theatre, in a conjectural model by Edward A. Langhans (1972). © Edward A. Langhans.

8. "God Bless Mr Henry Purcell 1682 September ye 10th". MU MS 88, fly leaf. By permission of the Fitzwilliam Museum, Cambridge.

9. Title-page of Purcell's *Sonatas of Three Parts* (1683). By permission of the British Library, London.

10. The crowning of James II in Westminster Abbey, showing Blow, directing the musicians in the gallery, wielding a long roll of paper as a baton. From *The History of the Coronation of . . . James II, King of England, and Queen Mary* (1687), by Francis Sandford, Lancaster Herald. By permission of the British Library, London.

11. "Poet Stutter": portrait of Thomas D'Urfey, oil on canvas, by John van der Gucht. By permission of Knole House, Kent.

12. "The Bashfull Thames": part of the Yorkshire Feast Song, *Of old, when heroes thought it base*, in Purcell's composing score. By permission of the British Library, London (Egerton MS 2956, f. 4v).

13. The masque in *Dioclesian*: conjectural model of the Dorset Garden stage and scenery by Frans Muller, 1993, based on the stage directions in the printed word-book. By permission of Frans Muller.

14. Queen Mary's funeral procession, showing the marching instrumentalists: engraving by Lorenz Scherm (1695). By permission of the Victoria & Albert Museum, London. Copyright © V&A Images/Photo Catalogue—All rights reserved.

15. Queen Mary's catafalque in Westminster Abbey, designed by Christopher Wren (from Francis Sandford, *Genealogical History of the Kings and Queens of England*). By permission of the British Library, London.

To Jana, my wife, who has made my work possible.

Contents

Acknowledgements

Although the writing of this book has involved much scrutiny of primary sources, any biographer of Purcell inevitably draws upon the work of previous scholars. In the 1920s Dennis Arundell published a compact and perceptive survey of the music, while Purcell's major stage works received particular attention from Edward Dent in his pioneering account of early English opera. The classic account of the composer's life and works by Sir Jack Westrup appeared in 1937. Franklin Zimmerman's magisterial biography, first published in 1967, is indispensable, not least for the wealth of original documents of which it includes full transcriptions. Curtis Price's detailed 1984 study of the theatre music remains unsurpassed. The tercentenary of Purcell's death elicited, *inter alia*, a searching biography by Maureen Duffy, a new appraisal of the works by Peter Holman (who had earlier chronicled the history of the royal violin band), an exhaustive analysis of Purcell's musical language by Martin Adams, and two important volumes of essays, one edited by Curtis Price and the other by Michael Burden. Renewed interest in the operas resulted in the publication in 2000 of an edition, co-ordinated by Michael Burden, of their complete texts accompanied by authoritative essays. Besides these volumes there are articles by many scholars on numerous aspects of Purcell's music and its context. I am fortunate to have had such a cornucopia available to me.

I must acknowledge a particular debt of gratitude to those who at various times have given me valuable advice, especially Dr Margaret Laurie, Professor James Winn, and Professor Sir Curtis Price. Helpful library staff, especially at the British Library and Westminster Abbey, did much to smooth my path. I owe most of all to Dr Andrew Pinnock, my research collaborator for nearly twenty years, who has been deeply inspiring. He has led me to sources of information about Purcell's music, and fresh ways of thinking about it, which I would never have explored without his prompting.

In one respect the book is entirely free of indebtedness: any errors that may have crept in are mine alone.

Bruce Wood

ONE

CHILDHOOD AND APPRENTICESHIP (1659?–1677)

A musical neighbourhood

The young Henry Purcell is a shadowy figure. Nearly all traces of his life during childhood have been obliterated by the passage of the centuries since, and the first surviving documents to mention him by name date from 1673, when he was already a teenager.[1] We do not even know exactly when he was born, for no record survives of either his birth or his baptism, and the only hard fact we have – from his memorial stone in Westminster Abbey – is that when he died, on 21 November 1695, he was in his thirty-seventh year. So he must have been born sometime between 22 November 1658 and 20 November 1659. Nowadays the year of his birth is invariably stated, without any caveat, to have been 1659, and that year is obviously the likelier, covering as it does nearly eleven of the possible months; but 1658, which used at one time to be accepted just as unreservedly, cannot be ruled out. Despite the lack of baptismal evidence, we do know that his godfather was a musician named John Hingeston (d. 1683), who had served as organist to Oliver Cromwell but was soon to prosper at the restored court of Charles II: a useful connection for the future.[2]

Purcell's lineage too has been debated. He was once believed to be the son of Thomas Purcell (d. 31 July 1682) and his wife Katherine, but it now seems fairly certain that his parents were another Henry (d. 11 August 1664) and his wife Elizabeth. There is compelling circumstantial evidence that Henry senior and Thomas were brothers. Both men were professional singers, Thomas a violinist too: and both were soon to secure prominent positions in the royal household. Their respective families also had a shared environment, for both men seem to have set up home in Westminster

---

[1] They are the two warrants quoted on p. 27, below.
[2] Hingeston's will included a legacy to "Henry Pursall (son of Elizabeth Pursall)": Zimmerman, *Purcell*, pp. 389–90.

during the 1650s. In late 1658 or early 1659 Henry and Elizabeth moved house, settling in Great Almonry, about a hundred and fifty yards from the west front of the Abbey – though this did not yet have the outline familiar to us nowadays: the imposing twin towers were not completed until 1740, when they were added to the medieval building by Nicholas Hawksmoor, a former pupil of Christopher Wren. The street pattern of the surrounding area has also changed a good deal over the years, and of Great Almonry itself no trace remains. It was roughly where the traffic now roars along Victoria Street that Henry Purcell the younger came into the world, to join two older brothers, Edward and Charles.

Westminster in 1659 was only a tiny city, joined to its larger neighbour London by a single urban artery: King's Street (now Whitehall). Yet among the Purcells' neighbours during Henry's early years were several of the most illustrious musicians in England. Christopher Gibbons (1615–76) had a house in the same street, and for a time Henry Lawes (1596–1662) lived next door, though he later moved across to Dean's Yard; while Henry Cooke (1615–72), in Little Sanctuary, John Banister (1624/5–79), in King Street, Thomas Farmer (d. 1688), in New Palace Yard, and John Wilson (1595–1674), in Dean's Yard, were all within a couple of minutes' walk. The reasons why this musical enclave had formed were not far to seek: the proximity of the Abbey itself, and that of the Palace of Whitehall, which lay immediately to the north. Whitehall Palace, a rambling warren of buildings of different periods and assorted styles, crammed together in a picturesque huddle, had been the principal residence of the kings and queens of England since time out of mind. Some of the distinguished musicians still living on in the neighbourhood had served its late royal master, while others had been members of the choral foundation at the Abbey.

At the time when Henry was born, all these men were eking out a precarious existence. The brutal Civil War of the 1640s had scattered what had been one of the most cultivated courts in Europe; and the same victorious Parliamentarians who had publicly executed the defeated King Charles I outside his own palace of Whitehall had also banned the services of the Church of England and, for good measure, one further potential source of at least some work for musicians – the professional theatre. But soon, while Henry was still a babe in arms, the palace would house a new king; later, when he had grown to adulthood, it would become one of the three focal points of his professional life, along with the nearby Abbey and a splendid theatre which would rise in 1671 a mile down the Thames from Whitehall.

His Majesty's return
In 1660, as the once vigorous Parliamentary republic collapsed in decay, Charles II was invited back to London, to be restored in due course to the

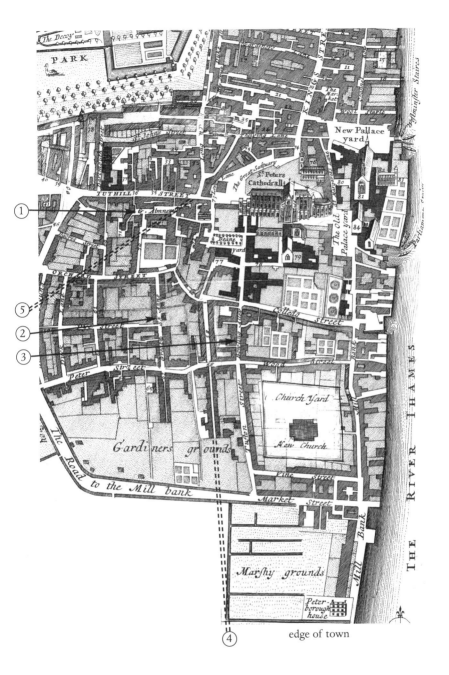

1. Map of Westminster in about 1680, drawn by William Morgan. The added numbers indicate the various addresses where Purcell lived: (1) Great Almonry, (2) Great St Ann's (1682–4), (3) Bowling Alley East (1684–92), (4) Marsham Street (1694–5), and (5) shows the line of modern-day Victoria Street.

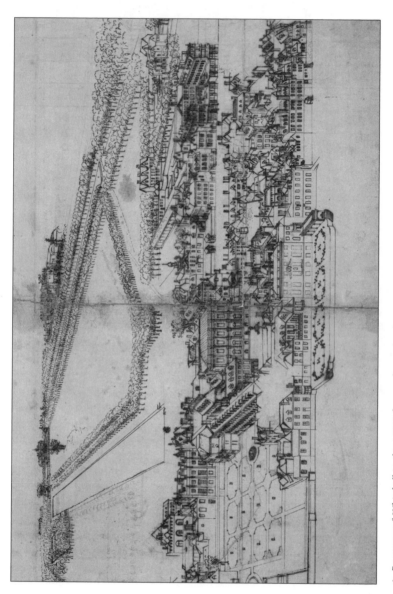

2. *Panorama of Whitehall in about 1680, by an unknown hand.*

throne of his father. He made a carefully stage-managed entry into London on 29 May, which was, by no coincidence, his birthday. The diarist John Evelyn (1620–1706) was enthralled by the euphoria of the occasion, as he watched a

> Triumph of above 20,000 horse & foote, brandishing their swords and shouting with unexpressable joye: the wayes strewed with flowers, the bells ringing, the streetes hung with Tapissry, fountaines running with wine; the Major [Mayor], Aldermen, all the Companies in their liver(ie)s, Chaines of Gold, banners; Lords & nobles & everybody clad in Cloth of Silver, gold & vellvet: the windows and balconies all set with Ladys: Trumpets, Musick, and (myriads) of people flocking the streetes and wa[y]s as far as Rochester, so as they were 7 houres in passing the Citty, even from 2 in the afternoon 'til nine at night: I stood in the strand, and beheld it, & blessed God: And all this without one drop of blowd . . . it was the Lords doing, such a Restauration was never seen in the mention of any history, antient or modern, since the returne of [the Jews from] the Babylonian captivity.[3]

All too soon afterwards, though, mundane reality had to be confronted. The task Charles faced was a daunting one: to restore as much of the kingdom of old as was possible, politically prudent, and affordable. The royal household, however straitened its finances might be after six years of civil war and twelve of republican government, had to be suitably imposing and, in particular, graced with all the arts of literature, painting, and music.

The musicians who had once served Charles I were dispersed far and wide: many had sought employment in wealthy households all over England. Now they were reinstated in the royal service, and singing-men were reassembled for cathedral and other choirs which had been silenced for a dozen years – Westminster Abbey among them. That lapse of time meant that there were plenty of fresh vacancies too. Both Thomas and Henry Purcell were promptly appointed Gentlemen of the Chapel Royal.[4] Henry also became a singing-man and master of the choristers at the Abbey.[5]

Recalling singing-men to restored choral foundations, and making any necessary new appointments, was a simple enough matter, but the business of recruiting boys was fraught with difficulty. Even the youngest of those who had been singing before the war now had broken voices, and choirmasters faced the unenviable task of recreating the top line of their

---

[3] Evelyn, 29 May 1660.
[4] Documentation relating to their swearing-in has not survived, but both are listed as Gentlemen at the coronation of Charles II in April 1661: *Cheque Book*, p. 128.
[5] WAM 61228A (Precentor's Book, 1660–71), f. 3 (entry dated 16 February 1661).

choirs from scratch, without being able to rely on any experienced boys (from whom juniors would normally glean as much of their craft as they would learn from the choirmaster). It must have been uphill work, especially at Westminster Abbey, which was in direct competition with the Chapel Royal – a formidable rival indeed, for Henry Cooke, the new Master of the Children of the Chapel, had an enormous advantage when it came to enlisting choristers. He revived the old system of impressment under the royal warrant, enabling promising boys from other choral foundations to be conscripted.

Armed with this power, Cooke scoured the country on horseback, visiting provincial cathedrals, Oxbridge colleges, and even parish churches in order to select young recruits for the Chapel. His eye for talent must have been remarkable, for within a matter of months he had assembled the most brilliant group of boys ever to sing together in an English choir – among them two, Pelham Humfrey (1648–74) and John Blow (1649–1708), who were destined to become the leading composers of their generation, and to exert a profound influence upon the music of the young Henry Purcell.

The coronation of Charles II, an event for which by long tradition the two choirs combined, did not take place until 23 April 1661, St George's Day – nearly eleven months after his return to London. Even then, despite the labours of Cooke and of Purcell senior, ambitious choral music was out of the question, and it seems that the boys were discreetly reinforced by men singing falsetto (a vocal technique much less common then than now).[6] The sheer pomp of the occasion, though, was more than enough to impress onlookers who had, during all the drab years of Puritan rule, been denied any spectacle on occasions of state – let alone a glittering pageant like this one – just as they had been starved of liturgical music. The pen of Samuel Pepys (1633–1703) fairly dripped with excitement as he wrote in his diary about the royal procession from the Tower of London to Whitehall on the eve of the coronation:

> saw the Shew very well – in which it is impossible to relate the glory of that this day – expressed in the clothes of them that rid – and their horses and horse-cloths. . . . Imbroidery and diamonds were ordinary among them. The Knights of the Bath was a brave sight of itself. And their Esquires . . . The King, in a most rich imbroidered suit and cloak, looked most nobly. . . . a fine company of Souldiers, all young comely men, in white doublets. There

---

[6] The polemical Matthew Locke observed scornfully that 'above a Year after the Opening of His Majesties Chappel, the Orderers of the Musick there, were necessitated to supply the Superior Parts of the Musick with Cornets and *Mens feigned Voices*, there being not one Lad, for all that time, capable of Singing his part readily': *The Present Practice of Musick Vindicated* (London: Brooke and J. Playford, 1673), p. 19.

followed the Vice-Chamberlin, Sir G. Carteret, a company of men all like turkes . . . The Streets all gravelled; and the houses, hung with Carpets before them, made brave show . . . So glorious was the show with gold and silver, that we were not able to look at it – our eyes at last being so much overcome with it.[7]

On the following day, Evelyn tells us, there was another 'splendid cavalcade' from Whitehall Palace to the Abbey; the king and his immediate entourage travelled as far as Parliament Stairs in the royal barge (a mode of transport he was to favour throughout his reign). The service itself gave Pepys rather less satisfaction. He had arrived soon after four o'clock in the morning, thereby securing a seat which gave him a good view:

And a pleasure it was to see the Abbey raised in the middle, all covered with red and a throne (that is a chaire) and footstoole on the top of it. And all the officers of all kinds, so much as the very fidlers, in red vests. . . . the Deane and prebends of Westminster with the Bishops (many of them in cloth-of-gold Copes); and after them the nobility all in their parliament-robes, which was a most magnificent sight. Then the Duke [of York] and the King with a scepter . . . and Sword and mond [orb] before him, and the crowne too. The King in his robes, bare-headed, which was very fine.[8]

Unfortunately, like nearly everyone else in the Abbey, he was unable to hear much of the music because of the noise made by the packed congregation. (Partly in exasperation at this, and partly because of his early start, he went out to relieve himself before the ceremony was over.) Evelyn, who seems to have been better placed, remarks only that he heard 'Anthems and rare musique playing with *Lutes, Viols, Trumpets, Organs, Voices* &c'.[9]

The choral pieces that Pepys struggled vainly to hear were only modest in scale, and decidedly varying in quality, but they were certainly delivered with panache. The singers must have made a splendid sight, dressed not in their everyday robes but in brand new coronation liveries. And in several of the pieces they were joined by instrumentalists, equally resplendent in scarlet mantles: the royal wind band of cornetts and sackbuts and the royal string band, the Twenty-Four Violins (modelled on the French court orchestra, but reflecting in its numbers – six each of first and second trebles, tenors, and basses – the English preference for music in four parts, with two violins and one viola, rather than five in the French

---

[7] Pepys, 22 April 1661.
[8] Ibid., 23 April 1661.
[9] Evelyn, 23 April 1661.

manner, with one violin and three violas). Besides these there were trumpeters and kettledrummers, all in full-dress uniform, to sound flourishes. And hardly less imposing than the appearance of the performers was the way in which their forces were disposed, at several different locations within the great church. The Abbey choir sang in its customary place, the choir-stalls just east of the crossing; the main body of the Chapel Royal was accommodated in a specially built wooden gallery on the north side of the chancel, but sixteen of their number, four boys and twelve men, were placed in a similar gallery on the south side, where they had their own organist (presumably playing a chamber organ, also erected for the occasion). The instrumentalists occupied a third gallery, on the north side but a little further to the east than the main Chapel choir. This layout offered some intriguing possibilities which might not be obvious to the casual onlooker – at any rate until the music began.

No printed order of service has survived, but an eyewitness account appears in a history of the English monarchy published early in the new reign (a piece of opportunism that would not have been out of place three centuries later). The writer was infuriatingly, if perhaps unsurprisingly, vague about such trivial details as the music that was performed, but what he bothered to commit to paper, coupled with such copies as survive of the pieces themselves, gives us just enough to go on.[10]

The introit, *I was glad*, has not been preserved, but its performance – in procession from the west door – was the time-honoured prerogative of the Abbey choir alone, so the composer may well have been its own choirmaster, Henry Purcell senior. After that the Chapel Royal took the lion's share of the music, singing sometimes alone and sometimes with the Abbey choir. Following the Presentation of the new king to his people, the next anthem, *Let thy hand be strengthened* (also lost), was sung by the Chapel Royal alone, aloft in their twin galleries. Then, at the Anointing, the two choirs joined forces with some of the instrumentalists – probably the cornetts and sackbuts – in an anthem by Lawes, one of the most senior of the royal composers: *Zadok the priest*, a dignified piece entirely in block chords.[11] *The King shall rejoice*, which followed the putting on of the crown, is usually said to have been a short and old-fashioned polyphonic anthem (now surviving only in a fragmentary state) by William Child (1607–97) – another veteran lately reappointed to posts he had held before the Civil War, both in the king's Private Music and as organist of St George's Chapel, Windsor. But it seems much likelier that

---

[10] Baker, *Chronicle*, pp. 811–18. Baker had died in 1645; the account of the coronation, one of numerous additions to the enlarged 1665 edition, is by an unknown hand. The account of Charles II's restoration in the 1665 edition of the *Chronicle* has been attributed to General Monck's brother-in-law, Sir Thomas Clarges: G. H. Martin, 'Baker, Richard', *Oxford DNB*.
[11] The piece survives in scattered sources, including York Minster, MSS M–1/5–8 (S) (all four vocal parts), and Oxford, St John's College, MS 315 (organ).

a very different setting was performed: expressly composed by Henry Cooke in the latest Italianate style, and fully exploiting all three vocal groups in the Abbey together with the Twenty-Four Violins.

Cooke, though a fine choir-trainer, was short-winded and technically clumsy as a composer, but he knew how to employ spatial separation to give music what was quite literally an extra dimension, and in the great spaces of the Abbey he exploited it to the full. His setting of *The King shall rejoice* opens with a substantial symphony played by the violin band, and for the remainder of its length it alternates 'verse' passages – scored for soloists and various larger combinations of voices (which would have been sung by the semichorus in the south gallery) – with sections for the full choir (north gallery and choir-stalls), complete with antiphony between the two sides, *decani* (the side on which the dean sat) and *cantoris* (the precentor's side); still more internal contrast is provided by short passages for the strings (north again). Cooke's setting extends to over two hundred bars – a considerably grander piece than any of the others described here – and it would have formed a fitting musical counterpart to the Crowning, which was, of course, the liturgical climax of the coronation service.[12]

The two pieces that followed were both composed by Cooke, and both performed by the Chapel Royal and the violin band. His *Behold, O God our defender*, which is preserved in the same manuscript as *The King shall rejoice*, is laid out in exactly the same way and scored for very similar forces, though it is a good deal shorter.[13] It was sung by the Chapel Royal alone, with the violin band first playing a sprightly symphony full of dotted rhythms, then 'answering [the voices] alternately'. Cooke's setting of the Nicene Creed, which came next, is lost, but we know that it employed the same layout.[14] At the Communion came a short piece for full choir, *Let my prayer come up*, setting a single psalm verse and sung probably by the Abbey choir alone, and finally, at the Post-Communion, *O hearken unto the voice of my calling*, sung by the Chapel Royal. Again, both pieces were by Cooke; both are lost. That concluded the coronation service itself, but at the ensuing banquet in Westminster Hall the table music, as well as the feasting, continued for the rest of the day.[15]

Besides being largely inaudible to the frustrated Pepys, as he sat in the Abbey on coronation day, all this music would no doubt have passed clean over the head of the two-year-old Henry Purcell if he ever happened to hear it being rehearsed. But, inconsiderable and crude though much of it was – a paltry achievement, compared with the music

---

12 The autograph score is preserved in University of Birmingham, Barber MS 5001, pp. 147–56.
13 University of Birmingham, Barber MS 5001, pp. 118–25.
14 The account in Baker's *Chronicle* records that it was 'sung by the *Gentlemen* of the *Chappel*, with *Verse*, and *Chorus*, . . . The *Violins*, and other *Instrumental Musick* placed in the *Gallery* over against them, alternately playing'.
15 Pepys, 23 April 1661.

of the next coronation, a quarter of a century later, when Purcell himself would preside at the Abbey organ – it had some prophetic features. The varied semichorus and solo writing in Cooke's *Behold, O God our defender* (and in his setting of *The King shall rejoice*) points the way to the mature Restoration verse anthem; both *Behold, O God our defender* and Lawes's *Zadok the priest* have a lively triple-time 'Hallelujah' ending of the kind that later came to typify it; while spatial effects would soon be delighting the ears of Londoners not only in church but in the theatre too, and would be handled in both contexts with consummate skill by Henry Purcell.

The new king had a genuine interest in music. He had never cultivated the skills in performance which had enabled his father to play in consort with some of his leading musicians, and his tastes were not exactly sophisticated. But it was at his instance that the royal composers began producing anthems of a new type, enlivened with preludes and interludes scored for a consort of violins – instruments generally associated with dancing, not worship. And in his easy-going way he took an interest in his Chapel choristers, and encouraged their efforts at composition. Many years later Thomas Tudway (c.1650–1726), a fellow chorister with Blow who went on to become organist of King's College, Cambridge, reminisced:

> His Majesty who was a brisk, & Airy Prince, comeing to ye Crown in ye Flow'r, & vigour of his Age, was soon . . . tyr'd wth ye Grave & Solemn way, And Order'd ye Composers of his Chappell, to add Symphonys &c wth Instruments to their Anthems; and therupon Establish'd a select number of his private Music, to play ye Symphonys, & Retornellos, wch he had appointed . . . He . . . appointed this to be done, when he came himself to ye Chappell, wch was only upon Sundays in ye Morning, on ye great festivals, & days of Offerings . . . In about 4 or 5 years time, some of the forwardest, & brightest Children of ye Chappell, as Mr Humfreys, Mr Blow, &c. began to be Masters of a faculty in Composing; This, his Majesty greatly encourag'd, by indulging their youthfull fancys, so that ev'ry Month at least, & afterwards oft'ner, they produc'd something New, of this Kind; In a few years more, severall others, Educated in ye Chappell, produc'd their Compositions in this Style, for otherwise, it was in vain to hope to please his Majesty.[16]

The Chapel choristers were not the only ones to benefit from royal encouragement. In September 1662, as part of a general overhaul of the remuneration of court employees, the king raised the salaries of the

---

[16] London, British Library, Harl. MS 7338, ff. 2v–3.

Gentlemen of the Chapel from £40 to £70 per annum.[17] Unfortunately this did not even make up for inflation – not surprisingly, since they had not received a pay increase for nearly sixty years![18] Worse, the dire state of the royal finances, which was to continue for most of the reign, meant that all such payments were invariably made months or even years in arrears. And the increase itself was more than a little precarious: only a year later it was being granted a specific exemption from spending cuts – and nine months after that it had to be reasserted by the king, in a warrant addressed to the court officials responsible for paying it.[19]

Even so, for Henry Purcell senior the announcement of the increase must have been welcome. In the spring of 1662 his wife had presented him with a sister for young Henry and his brothers, who was christened Katherine. It may have been this additional pressure on the household budget that caused him to seek an additional appointment, and in mid-November he secured one, as royal musician-in-ordinary for the lutes and voices, but it brought him no immediate increase in earnings, for he shared the post with the veteran violinist Angelo Notari.[20] (Job-sharing of this kind was not unusual in the royal musical establishment. When the holder of a post had become too old and infirm to discharge his duties, such an arrangement allowed him to retain his salary – a generous pension, in effect – while the man appointed to share with him would work unpaid until he should succeed to the entire post. Since Notari had been a royal musician since 1610, and was by now almost 97 years old, Purcell cannot have expected to share with him for very long, but in the event the old man survived a further year.) On the following day, by a curious coincidence, his brother Thomas gained an identical position – though this one was salaried from the outset – and, a day later again, a further appointment as a composer for the violins.[21] Both posts had fallen vacant on the death, three weeks previously, of another elder statesman among the royal musicians – Henry Lawes, Henry Purcell's erstwhile next-door neighbour, whose passing at the age of 76 severed another link with the pre-war court.

'In the midst of life we are in death'

The next couple of years brought Henry and Elizabeth two further sons, Joseph and Daniel, though no record survives of the birth or baptism of

---

[17] Order dated 2 September 1662: *CSP Dom.*, 1661–2, p. 476.
[18] In petitioning the king for an increase, the Gentlemen had pointed out that a salary of £80 would be worth less than one of £40 had been in the reign of James I, who 'raised their salary in 1604 from 30*l.* to 40*l.*, and their diet from 6*d.* to 10*d.* daily': ibid.
[19] *Cheque Book*, pp. 95–6, 96–7. As late as 1693 treasury officials were still referring to the annual salary of musicians as being £40: see p. 154, below.
[20] *RECM*, vol. 1, p. 38. The warrant, dated 14 November 1662, was operative – as indicated by Zimmerman, *Purcell*, p. 7, quoting it more fully than *RECM* does – from 24 June 1660; but since the post was shared, this backdating entailed no cost to the royal household.
[21] Ibid., p. 38 (warrant dated 15 November 1662); p. 219 (warrant dated 16 November 1662).

either child. And with Henry and Thomas both enjoying advancement in the royal service, their families must have seemed set for a secure and prosperous life. But on 11 August 1664, seemingly with the suddenness of lightning out of a clear sky, Henry died. Two days later he was buried in the east cloister of the Abbey, near to several other musicians including Lawes, whose neighbour he thus became in death as he had once been in life.[22] His widow Elizabeth was left in straitened circumstances to bring up six children, of whom the youngest, Daniel, was probably not even born at the time of his father's death. An immediate consequence was that the family had to move to a more modest home, in Tuthill (now Tothill) Street, to the north of Great Almonry; the house they had vacated kept its musical connection, for Christopher Gibbons moved in.[23] Very fortunately Thomas Purcell, it seems clear, took an interest in the continued well-being of his late brother's family, especially Henry, whom in later years he would describe as 'my son' (hence, of course, the later confusion as to the boy's parenthood). An uncle who was increasingly prominent among the royal musicians, and who was prepared to regard his talented nephew as his foster-son, could do much to compensate the boy, at least in practical terms, for the death of his father.

All the same, the bereavement must have left a deep scar on the five-year-old Henry – one of several events in his childhood that are often said to account for his extraordinary power as an adult composer to express profound melancholy with unforgettable eloquence. A second such occurrence was to come before another year had elapsed, and this time it would leave not merely the family but the entire nation stricken to the heart.

In March 1665 the government, impelled by trading rivalries and unwisely disregarding the neglected state of the navy, began what turned out to be a disastrous war against the Dutch. The series of defeats that ensued would have been bad enough, but within weeks of the declaration of war came an outbreak of plague, which the previous year had ravaged Amsterdam and which may have been brought to London by ship (though there had earlier been a small outbreak in Westminster).[24] 'God preserve us all!', wrote an apprehensive Pepys on 30 April – though he can scarcely have imagined that before it ran its course the pestilence would carry off more than 70,000 Londoners. Before long Londoners began to flee – at any rate those who could afford to – and the court ensconced

---

[22] WAM 61228A (Precentor's Book, 1660–71), f. 148: 'Mr Henry Purcell one of the gentlemen of his Majestyes Chapell Royall and Master of the boyes of Westminster was buried in the great Cloysters near Mr Lawes' on 13 August.
[23] Their new home was leased from the Abbey: for details see Zimmerman, *Purcell*, p. 271.
[24] Hodges, *Loimologia*, pp. 1–2.

itself up-river at Hampton Court, to sit out the epidemic in something approaching safety.[25]

But for those of the citizenry who had no means of escape – the widow Purcell and her six youngsters no doubt among them – daily life was beset with horrors: the fast-shut doors, each daubed with a warning red cross, of the houses 'visited' by the infection; the wailing of the sick and the dying, and the tolling of passing-bells; the ceaseless cart traffic that bore away the shrouded dead, and the stench of the corpses. A solemn day of fasting, declared for the first Wednesday of each month (as Pepys noted on 12 July), failed to bring about any miraculous abatement of the plague. On the contrary, its virulence doubled and then redoubled, thrusting the city to the very brink of communal breakdown. A physician, Nathaniel Hodges, described the situation in graphic terms:

In the Months of *August* and *September*, the Contagion chang'd its former slow and languid Pace, and having as it were got Master of all, made a most terrible Slaughter, so that three, four or five Thousand died in a Week, and once eight Thousand; who can express the Calamities of such Times? The whole *British* Nation wept for the Miseries of the Metropolis. In some Houses carcases lay waiting for Burial, and in others, Persons in their last Agonies; in one Room might be heard dying Groans, in another the Ravings of a Delirium, and not far off Relations, and Friends, bewailing both their Loss, and the dismal Prospect of their own suden Departure. Death was the sure Midwife to all Children, and Infants passed immediately from the Womb to the Grave; who would not burst with Grief, to see the Stock for a future Generation hang upon the Breasts of a dead Mother? Or the Marriage-Bed chang'd the first Night into a Sepulchre, and the unhappy Pair meet with Death in their first Embraces? Some of the infected run about staggering like drunken Men, and fall and expire in the streets; while others lie half-dead and comatous, but never to be waked but by the last Trumpet; some lie vomiting as if they had drunk Poison; and others fall dead in the Market, while they are buying Necessaries for the Support of Life. . . . The Divine was taken in the very exercise of his priestly Office, to be inrolled amongst the Saints above; and some Physicians . . . could not find Assistance in their own Antidotes, but died in the Administration of them to others; . . . of the Female Sex most died; and hardly any Children escaped; and it was not

---

[25] The court stayed at Hampton Court from 2 to 27 July, before removing to Salisbury and thence to Oxford, and the king did not return to London until the following February: Falkus, *Charles II*, pp. 102–5.

uncommon to see an Inheritance pass successively to three or four Heirs in as many Days; the number of Sextons were not sufficient to bury the Dead; the Bells seemed hoarse with continual tolling, until at last they quite ceased; the burying Places would not hold the dead, but they were thrown into large Pits dug in waste Grounds, in Heaps, thirty or forty together; and it often happened that those who attended the Funerals of their Friends one Evening, were carried the next to their own long Home:

——*Quis talia fundo* [*sic*]
Temperet à Lachrymis?——

In the course of one month more than twelve thousand died in a week.[26]

What impressionable and sensitive six-year-old, left fatherless only a year earlier, could avoid being marked for life by such an experience? But fate was soon to strike a further blow. As the plague gradually abated through the autumn of 1665, and the traumatized survivors began piecing their lives together again, they little suspected that the following year was to bring another nightmare, quite different in kind but just as destructive – and much more spectacular.

Early on 2 September 1666, there was a mishap in the royal bakehouse situated in Pudding Lane, in the heart of London. The small fire that resulted spread rapidly to the surrounding buildings – many of them timbered, and closely packed together in the narrow streets and alleys – and within hours had burgeoned into the Great Fire, ferocious in its destructive power. Whipped up by a southerly wind, the conflagration consumed all before it. Pepys looked on aghast:

So near the fire as we could for smoke; and all over the Thames, with one's face in the wind you were almost burned with a shower of Firedrops . . . so as houses were burned by these drops and flakes of fire, three or four, nay five or six houses, one from another. . . . and as it grow [*sic*] darker . . . in Corners and upon steeples and between churches and houses, as far as we could see up the hill of the City, . . . a most horrid malicious bloody flame,

---

[26] Hodges, *Loimologia*, pp. 16–19. (Modern analysis, such as that given by Stephen Porter, *The Great Plague* (Stroud: Sutton, 1999), pp. 33–78, suggests that the last figure given by Hodges is too high, and that the epidemic peaked at around eight thousand deaths per week, in late September.) The Latin quotation, taken selectively from Virgil's *Æneid*, ii. 6, 8, may be translated as 'Who could keep from tears over such things?' (Its third word should read *fando.*) The context is Aeneas's account of the destruction of Troy.

not like the fine flame of an ordinary fire. . . . We stayed till, it being darkish, we saw the fire as only one entire arch of fire from this to the other side the bridge, and in a bow up the hill, for an arch of above a mile long. It made me weep to see it. The churches, houses, and all on fire and flaming at once, and a horrid noise the flames made, and the cracking of houses at their ruine. So home with a sad heart . . . but . . . the noise coming every moment of the growth of the Fire . . . we were forced to begin to pack up our own goods and prepare for their removal. And did by Moone-shine (it being brave, dry, and moonshine and warm weather) carry much of my goods into the garden, and . . . did remove my money and Iron-chests into my cellar – as thinking that the safest place. And got my bags of gold into my office ready to carry away . . . So great was our fear.[27]

As it turned out, Pepys was lucky: his house, unlike thousands of others, was spared. The fact that anything at all of the city escaped the holocaust was due in no small part to the exertions of the king and his brother, the Duke of York, who between them personally oversaw the demolition of houses in the path of the relentlessly advancing flames, so as to create firebreaks (a task carried out in the face of opposition from affected property-owners).[28] This desperate expedient brought the fire at last under control – four days later. By then it had utterly destroyed close to a square mile of the city – over 13,000 houses – and rendered two thirds of the population homeless.

A Child of the Chapel

Westminster escaped the fire unscathed, but its inhabitants could scarcely hope to do so. Within days, huge numbers of woebegone refugees arrived from the wilderness of rubble and cinders that had lately been the capital city of England. How such an influx appeared to a bewildered seven-year-old, and what impact it may have had on the life of his family, we can only guess. But around this dark time came a happier event, and one that concerned young Henry more directly and more personally than fire or pestilence: he became one of the Children of the Chapel Royal, set to learn his business as a chorister from the formidable Henry Cooke, while his uncle Thomas no doubt looked on approvingly from the back row of the choir. We do not know exactly when Henry was admitted to this select group of musicians, for it was customary to record only the date of a boy's departure, after his voice had broken. But seven or, at most, eight years old was probably usual.

---

[27] Pepys, 2 September 1666.
[28] Evelyn, 4 September 1666.

It is just possible that he was already a chorister when, on 14 August 1666, one of the most striking of all the new anthems of the period was performed in Whitehall Chapel. A naval victory in the Dutch war, the battle of Sole Bay (a victory claimed, admittedly, by both sides), was made the occasion of an official celebration, so as to keep up the morale of an increasingly war-weary public. The thanksgiving anthem – its text judiciously selected so as to cast the best possible scriptural light on the affair – had been commissioned from Matthew Locke (who, being a Roman Catholic, had no formal connection with the Chapel Royal but willingly composed English anthems for it, just as William Byrd had done a hundred years earlier). Locke responded with an astonishing *tour de force* of polychoral writing, scored for twelve-part full choir divided into three separate groups, each of which also included solo voices; the instrumental movements are laid out alternately for the violin band and for a 'broken', or mixed, consort of violins, viols, theorbos, and organ, and both these instrumental groups also accompany the voices.[29] The reaction of the listeners in the chapel on that Sunday morning is not known, but certainly they can never have heard any music as sumptuous as *Be thou exalted, Lord* – and they would rarely do so again, even 15 years later, when elaborate new anthems by Purcell were performed regularly.

After the calamities of the last eighteen months, including a humiliating peace perforce concluded with the Dutch, 1666 drew to its close in a more positive mood. On 10 October the citizens of London held a feast day for their deliverance from the Great Fire, and on 20 November there was a general thanksgiving for the end of the plague.[30]

With these tribulations now past, the city regained its confidence with remarkable speed. So did the court. On 23 April 1667, St George's Day – and also the sixth anniversary of Charles II's coronation – a ceremony was held for the Order of the Garter. Purcell, if he was already a Chapel chorister, will have been wide-eyed at the glitter of the event, with its liberal helpings of music as well as dignified ceremonial and rich food. For all his maturer years John Evelyn, who was present, found it hard to contain his own excitement:

> In the morning His Majestie went to Chapell, with the Knights all in their habits, & robes, ushered in by the Heraulds. After the first service they went in Procession, the youngest first, the Sovraigne last, with the Prelate of the Order, & Dean, who had about his neck the booke of the Statutes of the Order, & then the Chancelor of the Order . . . who wore the Purse about his: then Heraulds & Garter King at Armes . . . Black Rod: but before the

---

[29] Included in *Musica Britannica*, vol. 38 (1976), pp. 52–73.
[30] Pepys, 10 October and 20 November 1666.

Prælate & Deane of Windsor, went the Gent[lemen] of [the] Chapell, Choristers &c. singing as they marched, behind them two *Doctors of Musick* in damask robes: This proceeding was about the Courts of White-hall, then returning to their Stalles & Seates in the Chapell, placed [seated] under each knights coate armour, & Titles. Then began Second Service, then the *King* Offered at the *Altar*, an Anthem sung, then the rest of the knights offered, and lastly proceeded to the Banqueting house to a greate feast: The King sate on an elevated Throne at the upper end, at a Table alone: The Knights at a Tab: on the right-hand reaching all the length of the roome; over against them a cuppord of rich gilded Plate &c: at [the] lowere end the Musick; on the balusters above Wind musique, Trumpets & kettle drumms: The King was se[r]ved by the lords, and pensioners, who brought up the dishes: about the middle of dinner the Knights drank the Kings health, then the King theirs: Then the trumpets, musique &c: plaied and sounded, the Gunns going off at the Tower: At the banquet came in the *Queene* & stood by the Kings left hand, but did not sit: Then was the banqueting Stuff flung about the roome profusely. . . . The Cheer was extraordinary, each Knight having 40 dishes to his messe: piled up 5 or 6 high. The room hung with the richest Tapissry in the World . . .[31]

Almost a quarter of a century after this spectacular event took place, Charles II's love of the Order of the Garter and its ceremonial would find belated expression in Purcell's music.

Discord and debt

Behind the glittering façade, however, all was not well. There were murmurings that the nation's late travails had been sent by God, as a punishment for the sins of its adulterous monarch; one preacher in the Chapel Royal, whose sermon may have been heard by young Purcell and was certainly heard by the king, went so far as to take as his subject the wrath of the Lord on finding King David committing the same sin.[32] And some among the royal musicians, however glamorous their role might be on state occasions, were far from contented. Towards the end of 1666 the members of the Twenty-Four Violins had begged the king for payment of the arrears (or at least part of them: they were realistic enough not to ask for the whole lot) into which their salaries had fallen amid the financial chaos of the royal household. They had, as their petition sourly observed,

[31] Evelyn, 23 April 1667.
[32] Pepys, 29 July 1667. (The same entry – an extraordinarily garrulous one – gives Pepys's credulous reaction to a lubricious and sensational piece of gossip, to the effect that the Archbishop of Canterbury 'doth keep a wench, and that he is as very a wencher as can be'.)

attended His Majesty and the Queen in their progresses, besides daily attendance; are 4¾ years in arrear [!], and have had houses and goods burned in the late fire.[33]

So they had not been paid since the beginning of 1661 – in other words, they had received their salaries on only one quarter day since they were first appointed – and now some of them were destitute.

It was not long before the disaffection already felt among the rank and file went right to the top. On 24 November, amid a vogue at Charles's court for Frenchified culture in all its manifestations (a craze fuelled by French moral support for England in the Dutch wars), a Parisian-trained Catalan named Louis Grabu (*fl.* 1665–94) was sworn in as Master of the King's Music in place of Nicholas Lanier, who had died aged 77 in February.[34] Grabu promptly set about undermining the position of John Banister, who, as a leading member of the Twenty-Four Violins and trainer of a select group of twelve of their number, had probably been cherishing hopes of succeeding Lanier himself. On Christmas Eve the Lord Chamberlain issued an order

> that Mr Bannister and the 24 violins appointed do practice with him and all His Majesty's private musick do, from time to time, obey the directions of Louis Grabu, master of the private musick, both for their time of meeting to practise, and also for the time of playing in consort.[35]

Banister, understandably, was furious, and of course the whole business set tongues wagging. Pepys recorded the tittle-tattle with relish:

> They talk . . . how the King's Viallin, Bannister, is mad that the King hath a Frenchman come to be chief of some part of the King's Musique – at which the Duke of York made great mirth.[36]

And by the middle of March the unfortunate Banister had been ousted from his position at the head of the smaller group (though he doggedly clung on as a rank-and-file member of the Twenty-Four).[37] The interloper Grabu had lived for a time in Paris, where he had evidently learnt from the example of Lully (1632–87), and not only in musical matters. But whereas

---

[33] 7 November 1666: *CSP Dom.*, 1666–7, p. 245.

[34] *RECM*, vol. 1, p. 74. Grabu had been appointed on 31 March 1666 (not 1665, as erroneously entered in the royal establishment books; see Holman, *Fiddlers*, p. 294).

[35] 24 December 1666: *RECM*, vol. 1, p. 75.

[36] Pepys, 20 February 1667.

[37] *RECM*, vol. 1, p. 75. He kept his place until his death in 1679, when he was succeeded by his son, also John: ibid., p. 186 (warrant dated 6 November 1679).

the scheming Lully always contrived to best any potential rival once and for all, Grabu's own swift rise to prominence at the English court was only temporary, and sowed the seeds of trouble nearly twenty years later – trouble in which, it appears, Purcell himself was directly involved.

It was not the mere vagaries of fashion that had caused Banister's fall from grace. There had also been repeated complaints from the entire violin band that he had pocketed fees and expenses which should have been passed on to them.[38] And, reading between the lines, we may guess that musical standards also came into the equation, and that Grabu's brief was not merely to coach the Twenty-Four Violins in the latest French style but also to improve the quality of their playing as an ensemble. If so, he seems to have succeeded; certainly he was soon gaining good reports. Among the first to record his impressions was Pepys, who, on 1 October 1667, judiciously admitted to being impressed by the disciplined playing even though the music itself found no favour with him:

> to White-hall and there in the Boarded-gallery did hear the music with which the King is presented this night by Monsieur Grebus, the Master of his Music – both instrumental (I think 24 violins) and vocall, an English song upon peace; but God forgive me, I was never so little pleased with a concert of music in my life – the manner of setting of words and repeating them out of order, and that with a number of voices, makes me sick, the whole design of vocall music being lost by it. Here was a great press of people, but I did not see many pleased with it; only the instrumental music he had brought by practice to play very just.[39]

Six weeks later Pepys reported a different reaction to Grabu – though it was, as he shrewdly noted, a far from disinterested one. Pelham Humfrey, who had been sent at the royal expense to study in France when his voice broke (a most singular privilege not extended to any other Chapel Royal ex-chorister, either then or later), returned home in October, full of French manners and even more full of himself – to the disgust of Pepys, who entertained him to dinner on 15 November:

> I away home . . . and there I find, as I expected, . . . little Pellam Humphrys, lately returned from France and is an absolute Monsieur, as full of form and confidence and vanity, and disparages everything and everybody's skill but his own. The truth is,

---

[38] These complaints came to a head two weeks after his dismissal from the select group, but they dated back four years: Holman, *Fiddlers*, pp. 294–5.

[39] Pepys, 1 October 1667. Although Pepys is not explicit about the matter, he appears to be attributing the 'English song' to Grabu, whose setting of English words in his opera *Albion and Albanius* has been harshly criticized: see p. 106, below, note 32.

everybody says he is very able; but to hear how he laughs at all the King's music here, as Blagrave and others, that they cannot keep time [i.e. play in the appropriate rhythmic style] nor tune nor understand anything, and that Grebus the Frenchman, the King's Master of the Musique, how he understands nothing nor can play on any instrument and so cannot compose, and that he will give him a lift out of his place, and that he and the King are mighty great, and that he hath already spoke to the King of Grebus, would make a man piss.[40]

So Humfrey too had learnt from Lully's unsavoury manoeuvrings against fellow musicians. And indeed Grabu was eventually given 'a lift out of his place'. But several years were to pass before this happened, and when it did it was due not to Humfrey's whispering campaign, for he was already dead, but to anti-Catholic legislation. In the meantime Grabu's work continued to meet with approval; in April 1668, for instance, Pepys went 'to the fiddling concert and heard a practice [rehearsal] mighty good of *Grebus*'.[41] Humfrey had to content himself with an appointment as a Gentleman of the Chapel Royal.

Intrigue and restlessness among the royal instrumentalists no doubt fuelled plenty of gossip among the Gentlemen of the Chapel during 1667. The two groups enjoyed plenty of contact, not least in the regular weekly rehearsal and performance of symphony anthems. The presence of the bumptious young Humfrey must have fluttered the dovecotes, too, at least until the novelty of his Frenchified airs had worn off. But otherwise the closing years of the 1660s were comparatively quiet ones, at least outwardly, for the court musicians. They will certainly not have seemed so to young Henry Purcell, however. Learning the duties of a chorister in the finest choir in England – something demanding enough in itself – was only part of his daily routine. Chapel boys were also taught to play the theorbo, a bass lute with re-entrant tuning (that is, with the tuning of its strings breaking back down the octave at one point). It was on this awkward instrument that they learnt to play from a figured bass – not the easiest way to study harmony! The more able among them also had lessons on keyboard instruments and on the violin. And by the time he was ten or eleven years old Purcell was probably taking his first steps in composition. Although nothing has survived of any such childhood efforts, the works he was to create in his late teens are, as we shall see, nothing short of astounding in their assurance, both technical and emotional, and it can only have been a rigorous apprenticeship that made them possible.

---

[40] Pepys, 15 November 1667.
[41] Pepys, 15 April 1668.

Once again, however, all was not well behind the scenes. In 1667 the chaotic state of the royal finances – perennially squeezed by a suspicious and niggardly Parliament, which refused to vote the king adequate monies – had led to the trimming of expenditure on anything deemed less than indispensable. The Chapel Royal and the Twenty-Four Violins were specifically exempted from these cuts, but the treasury officials ignored the king's instructions in the matter. By the late spring of 1670 Cooke, who was responsible not only for the boys' music-making but for their domestic well-being too, was at the end of his tether and, resolute as he had been during his earlier career as a soldier, resorted to the cunning ploy of withholding his young charges from their duties in the royal service.

> Petition of Henry Cooke, Master of the Children of the Chapel Royal to the King. The children not receiving their liveries as usual, are reduced to so bad a condition that they are unfit to attend His Majesty, or walk in the streets. Begs an order for their liveries, the charge not being great, and His Majesty having signified to the Bishop of Oxford that they should have their liveries continued.[42]

The response came on 30 June 1670. Its curtness suggests that the broadside had found its target:

> Order on the above petition, that the children of the chapel be for the future entertained and clothed, as they were before the late retrenchments.[43]

But the royal finances were in so precarious a condition that the order could not be carried out. Cooke, however, was not the man to take this lying down. Six days later a harassed functionary recorded that

> Mr. Newport [Francis, Viscount Newport, Comptroller of the Household] and Mr. Reymes [Col. Bullen Reymes, Surveyor of the Wardrobe] called in with Capt. Cook about the clothes for the Children of the Chapel. [It had been] Ordered that the King will have them made as formerly. The officers of the Wardrobe say they have no money. My Lords desire Capt. Cook to furnish the money by loan on the funds on which the Wardrobe has orders: which he promised.[44]

---

[42] [June] 1670: *CSP Dom.*, 1670, p. 306.
[43] 30 June 1670: ibid.
[44] 6 July 1670: *Cal. Tr. Books*, vol. 3: 1669–72, part i, p. 473.

It must have been a lively meeting. The total sum involved was £300, of which Cooke was asked to raise nearly three-quarters; his annual salary at the time as Master of the Children was £40.

Help was at hand for the hard-pressed finances of the royal household. But it was help of a decidedly unsavoury kind, it had come from a deeply suspect source, and the king had accepted it only reluctantly and after putting off the evil day as long as he could. On 22 April that year he had signed the secret Treaty of Dover with Louis XIV, which bound him to convert to Catholicism, and to provide military help in France's war against the Spanish and the Dutch, in return for a subvention of £225,000 from the French treasury. This was enough to alleviate his dependence on an obdurate and tight-fisted Parliament, though, as Louis no doubt intended, it fell a long way short of ending it. Nevertheless, once the subsidy came through, it eased the acutest of the royal financial problems – such as Chapel Royal choristers whose clothes were not fit to be seen in public.

Young Henry Purcell's view of the privations he and his fellows had suffered may readily be imagined. At home he was no doubt accustomed to a frugal life, but being reduced to wearing rags was a different matter. And the family's circumstances were eased somewhat – sharpening the contrast – when, around this time, his eldest brother Edward became a page at court, and before long a gentleman usher. He had probably received a helping hand from his uncle Thomas, who had himself become a groom of the robes – a useful sinecure.[45] Thomas's own offspring continued to prosper. From the Michaelmas term of 1670 his son Charles became a scholar at Westminster School, thus coming under the tutelage of the formidable Dr Richard Busby, the greatest public-school headmaster of the age, who had headed the school since the days of the Commonwealth and would continue to do so for many more years. Charles was one of four 'Bishop's Boys' holding awards founded half a century before by the Rev. John Williams, Dean of Westminster; he had also been granted a generous bursary by the school. When, in 1678, he relinquished the scholarship, it was awarded to another young Purcell – whose Christian name happened to be Henry. For many years it was assumed that the recipient was indeed Charles's cousin, but this seems unlikely, for he was already employed as a royal musician and clearly destined for great things, his lean times as a chorister long forgotten. He could hardly, given his age and status, have been a pupil of the school in any conventional sense; more probably the new scholar was another lad

---

45 Edward Chamberlayne, *Angliæ Notitia*, 12th edn (London: Martin, 1679), vol. 1, pp. 162, 171; ibid., 14th edn (London: Littlebury, Scott, and Wells, 1682), vol. 1, pp. 166, 178; *Cal. Tr. Books*, vol. 7: 1681–5, part i (8 June 1681, 2 December 1682).

of the same name.[46] Whatever the truth of the matter, Purcell evidently came to be held in high and warm regard by Busby, who on his death many years later – only seven months before that of Purcell himself – left him a mourning ring. This was sufficiently treasured to be passed on to Purcell's son Edward in his mother's will.[47]

At the end of May 1671 the king and members of the court – among them Cooke and the Chapel choir – went to Windsor for several weeks. The king enjoyed country life, and went regularly to Newmarket for the racing, but this seems to have been the first stay in Windsor. The royal apartments in what was then a draughty and comfortless medieval pile were soon to be luxuriously refurbished by Christopher Wren, allowing the court a 'remove' to Windsor every summer. It quickly became customary for the king, on his return to London, to be greeted by the leading citizens in a formal ceremony of welcome – an event which, in future years, would regularly be graced with an elaborate new composition by Purcell.

New perspectives

The autumn of 1671 brought an event that London theatregoers had been eagerly awaiting, and whose consequences were later to be of incalculable importance for Purcell. On 9 November the Duke of York's Men – one of two acting companies set up at the Restoration, each with its royal patent – opened a new theatre at Dorset Garden, on the north bank of the Thames near the present Blackfriars Bridge. The company, headed by the enterprising William Davenant (1606–68) (an actor-manager and a leading court poet before the Civil War, who claimed to be Shakespeare's illegitimate son and was almost certainly his godson),[48] had long chafed at the limitations of its previous house in Lincoln's Inn Fields. This was nothing more than a covered tennis court which had been hurriedly converted into a rudimentary playhouse at the Restoration (an expedient necessitated by the fact that the Puritans had systematically demolished London's existing theatres, after suppressing public play-acting in fear of its satirical power and its alleged immorality).

---

[46] For further discussion see Zimmerman, *Purcell*, pp. 29–30, 52–5, and Duffy, *Purcell*, pp. 54–5. Duffy speculates that the boy concerned may have been from another branch of the family. The payments did not cease until Michaelmas 1680, making it even more unlikely that they were made to Henry Purcell the musician, who had by then been serving for a year as organist of the neighbouring Abbey.

[47] Zimmerman, *Purcell*, p. 315. It may well be that Busby had got to know Purcell after inviting him to play on the chamber organ of which he was the proud owner: see James Winn, *John Dryden and His World* (New Haven and London: Yale University Press, 1987), p. 40.

[48] The entry by Mary Edmond on Davenant in *Oxford DNB* discounts Shakespeare's paternity, but John Aubrey, *Brief Lives*, ed. Oliver Lawson Dick (London: Secker and Warburg, 1949), p. 85, states that he was a regular guest at Davenant's parental home, an Oxford tavern, and recounts that Davenant, 'when he was pleasant over a glasse of wine . . . seemed contented enough to be thought his Son. He would tell . . . the story [of Shakespeare's visits], in which way his mother had a very light report, whereby she was called a Whore'.

Davenant had long harboured an ambition to mount elaborate productions, with spectacular scenic effects and stage machines. Before the Civil War these had been unknown in the public theatre, which was still of the 'Jacobethan' type – thrust stage, inner stage, balconies, and uncovered auditorium, like those of the reconstructed Globe on Bankside in London: the theatre of Shakespeare's plays, which often include a prologue inviting the audience to imagine the setting, and plenty of descriptive imagery to help them. Scenery was the preserve of the private theatre, specifically of the Jacobean and Caroline court masque, for which such luminaries as Inigo Jones had designed both painted flats and elaborate machines. And in the masque these had been associated with productions that included substantial episodes of music. Now, Davenant dreamed of offering something similar on the public stage.

During the Commonwealth years he had been involved in a series of all-sung dramatic productions – a possibility the Parliamentary draftsmen had overlooked when they banned play-acting: in 1656 *The Siege of Rhodes* (put on in a back room in Rutland House in Aldersgate Street, where he was living at the time, with Henry Purcell senior in a leading role and Christopher Gibbons in the orchestra), and in 1658 and 1659 *The Cruelty of the Spaniards in Peru* and *The History of Sir Francis Drake* (both mounted in a converted cockpit in Drury Lane). The wordbooks of all three described them in much the same terms: 'a Representation by the Art of Prospective in Scenes, and the Story sung in *Recitative* Musick'.[49] The stage sets were purely static, though the illusion they created of deep vistas was a novelty calculated to impress the public; as for the music, to judge from the few surviving fragments, it was far from elaborate, most of it being merely recitative accompanied by continuo. But these makeshift works – all-sung not from choice but for purely legal reasons – were the true starting point of English opera.

After the Restoration it had taken a frustratingly long time before Davenant could begin picking up the threads. For years he had been obliged to concentrate on a bread-and-butter repertory of straight plays; money had always been tight; and in the Lincoln's Inn Fields playhouse, staging any technically complex show was out of the question. Davenant's productions did include music, in the shape of act tunes (that is, played between the acts), and inset songs, dances, and even instrumental numbers, which were sometimes slipped in on the thinnest of pretexts – a practice that continued for many years. 'Here Gentlemen', says a character in one play, to a group of musicians who conveniently drop by, 'place yourself upon this spot and pray oblige me with a Trumpet Sonata.'[50]

[49] Secondary title of *The Siege of Rhodes* (London: Herringman, 1656).
[50] Colley Cibber, *Love's Last Shift* (III. ii); cited in Curtis A. Price, *Music in the Restoration Theatre: With a Catalogue of Instrumental Music in the Plays 1665–1713* (Ann Arbor, MI: UMI Research Press, 1979).

Adding music, though, was not the whole story. In 1663 *The Siege of Rhodes* had been revived with much less music. The wordbook indicates that the acting text, formerly sung in recitative, was now spoken, padded out with additional incidents, and that the only musical numbers were the choruses that end each of the five sections (still termed 'entries', like those in the Jacobean court masque); a sequel, tacked on for the revival, was printed without any lyrics at all, and was presumably spoken throughout: altogether an ironic fate for the first all-sung English opera![51]

At last, in the later 1660s Davenant had been able to commission designs – from Christopher Wren, according to some historians – for a commodious new theatre with state-of-the-art equipment. Sadly, Davenant did not live to see Dorset Garden built; he died in 1668. But his successor, Thomas Betterton (1635–1710), fired with the same ambition, carried the project forward to completion. In the summer of 1671, with the new theatre almost ready, he visited Paris to study theatrical practice in that sophisticated city. The hit of the Paris season was a comedy-ballet, *Psyché*, a play by Quinault, Corneille, and Molière, designed to accommodate musical episodes by Lully, plenty of dancing, and opulent stage spectacle. Betterton saw it, observed how it worked as an entertainment, no doubt discussed its technical demands with the French stage crew, and came back determined to mount an English musical re-telling of the same mythical tale. He commissioned the play and the lyrics from Thomas Shadwell (1640/1–92), the main musical score from Matthew Locke (b. 1621–3, d. 1677), and the act tunes and dances from Giovanni Battista Draghi (*c*.1640–1708), an Italian-born composer long resident in England. Betterton made no secret of what was planned, and in the meantime did what he could to satisfy his patrons' craving for a Parisian flavour – adding relish to the regular play repertory with a sprinkling of French dressing. The technical resources of Dorset Garden were put to work on exotic scenes and special effects shamelessly mimicked from the latest French originals. As things turned out it was nearly four years before the English *Psyche* finally opened, after a turn of events which took everyone by surprise, and which was to have a direct bearing on Purcell's major operatic works of the 1690s.[52]

Royal progress

Back in Westminster, meanwhile, Henry's uncle Thomas was continuing to accumulate posts in the royal music. In January 1672 he was appointed

[51] The evidence of the complete wordbook, *The Siege of Rhodes: The First and Second Part . . .* (London: Herringman, 1663), is clear, but other sources are more equivocal about how much was changed. See James Winn, 'Heroic Song: A Proposal for a Revised History of English Theatre and Opera, 1656–1711', *Eighteenth-Century Studies*, 30 (1997), pp. 113–37.
[52] For a full account of the genesis of *Psyche*, see Colin Visser, 'French Opera and the Making of Dorset Garden Theatre', *Theatre Research International*, 6 (1981), pp. 163–71.

composer-in-ordinary, jointly with Pelham Humfrey and for the time being unpaid.[53] The titular holder of the post, George Hudson, was elderly and ill, and died later that year, whereupon Humfrey and Thomas Purcell began to share the salary; on Humfrey's death two years later, Thomas became entitled to the whole of it.[54] And meanwhile, in the summer of 1672, he replaced Henry Cooke, who had retired through terminal ill health, as Marshal of the Corporation of Music (a body which attempted, with royal backing, to regulate the profession in an orderly manner, and which Thomas had previously served as an assistant).[55]

Cooke died in July, and was buried in the cloisters of Westminster Abbey; it may have been for this occasion that Purcell set to music part of the funeral service, the second dirge anthem (now termed the second group of burial sentences), to complement Cooke's own setting of the first and third anthems.[56] Purcell's setting is technically awkward – he subsequently revised it thoroughly – but if it is indeed the work of a boy of thirteen it is remarkable, full of hauntingly angular vocal lines and dissonant harmonies.[57] Cooke was succeeded as Master of the Children by Humfrey, with whom Purcell was thus brought directly into contact, and by whom he presumably began being instructed in composition. It must have been around this time, too, that Henry's youngest brother Daniel, now about eight years old, became a Chapel chorister.

One further event in 1672 demands mention, though at the time it struck no one as being of any great importance. The *London Gazette* for 26–30 December that year carried the following advertisement:

> at Mr *John Banister*s House, (now called the *Musick-School*) over against the *George Tavern* in *White Fryers*, this present Monday [30 December], will be Musick performed by excellent Masters, beginning precisely at 4 of the clock in the afternoon, and every afternoon for the future, precisely at the same hour.

Had Banister still been a respected musical director at court, he would scarcely have had the time, the energy, or the motivation for such a novel enterprise. So it was ultimately his demotion and disgrace that lay behind this, the establishment of one of the first professional concert series in Europe.

Two laconic memoranda from the Lord Chamberlain, respectively to the Great Wardrobe and to the Treasurer of the Chamber, both dated

---

[53] Warrant dated 10 January 1672: *RECM*, vol. 1, p. 111.
[54] Warrant dated 15 July 1673: *RECM*, vol. 1, p. 128.
[55] London, British Library, Harl. MS 1911, f. 5v (9 July 1664), f. 10 (24 June 1672); both entries quoted in full in Zimmerman, *Purcell*, pp. 366–7.
[56] See Wood, 'First Performance'.
[57] Purcell Society Edition, vol. 13 (1988), pp. 58–68.

17 December 1673, make it clear that young Henry Purcell was expected to have a bright future:

> Warrant to provide the usual clothing for Henry Purcell, late child of his Majesty's Chapel Royal, whose voice is changed and who is gone from the Chapel.

> Warrant to pay Henry Purcell £30 a year, beginning at Michaelmas 1673.[58]

So his years as a chorister were at an end, but not his connection with the Chapel Royal. Along with his friend Henry Hall, who had left the choir a few months before, he was to be kept on at the royal expense: an arrangement made only for the most talented boys, allowing them to further their studies. It was an enlightened policy, and £30 a year was perfectly adequate for the purpose, though it would scarcely finance a lavish lifestyle. Likewise, the 'usual clothing' – Hall's, unlike Purcell's, was itemized in the memorandum dealing with the provision to be made for him – made a modest enough wardrobe:

> two suites of playne cloth, two hatts and hatt bands, four whole shirts, four half shirts, six bands, six pair of cuffs, six handkerchiefs, four pair of stockings, four pair of shoes, and four pair of gloves.[59]

Little encouragement there for Purcell to develop into a self-satisfied young exquisite like Humfrey – to whom, in his capacity as Master of the Children of the Chapel, the outfit for Purcell and Hall was now issued.

Besides having his studies to pursue, Purcell already held a significant post in the royal music, to which he had been appointed in June, several months before his voice broke – testimony, surely, not only to exceptional musical ability but also to a solidly practical turn of mind. He was to serve – unpaid at first – as 'keeper, mender, maker, repairer, and tuner of the regals, organs, virginals, flutes, and recorders, and all other kind of wind instruments whatsoever' as assistant to the elderly John Hingeston, his godfather, to succeed to the post and its salary in due course.[60] In the event, Hingeston lived until 1683, at which date Purcell, by then one of the leading musicians in England, was still dutifully serving as his 'assistant'. (An instrument-repair man in Restoration London, though, enjoyed a status very different from that of his modern counterpart.

---

[58] *RECM*, vol. 1, pp. 131–2.
[59] *KM*, p. 251. The list of the items issued is summarized as 'the usual clothing' in *RECM*, vol. 1, p. 121.
[60] Warrant dated 10 June 1673: *RECM*, vol. 1, p. 126.

Besides maintaining the royal collection of wind instruments Hingeston was widely respected as a most distinguished musician: not only an organist of repute but also a viol player in the Private Music, and a skilled composer and teacher.)

In February 1674 Purcell's uncle Thomas acquired yet another royal post – his sixth – as musician-in-ordinary in the Private Music, in succession to John Wilson, a respected vocal composer, whose death severed one of the last remaining links with the pre-Cromwellian era.[61] But young Henry must have had little attention to spare for family matters, however satisfactory (his uncle was by now so prosperous that he was living in Pall Mall, as desirable an address then as now), for one of the most exciting musical developments in London for many years was under way.

A multimedia spectacular

In September 1673 Robert Cambert (c.1628–77), a leading Parisian composer who had fallen victim to the ruthless intrigues of Lully, had arrived in London to join his erstwhile pupil Grabu. The two of them formed a plan to mount a production of one of Cambert's operas, in association with the King's Men and their manager Thomas Killigrew – sworn rivals of Betterton and the Duke's Men.[62] (Killigrew, like Betterton and Davenant, had long been hankering after opera: as early as 1664 he had shared with Pepys his vision of putting on four major productions a year, in a new purpose-built theatre, though the project never came to fruition.)[63] The Duke's Men, once news of this French threat leaked out, needed a competing attraction in a hurry. With *Psyche* still nowhere near ready, Betterton hastily dusted off an adaptation of Shakespeare's *The Tempest*, made seven years earlier by Davenant and John Dryden (1631–1700), and set about turning it into an opera, or at any rate what he hoped Londoners would accept as an opera. The 1667 production had already contained a fair amount of music, with the play heavily cut to make room for it; the reworking went a good deal further. Thomas Shadwell wrote the lyrics for some new songs and also – most significantly for the future development of opera – for a substantial Masque of Neptune in the last act, which was set to music by Humfrey. Locke composed the First and Second Music (played as the audience took their seats), the Curtain Tune (overture), the act tunes, and the Conclusion (a short instrumental finale), while Draghi supplied the dance tunes. Anonymous designers added elaborate painted scenery and special effects, not least an ostentatious lighting plot – all, of course, to be executed by candle-power – and at the very outset there was to be a spectacular contribution from

---

[61] Warrant dated 9 March 1674: ibid., p. 134.
[62] A full account appears in White, *Grabu*, pp. 14–15.
[63] Pepys, 2 August 1664.

the machinists, with aerial spirits borne aloft on Dorset Garden's 'flying ropes':

> the Scene . . . represents a thick Cloudy Sky, a very Rocky Coast, and a Tempestuous Sea in perpetual Agitation. This Tempest (suppos'd to be rais'd by Magick) has many dreadful Objects in it, as several Spirits in horrid shapes flying down among the Sailers, then rising and crossing in the Air. And when the Ship is sinking, the whole House is darken'd and a shower of Fire falls upon 'em. This is accompanied with Lightning, and several Claps of Thunder, to the end of the Storm.[64]

Proudly though these effects are described in the wordbook for the production, they were not home-grown. Every one of them had been borrowed from a genuine French original, Lully's opera *Cadmus et Hermione*, premiered in Paris the previous spring. Presumably the canny Betterton, or one of his lieutenants, had been there again, keeping an eye on the latest line in French stagecraft.

But ambitious plans were not enough to head off the competition: the King's Men had stolen a march on their rivals. By the end of March the Royal Academy of Music, a body hitherto unheard of, was staging Cambert's *Ariane, ou Le Mariage de Bacchus* at the Theatre Royal in Bridges Street, Drury Lane – newly rebuilt following a disastrous fire, and opened only four days previously.[65] The opera dated from 1659, but for the London production a prologue was added, glorifying Charles II; this, the programme book implies, was set to music not by Cambert but by Grabu.[66] The latter had evidently pulled all the strings a Master of the King's Music could reach: three days before the production opened, the Lord Chamberlain sent a warrant to Christopher Wren, Surveyor of the Works,

> to deliver to Monsieur Grabu, or to such as he shall appoint, such of the scenes remaining in the theatre at Whitehall as shall be useful for the French opera at the theatre in Bridges Street.[67]

A new play was rated a success if it filled the theatre for three nights; *Ariane* had a triumphant run of nearly a month.

---

[64] *The Tempest, or The Enchanted Island* (London: Herringman, 1674; facsimile edition, London: Cornmarket Press, 1969), p. 1. Flying effects were a regular feature of spectacular productions in the Restoration theatre; they are called for in the libretti of *Dido and Aeneas*, *Dioclesian*, *King Arthur*, and *The Fairy Queen*, as well as those of *The Tempest* and *Psyche*.
[65] *London Stage*, pp. xxxviii, xli, 215.
[66] White, *Grabu*, pp. 15–16.
[67] Order dated 27 March 1674: *RECM*, vol. 1, p. 135.

Fortunately for Betterton, it did not sate the appetite of the London audience for music and spectacle. The 'operatic' *Tempest* – cobbled together so rapidly that it was able to open at the end of April, just after *Ariane* was taken off – succeeded brilliantly in its primary aim, which was to fill the house and turn a handsome profit.[68] It boasted an attraction calculated to outshine all the efforts of the King's Company: the participation of some of the finest singers in London, thanks to the personal intervention of the king. Already in Windsor for the summer, he gave orders that would supply the theatre at the cost of stripping his own chapel of weekday music:

> It is His Maties pleasure that Mr. Turner & Mr. Hart, or any other men or Boyes belonging to His Ma^ts Chapell Royall that sing in ye Tempest at His Royal Highnesse [i.e. the Duke's] Theatre do remain in Towne all the weeke (during His Maties absence from Whitehall) to performe that service, Only Saturdays to repaire to Windsor and to returne to London on Mondayes if there be occasion for them. And that [they] also performe ye like service in ye Opera in ye said Theatre Or any other thing in ye like nature where their helpe may be desired upon notice given them thereof.[69]

The inclusion of Chapel boys flatly contravened an express ban on their participation in theatrical entertainments. The royal patent of 1626, by which Charles I had conferred the power of impressment on the royal choirmaster, Nathaniel Giles, stressed the point in stern language:

> . . . we straitly charge and command that none of the said Choristers or Children of the Chapell, soe to be taken by force of this Commission, shall be used or imployed as Comedians, or Stage Players, or to exercise or acte any Stage plaies, Interludes, Comedies, or Tragedies; for it is not fitt or desent that such as should sing the praises of God Almighty should be trained or imployed in lascivious and prophane exercises.[70]

Lascivious and profane exercises! If it is hard for us now to view Shakespeare's *Tempest* in this light, even when tricked out in operatic garb, we have the Restoration to thank for a sea change in attitudes to such things.

The success of Grabu and Cambert with *Ariane* was followed by a royal command performance of other works. On 4 July 1674 twelve of the

---

[68] *London Stage*, pp. 215–16. According to Downes, p. 35, it was 'perform'd . . . so Admirably well, that not any succeeding Opera got more Money'.
[69] Order dated 16 May 1674: *RECM*, vol. 1, p. 138.
[70] Patent dated 26 August 1626: *KM*, p. 485.

Twenty-Four Violins were ordered to rehearse under Cambert for an entertainment to be mounted a week later at Windsor.[71] It included another Cambert opera, *Pomone*, and a recently composed *Ballet et musique pour le divertissement du roy de la Grand-Bretagne*, possibly a collaboration between the two composers.[72]

Master and pupil

On 14 July, also at Windsor, Pelham Humfrey died suddenly, at the age of only 26. He was replaced as Master of the Children of the Chapel by Blow, a year younger.[73] Blow, though every bit Humfrey's equal as a musician, had not enjoyed such rapid preferment in the royal service – he had been organist of Westminster Abbey since 1668, and a member of the Private Music since 1669, but it was only four months since he had been made a Gentleman of the Chapel – and he seems to have been a very different character from Humfrey. Purcell, who now began studying with him, seems to have taken to him at once. Blow was to remain a firm friend for life, and would prove in every way a generous one.

He was also a devoted teacher, as many of his pupils later testified. One of them, Purcell's friend Henry Hall, who besides becoming a distinguished minor composer himself also dabbled in poetry, gives us an affectionate glimpse of their studies together in a prefatory verse he contributed to Purcell's *Orpheus Britannicus*, when the first of its two posthumous volumes was published in 1698:

> Apollo's Harp at once our Souls did strike,
> We learnt together, but not learnt alike:
> Though equal care our Master might bestow,
> Yet only *Purcell* e're shall equal *Blow*:
> For Thou, by Heav'n for wondrous things design'd
> Left'st thy Companion lagging far behind.[74]

Thanks to Hall and his versifying – this time in a dedicatory poem for Blow's own retrospective collection *Amphion Anglicus*, issued in 1700 on the coat-tails of *Orpheus Britannicus* – we also know exactly what it was that Blow instilled into his young charges.

---

[71] Order dated 4 July 1674: *RECM*, vol. 1, p. 140.
[72] The *Ballet et musique* appears to have been commissioned by Charles II, and produced at court in a single performance during February 1674: *London Stage*, pp. 213–14; Pierre Danchin, 'The Foundation of the Royal Academy of Music in 1674 and Pierre Perrin's *Ariane*', *Theatre Survey*, 25 (1984), pp. 55–67.
[73] Warrant dated 23 July 1674: *RECM*, vol. 1, p. 140.
[74] Henry Purcell, *Orpheus Britannicus*, book 1 (London: H. Playford, 1698), p. vi.

3. "The English Amphion": portrait of John Blow, drawn and engraved by Robert White.

The Art of *Descant*, late our *Albions* boast,
With that of *Staining Glass*, we thought was lost;
Till in this Work we all with Wonder view,
What ever Art, with order'd Notes can do,
Corelli's Heights, with Great *Bassani's* too;
And *Britain's Orpheus* learned his Art from You. . . .
Others in Ayr [melody], have to Perfection grown,
But *Canon* is an Art that's Thine alone.[75]

Blow, then, taught old-fashioned counterpoint – the technique of creating harmony not by building up chords from a bass note but by meshing together musical lines that possess their own life and their own sense of direction. He had learnt this formidable discipline, the foundation of the art of the great Elizabethan and Jacobean polyphonists, from Christopher Gibbons, son of the illustrious Orlando (1583–1625).

If Blow was an unusually skilled and dedicated master, Purcell was an exceptionally apt pupil, taking to counterpoint like the proverbial duck to water: by the time he was in his early twenties he was composing contrapuntal music which, in its ingenuity and sheer intensity, outstrips

[75] John Blow, *Amphion Anglicus* (London: the author, 1700), p. ii.

anything else from the seventeenth century. It may be conjectured that he was given specific works by Blow as models. To take only one of several examples, the elaborate eight-part writing of the anthem *O Lord God of hosts*, building up from a single entry to a massive body of choral sound, owes more than a little to Blow's *God is our hope and strength* – interestingly, the two pieces share not only their style but also their home key – though Purcell surpasses his model both in ingenuity, with an immediate inversion of the brooding idea that opens the piece, and in sheer expressive intensity. The same is true of Purcell's only complete setting of the Anglican service (Morning, Communion, and Evening), which is heavily indebted to one of several such by Blow, that in G major. Purcell's setting is clearly the work of a prentice hand, and is not free from clumsiness – even the word-setting is awkward in places – but it is so technically adroit as not only to leave his fellow pupils 'lagging far behind' but also, in certain respects, to outdo his master.[76]

Vagaries of fashion

The popular success of Cambert and Grabu marked the high-water mark of French culture in London, and especially at court. The reasons for its decline were mainly political. Anti-Catholic feeling had found expression in the Test Act, passed in the spring of 1673 and enforced from that November, which excluded Catholics from holding public office. Grabu seems to have clung on to his post as Master of the King's Music for several months, but on 15 August 1674 he was replaced by Nicholas Staggins (*fl.* 1670–1700): the fall of his star had been as rapid as its rise.[77] (All the same, there may have been a feeling that Staggins, with his plain English musical background, would benefit in his new post from a veneer of cosmopolitanism: before long he was granted a full year's leave of absence to study, attended by his servants, 'in Italy and other foreign parts'.)[78] To make matters worse for Grabu, the Royal Academy of Music he and Cambert had set up proved a failure – presumably for financial reasons, though nothing certain is known.

The anti-Catholic prejudice to which the unfortunate Grabu and his plans for French opera had fallen victim resulted, somewhat illogically, in a rise in the popularity of Italian music. This was given a fillip by the arrival for the 1674–5 season of Nicola Matteis, a breed of virtuoso performer quite new to England. Evelyn, who heard him on 19 November, waxed lyrical:

---

[76] See Holman, *Purcell*, pp. 106–7.
[77] Warrant, dated 15 August 1674, to swear in Staggins: *RECM*, vol. 1, p. 140. (It is possible that Grabu had been removed earlier, for on 10 May 1675 Staggins was paid £100 a year, backdated to midsummer 1673, 'for such uses as the King shall direct': see Peter Holman, 'Grabu, Luis', *Grove Music Online*, ed. L. Macy (accessed 20 May 2008), <http://www.grovemusic.com>.
[78] Pass dated 26 February 1676, for Staggins and his servants: *CSP Dom.*, 1675–6, p. 581.

I heard that stupendious Violin Signor *Nicholao* (with other rare Musitians) whom certainly never mortal man Exceeded on that Instrument: he had a stroak so sweete, & made it speake like the Voice of a man; & when he pleased, like a Consort of severall Instruments [presumably by the novel technique of multiple stopping]: he did wonders upon a Note: was an excellent Composer also: . . . but nothing approach'd the *Violin* in *Nicholas* hand: he seemed to be *spiritato'd* [inspired as if by religious fervour] & plaied such ravishing things on a ground as astonish'd us all.[79]

It seems that Evelyn was more than willing to be astonished by Italian musicians, or even merely Italianate music-making: less than a fortnight later he had

> heard Signor *Francisco* on the *Harpsichord*, esteem'd on[e] of the most excellent masters in Europe on that Instrument: then came *Nicholao* with his *Violin* & struck all mute, but Mrs. *Knight*, who sung incomparably, & doubtlesse has the greatest reach [range] of any English Woman: she had lately be[e]n roaming in *Italy*: & was much improv'd in that quality.[80]

As 1674 drew to its close, the court was busy preparing a theatrical and musical entertainment which, in its way, would outshine any of those staged that year. This was the masque *Calisto*, a play by John Crowne with prologue, epilogue, and *intermedii* (episodes between the acts) all set to music by Staggins. *Calisto* was a true masque in the Caroline sense: that is, the principal parts were taken by royalty and nobility – the Duke of York's young daughters Mary and Anne, together with various ladies of the court and their maids of honour, all coached by Thomas Betterton and his wife. After some delay, the masque opened on 22 February 1675, and a short run of performances followed over the next few weeks, with at least one and probably several more in the early summer.[81] We may safely assume that Purcell managed to get into one or more of them.

Calisto must have been the most glittering affair the court had seen in forty years. The Hall Theatre in Whitehall Palace (see pp. 47–9, below) was magnificently refurbished for it; the costume of Margaret Blagge, one of the principals, was bejewelled to the tune of £20,000, a truly

---

[79] Evelyn, 19 November 1674. Another foreign violin virtuoso who had taken London by storm, the Swedish Thomas Baltzar (d. 1663), also 'used the double notes very much': North, p. 301.
[80] Evelyn, 1 December 1674.
[81] A comprehensive account of the masque and its production is given in Boswell, *Stage*, pp. 170–227. Andrew Walkling has shown ('Masque and Politics at the Restoration Court: John Crowne's *Calisto*', *Early Music*, 24 (1996), pp. 27–62) that the first performance, planned for Shrove Tuesday, 16 February, and already postponed from Epiphany, was prevented by a last-minute technical hitch, and did not take place until 22 February, at the start of Lent.

fabulous sum at that date – and she was a mere maid of honour![82] And the stage sets and machines, including a Temple of Fame which appeared in the clouds, were all that could be desired. Describing the music, alas, is more difficult, for we have no contemporary account of it, and only fragments of Staggins's score have survived. But the whole affair, though far too costly to follow up immediately, seems to have whetted the king's appetite for such entertainments. In years to come he would commission two more: they were very different from *Calisto* and from each other, yet each of them was, in its way, to bear directly on the music of Purcell.

A week after the premiere of *Calisto*, *Psyche* reached the stage at last.[83] Superficially it was like *The Tempest*, but beneath the dazzling surface there were major differences. Spectacular scenes, special effects, and stage machines were there in plenty, but the musical numbers had been systematically woven into the storyline – quite unlike the casual manner in which Shakespeare's play had been first gutted and filleted, then stuffed with musical episodes whose dramatic function is for the most part very slight. Yet for all the effort that had gone into it, *Psyche* was less profitable for the company than *The Tempest* had been.[84] Betterton no doubt asked himself the obvious question: why bother to expend energy and money on creating a carefully integrated musical drama, when the audience were quite happy to pay for a hotchpotch? The answer was equally obvious – and, like the two future court masques, it had important consequences for the kind of operatic works Purcell was later to write.

The latter, meanwhile, was continuing his thorough musical apprenticeship. Besides pursuing his studies with Blow, and assisting Hingeston in the task of tuning and maintaining instruments, he was paid £2 for tuning the organ in Westminster Abbey, presumably on his own responsibility.[85] This was no light matter for a boy in his mid-teens, but evidently the results were satisfactory, for the payment was repeated in 1676 and 1677.[86] In 1676 he also received a fee of £5 for 'pricking out' some organ parts for anthems: no mere chore of copying, for he will have been responsible for condensing into the parts the salient features of each score, as was customary.[87]

A steady diet of Anglican church music, though undoubtedly wholesome and nutritious for a growing contrapuntist, is perhaps not always appetizing; richer fare, when available, must have been welcome. In the summer of 1676 a veritable feast of French music offered itself – and

---

[82] The figure is given by Evelyn, 22 February 1675.
[83] *London Stage*, pp. 229–30.
[84] According to Downes, p. 36, 'It had a Continuance of Performance about 8 Days together, it prov'd very Beneficial to the Company; yet the *Tempest* got them more Money.'
[85] WAM 33709 (Treasurer's Account, 1675), f. 5.
[86] WAM 33710 (Treasurer's Account, 1676), f. 5; 33712 (1677), f. 5.
[87] WAM 33710 (Treasurer's Account, 1676), f. 5v. The rate per page was probably 6d, implying that he copied some two hundred pages.

Purcell will surely have devoured it with a young man's hunger. That June, Louis XIV sent three of his leading singers to London, to join French instrumentalists already in the city in performing excerpts from Lully's *Alceste*, *Cadmus et Hermione*, *Thésée*, and *Atys* (the last of which had been premiered only in February that year).[88] Although the performances were given in private – at the house of Louise de Quérouaille, Duchess of Portsmouth, for the entertainment of Charles II, whose mistress she was – it is almost inconceivable that Purcell, given his position on the fringes of the royal musical establishment, did not manage to get into a rehearsal, and perhaps even make contact with the visitors. If he did, it will no doubt have sharpened his interest in the latest French style; but it would be ten years before he had the opportunity to hear any of the Lully excerpts in the context of a complete performance.

In October 1676 another of England's senior composers, and another neighbour of the young Purcell's childhood years, was laid to rest in the Abbey cloisters: Christopher Gibbons. There is no record of Purcell's reaction to the death of this veteran musician of enormous distinction, whom he must have known well. But the death in August 1677 of Matthew Locke – the last important link with that distant past before the Civil War, save for the venerable Child who was to outlive Purcell – was a different matter. A long-standing family acquaintance, Locke had, despite the gulf of nearly forty years between them, become a personal friend of Purcell, who mourned him now in a compact but powerfully expressive elegy, *What hope for us remains now he is gone?* The music, which was published two years later in one of John Playford's songbooks under the subtitle 'On the memory of his worthy friend Matthew Locke', gives abundant evidence not merely of the depth of Purcell's feeling but also of his burgeoning skill as a composer.[89]

Locke's death had a further consequence – and a consolation – for Purcell. On 10 September the Lord Chamberlain issued a

> warrant to swear and admit Henry Pursell as composer in ordinary with fee for the violin to his Majesty, in the place of Matthew Lock, deceased.[90]

At the age of 18, Purcell had secured a major appointment in the royal music, in succession to one of the leading composers in England.

---

[88] The whole story is told in John Buttrey, 'New Light on Robert Cambert in London, and His *Ballet en Musique*', *Early Music* 23 (1995), pp. 198–220, and Sawkins, '*Trembleurs*', pp. 249–51.

[89] Printed in *Choice Ayres and Songs*, book 1 (London: J. Playford, 1679).

[90] *RECM*, vol. 1, p.173 (10 September 1677).

Hark! The echoing air

Purcell's music was performed in all kinds of rooms in London, ranging from taverns and private houses (which might, as we have seen, be opened to the public for informal concerts) to grand chambers in the royal palaces. But six venues were particularly important in the musical life of the capital: two churches, two halls, and two theatres. The two churches, both medieval but very different from each other, had of course been designed primarily for worship, of which music formed only a component part. Both the halls were new, but only one of them was purpose-built for concerts, while the building that housed one of the theatres had previously served a very different purpose for hundreds of years.

Two churches

Whitehall Chapel

The Palace of Whitehall was a sprawling medieval warren of buildings, with imposing state apartments huddling together cheek by jowl with humbler domestic quarters for the royal servants. The only significant addition made during the seventeenth century, and the only part of the palace still surviving today, was the Banqueting House, added at the beginning of the century by Inigo Jones. During the reign of Charles II (unlike that of his father) this was not normally used as a musical venue, except for table music played at state banquets. But three other buildings within the palace walls regularly housed performances of works by Purcell in the 1680s and 1690s: the Chapel, the Hall, and the Presence Chamber. All three were, alas, destroyed in the disastrous fire that swept the palace in 1698. We have almost no detailed information about the Presence Chamber, where the Private Music performed, but contemporary accounts tell us a great deal about the Hall and the Chapel.

The Chapel was modest in size: only about 70 feet by 30 feet in plan, with a roof perhaps 40 feet high internally. This suggests a lively but clear acoustic. The organ loft, which probably stood at the west end, was surprisingly spacious, and could on occasion provide seating for several visitors. A gallery, extending along both sides of the building at triforium level, was divided at intervals with curtains and wooden partitions. The rooms thus formed were presumably entered from a corridor at the rear, like

4. Interior of Whitehall Chapel, 1623, on the occasion of the ratification of the proposed Spanish marriage treaty, showing instrumentalists in a gallery.

boxes in a theatre. One of them served to accommodate the king when he attended services: it was known as the King's Closet. The same gallery housed at least one other apartment, for the ladies-in-waiting, who were discreetly curtained off from the royal person. (That at least was the theory, but Pepys, who often attended chapel, was amused on one occasion to observe that 'the Duke of York and Mrs Palmer did talk to one another very wantonly through the hangings that parts the King's closet and the closet where the ladies sit'.)[1] And on the other side of the King's Closet, separated from it not by hangings but by a solid partition, was the Music Room.[2]

The word 'music' here has its normal seventeenth-century sense of purely instrumental music, and this section of the gallery was used to accommodate instrumentalists. It had probably done so for many years: there had been an ensemble of cornetts and sackbuts at court since the days of Henry VIII, and accompanying the chapel choir was certainly one of their functions. In the early 1660s this 'ancient, grave and solemn wind musique', as John Evelyn regretfully described it,[3] was gradually superseded by a small consort of violins, numbering up to four players – two trebles, tenor (viola), and bass – probably with the regular addition of a theorbo and certainly with two or three woodwinds on occasion. In a gallery room that can hardly have been more than 15 feet long or 5 feet deep, it must have been a tight fit, and indeed in February 1671 Christopher Wren was ordered 'to cause the music room in his Majesty's Chapel Royal to be enlarged 3½ feet in length towards his Majesty's closet' – obviously by moving the partition.[4]

In addition to the King's Closet there was probably a separate Queen's Closet, on the opposite side of the building; but Charles II's queen, Catherine of Braganza, being a Roman Catholic, did not attend the Anglican services at Whitehall Chapel, instead maintaining a chapel of her own at Somerset House. It may have been the gallery space thus vacated, or another on the same side, which was known in Purcell's day as 'the singing loft', and which was used to accommodate a small group of singers – those allocated solo parts, or participating in 'verse' ensembles with only one or two voices to a part. This group, spatially separated, could exchange phrases antiphonally with the full choir in the stalls below. (A few anthems were laid out in spectacular fashion

[1] Pepys, 14 October 1660.
[2] For a full description see Holman, *Fiddlers*, pp. 388–93.
[3] Evelyn, 1 December 1662.
[4] *RECM*, vol. 1, p. 102 (order dated 8 February 1671).

for two or even three separate solo groups: the score of one of them, Blow's *O give thanks unto the lord, for he is gracious, for his mercy endureth for ever*, contains explicit directions for two groups to be placed 'above' and one 'below in yᵉ Quire'.)[5]

So in Whitehall Chapel the symphony anthems of Purcell, Blow, and their contemporaries had an important spatial element, not readily apparent in the score. Passages in which short phrases in block chords are passed among several vocal and instrumental groups gain enormously in impact from such treatment: an effect long taken for granted in the music of the Gabrielis and their disciples, and often exploited in modern-day performances of it, but not, sadly, in those of Restoration anthems.[6]

Westminster Abbey

This majestic church, standing next to Parliament Square at the end of Parliament Street, the southern extension of Whitehall, is one of the supreme expressions of the English Gothic style. Over 400 feet long from west to east and 150 feet across the transepts, it has a vault of stone, whose crown reaches 100 feet above the floor. The acoustic is spacious, with a reverberation time of about four seconds; this explains why some of Purcell's anthems are 'big-building music', with massive choral effects and a leisurely rate of harmonic change – very different from the lively style of the works which he composed for the intimate surroundings of Whitehall Chapel.

The Abbey is unusual in that the choir-stalls stand not in the chancel but instead at the eastern end of the nave, beyond a stone-clad wooden screen surmounted by the organ and its loft. (The area of the chancel immediately to the east of the crossing accommodates the Sanctuary and the High Altar, which to this day are reserved for the most solemn of occasions, such as coronations; there is a subsidiary altar west of the organ screen.) Purcell's everyday work would therefore all have been done in an area little more than 60 feet by 25 feet, occupying the four eastern bays of the nave, with the choir entering and leaving through the cloister door alongside. Only on major occasions of state were musicians placed elsewhere among the great spaces of the Abbey – instrumentalists and additional singers at coronations, for

---

[5] *Musica Britannica*, vol. 79 (2002), pp. 106–45.
[6] A solitary exception in modern times is a concert given by the Royall Consort (director, Andrew Manze) and Westminster Abbey Choir, under their then Master of the Choristers, Martin Neary, in St John's, Smith Square, London, on 22 November 1990, promoted by the Early English Opera Society and broadcast on BBC Radio 3.

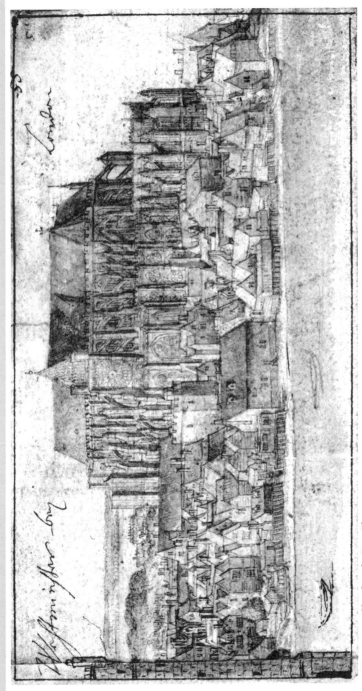

5. *Westminster Abbey from the River Thames.*

instance, in temporary wooden galleries. And it was only at special services of that kind that the choir entered by the great west door and moved in solemn procession along the full length of the nave to reach their stalls.

Two concert halls

York Buildings

In 1683, when Purcell and others founded the Cecilian festival, there was only one purpose-built concert room in London: the 'music house' in York Buildings, Villiers Street (part of a fashionable range of buildings erected in the mid-1670s between the western end of the Strand and the river). Roger North, writing many years later, explains that it was built because of overcrowding at the nightly concerts in the Castle tavern, which began after the play in the nearby Duke's Theatre had ended. He describes the 'music house' as 'built express and equipt for musick', '. . . a great room . . . with proper decorations as a theater for music, and . . . a vast coming and crowding to it'. Elsewhere he recalls that it was as

> frequented with coaches as the theatres, and for a long time the resort of all the idle and gay folk of the town. Here was consorts, fugues, lutes, oboes, trumpets, kettledrums, and what not . . . here it was that the masters began to display their powers afore the wise judges of the town, and found out the grand secret, that the English would follow music and drop their pence freely; of which some advantage hath been since made.[7]

Yet this bustling hub of London's concert life was tiny. In 1724, when its lease became available, a newspaper carried a full description:

> The GREAT ROOM in Villiers-street, York Buildings, 32 Foot 4 Inches long, 31 Foot 6 broad, 21 Foot high, the Sides and Roof adorn'd with Painting, Gilding, Pillars, Capitals and other Decorations, 4 Rows of Seats round the Room, stuff'd and cover'd with green Bayes, and rail'd in with Iron; besides an Alcove rais'd four Foot, with a Semicircle of Seats and Stands for Musick, 15 Foot 9 Deep, and 17 Foot in Diameter, towards the Room a

---

[7] North, p. 305.

Gallery over against the Alcove, handsomely rail'd with Iron.[8]

How so small a concert platform could ever have accommodated all the performers needed for even a scaled-down performance of Purcell's *Hail! bright Cecilia* – perhaps twenty singers plus a dozen strings, three wind, two brass, kettledrums, harpsichord, one or two theorbos, and possibly a chamber organ – remains a mystery!

Stationers' Hall

This handsome building still stands in the City of London; rebuilt by the Stationers' Company after the Fire of London, by great good fortune it survived the Blitz. The magnificent interior measures 58 feet by 33 feet, with a ceiling height of about 25 feet. It is lit by large round-headed windows – those on one side filled with richly coloured glass – which rise almost the full height of the walls.

The walls are panelled in heavily carved oak, the plaster ceiling, figured in gold leaf, is elaborately moulded, and the floor is of polished timber. These features combine to create an acoustic that is warm and sympathetic, though the sheer numbers of performers and listeners who must have crammed the room to capacity for concerts in Purcell's day will probably have made it feel much drier. The floor is on a single level, but for musical performances staging was erected to form a temporary concert platform, and for the Cecilian festival, at which the concert was followed by a grand dinner, tables and benches were brought in too. In 1692, when *Hail! bright Cecilia* was first performed, this was done without due care, as we may surmise from a minute in one of the books of the Stationers' Company:

> A mocon [*sic*] being made to [*illegible*] letting the Hall for the next St Cecilia's ffeast And the Court taking into consideracon of the damage that may be don to the Hall by setting up and fastning to the floore and wainscott scaffolds tables and benches[,] advised and ordered That the Hall should not be lett upon that occasion under five pounds.[9]

---

[8] *Daily Post*, 10 August 1724, quoted in Hugh Arthur Scott, 'London's First Concert Room', *Music & Letters*, 18 (1937), pp. 379–90.
[9] Stationers' Company, Court Book F (1683–97), f. 194 (minutes of meeting held on 6 November 1693; quoted with the permission of the Worshipful Company of Stationers and Newspaper Makers). I am grateful to Mrs Sue Hurley, Archivist of the Stationers' Company, for helping me decipher the clerk's idiosyncratic script. William

(This was a hefty increase: ever since the Cecilian celebrations had moved to Stationers' Hall from York Buildings in 1683, the hire fee had been only £2. Despite the Stationers' resolve, the stewards of the festival were successful in haggling; from 1694 onwards they were charged £4.)

Two theatres

Dorset Garden

The building of the Duke's (later the Queen's) Theatre in Dorset Garden was commissioned in the late 1660s by William Davenant, manager of the enterprising Duke's Company, specifically to house elaborate productions such as operas, which were as yet impracticable in London: existing theatres lacked the machinery necessary for spectacular displays of stagecraft (flying effects, magical transformations of the scene, and so on). The architect has not been identified with any certainty, but the name of Christopher Wren is often associated with the project, while that of Robert Hooke has also been mooted.[10] The theatre opened in 1671, and it prospered at first, but after the upheaval that rent the theatrical establishment in the mid-1690s it fell on hard times, and was demolished in 1708 after having stood empty for some years. It was home only to Purcell's most elaborate works for the stage, the more modest theatre in Drury Lane being used for ordinary plays.

The building was about 150 feet long by 60 feet broad; the auditorium was roughly 54 feet wide and 60 feet deep, and an internal height of around 40 feet accommodated three levels of seating – most of it on benches, allowing an audience of somewhere around eight hundred to be packed in.[11] The full-width forestage, flanked by proscenium doors for entries and exits, with stage boxes above, was about 20 feet deep; both it

Henry Husk, *An Account of the Musical Celebrations on St. Cecilia's Day in the Sixteenth, Seventeenth and Eighteenth Centuries* (London, 1857), pp. 33–4, quoting part of the minute, mistakenly dated the damage itself to 1693.

[10] See Diana de Marly, 'The Architect of Dorset Garden Theatre', *Theatre Notebook*, 29 (1975), pp. 119–24.

[11] Estimates vary, and so do conjectural descriptions. For a lively controversy over the details, see Edward A. Langhans, 'A Conjectural Reconstruction of the Dorset Garden Theatre', *Theatre Survey*, 13 (1972), pp. 74–93; John R. Spring, 'Platforms and Picture Frames: A Conjectural Reconstruction of the Duke of York's Theatre, Dorset Garden, 1669–1709', *Theatre Notebook*, 31/3 (1977), pp. 6–19, and 'The Dorset Garden Theatre: Playhouse or Opera House?', *Theatre Notebook*, 34 (1980), pp. 60–9; Robert D. Hume, 'The Dorset Garden Theatre: A Review of Facts and Problems', *Theatre Notebook*, 33 (1979), pp. 4–17, and 'The Nature of the Dorset Garden Theatre', *Theatre Notebook*, 35 (1981), pp. 99–109. See also Julia Muller and Frans Muller, 'Purcell's *Dioclesian* on the Dorset Garden Stage', in Burden, *Performing Purcell*, pp. 232–42.

7. *Cross-section of Dorset Garden Theatre, in a conjectural model by Edward A. Langhans, 1972.*

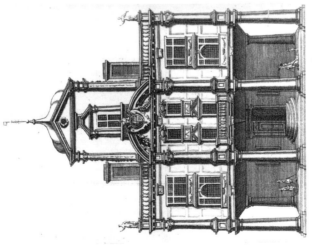

6. *Dorset Garden Theatre: engraving by William Sherman.*

and the scenic stage had trapdoors, allowing for such effects as spirits being conjured up. Behind the forestage stood the proscenium arch, perhaps 30 feet wide by 18 feet high. Behind that again the scenic stage extended back some 27 feet from the curtain line, and probably had five sets of wings and shutters, sliding in grooves in the floor (lubricated with a mixture of oil and soap) and supported above by cables and pulleys. Each pair of shutters, when closed, met to form a continuous backdrop, so that four different scenes could be 'discovered' by the drawing apart of the next pair downstage. This made possible the spectacular scenic transformations featured in Purcell's operas; even 'dissolves' (film-style, with one scene melting into the next) could be achieved by the carefully timed shifting of several sets of wings. All this mechanical activity, hectic at times, needed precisely co-ordinated teamwork and strong muscles to manhandle the shutters and wings, not to mention the elaborate machines used for flying effects and so on. The stage crew were mostly ex-sailors – pensioned off through age or injury, perhaps, but still capable of hauling lustily on a rope when the prompter blew his whistle!

The proscenium arch was surmounted, above the royal coat of arms, by a 'music room'. This extended across its full width, and was around 8 feet deep; a portion of it also projected forward, with angled sides rather like those of a bay window, and with curtained openings into the auditorium. Although this room would comfortably accommodate a small orchestra, there were several other spaces in the theatre where musicians might also be placed: in balconies above the stage doors, on either side of the music room proper; in a pit between the stage and the floor of the auditorium; under the stage; on the stage – either the forestage or the scenic stage (where musicians concealed behind closed shutters could supply echo effects); and even on stage machines, whether rising from the depths or descending from the heavens.[12] The 1674 operatic version of *The Tempest* exploited this variety to the full: the wordbook directs that the orchestra be placed, specifically, in the pit; the devils at first sing under the stage, then join in a chorus as they rise and appear to the human characters; Ferdinand is bewildered ('Where should this Musick be? i' th'air, or earth?') as Ariel sings 'Come unto these yellow sands' – obviously from the music room or one of the galleries;

---

[12] See Mark A. Radice, 'Theater Architecture at the Time of Purcell and Its Influence on His "Dramatick Operas"', *Musical Quarterly*, 74 (1990), pp. 98–130, and 'Sites for Music in Purcell's Dorset Garden Theatre', ibid., 81 (1997), pp. 430–48.

Ariel and Milcha sing 'Dry those eyes', both of them *'invisible'*, presumably behind a scenic flat, as is Ariel later on, singing the echoes to Ferdinand's 'Go thy way'; for the masque of Neptune the *'Scene changes to the Rocks, with the Arch of Rocks, and calm Sea'*, and there is *'Musick playing on the Rocks'* – on the scenic stage and in full view; and, just before the end, Ariel sings 'Where the bee sucks' while *'hovering in the Air'*.[13] The following year *Psyche* featured more airborne musicians, this time instrumentalists. Act V, Scene ii, presents a gorgeously ornamented Palace of Jupiter set in an arcadian landscape, beneath a sky that was sunny but not perfectly clear:

> Below the Heav'ns, several Semicircular Clouds, of the breath of the whole House, descend. In these Clouds sit the Musicians, richly Habited. . . . While the Musicians are descending, they play a Symphony . . .[14]

Purcell's operas will have been treated just as resourcefully: in *The Fairy Queen*, to take a single example, there are obvious implied cues in Act II for 'music in the air', in the tiny bird-call symphony that follows 'Come all ye songsters', and for echo effects within the scenic stage, in 'May the God of Wit' and its ritornello, which is actually entitled *Echo*, while in Act IV, for the Entry of Phoebus, the blazing trumpets, with their associated kettledrums, will surely have been placed in the music room, in order to make – in the words of the preceding duet – 'the arch of high heaven the clangour resound'.

The Hall Theatre
In 1662 Charles II gave orders for the medieval hall that had once formed the nucleus of Whitehall Palace, but which had been redundant ever since the building of the fine new Banqueting House by Inigo Jones, to be converted into a theatre. The result was evidently somewhat primitive, and in 1665 a more ambitious plan, by the experienced designer John Webb, was executed. Webb's theatre was small – some 80 feet by 40 feet internally – but well equipped, with a proscenium arch 25 feet wide and 23 feet high, and a slightly raked scenic stage 32 feet deep, with the usual four sets of sliding shutters, plus trapdoors. There was no forestage. Instead, in front of the proscenium was a pit 5 feet below stage level, extending back some 25 feet and flanked by

---

[13] *The Tempest, or The Enchanted Island* (London: Herringman, 1674), pp. 1, 31, 37, 42, 77, 81.
[14] Thomas Shadwell, *Psyche: A Tragedy* (London: Herringman, 1675), p. 66.

benches, and behind that a dais, again flanked by benches at floor level, occupied the remaining 20 feet, with a gallery over the rear part of it. A throne for the king was set up on the dais as necessary, in addition to the benches which filled most of it, and the theatre could easily be converted to serve for dancing by means of a temporary floor installed over the pit. Across the back of the hall was a gallery some 7 feet deep, which was fitted out with boxes. The windows that had originally lit the hall were boarded up, save for the great window over the gallery, which was dealt with even more unceremoniously: part boarded, part plastered, part curtained. But the lofty hammer-beam roof and the central lantern were of necessity left intact, which suggests an acoustic more congenial to musicians than to actors; at all events a steeply canted sounding board had to be installed over the stage.[15]

Not much of Purcell's theatrical music will have been heard here – by the 1690s command performances had all but ceased, and instead the queen and her maids of honour would have boxes reserved for them at Dorset Garden – but the Hall Theatre was used for the performance of welcome songs and royal birthday odes. The work of conversion into a theatre had inflicted various indignities on the ancient building, but they could not disguise its noble proportions, and it must have made an impressive setting for such important occasions in the court calendar.

Practical arrangements for the performers were made as necessary, with a frequency which testifies to the importance of music in court life. Purcell's own claim for arrears and expenses, described on p. 106, includes an item for 'the loan of a harpsichord, portage and tuning to three practices and performances of each song to the King' – that is, each royal ode in the preceding couple of years.[16] And on numerous occasions over the years, payment was authorized by the Office of Works for carpentry and other tasks related to music-making in the Hall: 'takeing downe yᵉ Musicke seats & laying two large floores & rayseing another floor with several degrees [different levels] for ye Musicke';[17] for 'Carryeing & recarryeing 4 musicke formes [i.e. benches for instrumentalists] from yᵉ Queenes pʳsence [the Presence Chamber] to & from yᵉ said Theater';[18] for 'takeing

[15] For a full description of the Hall Theatre, see Boswell, *Stage*, pp. 22–56.
[16] *Cal. Tr. Books*, vol. 8: 1685–9, part iii, pp. 1763–4 (18 February 1688); quoted in full in Zimmerman, *Purcell*, p. 155.
[17] November 1674; Works 5/17, quoted in Boswell, *Stage*, p. 253.
[18] May 1675; Works 5/24, Boswell, *Stage*, p. 256.

down pte of the musick seates and the Deskes where they lay
there bookes in the Pitt in the Theatre and the Surveyour of the
workes Box . . . fetching the musicke Seates out of the Queenes
Presence and placing them upon the Stage . . . [and] carrieing the
musicke Seates out of the Theatre into the Queene's presence';[19]
for 'setting up 2 rayles in ye gallery for the musick, and putting 2
flapps to them to keepe the people from the Musickque roome
there';[20] for 'inlarging the musick seats and desks in the
Theater';[21] for 'taking downe the musick seats at the Hall
Theater and bring[ing] them into the store';[22] for 'taking the
Musick seats out of the store in Scotland yard [part of Whitehall
Palace] and fitting & setting them vp on the Stage';[23] for 'making
two desk boards for the Musick 8 fo^t long a peice [the long
bench-like music stands of the period] and setting vp two bearers
[trestles] for the Harpiscall';[24] for 'mending . . . the floore where
the Musick playes, and putting vp boards to keep people out of
the Musick [room] . . . & carrying vp the Musick Seats and railes
in the Q^s. presence';[25] for 'mending the Musick Seats & formes in
the Hall Theatre . . . & carrying & recarrying ye musick Seats and
forms into the Drawing roome and bringing them back into the
Hall againe 2 Severall times';[26] and finally for 'mending the
musick Seats & the desks'.[27] Those last repairs, poignantly, were
made only weeks before the Hall was destroyed in the fire of
January 1698.

[19] November 1677; Works 5/27, Boswell, *Stage*, p. 260.
[20] February 1678; Works, 5/27, Boswell, *Stage*, p. 261.
[21] November 1683; Works 5/35, Boswell, *Stage*, p. 263.
[22] February 1684; Works 5/35, Boswell, *Stage*, p. 263.
[23] November 1684; Works 5/38, Boswell, *Stage*, p. 263.
[24] January 1685; Works 5/38; Boswell, *Stage*, p. 264.
[25] November 1693; Works 5/45, Boswell, *Stage*, p. 270.
[26] November 1694; Works 5/47, Boswell, *Stage*, p. 270.
[27] November 1697; Works 5/48, Boswell, *Stage*, p. 271.

TWO

EARLY MASTERY (1677–1685)

Early music

Purcell's new duties centred on providing music for courtly entertainment, which included dancing. Of his early dance music nothing has been preserved except a few fragments, though as successor to the illustrious Locke he must already have shown prowess at composing such pieces. But he was also busy composing church music, and some of his anthems from this period not only survive but can be dated, on clear evidence. In December 1677 his old teacher Blow was made a Doctor of Music, in recognition of his eminence as a church musician. This degree was conferred not by Oxford or Cambridge, but under special powers held by the Archdiocese of Canterbury.[1] It was a signal honour, and the music copyists of the Chapel Royal and Westminster Abbey promptly took account of it, by ascribing his compositions to 'Dr' instead of 'Mr' Blow. This change of style is a useful tool for the task of dating compositions. No fewer than six anthems by Purcell are found in the Abbey books before Blow begins to be referred to as 'Dr' – some of them many pages before – and it seems likely that all of them had taken their place in the choral repertoire weeks or even months before Purcell reached his eighteenth birthday.

They reveal two things about the young composer. First, although his technical skill was already astonishing, this is not what impresses most (indeed, the music still has some rough edges). Far more striking is its eloquence, especially when dealing with grief and penitence: something that was to be a hallmark of Purcell's adult compositions. Secondly, the range of style comes as a great surprise. The pieces range from *My beloved spake*, a vivacious symphony anthem, to *Blow up the trumpet in Sion*, a sombre

---

[1] London, Lambeth Palace Library, Register of Degrees, 1669–79 (FI/D). f. 169. The powers were held to flow from the Act of Exoneration from Exactions payable to the See of Rome (25 Henry VIII, cap. xxi); Blow's degree was the first in music to be conferred under them (and, until the nineteenth century, it remained the only one).

piece for eight-part choir in which arresting antiphonal exchanges between different vocal groups alternate with complex polyphony. A talented teenager might have been expected to revel in the up-to-date Frenchified manner displayed in the symphony anthem, so Purcell's equal enthusiasm for old-fashioned contrapuntal techniques might appear unexpected. Yet the reason for it is simple. His teacher Blow, himself a master of the art and craft of polyphony, had passed these skills on to him. In so doing he had made his pupil the heir of such luminaries as Tallis (*c.*1505–85), Byrd (*c.*1540–1623), and Orlando Gibbons, whose music had been among the cultural glories of Elizabethan and Jacobean England.

One of the last of those older masters, John Jenkins, died on 27 October 1678, at the venerable age of 86.[2] Although Jenkins was not among his Westminster neighbours, Purcell must have known him: they shared not only their connection with the court but also their acquaintance with Roger North, a prominent lawyer who was a cultivated musical amateur, and who had studied with Jenkins for some years.[3] Jenkins was an exceptionally distinguished composer of instrumental chamber music. His output, especially his fantasias – intricately crafted single-movement pieces in contrasting short sections, full of learned counterpoint – had fallen out of fashion at court many years before, but such music fascinated Purcell, who was soon to turn his own hand to this archaic genre with spectacular success.

Conspirators and concert promoters

He may have been glad to ponder such abstract and intellectual music in the closing months of 1678, as a relief from the fevered atmosphere that was besetting the court. In August and September that year allegations had surfaced of a Jesuit conspiracy to poison the king, install his Catholic brother James as his successor, fire London and massacre its inhabitants, and impose Papism on England by the sword. This so-called Popish Plot, attested to by a highly dubious character named Titus Oates, was in reality never laid. It was the purest fabrication, now being woven in order to discredit and destroy prominent Catholics at court and in the government. (The entourage of the Duke of Monmouth, the king's Protestant but illegitimate son who was seeking to succeed to the throne in place of the Duke of York, the legitimate but Catholic heir, was suspected of involvement.)

But the truth took a long time to emerge. Meanwhile Oates's story caused alarm and when Sir Edmund Godfrey, the magistrate who had

---

[2] Unusually, he had resigned his place in the private music seven months previously: *RECM*, vol. 1, p. 178 (warrants dated 19 April 1678).
[3] North, pp. 6, 21, 82, 347.

taken his deposition, was found murdered on 17 October, outright hysteria:

> Houses were barricaded against the imminent Catholic rising; fine ladies . . . carried pistols in broad daylight for protection; Catholic houses were ransacked for secret caches of weapons; Popish books and relics were ferreted out and publicly burned; priests were hunted down; innocent suspects dragged off to prison. One man wrote that if anything Catholic appeared, even a dog or a cat, it would be cut to pieces in a moment, while a commercially-minded cutler manufactured a special 'Godfrey' dagger with the words 'remember the murder of Edmund Berry Godfrey' engraved on one side and 'remember religion' on the other. Three thousand were sold in one day.[4]

The king, though, kept his nerve, took limited anti-Catholic measures for appearance's sake, and faced down an attempt to implicate his Catholic queen. As the months passed the city grew calmer, and public suspicion gradually abated. But it was not until 1681 that Oates was finally discredited, and only after three further years had passed was he brought to trial and, amid general satisfaction, sentenced to public whipping followed by imprisonment for life. And before the whole squalid affair was over Purcell's music was to be drawn into it, as we shall see.

In November 1678, when the hysteria was at its height, an event occurred that understandably went almost unnoticed – but its implications for the future were enormous. The *London Gazette* announced that

> On Thursday next the 22nd of this instant *November*, at the Musick School in *Essex* Buildings, over against St. *Clements* church in the *Strand*, will be continued a Consort of Vocal and Instrumental Musick, beginning at five of the Clock every evening. Composed by Mr. *John Bannister*.[5]

The significance of this was twofold. The inaugural event in the new premises occurred on 22 November, the day dedicated to St Cecilia, the patroness of music. No details of the programme for that day have survived, the baldly worded advertisement makes no mention of any Cecilian connection, and the enterprise seems not to have lasted very long. Five years later to the day, however, Purcell himself would launch just such a concert series: an annual celebration, which in years to come would spread from London to several other cities in England (and which,

---

[4] Falkus, *Charles II*, p. 174.
[5] *London Gazette*, 19–22 November 1678.

despite some lengthy interruptions in the meantime, still flourishes in the twenty-first century). More immediately important was the fact that Banister's concert series, begun six years previously in his own home, had at last moved into a formal venue for music-making.

This may have been in response to competition. A coal merchant named Thomas Britton had just started a concert series of his own, also on Thursdays, and held in a loft above the converted stable in Clerkenwell Street where he carried out his business. According to one account, Britton's premises were 'not much higher than a *Canary* Pipe [wine cask], and the Window of his State-Room, but very little bigger than the Bunghole of a Cask',[6] and another concurs: the concert room was 'very long and narrow, and had a ceiling so low, that a tall man could but just stand upright in it'.[7] Clearly it was something Banister might wish to improve on! (Despite the shortcomings of its venue, however, Britton's series was to continue for over thirty years – some of his last concerts may have given a platform to a young composer newly arrived from Germany, by the name of Handel – whereas Banister's was cut short by his death the following year.) The concerts in both series were on a modest scale, with only small numbers of performers and an informal atmosphere not far removed from that of a public house,[8] but they gave music-lovers their first opportunity of hearing public performances of music that was freed from serving the interests of other masters: court, theatre, or church.[9]

For the moment, though, the pre-eminent patrons were still the court and the church, and especially their conjunction, the Chapel Royal. In the spring of 1679 one of the finest singers in England came to London, summoned there to join the Chapel. John Gostling, a bass from Canterbury who was on friendly terms with Purcell's uncle Thomas, had a sensational voice.[10] Some of the solo parts that Purcell would write for him in years to come range down to bottom C, and contain firework displays of vocal technique which delighted the court throughout the 1680s, and which few singers since have ever managed to tackle convincingly. In one anthem, for instance, a single phrase (setting the words 'As for the proud, he beholdeth them afar off') swoops down through two octaves and a

---

[6] [Edward Ward], *A Compleat and Humorous Account of All the Remarkable Clubs and Societies in the Cities of London and Westminster* (7th edn, London: J. Wren, 1756), p. 302. Ward adds that Britton briefly rented a more spacious room next door, 'that the Company might not stew in Summer-Time like sweaty Dancers at a Buttock-Ball, or like Seamens Wives in a *Gravesend* Tilt-Boat, when the Fleet lies at *Chatham*', but that, finding the custom disappointing, he soon returned to his 'primitive Station' (his loft), which was open to 'any Body that is willing to take a hearty Sweat'.

[7] Hawkins, p. 790.

[8] Cf. Westrup, *Purcell*, pp. 100–1.

[9] Then as now, there were plenty of taverns that made a feature of music, though none of them could be said to mount a concert series. See John Harley, *Music in Purcell's London: The Social Background* (London: Dobson, 1968), pp. 135–51.

[10] It prompted Charles II to remark that it made all the other choirmen at Canterbury sound like geese: North, p. 270.

fourth, including one giddy leap of a twelfth![11] To carry such things off he must have been not merely a fine singer but something of a character too, and it seems he and Purcell got on famously together.

Gostling's happy arrival was soon followed by an equally sad departure. Louis Grabu had fallen on hard times in the years since the Test Act had forced him out of his post as Master of the King's Music. He had scraped a living of sorts, but in 1679, despairing of his prospects in the face of the anti-Catholic prejudice stirred up by the Popish Plot (and, no doubt, of his chances of recovering the considerable arrears owed him), he finally gave up the struggle, and on 31 March departed for France.[12] Little more than four years later the unfortunate man would be back, and once again his presence would have an unhappy outcome – this time impinging directly on Purcell's own career.

Responsibilities professional and personal

The autumn of 1679 marked a milestone in Purcell's professional life, and possibly brought one of the major events in his personal life too. Blow resigned his post as organist of Westminster Abbey, apparently in order to see Purcell appointed in his place. Why he did so has never been entirely clear. It was evidently not because he himself was finding the duties irksome, or his own workload excessive, for on Purcell's death he resumed the post, and held it for the rest of his life. It used to be said that he was simply making way for Purcell's superior genius, but this is just as implausible; he did not vacate any of his three royal appointments (Gentleman, Organist, and Master of the Children of the Chapel Royal), and far from being overawed by Purcell seems to have remained on the most cordial of terms with him, both personal and professional, until their friendship was cut off by the younger man's untimely death. A third possibility is that Blow acted as he did because he was anxious to see Purcell remain in London rather than move to a provincial cathedral, as Henry Hall, now organist of Hereford, had done – and this may be closer to the mark (though it is hard to imagine Purcell being content for long in some sleepy country town with limited musical resources).[13]

But the likeliest reason for Blow's resigning in Purcell's favour was that the young man was getting married. Exactly when he did so is unknown,

---

[11] *I will give thanks unto thee, O Lord*: Purcell Society Edition, vol. 17 (1996), bars 244–6.
[12] *CSP Dom.*, 1679–80, p. 338.
[13] In his dedicatory poem printed in Blow's *Amphion Anglicus* Hall bemoans his own provincial lot:

> Wh[il]e *British* Bard on Harp a *Treban* plays,
> With grated Ears I saunter out my days.
> *Shore*'s most Harmonious Tube [Matthias Shore's trumpet], ne'er strikes my Ear,
> Nought of the Bard, besides his Fame, I hear:
> No chaunting at St. *Paul*'s, regales my Senses:
> I'm only vers'd in *Usum Herefordensis*.

but a wedding sometime after Michaelmas 1679, when Purcell took up his post as Abbey organist, would fit the facts. Blow would have been only too well aware that his colleague would be needing an income that was more substantial, and paid more reliably, than the salary from his post as a royal composer, supplemented only by whatever he might be getting as Hingeston's assistant. Being himself a well-to-do pluralist, holding several salaried posts, he could give up one of them without feeling the pinch. Even so, if this was indeed what motivated him, Blow's action was undoubtedly generous.

The identity of Purcell's bride is another mystery. We know her Christian name, Frances, but not her maiden surname – at any rate not with any certainty. But it is generally believed that she was Frances Peters, the daughter of a Flemish immigrant, John Baptist Peters (or Pieters), and his wife Amy. It seems that John Peters, who had died in 1675, was a leather merchant, and that his widow managed a large and prosperous tavern, in Thames Street in the City, built near the remains of the church of All-Hallows-the-Less after the whole area had been destroyed in the Fire of 1666.[14]

The daughter of a tavern-keeper might seem a dubious match for an ambitious young court musician and organist of Westminster Abbey. Social considerations apart, the connection with the Peters family was questionable in another way too: in his native town of Ghent, John Peters had been baptized a Catholic. (In 1663, when he became an English subject, he declared himself as conforming to the Church of England, but this may have been merely for form's sake.) If Purcell's bride was herself a practising Catholic this was likely, given the deep-rooted prejudices against Papism in England, to spell trouble for him sooner or later.

The new and the old

The summer of 1680 brought Purcell a quite unexpected commission: music for the stage. It came from the enterprising Duke's Company, based at Dorset Garden. Purcell had no experience whatever as a theatre composer, but the score he produced for *Theodosius*, a tragedy by Nathaniel Lee, who was a disciple of Dryden's, proved brilliantly effective. Unlike most of his later suites of music for plays, it included no instrumental numbers: even the interludes between the acts – the 'act tunes' of which he was to produce so many superbly crafted examples in the 1690s – were replaced by songs, though this was not unusual at the time.

Purcell's score delighted the audience, as the company's prompter, John Downes, noted in his memoirs:

---

[14] For a concise summary of such evidence as survives, see Duffy, *Purcell*, pp. 61–5.

All the parts in't being perfectly perform'd, with several Entertainments of Singing; Compos'd by the Famous Master Mr. *Henry Purcell*, (being the first he e'er Compos'd for the Stage) made it a living and Gainful Play to the Company.[15]

Purcell was not yet a 'famous master' – Downes was writing many years later, with the benefit of hindsight – but he was on his way. And as far as the theatre management was concerned the bottom line, then as now, was the box office. Purcell's long-term future as a composer for the stage was assured. One of the songs from *Theodosius* must have been a particular hit, something that stuck in the audience's memory, for it later gained a life of its own. 'Hail to the myrtle shade', the third of the four interlude songs, reappeared a couple of years after the production in an anonymous printed broadside with fresh words, 'Hail to the Knight of the Post'[16] – a vitriolic attack on Titus Oates, whose world of lies and scheming was at last beginning to crumble.

In April 1680, meanwhile, the king, no doubt exhausted after all the tensions stirred up by the Popish Plot, ordered an unusually early remove to Windsor, and the court who accompanied him included a substantial contingent of musicians; Purcell may well have been among them.[17] Whether he was or not, his everyday duties that summer cannot have been heavy, for music began to pour from his pen: a succession of superb examples of, improbably enough, the instrumental fantasia.[18] (Purcell, with characteristic quirkiness, spelt it 'fantazia'.) He dated the first – in G minor, one of his favourite keys – 10 June; six more followed by the end of the month, and he added another two in August (though by then, as we shall see, he also had other things on his mind).

These are astonishing pieces. They are among the most profound and searching counterpoint of the seventeenth century – indeed of any period – and the harmonies woven by the individual parts are in places so dissonant and so chromatic that the listener is left unsure of the key and direction of the music. Composing such pieces in rapid succession would have been close to superhuman, and we must suspect that what Purcell was actually doing was revising and refining works he had drafted earlier. But even more surprising than the speed at which he was working was the fact that he was producing such pieces at all, for the genre they represent was simply archaic.

---

[15] Downes, p. 38.

[16] *Titus Tell-Troth: or The Plot-Founder Confounded* (London: Allen Banks, 1682).

[17] *RECM*, vol. 1, pp. 191–3 (warrants for riding charges dated between 23 October 1680 and 4 January 1681; Purcell's name is not among those reimbursed, but this does not prove that he did not go to Windsor).

[18] All the fantazias are included in Purcell Society Edition, vol. 31 (1959, rev. 1990).

The fantasia had a long pedigree, going back to the previous century, and by 1680 it had come to be regarded as hopelessly old-fashioned. Before the Civil War it had been highly regarded in court circles, and Charles I had been an enthusiastic and skilful performer of consort music, but his son, whose musical tastes were a great deal less cultivated and tended towards French dance music, 'had an utter detestation of Fancys'.[19] The fifteen fantasias that Purcell eventually completed, together with one he left unfinished, are the last examples of the genre ever to be composed – decades after other composers had abandoned it. Among them are two based on 'In nomine', and these do homage to an even older tradition than the fantasia itself. They are based on a plainsong fragment occurring at the words *in nomine domini* ('in the name of the Lord') in one of John Taverner's Latin Mass settings, composed back in the 1530s.

In all these works Purcell displays a formidable command of all the ancient techniques of polyphony, including inversion (turning a melodic idea upside down), augmentation (increasing its note values), and diminution (reducing them). Two of the fantasias, for instance (Nos 8 and 11), present us with mirror-image pairs of inverted entries in their opening bars, while a third (No. 4) contrives to cram into its first fifteen bars no fewer than twenty-four entries of the opening idea, not merely inverted but also cunningly halved in length, stretched out into double note-values and even doubled again. The musical miracle, though, lies not in this manipulation of line and rhythm but in the fact that the harmony, far from being shackled by it, is instead set free, to move in patterns of wrenching expressiveness. This is music in which the composer we nowadays regard as the greatest of all contrapuntists, Bach himself, would have taken immense pride. Its creator was only just out of his teens.

Altogether this was a very strange kind of music to be preoccupying a rising composer of twenty-one (and a good deal of what he produced is strange in itself). What attracted him to it? One reason is that he was a born contrapuntist: we have already observed him writing old-fashioned polyphonic anthems with evident relish, and weaving instrumental lines together to form intricate musical textures held the same fascination for him. Further evidence of a taste for the archaic lies in another piece he included among the fantasias in his copy. It is a solitary dance movement, but not one of the then fashionable French measures – far from it. It is a pavan. This stately measure had enjoyed its heyday, at any rate for dancing as such, during the reign of Elizabeth I; afterwards it became an abstract, purely musical form (much as the minuet was to do in central Europe a hundred years later, moving from the dance floor into the orchestral serenade and the symphony). As a dance it had already been superseded by newer and more fashionable measures when Dowland

[19] North, p. 350.

(1563–1626) composed his celebrated 'Lachrymae' pavans, which he published in 1604. By the time of the Restoration even the art-music pavan was rapidly falling into disuse;[20] yet here was Purcell twenty years later again, working on a pavan of his own – and one that rivals the fantasias in its contrapuntal ingenuity. It is laid out for three violins (or perhaps treble viols) and bass. This scoring is found nowhere else in his entire output [21] – but it had been used a great deal in the 1650s and 1660s by Jenkins, who was an arch-exponent of the pavan as well as of the fantasia. Purcell's haunting pavan, and four others which he scored for only two violins and bass, had probably been written eighteen months previously, as a tribute to Jenkins at the time of his death.[22]

How did Purcell occupy himself between the seventh of his fantasias, dated the last day of June, and the eighth which, as he revised more and more details of it, he dated successively 16, 17, and 19 August? Even if it gave him difficulty, its fifty bars of four-part writing can hardly have filled his time for seven weeks. The answer is that he had to turn from the most abstract kind of musical thought to the most utilitarian: a royal ode.

A royal reception

Ever since the early years of the Restoration, music had been pressed into service on two of the three major secular occasions of state: New Year's Day and 29 May, which was not only the king's birthday but also the date of his carefully timed return to England in 1660 from his continental exile. On both occasions there was a reception at court, during which the Lord Mayor and leading citizens of London presented loyal addresses to the king. (This was no mere formality. Control of the capital was essential to control of the kingdom, as Charles's father had found to his cost.) From about 1666 onwards, music was added to these ceremonies, in the shape of an ode. This was a poem penned for the occasion by one of the court poets (and, of course, putting a positive gloss on the recent actions of the king) and set to music for the occasion by one of the court composers. The ode was, in effect, part of the public-relations machinery of the court: a vehicle for political spin. It was thus a secular counterpart of the symphony anthem, and was broadly similar to it in scoring and musical style. The earliest odes were by Cooke, Locke, and Humfrey; since the death of the latter, Blow had shouldered nearly all the responsibility for

---

[20] Thomas Mace wrote that 'Pavines, are . . . very Grave, and Sober; Full of Art, and Profundity, but seldom us'd, in These our Light Days': Musick's Monument (London: the author, 1676), p. 129.
[21] The Fantasia: Three Parts on a Ground survives in manuscript (London, British Library, MS R.M. 20.h.9) only in a version for three violins and bass, but there is little doubt that this is an arrangement made by an unknown hand, and that the piece was originally scored for three recorders: see Purcell Society Edition, vol. 31 (1959, rev. 1990), pp. 52–60, 121.
[22] The others survive in a non-autograph manuscript of the same period (London, British Library, Add. MS 33236) – in the company, interestingly, of three of the fantasias.

ode composition. His efforts, like those of his predecessors, were dutiful rather than inspired.

In 1680 the decision was taken to add music in the same way to the third well-established occasion of loyal addressing: the formal welcome back to London after the summer remove of the court to Windsor. This decision was probably taken in the wake of the Popish Plot, and whichever official was responsible for it was probably not looking beyond the immediate opportunity to put out more propaganda. But with Blow already heavily committed, having to set an ode in January and May every year, the new task devolved upon the young Purcell. This choice turned out to be an inspired one.

Purcell himself, we might suppose, viewed his new task with little enthusiasm, and his dismay can be imagined when he was presented with the text he was to set. Its couplets, trite and limping, were scarcely calculated to inspire musical ideas:

> Welcome, Vicegerent of the mighty King
> That made and governs everything;
> Welcome from rural pleasures to the busy throne
> In this head city, this imperial town,
> The seat and centre of the crown . . .
>
> His absence was autumn, his presence is spring,
> That ever new life and new pleasure does bring.
> Then all that have voices, let 'em cheerfully sing,
> And those that have none may say, 'God save the King!'[23]

Dreadful stuff of this kind occurs in the texts of many of his royal odes, and as a result both words and music have been given short shrift by most writers nowadays. But that is misguided. The poets were engaged not in purely literary endeavour: what they produced is equivalent not to the canvases of a master painter but to the political cartoon. As for Purcell, he evidently recognized an opportunity to show his mettle, with the Chapel Royal participating at full strength, together with the Private Music and the Twenty-Four Violins, and with his music at the centre of an important state occasion. Accordingly he spared no effort, and his royal odes, though sometimes uneven in quality, contain some fine and sadly neglected music.[24]

Welcome, Vicegerent begins with an unblushing piece of showing off: the young composer was determined to be noticed. The second movement of

---

[23] Purcell Society Edition, vol. 15 (2000), pp. 1–28.
[24] See Ian Spink, 'Purcell's Odes: Propaganda and Panegyric', in Price, *Studies*, pp. 145–71; Martin Adams, 'Purcell, Blow and the English Court Ode', ibid., pp. 172–91; Bruce Wood, 'Purcell's Odes: A Re-appraisal', in Burden, *Companion*, pp. 200–53.

its introductory symphony is repeated in its entirety, note for note, as an accompaniment to the opening chorus. After this promising start, what follows is a good deal less impressive, but no matter. Purcell had made his mark, and initiated what would turn out to be one of the most important series of works in his career – one that stretches unbroken through to the magnificent offerings he was to compose for Queen Mary's birthday in his last years.

Play, Playford, parenthood

It was not long before the theatre beckoned again. This time the commission, a modest affair involving only a single song, came from the King's Company at the Theatre Royal, Drury Lane. The play was Shakespeare's *King Richard the Second*, heavily rewritten as *The Sicilian Usurper* by the Irish playwright Nahum Tate (1652–1715), and Purcell's song, performed during the prison scene in the final act, was the first of many collaborations between the two men. Tate, though he later rose to be Poet Laureate, would be forgotten nowadays were it not for the association between his words and Purcell's music – most famously, of course, in *Dido and Aeneas*. For the moment, though, all of that was unforeseeable, and the immediate signs were less than propitious. Tate's effort fell foul of the censors – the poison spread by the Popish Plot was enough to make any play dealing with an English king a risky proposition – and it was suppressed after only a couple of performances, taking Purcell's song with it into limbo.[25]

The year ended more happily. Purcell had the satisfaction of seeing his music in print: only the second time this had happened. Two years previously, three short songs of his, together with his rather more imposing elegy on the death of Matthew Locke, had been included in one of the numerous song-books published by John Playford (1623–87), the second volume in a series entitled *Choice Ayres and Songs to Sing to the Theorbo-Lute or Bass-Viol* – shrewdly aimed at musical amateurs, a rapidly expanding market. Now the third volume appeared, and this time Purcell's work featured far more prominently. The book included no fewer than nine of his songs, among them three from *Theodosius*; altogether these made up almost a sixth of its contents.[26] Purcell's name was beginning to catch the public eye.

In his preface to the volume Playford, after apologizing for a delay to its appearance caused by illness, had some important things to say about the composition of English songs – things that apply to Purcell perhaps above all other composers:

---

[25] *London Stage*, p. 293.
[26] *Choice Ayres and Songs . . . The Third Book* (London: J. Playford, 1681 – published on 16 December 1680: see *RMA Research Chronicle*, 1 (1961), p. 4). Two of Purcell's songs are among the fifteen unattributed items in the volume, which total more than one item in three.

I need not here commend the Excellency of their Composition, the ingenious Authors Names being printed with them, who are Men that understand to make *English* Words speak their true and genuine Sence both in good humour [expression] and Ayre [melodic line]; which can never be performed by either *Italian* or *French*, they not so well understanding the Proprieties of our Speech. I have seen lately published a large Volum of *English* Songs, composed by an *Italian* Master, who has lived here in *England* many Years; I confess he is a very able Master, but being not perfect in the true *Idiom* of our Language, you will find the Air of his Musick so much after his Country-Mode, that it would sute far better with *Italian* than *English* Words. But I shall forebear to censure his Work, leaving it to the Verdict of better Musical Judgments: only I think him very disingenious [*sic*] and much to blame, to endeavour to raise a Reputation to himself and [his] Book, by disparaging and undervaluing most of the best *English* Masters and Professors of Musick. I am sorry it is (in this Age) so much the Vanity of some of our *English* Gentry to admire that in a Foreigner, which they either slight or take little notice of in one of their own Nation; for I am sure that our *English* Masters in Musick . . . are not in Skill and Judgment inferiour to any Foreigners whatsoever.[27]

The Italian composer targeted was Pietro Reggio (1632–85), whose songbook – elegantly and expensively engraved, unlike the average Playford product, and dedicated to the king – had appeared earlier that year.[28] Playford's comments, and his attack on Reggio, show very clearly how much of an obstacle was placed in the way of native English composers by sheer snobbery. It was an obstacle that Purcell would soon surmount effortlessly – but he would also turn the snobbery to his own advantage.[29] For the moment, though, his prominent place in the new volume of *Choice Ayres* no doubt left him more than content.

There was good news at this time for another member of the Purcell family too. In February 1681 his cousin Francis, the second youngest of his uncle Thomas's seven offspring, was made a groom-in-ordinary to Charles II, gaining a welcome measure of financial security. But a more important family event was impending. That summer Frances Purcell presented Henry with a son. Their joy, however, all too quickly turned to sadness, for the baby, christened Henry at All-Hallows-the-Less on 9 July, was buried

[27] Playford, *Choice Ayres and Songs . . . The Third Book* (London, 1681), p. [i]. The preface is dated 2 November 1680.
[28] *Songs Set by Signior Pietro Reggio* (London: n. publ., 1680).
[29] Holman, *Purcell*, pp. 41–2, directly compares Reggio's and Purcell's 'She loves, and she confesses too', which employ the same ground bass, and concludes that Purcell's setting, published in *Choice Ayres*, book 3, 'may have been composed as a response and rebuke to Reggio' for his disparagement of English composers.

there only nine days later. (All these events were recorded in the All-Hallows registers, so presumably Purcell was still living with his in-laws, an arrangement which was not uncommon.)[30] Purcell may well have sought solace in a memorial composition for the dead infant, for it was around this time that he began a setting of George Sandys's 'Ah! few and full of sorrow are the days of man', a paraphrase of words taken from the Book of Job. The piece is a devotional song for four solo voices – music for domestic use, not public performance – and in Purcell's lifetime it was never published, nor even circulated in manuscript, adding to the sense that it was conceived as a private expression of grief. He never completed the fair copy, though he left space for it; perhaps he had not the heart.[31]

Infant deaths were commonplace – unsurprisingly, given the primitive living conditions of the period – and they were no doubt accepted with resignation as much as with anguish. Life, in any case, had to go on. Certainly the demands on Purcell to compose music for events at court did not slacken. By the time of his son's death he must have needed to begin work, if he had not already done so, on the autumn welcome song for 1681, *Swifter, Isis, swifter flow*, whose text depicts the king arriving back at Whitehall Palace in the royal barge. (This is almost certainly how the court party actually travelled when they returned on 27 August after their stay in Windsor. The Lord Mayor and aldermen who waited on the king four days later to present their loyal addresses at the welcome ceremony probably came by boat too; it was a common mode of transport in a city that had few paved roads and only one bridge.) Other verses refer to the spring tides that replenish the waters of the river, 'dead low' at the end of summer, and liken the king's return to that of the sun after its winter absence in remote northerly latitudes. (Identifying Charles II with the sun was a frequent image in royal odes; Louis XIV was not the only Sun King!) And raising his eyes from the riverside, the poet depicts the city's customary celebrations, both formal and informal, at the monarch's return: church bells ringing, bonfires blazing, and the big artillery pieces at the Tower firing a salute.[32]

Despite all this evocative imagery in the text, Purcell evidently had trouble with the music – not surprisingly, for the events of the summer must have left him with little appetite for such a task. Only by the skin of his teeth did he succeed in finishing the score in time. He managed to work up his sketches into a fair copy: it is the first piece he entered in a large score-book formed of luxurious and expensive paper, probably the official file copy from which instrumental and vocal parts would be drawn for the performance.[33] Fair copy or not, it shows more and more signs of

---

[30] Register of Baptisms, All-Hallows-the-Less, 9 July 1681; Register of Burials, 18 July 1681.
[31] Purcell Society Edition, vol. 30 (1965), pp. 109–16.
[32] Purcell Society Edition, vol. 15 (2000), pp. 29–58.
[33] London, British Library, MS R.M. 20.h.8.

haste towards the end, and in the final chorus the inner vocal parts are blank save for a few notes. No doubt scribbled on some scrap of paper and inserted in the parts at the last minute, to be performed more or less at sight, they have not survived.

Yet the musical quality of the remainder of the work is unaffected: *Swifter, Isis* represents a triumph for Purcell's professionalism, in what must have been very difficult circumstances. The piece is full of delightful pictorial touches: running quavers suggest the flow of the river, vigorous downward scales depict the pealing of bells, and so on. More interesting, though, is a movement constructed over a repeated or 'ground' bass. (This is one of the first examples in Purcell's music of a device in which he would soon come to excel, though at the moment he still had a lot to learn about handling it: this early effort is rather stiff, with an awkwardly fanfare-like bass pattern.) And the work employs a bigger orchestra than usual, with Purcell making imaginative and effective use of recorders and oboes as well as the usual strings. (The woodwind instruments, making their first appearance in a royal ode, had been introduced to the court by players from Paris, who arrived in 1673 with splendid French-made three-piece instruments – vastly superior to their English predecessors, obsolete single-piece renaissance recorders with their queasy tuning, and shawms incapable of soft or expressive playing.)[34]

The attractively naive description of loyal subjects eagerly awaiting the arrival of the royal barge took little account of current political realities. The anonymous poet gave these only one oblique mention, which came, rather uncomfortably, at the end:

> May no harsher sounds e'er invade your blest ears,
> To disturb your repose or alarm our fears;
> No trumpet be heard in this place, or drum-beat,
> But in compliment, or to invite you to eat;
> Nor this happy palace with any shouts ring
> Save the loud acclamations of 'God save the King!'

For us the sheer banality of these lines obscures their all-too-serious meaning, but no one among the listeners that day would have missed it. Politically it was still business as usual: even after the Popish Plot had been exposed as a chimera, an unscrupulous Whig faction remained hell-bent on excluding the Duke of York from the succession to the throne and, when the time should come, installing Monmouth as king. Their leader,

---

[34] Three French recorder players – Maxant de Bresmes, Pierre Boutet, and (Jean?) Guiton – first appear in the records in January/February 1675 (*RECM*, vol. 1, p. 146); together with a fourth, Jacques (James) Paisible, they had apparently travelled with Cambert, and all four of them plus a fifth, Bejard, are also referred to as playing the oboe (ibid., p. 150). For a fuller account of their work in England see David Lasocki, 'Professional Recorder Playing in England 1500–1740, II: 1640–1740', *Early Music*, 10 (1982), pp. 183–91.

the Earl of Shaftesbury, had been arrested for treason during the summer – perhaps even Purcell was not too busy to notice – and was brought to trial in October, provoking popular demonstrations in his support. On 1 November a resolutely Whig jury brought in a verdict of *ignoramus* (equivalent to a Scottish verdict of 'not proven'), allowing Shaftesbury to escape execution, though he and his party were broken: he fled to Holland in December and died there little more than a year later. The equivocal verdict nevertheless paved the way for continuing political strife and intrigue, whose consequences would involve Purcell, in his capacity as a court composer, more and more as time went on.

Not long after the welcome ceremony Purcell was busy with a very different task: composing a roistering sea song, 'Blow, Boreas, blow', for a new comedy by Thomas D'Urfey (*c*.1653–1723), *Sir Barnaby Whigg*, which was produced that autumn.[35] This was only a modest commission, but times were hard in the theatrical world. The following year the two London companies, both of them exhausted by ceaseless competition and the King's Company impoverished by it, would merge, on what were effectively takeover terms dictated by Betterton. Even after the merger it would be years before Purcell began to receive more substantial commissions from the new United Company.

Early in 1682 the Purcells moved into a new home, in Great St Ann's, just behind the Abbey, and offering a convenient short cut to the organ loft through the back gate of Dean's Yard and the cloisters.[36] (The street still stands, and the short cut can still be made, though the house itself was demolished in the eighteenth century.) And it was not long before another, more temporary move was in prospect, for the court's annual stay in Windsor. They made the short journey on 17 May, among them Purcell's cousin Francis, in attendance on the king, and his youngest brother Daniel, still a Chapel chorister.

Purcell himself was faced with an unusual prospect: the performance of a royal welcome song at Windsor instead of Whitehall. The king had at last judged it safe to bring back the Duke of York from Scotland. (He had packed him off there at the height of the Exclusion Crisis in the wake of the Popish Plot, ostensibly to serve as High Commissioner but actually to keep him out of the way and prevent him from fuelling the political flames with some tactless remark, as he was inclined to do.) On 27 May his ship docked in the Pool of London, and two days later – on the king's birthday, by a happy coincidence – Purcell's *What shall be done in behalf of the man* was performed before the two royal brothers. Its anonymous text is outspoken about Monmouth and his backers:

---

[35] *London Stage*, p. 302; Purcell Society Edition, vol. 21 (forthcoming).
[36] St Margaret's, Westminster, overseer's accounts of rates for 1682.

The mobilè crowd [the London mob]
Who so foolishly bow'd
To the pageant of royalty [Monmouth], fondly mistaken,
Shall at last from their dream of rebellion awaken.[37]

This prediction, though, was to prove wide of the mark. That summer there was a prolonged stand-off between the king and the City of London, whose voters, at the polls held on Midsummer's Day, 24 June, elected Whigs to the two positions of sheriffs. The royal party cried foul, and the elections had to be re-run, twice, before they yielded an outcome satisfactory to the king: the election of his own candidates. This was the first rent in the Whigs' armour; from now on the king, not they, would be on the attack, and before another year was out he would be triumphant.

Purcell must have been aware of these goings-on, but he had more immediate things on his mind. That same month his cousin Charles, Thomas's third son, who was a naval officer, set sail on an expedition to Africa, prudently making his will before he left. On the same day Thomas made his own will. It seems likely that he was seriously ill, for two weeks previously he had given another of his sons, Matthew, power of attorney to manage his affairs and draw his salary.[38] At all events he died on 31 July, and was buried three days later in the Abbey cloisters, where so many musicians had been laid to rest. But the mourning family soon had their spirits lifted. It may have been on that same day – it was certainly within a week – that a second son was born to Henry and Frances. On 9 August he was christened John Baptista, in the Abbey. Like his elder brother, alas, he had but a short time to live; he died a little over two months later.[39]

Gentleman of the Chapel

A third death at this time directly affected Purcell: that of Edward Lowe, a Gentleman of the Chapel Royal and one of its three organists, on 11 July 1682. Purcell must have had his hopes set on membership of the Chapel for a long time, but vacancies for Gentlemen came up only infrequently. (There had been only three – two for countertenor and one for bass – in the preceding three years, and in any case it seems likely that Purcell did not possess a good voice as an adult, since we never hear of him as a singer save for one highly suspect mention.)[40] Because the court was at Windsor there was a lengthy wait – more than two months – before the vacancy created by Lowe's death could be formally filled. At last, on 16 September, Purcell was sworn in as his successor. His appointment and salary were to take effect retrospectively, from the date, three

[37] Purcell Society Edition, vol. 15 (2000), pp. 59–89.
[38] All three documents are quoted in full in Zimmerman, *Purcell*, pp. 293–4, 368–9, 94–5.
[39] WAR, Baptisms 1607–1705, f. 10, Burials 1606–1706, f. 37v.
[40] See p. 151, below.

days after Lowe had died, on which he received a warrant for the post – in other words a written promise of it.[41]

The new appointment brought with it responsibilities which were not even hinted at in its title. There was, anomalously, no post of Composer to the Chapel Royal, yet its services had a continual need for new music, and for anthems in particular. Blow, who was another of the three organists (the third being a lesser light named John Dusharroll) and also Master of the Children, had since his appointment in 1674 produced a large corpus of church music, much of it specifically for the Chapel: upwards of thirty anthems, half of them elaborate pieces with instrumental symphonies. Purcell too had been contributing ever since 1677 and possibly earlier, on an entirely unofficial basis since he had no formal connection with the Chapel: he composed at least three symphony anthems (though two of them survive only as fragments) before his appointment as Chapel organist.[42] In future he would produce a great deal more.

To mark this new point of departure, Blow presented Purcell with a handsome score-book containing, among other music, several anthems he had copied himself.[43] (This was not just another instance of Blow's generosity, for the book almost certainly had an official purpose – serving, probably, as a file copy for the preparation of performing material.) Some of these anthems are by Blow himself, others are by Humfrey and Locke. Purcell too had been contributing to the collection for several years, probably at first under Blow's supervision; he had finished an incomplete transcription of one of Blow's anthems, and added other pieces of Blow's and of his own. He had also transcribed pieces by his great Tudor and Jacobean forebears, including Tallis, Byrd, and Orlando Gibbons – not, as some have claimed, in order to study their music, but in order to sort out the correct word-underlay, which is very sketchy and unsatisfactory in the printed vocal partbooks from which he was copying.[44] After the volume came permanently into his possession he filled most of the remaining pages with new works of his own.

On the rear flyleaf of the book, below an elaborate rebus formed of Blow's initials, Purcell proudly signed his name. It forms part of an inscription which has been a source of puzzlement and speculation ever since:

---

[41] *Cheque Book*, p. 17.

[42] *If the Lord himself* and *Praise the Lord, ye servants* (vocal bass parts only), in Tokyo, Nanki Library, MS N–5/10, and *My beloved spake* (countertenor, tenor, and bass parts only), in London, Westminster Abbey, Triforium Books, all precede pieces attributed to 'Mr' Blow – copied, therefore, before December 1677, when Blow received his doctorate. Several of Purcell's anthems with organ can also be dated before 1682, but these cannot with certainty be linked to the Chapel rather than the Abbey.

[43] Cambridge, Fitzwilliam Museum, Music MS 88.

[44] *The First Book of Selected Church Musick* (London: Griffin, 1641), compiled by John Barnard, minor canon of St Paul's Cathedral. The publication comprises ten books, but Purcell seems not to have had a complete set, for he omitted one part in Byrd's *O Lord, make thy servant* – though this may be a mere oversight.

8. *"God bless M* *Henry Purcell 1682 September y* *10*th*": Cambridge, Fitzwilliam, MS 88, flyleaf.*

'God bless Mr Henry Purcell September ye 10th 1682'. Why on earth should Purcell write such a thing on his own book? – why indeed should he style himself 'Mr', in such a formal manner? All kinds of ingenious explanations have been offered: that it was somehow connected with young John Baptista, who may already have been mortally ill; that it was Purcell's birthday; that it was the fifth anniversary of his appointment as a royal musician in succession to Locke. The last point is certainly true, and may even have some relevance, but there is a perfectly straightforward explanation for both the wording and the date. Even though a few days were to elapse before Purcell was sworn in as Chapel organist, his appointment must have been agreed unofficially (hence its eventual backdating). The court had returned from Windsor only the previous day, so Blow gave him the book at the first opportunity.[45] And close inspection reveals that most of the apparently puzzling inscription is in Blow's handwriting: all that Purcell wrote was his own name. What could be more natural than for Blow to add the words which he did, framing the signature, to mark the passing of the book from an erstwhile master to a pupil who had at last become a colleague?

The return of the court from Windsor did not, on this occasion, entail the usual welcome ceremony. Purcell still had more than a month's grace in which to complete a new ode for that event, for the king was off to Newmarket for the races. *The summer's absence unconcern'd we bear* was duly performed on 22 October, the day after his return.[46]

Meanwhile Purcell, as a royal musician, found himself being sucked repeatedly into the political whirlpool. The text of *The summer's absence*

---

[45] Luttrell, vol. 1, p. 218. See also Shay and Thompson, *Manuscripts*, pp. 41–3, where the date of the court's return is given as 10 September.
[46] Purcell Society Edition, vol. 15 (2000), pp. 90–122.

unconcern'd we bear had not sailed nearly as close to the wind as that of *What shall be done in behalf of the man*: the anonymous poet confined himself for most of its length to a pious reminder of the martyrdom of Charles I and the public rejoicing at the Restoration of his son, a couple of digs at the expansionist militarism of Louis XIV, and a celebration of the blessings of peace, which the policies of Charles II had secured for England. As he approached the end of the poem, however, he could no longer avoid mentioning tensions at home:

> But amidst all our stores [plenty], some who surfeit on peace
> The infection had spread of a mortal disease:
> To the plague of rebellion the mischief was growing,
> And the life of the State to your conduct is owing.

And as if this were not enough (though Purcell managed only what seems a curiously inappropriate setting of these lines, as a tenor air in a sprightly dance measure), one of his song tunes was appropriated by the loyal party in the political in-fighting, just as 'Hail to the myrtle shade' had been two years earlier. The present occasion was the installation, on 29 October, of Sir William Pritchard, a supporter of the king, as Lord Mayor of London. Exactly as before, it was a number from *Theodosius* that was adapted to political doggerel, a fact which speaks volumes for the popularity of Purcell's score. The tune of 'Now, now the fight's done' had already done duty, when the king contemptuously dissolved an uncooperative Parliament the previous year, for

> Now, now the work's done, and the Parliament set [sitting]
> Are sent back again like fools as they met.[47]

Now it reappeared in a new guise:

> Now, now the time's come, noble *Pritchard* is chose
> In spight of all people that would him oppose.[48]

So Purcell, willy-nilly, had become firmly identified with the loyal party. He does not seem to have taken this amiss, for whatever he may have thought in private about having doggerel force-fitted to his music, he composed a new catch expressly for this same occasion. The anonymous poet did not mince his words:

---

[47] Ebsworth, *Ballads*, p. 22.
[48] Martin, Joseph, *The contented subjects; or, the Citizens joy* ([London], [1682]); included in Ebsworth, *Ballads*, p. 166.

Since the Duke [of York] is return'd we'll slight all the Whigs,
And let 'em be hang'd for politic prigs;
Both Presbyter Jack [James, Duke of Monmouth] and all the old crew
That lately design'd Forty One to renew.[49]

The reference is to 1641, the year when open hostilities had broken out between king and Parliament – leading to the Civil War. Neither the poet nor the composer (who subsequently published the piece) could have nailed his colours more firmly to the royal mast.

In such a fevered atmosphere, though, even Purcell's loyalty was not enough to save him from embarrassment. On 4 February 1683 he was obliged, on the insistence of the Abbey authorities, to take the Anglican Holy Communion in public, before four witnesses who would testify that he had done so; two of them would later be called into court to swear that they had been present at the event, and observed the other two signing their own depositions to the same effect.[50] These extraordinary precautions can hardly be explained away by mere generalized paranoia: there must have been some definite suspicion of Catholic sympathies on Purcell's part. The likeliest reason was that he had a Catholic wife. Eventually the affair passed over, though it must have left an unpleasant taste in Purcell's mouth.

Songs and sonatas

Music offered some timely consolation, with the publication of another volume of Playford's *Choice Ayres and Songs* – the fourth in the series. As in the third, Purcell's music made up a substantial part of the contents: eight of the songs were his (and one by Blow was credited to Purcell by mistake, no doubt to the amusement of both men).[51] Four of these are of particular interest. The impressive 'Retir'd from any mortal's sight' was now no longer doomed to oblivion along with Tate's *King Richard II*.[52] There are two ground-bass songs, 'She loves, and she confesses too' and 'Let each gallant heart'; the latter, a brisk and cheerful number, uses a ground which is a diatonic version of that in the famous Lament in *Dido and Aeneas*, showing just how flexible this seemingly rigid formula could be in Purcell's hands. But easily the most impressive of the eight songs is the largest: 'From silent shades', an example of the then fashionable 'mad song', depicting insanity brought on by unrequited love.[53] It gives us a haunting and unforgettable portrait of poor Bess of Bedlam (the song's

[49] Purcell Society Edition, vol. 22a (2000), p. 23.
[50] The relevant documents are quoted in full in Zimmerman, *Purcell*, pp. 100–1.
[51] Blow's 'Why does the morn in blushes rise' – subsequently published with the correct attribution in Henry Playford's *Wit and Mirth . . . The Second Part* (London: H. Playford, 1700).
[52] Purcell Society Edition, vol. 20 (1998), pp. 45–6.
[53] Purcell Society Edition, vol. 25 (1985), pp. 18–21, 31–2, 26–30 respectively.

subtitle). The song is full of violent internal contrasts and swerving shifts of time signature (twelve in less than sixty bars); feverish declamatory writing and searingly vivid touches of word-painting occur cheek by jowl with naive lyrical fragments that resemble distorted nursery rhymes half remembered from a nightmare. This is the work of a musical dramatist of exceptional power.

A project that was first mooted in the spring of 1683 offered Purcell the prospect of some light relief. A new organ was required for the Temple Church, and the Benchers of the Temple – shrewd lawyers one and all – decided on a competitive contract. Their idea was ingenious. Two leading organ-builders were invited to take part. Each had not merely to submit a scheme but actually to build an organ, and each instrument was to be given a public demonstration once it was ready. The Benchers of the Inner Temple championed Bernard Smith (c.1630–1708), while those of the Outer supported Renatus Harris (c.1652–1724), and the two builders in turn engaged leading players to show off their wares: Draghi for Harris, Blow and Purcell for Smith.[54] The stage was set for what was to become the famous Battle of the Organs – though this would not be joined in earnest for another year. Both instruments had first to be designed, built, and installed.

This was probably just as well, for the late spring was a busy time for Purcell. In the *London Gazette* for 24–8 May he advertised his first instrumental publication:

> These are to give Notice to all Gentlemen that have subscribed to the Proposals published by Mr Henry Purcel for the Printing his Sonata's of three Parts for two Violins and Base to the Harpsecord or Organ, That the said Books are now compleatly finished, and shall be delivered to them upon the 11th of June next: And if any who have not yet subscribed, shall before that time subscribe, according to the said Proposals (which is Ten Shillings the whole sett) which are at Mr. William Hall's house in Norfolk-street, or at Mr. Playford's and Mr. Carr's Shops in the Temple; for the said Books will not after that time be sold under 15s. the Sett.[55]

He was as good as his word. On the appointed day the *Gazette* contained a second notice, directing subscribers to collect their copies – not, however, from Playford and Carr, but from Purcell's own house. This was probably because, although the books had been elegantly engraved, some misprints

---

[54] Hawkins, vol. 2, p. 691; Charles Burney, *A General History of Music*, vol. 2 (London: the author, 1782), p. 344.
[55] *London Gazette*, 24–8 May 1683. The sonatas were also advertised in book 5 of Playford's *Choice Ayres and Songs* (London, 1684).

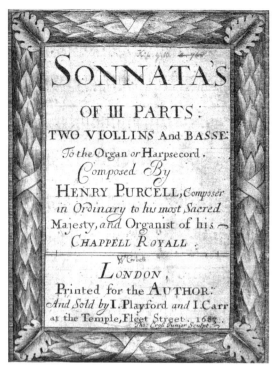

9. Title-page of Purcell's Sonatas of Three Parts (1683).

had inevitably slipped through; surviving copies contain meticulous hand-corrections, inserted probably by Purcell's wife.[56] Great care was lavished on every aspect of the publication. Purcell had even ordered the sonatas in an ingenious and near-symmetrical pattern. The keys of the first eight, alternately minor and major, rise by thirds from G minor to G major, while those of the last four mirror this, falling by thirds from C minor to D major; they thus cover all the keys that were available with a keyboard instrument tuned in unequal temperament.

The publication was a major event: these were the first examples to be published in England of a chamber-music genre that would, within 20 years, prove all-conquering. The sonatas were inscribed:

---

[56] Margaret Laurie has suggested that these corrections may have been inserted after Purcell's death, together with those in some copies of *Dioclesian*, the Te Deum and Jubilate in D major, *Ayres for the Theatre*, etc. On 6 November 1699 Frances advertised that she had 'taken into her own hand the Te Deum, Aires, the Opera of Dioclesian, first and last Sonata's, with Instructions for the Harpsichord . . . and [they] may be had at her House . . . with all the Errata's carefully corrected' (Michael Tilmouth, 'A Calendar of References to Music in Newspapers Published in London and the Provinces, 1660–1719', *RMA Research Chronicle*, 1 (1961), p. 30).

May it please yor Maj^{ty} /
I had not assum'd the confidence of laying ye following Compositions
at your Sacred feet; but that (as they are the immediate Results of your
Majesties *Royall favour, and benignity to me (which have made me*
what I am) so, I am constrain'd to hope, I may presume, amongst Others
of your Majesties *over-oblig'd and altogether undeserving Subjects,*
that your Maj^{ty} *will with your accustom'd Clemency, Vouchsafe to*
Pardon the best Endeavours of

> Yo^r Maj^{ties}
> *Most Humble and*
> *Obedient Subject and Servant*
> H. Purcell

After this flowery and conventional dedication, though, comes something altogether more informative.

Ingenuous Reader,

INstead of an elaborate harangue on the beauty and the charms of
Musick (which after all the learned Encomions that words can contrive)
commends it self best by the performances of a skilful hand, and an
angelical voice:) I shall say but a very few things by way of Preface,
concerning the following Book, and its Author: for its Author, he has
faithfully endeavour'd a just imitation of the most fam'd Italian
Masters; principally, to bring the seriousness and gravity of that sort of
Musick into vogue, and reputation among our Country-men, whose
humor, 'tis time now, should begin to loath the levity, and balladry of
our neighbours: The attempt he confesses to be bold, and daring, there
being Pens and Artists of more eminent abilities, much better qualify'd
for the imployment than his, or himself, which he well hopes these weak
endeavours, will in due time provoke, and enflame to a more acurate
undertaking. He is not asham'd to own his unskilfulness in the Italian
Language; but that's the unhappiness of his Education, which cannot
justly be accounted his fault, however he thinks he may warrantably
affirm, that he is not mistaken in the power of the Italian Notes, or
elegancy of their Compositions, which he would recommend to the
English Artists. There has been neither care, nor industry wanting, as
well in contriving, as revising the whole Work; which would have been
abroad in the world much sooner, but that he has now thought fit to
cause the whole Thorough Bass to be Engraven, which was a thing quite
besides his first Resolutions. It remains only that the English
Practitioner be enform'd, that he will find a few terms of Art perhaps

unusual to him, the chief of which are these following: Adagio *and* Grave, *which import nothing but a very slow movement:* Presto Largo, Poco Largo, *or* Largo *by it self, a middle movement:* Allegro, *and* Vivace, *a very brisk, swift, or fast movement:* Piano, *soft. The author has no more to add, but his hearty wishes, that his Book may fall into no other hands but theirs who carry Musical Souls about them; for he is willing to flatter himself into a belief, that with such his labours will seem neither unpleasant, nor unprofitable.*

Vale.[57]

What a tempting sales pitch, in an age and a country that loved both all things new and all things Italian! (A distinctly self-conscious sales pitch too: Purcell hardly ever used those new-fangled Italian tempo markings except in his trio sonatas.) And there was the bonus of a sideswipe at the 'levity and balladry' of French music, which like all things French was becoming increasingly unpopular in England, thanks to Louis XIV and his threatening territorial ambitions. The music, though, was not quite what Purcell claimed. True, the sonatas contain all the latest Italian tricks: brilliant passages in parallel thirds, vigorous fugal writing, 'walking' basses, and so on. But they are also unmistakably English, the direct descendants of Purcell's fantasias. Like those antecedents, they contain powerfully expressive dissonances, startling chromatic harmonies, and astonishing feats of counterpoint (one begins with the same idea in all three stringed instruments, simultaneously at three different speeds; another opens with a movement that crams its twenty-six bars with seventeen entries of a single idea, presenting many of them upside down or at half speed, or both).[58] Mixing English and Italian characteristics in this manner might, in the hands of a lesser composer, have produced incongruous results. But Purcell did something more than mix them: he fused them together indissolubly. In the process he created some of the finest instrumental chamber music of all time – on a par even with that of such later masters as Haydn, Mozart, Beethoven, or Bartók.

Why was a collection of sonatas published in four partbooks entitled *Sonatas of Three Parts*? (The *Sonatas of Four Parts*, published after Purcell's death, are identical with these in scoring and presentation, and were probably composed over the same period.) The explanation is amusing. Evidently after Purcell had, as he explains, decided on including a separate keyboard part, not just a second copy of the bass line, Playford was too tight-fisted to allow the title page to be re-engraved! London's

---

[57] Purcell, *Sonatas of Three Parts* (London: J. Playford and Carr, 1683), prefatory pages in each partbook. The last word of the preface, 'vale', is latin for 'farewell'.
[58] Sonatas Nos 6, in C major, and 7, in E minor. All twelve are included in Purcell Society Edition, vol. 5 (1977).

musical amateurs, though, did not mind. The sonatas sold briskly, and over the next year or so went through three editions. Roger North admired them as 'very artificiall [that is, skilfully composed] and good musick', and even though he privately regretted their being 'clog'd with somewhat of an English vein', he considered that Purcell had 'outdone' the famed Italian masters, even if the results betrayed 'a litle too much of the labour'. He wrote of the sonatas with artless enthusiasm after he had spent an evening playing them – with the composer, no less, at the keyboard. North explains that his brother Francis, the Lord Chancellor, who like himself was a musical amateur, had

> caused the devine Purcell to bring his Itallian manner'd compositions; and with him on the harpsicord, myself and another violin, wee performed them more than once, of which Mr Purcell was not a little proud, nor was it a common thing for one of his dignity to be so entertained.[59]

This no longer reads quite as North intended. While praising the greatest musician of the age, he tells us without embarrassment that 'the devine Purcell' was 'not a little proud' to be 'entertained' by a couple of wealthy lawyers.

Odes, royal and Cecilian

Meanwhile yet another political storm had broken – this time one that would finally clear the air. In March 1683 the king had gone off to enjoy another stay in Newmarket, but on 22 March a careless stable-groom who was smoking had started a fire that destroyed much of the town, forcing the king to return to the capital earlier than planned. Unbeknown to him, this saved his life. Prominent members of the Whig faction had plotted an ambush for the royal party at Rye House, on the Newmarket Road about 20 miles from London, with forty or fifty armed men. Both the king and his brother were to be assassinated, and Monmouth placed on the throne.

Unlike the Popish Plot this one had been real, and it was not long before the secret began to leak out. Some of those involved tried to save their own skins by turning informer. By the summer the whole conspiracy was laid bare. Monmouth went into hiding (and later into exile); a few of his principal backers fled abroad, but others were tried and sent to Tyburn. The royal propaganda machine, musicians included, went into overdrive. A symphony anthem by Blow, *Hear my voice, O God*, setting a blood-curdling text about God's vengeance on conspirators, was sung at Whitehall before the king on the Sunday between the guilty verdicts, delivered on 12 July, and the executions, on 20 and 21 July. Over three

---

[59] North, pp. 47–8.

hundred bars long, it had been composed, copied, and rehearsed in six days flat (unless, of course, Blow had been tipped off to expect a guilty verdict).[60] And two symphony anthems by Purcell, *In thee, O Lord, do I put my trust* and *The Lord is my light*, both of them unusually powerful settings of texts that deal with similar matters, also belong to this period, though their performance dates are not known.[61]

It may seem surprising that Purcell's next royal ode, which was performed only a matter of days after the execution of the Rye House conspirators, made no mention of the affair. Nor did it mention another victory which the king was able to savour that summer, when he succeeded at last in mastering the City of London by browbeating its common council to surrender its charter and accept a reduction in its powers. But events in both arenas had moved so fast that the poem had almost certainly been written, and Purcell's setting of it composed, too early to take account of them. In any case, the piece has a special purpose all its own. It is a marriage ode for the Duke of York's younger daughter, Princess (later Queen) Anne, and Prince George of Denmark, who had arrived in England on 19 July to claim her hand. *From hardy climes* accordingly confines itself to conventional compliments to the prince and good wishes for the future of the royal pair.[62]

The autumn welcome song for the king is very different. The anonymous poet, as he surveyed the destruction of the plotters and the Whig faction in the City, and went on to chide the London mob who had so often supported them, exulted in his task:

> Fly, bold Rebellion! make haste and be gone!
> Victorious in Council, great Charles is return'd.
> The Plot is display'd, and the traitors, some flown
> And some to Avernus by Justice thrown down. . . .

> Come then, change your notes, disloyal crowd,
> You that already have been too loud
> With importunate follies and clamours;
> 'Tis no business of yours
> To dispute the high powers
> As if you were the government framers . . .

---

[60] *Musica Britannica*, vol. 79 (2002), pp. 27–47. The anthem sets Psalm 64, vv. 1–9.
[61] Purcell Society Edition, vol. 14 (2003), pp. 78–103 (setting Psalm 71, vv. 1, 4, 5, 18, 20, 21), and pp. 104–24 (setting Psalm 27, vv. 1, 3, 5, 6).
[62] Purcell Society Edition, vol. 15 (2000), pp. 123–51. In the preface to that volume I suggest (p. xi) that the piece is a welcome song for the prince, performed soon after the day of his arrival, but James Winn has kindly pointed out in private correspondence that nuptial references in the text, and the lack of much forewarning of George's visit, indicate that the performance is more likely to have been given on 28 July, the wedding day itself, or on the following day, when the prince and princess received official visitors.

And Purcell exulted with him: the ode is easily his finest so far.[63] After its fleet-footed overture comes a grand sweep of music, extending to almost a hundred bars, before the piece first pauses for breath. Later on the 'disloyal crowd' are berated in the teeth-grating key of F minor. (In most of the various unequal temperaments which were current in Purcell's day, the flatness of its third gives the music a sinister quality – which is presumably why Purcell chose the key for this passage, and subsequently for the Sorceress's scene in *Dido and Aeneas*.) Towards the end of the ode comes an exquisitely poised solo air over a ground bass of steadily pacing quavers ('Be welcome, then, great Sir'), which blossoms into a meltingly beautiful string ritornello, and finally a seven-part ensemble full of ingenious part-writing and a dignified six-part chorus with sumptuous harmonies.

The late autumn was just as fruitful for Purcell as the summer had been. He composed yet another substantial ode – his third in four months. This one, *Welcome to all the pleasures*, was not for the court, but its occasion was every bit as momentous as that of *Fly, bold Rebellion!* For in November Purcell was a prime mover in the launch of an annual Cecilian festival in London. (The saint's day, 22 November, was well established and widely observed, but the idea of marking it with a secular celebration seems to have been an innovation.) The first concert was held in the 'musick house' at York Buildings, in Villiers Street near the Strand – at the opposite end from where, on the same day five years earlier, John Banister had given his concert series a new home in the Music School.

We do not know what else was on the programme for this first Cecilian concert. One possible contender is yet another ode by Purcell: *Laudate Ceciliam*, which he dated 1683 in his manuscript, though he may have intended the piece for the university concert series in Oxford (hence its Latin text).[64] But *Welcome to all the pleasures* will have needed no supporting cast to help it make an impression on the audience, for it is as finely crafted as *Fly, bold Rebellion!*, though quite different in character. Its text is by Christopher Fishburn, a very minor poet and song composer. Since his chief claim to fame (or infamy) is his possible authorship of an obscene play entitled *Sodom*, he seems an unlikely contributor to the noble Cecilian enterprise, but Restoration minds were broad. Purcell's setting employs various formulae on which he was coming to rely in his court odes – an elaborate ground-bass air plus a suitably lush ritornello, a solo number more lyrical in character – but one feature of it was quite novel: the

---

[63] Purcell Society Edition, vol. 15 (2000), pp. 152–91.
[64] Both Cecilian pieces are in Purcell Society Edition, vol. 10 (1990). The autograph of *Laudate Ceciliam*, uniquely among Purcell's music, employs a style of notation with void crotchets and quavers that is sometimes encountered in music by Italian composers such as Carissimi, and occasionally in Italianate music by English composers, which featured prominently in the Oxford concert series. See Martin Adams, *Purcell*, p. 38, and his 'Purcell's *Laudate Ceciliam*: An Essay in Stylistic Experimentation', in Gerald Gillen and Harry White (eds), *Musicology in Ireland*, Irish Musical Studies, 1 (Dublin: Irish Academic Press, 1990), pp. 227–47.

celebratory final chorus, interestingly, is in E major. This is the sharpest key ever used in the music of the period – as far removed from C major on the sharp side as F minor is in the other direction, and sounding just as distinctive for the opposite reason: the major thirds, particularly that from B to D sharp, are over-bright, giving a feeling of almost hectic jubilation.

Impressed the audience certainly were: so much so that Purcell was able to publish the piece – the first ode setting ever to be printed in its entirety. Playford issued it the following spring, complete with a most informative preface by the composer:

TO THE GENTLEMEN OF THE Musical Society, *And particularly the* STEWARDS for the YEAR ensuing. *William Bridgman,* Esq; *Nicholas Staggins,* Doctor in *Music; Gilbert Dolben,* Esq; and Mr. *Francis Forcer.*

GENTLEMEN, Your kind Approbation and benign Reception of the Performance of these *Musical Compositions* on St. *CECILIA*'s day, (by way of Gratitude) claim this DEDICATION; which likewise furnishes the Author with an opportunity of letting the World know the Obligation he lies under to you; and that he is to all Lovers of Music, *A real Friend and Servant,* HENRY PURCELL.[65]

This reveals a solid organization behind the event, and gives us a useful snapshot of its committee: two professional musicians and two wealthy leading citizens. It was a sound formula to carry the festival forward.

Glamorous music festivals were all very well, but everyday life, and death, continued regardless of them. Just before Christmas 1683 the aged John Hingeston died, and Purcell at last succeeded to his place as keeper of the king's wind instruments. The royal bill for his appointment gives a fascinating list of what was involved. Purcell was named

keeper, maker, repairer and mender and tuner of all and every his Majesty's musicall wind instruments; that is to say all regalls, virginalls, organs, flutes, recorders and all other kind of wind instruments whatsoever

– and in return for a salary of £60 a year he was to be responsible for

workinge, labouringe, makeing and mending any of the said instruments aforesaid . . . [and was required] to take up within ye

[65] Henry Purcell, *A Musical Entertainment Perform'd on November XXII. 1683* . . . (London: J. Playford and J. Carr, 1684), pp. [iii–iv].

realme of England all such mettalls, wyer, waynscote and other wood and things as shalbe necessary to be imployed about the premisses, agreeing, paying and allowing reasonable rates and prices for the same. And also in his Majesty's name and upon reasonable and lawfull prices, wages and hire, to take up such workmen, artificers, labourers, worke and store houses, land and water carriages and all other needeful things as the said Henry Purcell or his assignes shall thinke convenient to be used on ye premisses. And also . . . to take up all tymber, strings, and feathers, necessary and convenient for the premisses, agreeing, paying and allowing reasonable rates and prices for the same, in as full and ample manner as . . . John Hingston . . . formerly had.[66]

There must obviously have been one further, unwritten requirement: to know how to delegate.

The great frost

It was the bitterest winter anyone could remember. Off the south coast of England the sea was covered with a sheet of ice for two miles out from the shore, while in London the Thames froze to such a depth that it would bear the weight of horses and carriages. Three hundred years before home insulation and central heating were heard of, it must have caused misery. But not everyone was unhappy about it. The ingenious merchants of London soon turned these extreme conditions to advantage, by holding a 'frost fair' out on the ice,

planted with bothes in formal streetes, as in a Citty, or Continual faire, all sorts of Trades & shops furnished, & full of Commodities, even to a Printing presse, where the People & Ladys tooke a fansy to have their names Printed & the day & yeare set downe, when printed on the *Thames*: This humour tooke so universaly, that 'twas estimated the Printer gained five pound a day, for printing a line onely, at six-pence a Name, besides what he gott by Ballads &c: Coaches now plied from Westminster to the Temple, & from severall other staires too and froo, as in the streetes; also on sleds, sliding with skeetes; There was likewise Bull-baiting, Horse & Coach races, Pupet-plays & interludes, Cookes & Tipling, & lewder places; so as it seem'd to be a bacchanalia, Triumph or Carnoval on the Water, whilst it was a severe Judgement upon the Land: the Trees not onely splitting as if lightning-strock, but Men & Cattell perishing in divers places, and the very seas so locked up with yce, that no vessells

---

[66] *RECM*, vol. 1, p. 210 (16 February 1684).

could stirr out, or come in: the fowle[,] Fish & birds, & all our exotique Plants & Greenes universaly perishing; many Parks of deere destroied, & all sorts of fuell so deare that there were greate Contributions [public collections] to preserve the poore alive . . .[67]

Without the river to flush away its filth, the city was in fear of an outbreak of smallpox, which duly arrived, though it proved less terrible than many had feared. And to cap it all the iron frost brought another pestilence, one that was not to be finally banished from the city until nearly three hundred years later:

London, by reason of the excessive coldnesse of the aire, hindring the ascent of the smoke, was so filld with the fuliginous steame of the Sea-Coale, that hardly could one see crosse the streete, & this filling the lungs with its grosse particles exceedingly obstructed the breast, so as one could scarce breathe: There was no water to be had from the Pipes & Engines [pumps], nor could the Brewers, and divers other Tradesmen work . . .[68]

One of the tradesmen affected was Playford. A novelty printer of one-liners may have made fat profits out on the ice, but the serious printing industry was at a standstill. The reason was simple. Before each sheet was printed the type had to be inked using balls of stuffed sheepskin, which once or twice a shift were washed out in urine (the stench is said to have been breathtaking).[69] Now, even indoors, this froze. Playford alluded to the problem in his preface to the fifth volume of *Choice Ayres and Songs*: 'the last dreadful frost', he explained delicately, 'put an Embargo upon the Press for more than ten Weeks'.[70] But he had been helped through these difficulties, he added, by a new partner, John Carr, who had gone around town collecting copy from the composers. Among these, by now inevitably, was Purcell, represented in the volume by seven songs.

Staging a celebration
During 1683 one of the most crucial sequences of events in Purcell's life had begun to unfold. The king, conscious that the twenty-fifth anniversary

---

[67] Evelyn, 24 January 1684.
[68] Evelyn, 24 January 1684. As late as 8 February he reported 'an absolute Thaw & raine, but the Thames still hard'.
[69] For a full description of hand-press printing, see Philip Gaskell, *A New Introduction to Bibliography* (Oxford: Clarendon Press, 1972), pp. 9–141. An illuminating account of how contemporary printing techniques shaped printed sources of Purcell's operas is given in Andrew Pinnock, ' "From Rosy Bowers": Coming to Purcell the Bibliographical Way', in Michael Burden (ed.), *Henry Purcell's Operas: The Complete Texts* (Oxford: Oxford University Press, 2000), pp. 31–93.
[70] *Choice Ayres and Songs . . . The Fifth Book* (London, 1684), p. [iii].

of the Restoration was only two years away, determined to celebrate in style – with opera, served up in the grandest French manner. Thomas Betterton was accordingly dispatched to Paris, once the theatrical season had ended in July, 'to carry over the opera': that is, arrange for the company there to visit London. When this proved, not surprisingly, to be impracticable, he settled instead for bringing back a composer who was willing 'to endeavour to represent something at least something like an Opera . . . for his Majestyes diversion' on the occasion of the jubilee.[71] This composer proved to be none other than the ill-starred Louis Grabu, who duly arrived in London that autumn – no doubt to the great displeasure of Blow and Purcell.

It may have been the king's operatic ambitions that prompted Blow to compose his only stage work, the court masque *Venus and Adonis*, in order to show his own mettle. He evidently managed to secure a royal commission, for the masque, which appears to have originated in the household of the Duke of York,[72] was actually performed before the king, as John Walter (*c.*1660–1708), the copyist of its principal manuscript, duly noted.[73] Its production had a feature which linked it back through *Calisto* to court masques in the reign of Charles I and James I: the inclusion of royalty in the cast. On this occasion, though, the royal participants, unlike the bejewelled princesses and ladies in *Calisto*, were slightly down-at-heel members of the court circle: the king's illegitimate daughter, Mary Tudor, who sang Cupid, and her mother, his discarded mistress Moll Davies, a one-time singing actress, who sang Venus.[74] (The fact that Venus in the masque is, of course, Cupid's mother no doubt occasioned lubricious amusement.) The date of the production is not known, but it can hardly have been earlier than the beginning of 1683, for Mary Tudor did not reach her tenth birthday until 16 October that year: even then she would have been very young to sing difficult declamatory music.[75] Furthermore, when a performance given the following April at the same girls' school in Chelsea where *Dido and Aeneas* was to be staged in 1689, it was proudly announced on the front of the programme that the piece had been 'Perform'd before the KING. Afterwards at Mr. *JOSIAS*

---

[71] Letter from Lord Preston to the Duke of York: London, British Library, Add. MS 63759, p. 91.
[72] James A. Winn, '"A Versifying Maid of Honour": Anne Finch and the Libretto for *Venus and Adonis*', *Review of English Studies*, 59 (2008), pp. 67–85.
[73] London, British Library, Add. MS 22100, f. 126.
[74] Ibid.
[75] I am grateful to Sandra Tuppen, who has very recently drawn my attention to evidence of an entertainment put on for the king on 19 February 1683 – Shrovetide, the traditional masquing season – for which substantial refreshments were provided 'for the Musick and Dancing Masters' (i.e. instrumentalists and professional dancers), and coal was ordered 'for Ayring the Tiring roomes' (dressing rooms); this event may have been the premiere of *Venus and Adonis*. The expenditure on it is documented in Kew, National Archives, LS 1/25 (Lord Steward's accounts book, unfoliated).

PREIST'S Boarding School'.[76] 'Afterwards' obviously implies a lapse of months – with the original event still remembered – rather than years.

Purcell, in turn, responded to *Venus and Adonis* by composing *Dido and Aeneas*. Again we have no certainty as to its date, or whether it was ever staged – at any rate in its entirety – before the Chelsea performance in 1689. But several features of it are modelled unashamedly on *Venus and Adonis*, including the vocal scoring, some of the specific musical ideas, and certain aspects of the tonal design, with a tragic culmination in G minor (though Purcell's scheme is much more tightly controlled than Blow's). These are exactly the kind of borrowings that Blow and Purcell, throughout the 1680s, delighted in making from each other's works – invariably their most recent works. It seems likely that Purcell's little opera was intended, like *Venus and Adonis*, as part of a counterstrike against Grabu.

Dido and Aeneas, probably the best known of all Purcell's works, is ironically also perhaps his most misunderstood. It was long presumed to have been written for Priest's school, and therefore to date from the year of its known production there. But there is no evidence for either belief. The libretto demands the full resources of the professional theatre, including several painted scenes, a space for musicians beneath the stage (for the echo chorus and dance in the 'deep vaulted cell' in Act II), and even a flying machine (for the cupids who appear in the clouds above Dido's tomb): none of these is likely to have been available in a school, and nor, at least in an all-girls' establishment, are the countertenors, tenors, and basses required in all the chorus numbers. As for the date of composition, it was certainly not 1689, for very recent research has uncovered evidence of a performance at the school some time before the one in 1689 – in 1685, 1686 or 1687, though it is not clear which.[77] The musical language of the opera suggests an even earlier date: it has a great deal in common with works Purcell is known to have composed around 1683.[78] The musical sources, unfortunately, present intractable problems. All the principal manuscripts date from the late eighteenth century, many decades after the piece was composed, and all are defective in one way or another, not least in that they lack both the substantial sung prologue, in two scenes, and the chorus and dance for the enchantresses which originally rounded off Act II. Even the vocal scoring is debatable. There

---

[76] Cambridge, University Library, Sel. 2.123[6].

[77] Bryan White, 'Letter from Aleppo: Dating the Chelsea School Performance of *Dido and Aeneas*', *Early Music*, 37 (2009, August issue, forthcoming).

[78] See Bruce Wood and Andrew Pinnock, ' "Unscarr'd by turning times"? The Dating of Purcell's *Dido and Aeneas*', *Early Music*, 20 (1992), pp. 373–90. This article provoked a lively controversy, aired in subsequent issues of *Early Music*, about the dating of the opera, which has still not been conclusively settled. For further evidence that the work was composed before the end of 1684, see Tuppen, *French Influence*, vol. 1, pp. 336–7.

is evidence that the role of the Sorceress, the third most important character in the opera, may have been intended not for a female singer but for a baritone – male actors conventionally played such parts on the Restoration stage – and that it was indeed sung by one in a professional production in 1700.[79]

Yet the work, for all the mutilations it has suffered down the years, and despite its modest scale, is one of Purcell's masterpieces. Some modern critics have looked askance at the swift pace of its action and the absence of any contextual matter, but such strictures are misguided. Tate's plot is very properly confined to a period of 24 hours, in accordance with the theatrical convention of unity of time, while an educated audience in his day – unlike ours – will have been thoroughly familiar with classical myth, needing no enlargement upon a narrative derived from it. Purcell's music brings both the storyline and the characters into needle-sharp focus. It is hard to say what is the chief glory of the opera: its wonderfully vivid declamatory writing; its handful of airs, at once tautly constructed – three of them on ground basses – and perfectly judged in expressive terms; its sprinkling of choruses, their textures varied with masterly resourcefulness; or its dances, ranging from dignified courtly examples to movements whose jagged lines, sudden held chords (suggestive of leering gestures from the dancers), and abrupt swerves between metres mark them as lineal descendants of the most grotesque and sinister elements in the Jacobean antimasque.[80]

If *Dido* was indeed composed around 1683–4, its subsequent neglect is easily explained. Whether or not it received a first performance at the court of Charles II – and it may have fallen by the wayside after his sudden death – the succession of his Catholic brother James would have precluded any revival, whether at court or in public, of an opera whose tragic denouement hinged on the evil machinations of a sorceress and her enchantresses – characters who, in the England of the period, were stock symbols of Papism (even though sophisticated people no longer believed in witchcraft itself). By 1689, with the Protestant William on the throne, the piece once again became revivable, at least in a school context, but opera on the public stage was simply not in prospect; and by the time it was, the following year, the theatre company was seeking financial safety in old-fashioned dramatic opera, while Purcell himself had something much more ambitious in mind than *Dido*. This small masterpiece seems simply to have fallen prey to the vagaries of political and musical history.

---

[79] Anthony Harris, *Night's Black Agents: Witchcraft and Magic in Seventeenth-Century English Drama* (Manchester: Manchester University Press, 1980), p. 159; Curtis Price and Irena Cholij, 'Dido's Bass Sorceress', *Musical Times*, 127 (1989), pp. 615–18.

[80] For numerous examples of antimasque dances, see *Four Hundred Songs & Dances from the Stuart Masque*, ed. Andrew J. Sabol (Providence, RI: Brown University Press, 1978; enlarged 2nd edn, 1982).

Any hopes which Blow or Purcell may have cherished of recapturing the jubilee operatic commission were soon dashed, in a sequence of events that will not have endeared Grabu to either of them. First, Betterton commissioned him to compose the music for a revival of John Wilmot's *Valentinian* – staged in February 1684, and opening, most unusually, as a royal entertainment in the Hall Theatre; Grabu obliged with an unusually lavish score.[81] As if to rub salt into the wound, the musical contract for a second revival, at the beginning of April, also went to Grabu: the title of the play, Thomas Southerne's *The Disappointment*, must have seemed cruelly apt to Purcell at a time when theatrical commissions were few and far between.[82] To cap it all, word soon got around that the king had commanded Dryden, Poet Laureate and the doyen of English dramatists, to write an opera libretto for Grabu. Blow and Purcell must have been furious: one of the most desirable musical commissions London had ever been able to offer, a full-scale opera, had been handed on a plate to a foreigner. But there was nothing they could do to vent their frustration. Through the spring and early summer of 1684 Dryden's and Grabu's new work steadily took shape. Only much later would it be stricken by disaster.

Indian summer

The last year of Charles II's reign was a time of unaccustomed political quiet. His enemies were finally neutralized, and even the royal finances were in tolerable order (which, for his musicians, had the welcome consequence that their salaries began to be paid on time – though the accumulated arrears were another matter). The king was at last able to relax. On 5 April, earlier than in any previous year, the court left London for its summer remove. Three days later, at Windsor, Prince George of Denmark was installed as a Knight of the Garter. The ceremony was no doubt graced with elaborate music, though no details have come down to us.

At some point during the summer Purcell was obliged to return to London, along with Blow. The Battle of the Organs, initiated in the spring of the previous year, was finally to be joined, for both Smith's and Harris's instruments had by now been installed in the Temple Church. At first the contestants performed on alternate days, but this failed to settle the matter, so later on they competed directly. Even this did not produce a result. The lawyers of the Temple did eventually reach a decision – in favour of

---

[81] Peter Holman, '*Valentinian*, Rochester and Louis Grabu', in John Caldwell, Edward Olleson, and Susan Wollenberg (eds), *The Well Enchanting Skill: Music, Poetry, and Drama in the Culture of the Renaissance* (Oxford: Oxford University Press, 1990), pp. 127–41, at p. 129. Holman gives (p. 127) the complete text of Lord Preston's letter to the Duke of York (see p. 80 and note 71, above).
[82] *London Stage*, pp. 325–6, 327.

Smith – but not until four years later. How this disgraceful delay was viewed by Purcell, Blow, and Draghi (not to mention Smith and Harris, who had to wait for their payment) is best left to the imagination.

Purcell in particular must have found the Templars' prevarication irksome, for he had other things on his mind than demonstrating an organ day after day. He and his wife were preparing to move house, which they did around the end of September. Their new home was in Bowling Alley East, one of the huddle of narrow streets behind the Abbey. (The name has disappeared, along with the Purcells' house, but the line of the alley itself is still traceable, as a bustling thoroughfare – the northern end of Tufton Street.)[83]

The king, too, was planning to move to a new home: a vast and imposing palace which Christopher Wren was building for him near Winchester. In the autumn of 1684 he and the Duke of York, freed at last from the pressures of political turmoil, travelled there from Windsor to inspect the works, before making a leisurely progress back to London. They arrived at Whitehall on 25 September, to be greeted with Purcell's *From those serene and rapturous joys*. In the poem, by Thomas Flatman, political comment is muted, and kept to a minimum; instead, the king is depicted as a welcome bringer of mercy and peace. Purcell responded with a score of unusually tranquil beauty.[84]

In late October a new series of songbooks was launched by Henry Playford (1657–1709) – who had taken over from his father as head of the publishing firm – and his new partner, Richard Carr. The inaugural volume of *The Theater of Music* was dedicated jointly to Purcell and Blow, with a preface thanking the two of them for helping to edit the contents. They had, Playford gratefully explained, proof-read other people's music, added figuring to the basses, and so on: unlikely work for the two leading composers in the land to find time for! The volume added five songs to the growing tally of Purcell's published work.

The Playfords were careful not to neglect the other end of the cultural scale. One of the last volumes issued by Playford senior, not long before his son announced the first *Theater* volume, is a collection of catches – drinking songs in which a single line is passed among three or four voices, in the manner of a round. Purcell wrote nearly sixty of these all told, some lewd and a few frankly obscene. The new volume, with the rather obvious title *Catch that catch can*, included a dozen of them, with more added to later editions.

---

[83] John Ogilby's famous 1677 map of London does not extend to the separate City of Westminster. But Bowling Alley is clearly shown in John Strype's revision (1720) of John Stow's famous Survey of London and Westminster (1598), to which Strype added the first maps. These are from a variety of sources considerably earlier than Strype's publication; the map of Westminster, originally drawn by William Morgan, dates from 1680. For full details see the commentary by Ralph Hyde to *Find Your Way round Early Georgian London* (CD-ROM, Guildford: Motco Enterprises, 2003).
[84] Purcell Society Edition, vol. 18 (2003), pp. 1–39.

Preparations must have been already afoot for the Cecilian celebrations two months later. Evidently the 'musick house' at York Buildings had proved uncomfortably small, for this year's concert was held amid the splendours of Stationers' Hall, in the City, which was to remain the usual venue (with the Merchant Taylors' Hall occasionally substituted) for the rest of Purcell's life and beyond. The ode this year was Blow's *Begin the song!*; like *Welcome to all the pleasures*, it was published by Playford in the new year. The festival which Purcell had helped to establish seemed to be set fair for continuing success.

January 1685 brought the traditional round of musical activities at court: on New Year's Day an ode (Blow's *How does the new-born infant year rejoice!*) and, at the end of the month, a ball.[85] A glimpse of more unusual music-making is provided for us by Evelyn, who had been to a dinner party at Lord Sunderland's,

> invited to heare that celebrated voice of Mr. *Pordage* newly come from *Rome*, his singing voice was after the Venetian Recitative, as masterly as could be, & with an excellent voice both treble and bass. . . . *Pordage* is a *Priest* as Mr. *Bernard Howard* told me in private.[86]

Evelyn's account implies that falsetto singing was out of the ordinary; so it seems likely that in Purcell's day English countertenors, like French *haute-contres*, were high tenors who sang with the natural voice, perhaps slipping into falsetto if necessary only at the top of the range.[87] But this was not the only respect in which Pordage differed from English singers familiar to Evelyn. Before long he and several of his compatriots would gain prominent positions as court musicians, importing not only the vocal style of Italy but also the devotional practices of Rome.

The following day, this time at Lord Arundell's, Evelyn heard Pordage again (along with Gostling, whom he described as 'that stupendious Base'), accompanied on the harpsichord by Draghi. Four days later, on 1 February, he attended a soirée at court, though on this occasion it was not the music that most struck him but the decadent atmosphere:

> I am never to forget the unexpressable luxury, & prophanenesse, gaming, & all dissoluteness, and as it were total forgetfulnesse of God (it being Sunday Evening), which . . . I was witness of; the King, sitting & toying with his Concubines Portsmouth,

---

[85] The ode is preserved in London, British Library, Add. MS 33287, ff. 63–9; *RECM*, vol. 1, p. 214 (order dated 26 January 1685).

[86] Evelyn, 27 January 1685.

[87] Cf. the reference to 'Mens feigned Voices' quoted in note 6 on p. 6, above. See also Neal Zaslaw, 'The Enigma of the Haute-Contre', *Musical Times*, 115 (1974), pp. 939–41, and p. 153, below.

Cleaveland, & Mazarine: &c: A French boy singing love songs, in that glorious Gallery, whilst about 20 of the greate Courtiers & other dissolute persons were at Basset round a large table, a bank of at least 2000 in Gold before them, upon which two Gent: who were with me made reflexions with astonishment, it being a sceane of uttmost vanity; and surely as they thought would never have an End: six days after was all in the dust.[88]

Indeed it was. The very next morning the king suffered a severe stroke. After initially seeming to rally he gradually weakened, and his life was despaired of, causing public consternation. Purcell, working at breakneck speed, managed to complete a symphony anthem, *O Lord, grant the king a long life*, presumably for performance the following Sunday, but events moved faster still. On the evening of Thursday 5 February, amid the utmost secrecy, the king was received into the Roman Catholic church, and was given the Sacrament and extreme unction. By noon the next day he was dead.

Inevitably, rumours of his conversion were soon circulating, and they horribly complicated the arrangements for his funeral. There was no lying-in-state, no period of official mourning. The king was laid to rest, almost furtively, in the late evening, on 14 February. The *London Gazette* announced that his catafalque had been greeted by the Abbey choir and prebendaries, and that the funeral had been observed with all the custom-ary rituals, including the breaking of their white staves by the officials of his household.[89] But this, it seems, was merely for public consumption. John Evelyn's diary, a private document in which he had no reason to be less than truthful, tells a different story: the king, he states flatly, was buried by night, 'obscurely and without any manner of pomp', even his grave being left unmarked.[90]

A state funeral would have been a major musical event in the Abbey, and Purcell evidently began preparing for one. He set to work on an anthem for the occasion, *Hear my prayer, O Lord*.[91] All that survives is a noble torso: an eight-part opening chorus only 34 bars in length, setting the first verse of Psalm 102. It begins very softly with a single voice, then entry is piled upon entry, building up to a dissonant climax of awe-inspiring grandeur. Purcell seems never to have finished the piece; certainly the fair copy – the only source that survives – stops short at the end of this chorus (there is no double bar-line, and Purcell left space to continue).[92] Probably he put

---

[88] Evelyn, 4–6 February 1685.
[89] *London Gazette*, 12–16 February 1685.
[90] Evelyn, 14 February 1685.
[91] Purcell Society Edition, vol. 28 (1959), pp. 135–8.
[92] Cambridge, Fitzwilliam Museum, Music MS 88, ff. 83v–83 of the volume reversed; followed by blank folios. For the dating of this fragment, see Shay and Thompson, *Manuscripts*, pp. 44–6.

down his pen as soon as he heard that the king's obsequies were to be curtailed. We can only imagine what a towering masterpiece he might have been inspired to create by the next few verses of the psalm:

> My days are consumed away like smoke: and my bones are burned up as it were a fire-brand.
> For the voice of my groaning: my bones will scarce cleave to my flesh.
> For I have eaten ashes as it were bread: and mingled my drink with weeping.
> My days are gone like a shadow: and I am withered like grass.

Instead, his principal tribute was a secular one: the haunting solo song 'If prayers and tears', subtitled 'Sighs for our late Sovereign'. The extravagant imagery of the poem is perfectly reflected in Purcell's superb declamatory writing – not least in the closing bars, which lament

> . . . our former crimes,
> Treasons, rebellions, perjuries,
> With all the iniquities of the times.
> Whole legions do against us rise:
> These be the powers that strike the kingdom dead,
> And now the crown is fall'n from our Josiah's head.[93]

The country mourned. The exasperatingly complex man whom an ignorant posterity would dub the Merry Monarch had achieved the near-impossible: stayed for a quarter of a century on the most difficult throne in Europe, helped rebuild whole areas of cultural life that civil war and subsequent repression had all but destroyed, seen off his enemies, and finally come to be much loved. Purcell, having known him, no doubt mourned him as sincerely as anyone – though he may well have harboured private hopes that a new reign would bring greater order and stability to the finances of the royal household.

---

[93] Purcell Society Edition, vol. 25 (1985), pp. 90–6.

The energy of English words

The first volume of *Orpheus Britannicus*, published by Henry Playford three years after Purcell's death, parcels up between one pair of covers some eighty of his solo songs, duets, and dialogues, more than half of them excerpted from bigger works – operas and odes – or written for inclusion in plays. The sheer variety of the music is astonishing, but one common thread runs through it all, and the publisher alluded to it in an address from 'The Bookseller to the Reader' printed at the beginning:

> *The Author's extraordinary Talent in all sorts of Musick is*
> *sufficiently known, but he was especially admir'd for the* Vocal,
> *having a peculiar Genius to express the energy of* English *Words,*
> *whereby he mov'd the Passions of all his Auditors* [hearers].

How exactly did Purcell do this? Part of his 'extraordinary talent' lay in composing vocal lines that reflected verbal rhythms, stress patterns, and syllabic lengths, as Henry Hall explains in his dedicatory poem published in *Orpheus Britannicus* itself:

> Each syllable first weigh'd, or short, or long,
> That it might too be Sense, as well as Song.

But this was, as Hall indicates, merely the first step: something that many lesser composers of the period, among them Hall himself and Purcell's brother Daniel, could manage – yet they all too often produced results that were bland in comparison with Purcell's eloquence. And indeed Purcell sometimes went directly against naturalistic declamation, in order to create some specific effect (a rhetorical trick employed by English composers for several decades).[1] For instance, in the first of his birthday odes for Queen Mary, *Now does the glorious day appear*, the first phrase of a bass solo reverses both the expected rhythm and the natural length of two successive pairs of words, 'full as' and 'great a' – each pair being set as short–long instead of long–short – in order to place emphasis on the next word, 'weight', with a leap down onto a sonorous bottom G, before clambering a full octave to the climactic word 'power'. One other detail is worth noting here: the shift at the end from dotted or reverse-dotted rhythms onto a pair of even quavers – giving apt equality to the two syllables of 'selfsame'.

---

[1] For a full discussion see Ian Spink, *Henry Lawes, Cavalier Songwriter* (Oxford: Oxford University Press, 2000), pp. 17–18.

BASS SOLO

It was a work of full as great a weight, And did re-quire the self-same pow'r

Now does the glorious day appear, bars 249–51[iii] [2]

Such deftness and economy of means are the very essence of Purcell's declamatory writing. But rhythm is only part of the story. His word-setting owes its eloquence to the accretion and subtle interaction of a host of other features too: the intervals, stepwise or disjunct, that shape the musical line and determine the direction of the phrase; the length of individual notes, and their pitch within the line; written-out ornamentation, including roulades on individual syllables; chromatic alteration; and the supporting harmony, including the amount of activity in the bass line.[3] The word-setting in a much more familiar example than the preceding one – the conversation between Belinda, the Second Woman and the Queen in Act I of *Dido and Aeneas* – displays a wide range of technical devices: rhythmic pointing is one of them, of course, but by no means the most important.

Here the reversed dotted rhythms in the first and third bars, unlike those in the preceding example, are naturalistic, but again each has the effect of concentrating the listener's attention on the word that follows. There are also flourishes of semiquavers spanning nearly an octave, on 'storms' and 'fierce' – obvious, perhaps, but telling; the second of them soars up to a momentary apex on 'how', set to the highest note of the phrase but placed on a weak quaver so as to highlight the next word, 'fierce'. A flourish three bars earlier on 'valour' is subtly modified by its dotted rhythms and triadic outline into suggesting a trumpet call, before the line sinks flatwards towards 'charms' and 'soft' – the latter word repeated for emphasis, and given a sighing suspension each time. Belinda's rejoinder contains two upward appoggiaturas, a dissonant one occupying a full beat, emphasizing 'strong', and a minor–major one in quavers, colouring 'woe', before the line momentarily trickles downwards on 'melt'. The Second Woman has another reversed dotted rhythm, giving natural accentuation to 'stubborn', and another upward appoggiatura on 'unmov'd' – the

---

[2] Purcell Society Edition, vol. 11 (1993), p. 24.
[3] For a detailed discussion of the techniques on which Purcell drew in his songs, see Ian Spink, *English Song: Dowland to Purcell* (London: Batsford, 1974), pp. 208–40, and Kathleen Rohrer, *'The Energy of English Words': a Linguistic Approach to Henry Purcell's Methods of Setting Texts* (PhD diss., Princeton University, 1980).

Dido and Aeneas, No. 6, bars 1–15[ii] [4]

line here laboriously heaving itself up onto a dissonance before returning to the original note – with yet a further upward appoggiatura on 'distress'. All these tiny but vivid musical images, densely packed into a mere fifteen bars, are combined with rhythms that sensitively reflect those of speech, and with melodic lines that possess an unerring sense of direction in rise and fall, step and leap; and the result is both supported and complemented by a bass which is mostly static or slow-moving but which, when occasion demands, as beneath 'fierce', drives forward resolutely. Surely no hearer, as Playford indicates, could resist the power of this passage – or uncounted others in Purcell's music – to stir the emotions.[5]

---

[4] Purcell Society Edition, vol. 3 (1979), pp. 13–14
[5] For a brilliant dissection of another declamatory passage in *Dido and Aeneas* see Imogen Holst, 'Purcell's Librettist, Nahum Tate', in Imogen Holst (ed.), *Henry Purcell, 1659–1695: Essays on His Music* (London: Oxford University Press, 1959), pp. 35–41.

Purcell's task was not made easier by some of the verse he had to set: not because of its poor literary quality (though that was true enough of some), but because of a specific technical limitation affecting opera libretti in particular but a good deal of other verse too: the overwhelming preference of English poets for duple rather than triple metre. This stemmed in part from the natural rhythms of the language and partly from a classical mindset – a combination of factors that had led John Dryden, the doyen of English dramatic poets, to make the Olympian pronouncement that 'No man is tied in modern Poesie to observe any further rule in the feet of his verse, but that they be dissylables; whether *Spondee*, *Trochee*, or *Iambique*, it matters not; onely he is obliged to rhyme'.[6] In the libretto of *Dido and Aeneas* there are only some twenty-five triple-metre lines among a total of about three hundred; in that of Blow's *Venus and Adonis* none at all; and neither contains any lines that do not rhyme, a consideration which for musical purposes Dryden elevated above metre (a bizarre decision). If a composer wished to write in triple time, then – whether for the sake of characterization, of dramatic effect, or simply of musical variety – he was frequently obliged to go behind the librettist's back and impose triple rhythms on duple-metre verses: there is no evidence of feedback from composers to poets, leading to the writing of more accommodating lines (at any rate until Purcell came to collaborate with Dryden on the opera *King Arthur*, when the two men had a stand-off over whether some of the lyrics were suitable for setting to music in the style Purcell intended – and we do not know the details of that disagreement, which may have involved other issues).[7] Composers became so skilled at performing the duple-to-triple trick that listeners today are barely aware of it; yet a trick it is – and some of the most effective music in Purcell's output depends on it. To take a single work as an example, in *Dido and Aeneas* no fewer than five numbers, 'Ah! Belinda', 'Fear no danger', 'Harm's our delight', 'Thanks to these lonesome vales', and 'When I am laid in earth', were conceived by Nahum Tate in duple metre and dressed in their now-familiar triple-time guise – each of them utterly different in style from the others – only by unnoticed sleight of hand on Purcell's part.

---

[6] Dryden, *An Essay of Dramatick Poesie*, in *Works*, vol. 17, p. 71.
[7] See Andrew Pinnock and Bruce Wood, 'A Mangled Chime: The Accidental Death of the Opera Libretto in Civil War England', *Early Music*, 36 (2008), pp. 265–84.

THREE

SERVING A CATHOLIC MONARCH (1685–1688)

Regal splendour

James II and his queen, Mary of Modena, were crowned in Westminster Abbey on 23 April – St George's Day. Their coronation procession was the most spectacular public event seen in London since that of Charles II, exactly 24 years earlier. But unlike that event it was recorded in exhaustive detail, in a sumptuous souvenir book by Francis Sandford, Lancaster Herald-at-Arms, full of vivid descriptions and magnificent engraved illustrations: a book so elaborate that its preparation and printing took two years.[1] It tells us that the entire length of the processional route, running from Westminster Hall down King's Street and along the Great Sanctuary to the west door of the Abbey, had been railed off and spread with a blue carpet wide enough for four men to walk abreast.

On the great day the carpet was strewn with sweet-smelling herbs, and along it, between the cavalry and infantry that lined it on either side, trod the stately procession, led by a fifer in scarlet livery trimmed with gold. There followed four military drummers and their drum major, and two ranks each of four trumpeters, with their kettledrummer, all similarly arrayed; the banners of the trumpets and the valances of the kettledrums were of damask, embroidered with the royal coat of arms. Next came court officials in their finery, also in fours. In the centre of the procession were the Children and Gentlemen of the Chapel Royal – the Gentlemen all named individually in the book, with Purcell and Blow among the basses – resplendent in their surplices and mantles (that of Blow, according to a marginal note, containing five yards of fine scarlet cloth). With the Chapel were the choir of Westminster (a dowdy lot, in mere cassocks

---

[1] Francis Sandford, *The History of the Coronation of . . . James II, King of England, . . . and of . . . Queen Mary* (London: Newcomb, 1687).

10. *The crowning of James II in Westminster Abbey, showing Blow, directing the musicians in the gallery, wielding a long roll of paper as a baton.*

and surplices) and members of the royal wind band of cornetts and sackbuts (scarlet mantles again). Accompanied by the wind players, the two choirs were singing *O Lord, grant the king a long life*, an anthem for full choir by the veteran William Child, who had been a Gentleman of the Chapel since the 1660s and was now nearly eighty years old. Finally came dignitaries from the court, the Abbey, and the City of London, and the king and queen themselves, attended by all the nobility of England.

Once everyone had filed into the Abbey – a lengthy business – the service was celebrated with perhaps the most impressive music ever heard on such an occasion in England. Purcell, as Abbey organist, took a leading part in it, as he had already done in the preparations. In addition to composing and rehearsing new anthems, his numerous duties had included installing a chamber organ in one of the temporary wooden galleries that were put up in the Abbey.

Members of the congregation who could remember the coronation of Charles II found some novel features in the ceremony they now witnessed. James, being a Catholic, had refused to allow the customary Communion to be included, so William Sancroft, the Archbishop of Canterbury, had recast the liturgy to disguise this curtailment. Among other changes he introduced several new anthem texts. Altogether there were eight anthems. Blow, as the senior composer, provided three of these to Purcell's two, but it was the younger man's music that took pride of place, at the beginning and end of the service.

The introit was sung in procession from the west door by the Abbey choir alone, in accordance with their ancient prerogative. *I was glad*, a traditional text, was newly set by Purcell.[2] This was a wonderful opportunity for him to display his art, and he duly seized it – though his approach was also thoroughly practical. For most of its length the piece, which is for five-part full choir, moves in stately block chords. But towards the end, by which time the singers would have been safely in their places and able to watch a conductor, it breaks out into a dazzling exhibition of Purcell's skill as a polyphonist. The words 'world without end, Amen' are set to a single phrase which enters again and again, in single, double, and quadruple note-values, and in inversion too – all simultaneously.

At the Acclamation of the new king came *Let thy hand be strengthened*, another traditional text set by Blow and performed, like all the music that followed, by both the Abbey choir and that of the Chapel Royal.[3] At the Anointing the choirs sang William Turner's *Come, holy Ghost* (now lost), and *Zadok the priest*, composed by Henry Lawes for the coronation of

---

[2] See Bruce Wood, 'A Coronation Anthem – Lost and Found', *Musical Times*, 118 (1977), pp. 466–8. The anthem, not yet issued in a Purcell Society volume, is published by Novello, and by Oxford University Press in *A Purcell Anthology: 12 Anthems*, ed. Bruce Wood (1995).

[3] The texts of these anthems, together with the names of their composers, are given in full in the order of service included in Sandford's volume.

Charles II and the only piece retained from that occasion. The Anointing was followed by Blow's second contribution, *Behold, O God our defender*, to another traditional text. Next came Turner's *The King shall rejoice* (also lost) and a setting of the Te Deum by Child.

All this music was sung by full choir without soloists, and accompanied by organ alone. Now came the two most magnificent of the anthems. The first was Blow's *God spake sometime in visions*, scored for eight-part choir and strings. Three groups of musicians – solo voices, the main choir, and the Twenty-Four Violins – were placed in separate galleries, just as at the coronation of Charles II. The piece was performed while the Treasurer of the King's Household, attended by Garter King of Arms and Black Rod, scattered among the people the gold and silver medals of the King's Largesse. Afterwards, according to an eyewitness account, the trumpets sounded and the drums beat, and the congregation shouted 'God save the king!'.

There followed the coronation of the queen, whose part of the cere-mony was briefer and less ostentatious, for she was not a queen regnant but merely a consort. The anthem that followed, however, was the longest and most elaborate of all – and the finest. Purcell's *My heart is inditing* is scored for the same forces as *God spake sometime in visions*, but is very different in character.[4] In contrast to the blunt masculine vigour of Blow's piece, Purcell's is sensuous and full of feminine grace. Purcell uses the strings differently too, and more prominently. Blow's anthem has a sizeable and imposing prelude, but Purcell's opens with a spacious two-movement symphony, which is repeated in its entirety at the midpoint of the work, buttressing the grand design. And whereas in Blow's anthem the upper strings double the voices in solid unison, Purcell places them an octave and sometimes two octaves higher, creating a combination of bril-liance and richness that was quite new in English music.

An ill-fated opera

After the coronation, everyday life had scarcely time to grow humdrum before fresh excitements came along, in the shape of Grabu's opera. It had been a long time in preparation. Dryden's libretto, an allegory cele-brating the reign and achievements of Charles II (Albion) and his loyal brother (Albanius), demanded lavish sets, stage machines, and costumes. The second act, for instance, is set in Hell:

> There is the Figure of Prometheus *chain'd to a Rock, the Vulture gnawing his Liver;* Sisiphus *rowling the Stone, the* Belides, &c. *Beyond, abundance of Figures in various Torments. Then a great Arch*

---

[4] *God spake sometime in visions* is included in *Musica Britannica*, vol. 7 (1953), pp. 1–45; *My heart is inditing* in Purcell Society Edition, vol. 17 (1996), pp. 78–138.

of Fire. Behind this, Three Pyramids of Flames in perpetual agitation. Beyond this, glowing Fire . . .[5]

Part of the opera had been presented before the king over a year earlier, on his birthday in 1684, though on that occasion it may have been merely the libretto, read aloud by Dryden. Rehearsals went on all through the autumn, and by the new year the work was finally ready, as a court insider reported:

> Wee are in expectation of an opera composed by Mr. Dryden and set by Grabuche, and so well performed at the repetition [rehearsal] that has been made before His Majesty at the Duchess of Portsmouth's, pleaseth mightily, but the rates [ticket prices] proposed will not take so well, for they have set the boxes at a guyney a place, and the Pitt at halfe. They advance 4,000*l* on the opera, and therefore must tax high to reimburse themselves.[6]

Half a guinea for a seat in the stalls was more than four times the price for a play. Equally, though, £4000 was a colossal sum, nearly half the company's entire annual budget. The backers must have been holding their breath. Then, with the show about to open, came the sudden death of the king, in whose honour the work had been created. All appeared lost. Dryden, however, ingeniously saved the situation by adding two scenes at the end, the first depicting the apotheosis of Charles, the second the Garter ceremony at Windsor (whose ritual he had loved). Grabu hastily set these to music, and the production went ahead. On 3 June came the opening night.

By now a powerful feeling of resentment had built up against the whole enterprise – not only from English musicians but also from the members of the acting company, for an all-sung opera did not require their services, and hence threatened their earnings. A vicious pamphlet campaign set out to vilify Grabu. One of the pamphlets, a satirical poem entitled *The Raree-Show*, poked fun at the extravagant staging and what it had cost the shareholders:

> *Betterton, Betterton*, thy decorations,
> > And the machines [the elaborate staging] were well written
> > we knew;
> But all the words were such stuff we want Patience,
> > And little better is Monsieur *Grabu*.

---

[5] Dryden, *Works*, vol. 15, p. 30.
[6] Letter dated 1 January 1685 from Edward Bedingfield to the Countess of Rutland: *HMC Rutland*, V/ii, p. 85.

D— me, says *Underhill*, I'm out of two hundred,
  Hoping that rainbows and peacocks would do [both appear
    in the opera];
Who thought infallible Tom [Betterton] could have blunder'd,
  A plague upon him and Monsieur *Grabu*.

Bayes [Dryden], thou wouldst have thy skill thought universal,
  Tho' thy dull ear be to music untrue;
Then whilst we strive to confute the Rehearsal,[7]
  Prithee learn thrashing of Monsieur *Grabu*.[8]

Dryden, in the programme book of the opera, mounted a vigorous counter-attack:

I may without vanity, own some Advantages, . . . as have given the composer Monsieur *Grabu* what occasions he cou'd wish, to show his extraordinary Tallent, in diversifying the Recitative, the Lyrical part, and the Chorus: In all which, (not to attribute any thing to my own Opinion) the best Judges, and those too of the best Quality [social rank], who have honor'd his Rehearsals with their Presence, have no less commended the happiness of his Genius than his Skill. And let me have the liberty to add one thing; that he has so exactly express'd my Sence, in all places, where I intended to move the Passions, that he seems to have enter'd into my thoughts, and to have been the Poet as well as the Composer. This I say, not to flatter him, but to do him right; because amongst some *English* Musicians, and their Scholars, (who are sure to judge after them,) the imputation of being a *French-man*, is enough to make a Party, who maliciously endeavour to decry him. But the knowledge of *Latin* and *Italian* Poets, both which he possesses, besides his skill in Musick, and his being acquainted with all the performances of the *French Opera's*, adding to these the good Sence to which he is Born, have rais'd him to a degree above any Man, who shall pretend to be his Rival on our Stage. When any of our Country-men excel him, I shall be glad, for the sake of old *England*, to be shown my error: in the mean time, let Vertue be commended, though in the Person of a Stranger [foreigner].[9]

The remark about Grabu's knowledge of Latin and Italian was a shrewd dig. Purcell had, after all, ruefully admitted in the Preface to his *Sonatas of*

[7] An oft-revived play by Buckingham, poking fun at Dryden.
[8] Quoted in Hawkins, vol. 2, p. 107.
[9] Dryden, *Works*, vol. 15, pp. 8–9.

Three Parts that he was ignorant of Italian. But this war of words, inconclusive at the time, has subsequently had one negative effect: it has obscured what really happened that fateful June. Most music historians have claimed that the opera was a ludicrous flop, laughed off the stage for the feebleness of its music. In fact, it seems to have succeeded well, despite Grabu's occasional clumsiness in setting English words. But only six performances had been given – not nearly enough to repay the company's huge investment – before disaster struck.

On 13 June news reached London that the Duke of Monmouth had landed in Dorset with a large body of troops, intent on deposing the king and seizing the throne. This instantly turned the opera, with its extravagant praise of both Charles II and James II, into a political risk, and it was promptly taken off. As it turned out, the rebellion was swiftly and brutally put down, and on 15 July Monmouth paid for his foolhardiness with his head. But by then the public mood had changed: the opera was never revived, and its promoters were nearly bankrupted. It would be five years before they plucked up courage to commission another new opera – a fact that altered the course of Purcell's career. He himself, though, had evidently listened to Grabu's music with keen attention, and stored up a number of ideas for the future.

Songs: solo, symphony, ceremonial

The same issue of the *London Gazette* that announced Monmouth's execution also contained an advertisement for a new songbook. This was the second volume of *The Theater of Music*. Among the pieces by Purcell which it includes is one of his biggest and most elaborate vocal works other than the court odes. Ironically, though, this item is very carelessly printed – in the second volume, which unlike the first was evidently not proofread by Purcell or Blow. *Soft notes, and gently rais'd* is a symphony song: that is, introduced and accompanied by instruments (in this case recorders).[10] Purcell had composed it, along with several other such pieces, for the Private Music at court, and had accordingly laid it out for accomplished professional players. It may seem surprising that Playford's book, aimed at the amateur market, should have found space to present such a big piece in full score and unabridged. (Blow's ode *Awake, awake, my lyre*, a piece on a comparable scale, had appeared in the third volume of *Choice Ayres and Songs* shorn of all its instrumental and choral passages, and his elaborate symphony song *Go, perjur'd man* in the fourth volume in a version for voices and continuo only.) But the recorder, only a few years earlier an exotic novelty confined to the court, was now in vogue among London's gentlemen amateurs, and printed music for it was starting to appear in increasing quantities.

---

[10] Purcell Society Edition, vol. 27 (2007), pp. 88–97.

Having suppressed the rebellion, the king turned to a more mundane task: sorting out the administrative mess in which his late brother had left the royal household, including its musical establishment. On the last day of August the Lord Chamberlain issued an order for the swearing-in of musicians.[11] First come members of the violin band, then the Private Music: one recorder player, two countertenors, one tenor and two basses, plus three other instrumentalists. The continuo team consisted of harpsichord – Purcell himself, who now began to receive the standard salary of £40 for work he had doubtless been doing for years – and bass viol; Blow is named as composer, a post he had held since 1674, and Brockwell as keeper of the instruments (the strings, that is, for Purcell was still responsible for wind and keyboard instruments). The new administration, to its credit, made a serious effort to clear at least some of the arrears of payments: an enormous relief to musicians who had been treated shabbily for almost the whole of the previous reign.

In the autumn came the welcome ceremony, held on 10 October, two days after the court returned to Whitehall. In subsequent years it was combined with the celebration of the king's birthday, 14 October, but in this first year of the reign the two events were kept separate. Among those present at the welcome was Pepys. He was no longer keeping a diary, but a letter he wrote to a friend gives us a glimpse of the magnificent function: 'a mighty Musique-Entertainment at Court for the welcomeing home the King and Queene', he called it.[12] On the birthday itself there was a great ball, and this, as it happened, was attended by Evelyn, who enjoyed 'Musique of Instruments & Voyces before the Ball' – and chatting about it with the king and queen, who happened to be standing next to him.[13] On both days the church bells rang out all over London, and as dusk fell the bonfires blazed.

Purcell evidently considered this particular welcome song, *Why are all the Muses mute?*, to be unusually important. He proudly noted at the head of the score that it was 'yᵉ first Song performd to King James', and it is his longest and most elaborate ode so far.[14] It begins, daringly, not with the customary symphony but with a single voice plaintively demanding to know why 'the viol and the lute' are asleep, and calling on them to awaken in order to praise Caesar. They duly oblige, and the symphony

[11] *RECM*, vol. 2, pp. 2–3.
[12] Pepys, letter to Sir Robert Southwell, 10 October 1685, in R. G. Howarth (ed.), *Letters and the Second Diary of Samuel Pepys* (London: Dent, 1932), p. 171. Pepys muddies the water, however, by adding waspishly that 'the fraequent Returnes of the Words, *Arms, Beauty, Triumph, Love, Progeny, Peace, Dominion, Glory* &c. had apparently cost our Poët-Prophet more paine to finde Rhimes than Reasons': of these words only 'arms', 'triumph', 'glory', and (stretching a point) 'lov'd' occur in the welcome song – raising a faint doubt as to whether this was actually the work he heard. But perhaps he was exaggerating for effect: it seems unlikely that a court poet would have been so tactless as to mention progeny when the king and queen had none.
[13] Evelyn, 15 October 1685.
[14] Purcell Society Edition, vol. 18 (2005), pp. 40–91.

follows. The centrepiece of the work is a gripping bass solo, 'Accurst Rebellion rear'd her head' (curious that Rebellion should be personified as female!), unmistakably intended for John Gostling. The vocal line plunges down to cavernous bottom notes – predictable, but by now obligatory in such showpieces – when the text depicts the threatening monster being driven 'back from whence it rose, to Hell'. Equally striking is the setting of the concluding lines (a confident prophecy that was to prove wildly inaccurate):

> His fame shall endure till all things decay;
> His fame and the world together shall die,
> Shall vanish together away.

Taking this unusual cue, Purcell brought the work to an end with quiet, almost wistful music: his first royal ode to conclude with anything but pomp.

Later in the autumn life returned to something like normal. The Cecilian festival the following month seems to have been less of a success than in its first two years. The ode, by Tate, is no worse than Fishburn's poem in 1683 or Oldham's in 1684, but the music, by William Turner, never appeared in print. (Does this reflect on its quality? There is no way of knowing, for no manuscript of the piece has survived either.) Publication of the score had looked set to become a custom. But this now lapsed, and it was never resumed, even for the magnificent works that graced the festival in some subsequent years.

Another opera, and another ode

The unhappy fate of *Albion and Albanius* had evidently not brought French opera into disrepute, for early in the new year came news that a work by Lully was to be staged in London. *Cadmus et Hermione* had been composed 13 years previously, and some of its special effects would have been familiar to theatregoers who had seen *The Tempest*, either back in 1674 or in any of its numerous revivals. But they had never seen the originals of those effects. And they must have started to wonder if they were ever going to, for preparations ran far from smoothly – as a series of letters to an interested noblewoman in the country makes clear:

> *23 January:* Next week begins the French Opera.
> *28 January:* The French Opera will begin the week after next.
> *11 February:* Today was the French Opera. The King and Queen were there, the music was indeed very fine, but all the dresses the most wretched I ever saw.[15]

---

[15] Letters from Peregrine Bertie to the Countess of Rutland: *HMC Rutland*, V/ii, pp. 102, 103, 104.

This was a sad comedown after the no-expense-spared finery of *Albion and Albanius*. Even so, Purcell no doubt seized the opportunity to see and hear the work. He seems to have taken a particular interest in the music of a powerful sacrifice scene in the third act; its influence can be detected in several of his own scores of the 1690s.[16]

More immediately, however, Purcell was hard at work on smaller projects. His songs were being published in increasing numbers: five of them in the third volume of *The Theater of Music*, and three more in an enlarged edition of *The Pleasant Musical Companion*, while the fourth and last volume of *The Theater of Music*, published that autumn (though, like many songbooks of the period, post-dated the following year), included no fewer than ten – the lion's share of the 53 songs it contained. A further eight were by Blow; in his preface Henry Playford thanks both of them for helping to see the book through the press. He describes 'the eminent Dr. *John Blow*, and Mr. *Henry Purcell*' as 'my ever kind Friends', and no doubt they were: being associated with an honest publisher must have been very welcome to both of them, for copyright law did not yet exist and pirate editions were as rife as illegally copied CDs are today. Playford's preface also refers slightingly to '*New Pretenders*' who might be 'disparaging this Book'. Who were these? The answer lies on the title page, on which the name of his former partner is conspicuous by its absence. Carr had set up in competition.

Although he was busy not merely composing songs but also editing other people's, 1686 appears to have been a quiet time for Purcell at court. Only one piece, the boozy duet 'Here's to thee, Dick', appears in the autograph score-book between *Why are all the Muses mute?* and the autumn welcome song for 1686, *Ye tuneful Muses*. But for much of the time domestic matters will have been demanding his attention. On 3 August, while the court was enjoying its stay at Windsor, he himself was at home, engaged on the sorrowful task of burying a third son, Thomas. When the boy had been born is not known.[17]

At the end of September, along with Blow and various others, he served on a committee set up to approve a new organ, built by Bernard Smith, at the City church of St Katherine Cree. They were also charged with appointing an organist. After they had heard all the short-listed candidates their choice fell on Moses Snow (1661–1702), who was also a Gentleman of the Chapel Royal. Cronyism might be suspected, but the appointment committee had seven members besides Purcell and Blow, including the churchwardens and the vicar, Nicholas Brady, who was something of a poet. This may have been how he and Purcell met: at all events, he was

---

[16] Invocation scenes in *King Arthur*, *Oedipus*, *The Libertine*, and *Bonduca* are all indebted to *Cadmus et Hermione*: see Laurie, *Stage Works*, pp. 341–3.
[17] WAR, Burials 1606–1706, f. 38.

later to write the text for the greatest of all Purcell's odes, *Hail! bright Cecilia*. The affair has one other point of interest, in the light it casts on the earnings of ordinary church musicians in London, for Purcell's fee, fourteen shillings, and his travelling expenses, a further five shillings for 'coach hire', added up to very nearly a fifth of Snow's quarterly salary.[18]

Money in the Purcell household was tight at the time. An adult pupil who had boarded there owed a large sum for his keep and his lessons, and Purcell found himself faced with the irksome task of pursuing a bad debt. Eventually, at the beginning of November, he sought the help of the Dean of Exeter, who was evidently an acquaintance of the pupil:

> I have wrote severall times to Mr Webber concerning what was due to me on Hodg's account and recvt no answer, which has occasion'd this presumption in giving you the trouble of a few Lines relating to the matter; It is ever since ye begining of June last that the money has been due: the sum is £27, *viz*. £20 for half a years teaching & boarding the other a bill of £7 for nessecaries [*sic*] which I laid out for him, the Bill Mr Webber has; Compassion Moves me to acquaint you of a great many debts Mr Hodg contracted whilst in London and to some who are so poor 'twere an act of Charity as well as Justice to pay 'em . . .[19]

Who the elusive Hodge was, how he had come to be studying with Purcell, and whether he (or Webber, or the Dean) ever paid up, we do not know.

Meanwhile, on 14 October, the king's birthday had been celebrated, with a carefully planned public-relations exercise aimed at the London dignitaries who would be attending. Just over three months previously, in June, the king had ordered thirteen thousand regular troops into camp on Hounslow Heath – an unsubtle hint that if the pro-Catholic policies on which he was intent were thwarted by political means, he would impose them by force, starting in the capital. Now, on the morning of the birthday, he carried out a formal review of the troops. The anonymous court poet who penned the birthday ode had done his best to put a positive spin on this plan:

> From the rattling of drums, and the trumpet's loud sounds,
> Wherein Caesar's safety and his strength abounds,

---

[18] Vestry Minutes of St Katherine Cree (now in London, Guildhall Library, MSS 1196/1, 1198/1); quoted in full in Zimmerman, *Purcell*, pp. 137–8.
[19] Reproduced in facsimile in Westrup, *Purcell*, facing p. 236; the original is in Exeter Cathedral Library.

The best protectors of his royal right
'Gainst fanatical fury and sanctified spite
By which he first did glory gain
(And may they still preserve his reign!)

Purcell too must have been in on the plan, and he evidently decided to make sure the message was put across loud and clear – though what he thought privately we can only guess. The music to which he set these lines is trite as well as bombastic, and is padded out with endless internal repeats. Most of the other movements in the ode are far superior – especially the rousing bass solo 'In his just praise', obviously intended for Gostling and complete with plenty of low notes, and a delicate ground-bass air, 'With him he brings the Partner of his throne', written for Turner.[20] But one movement is less satisfying, and like 'From the rattling of drums' it is a heavily political one. Most unusually, though, the politics lie not in the words but in the music. The bass line of a solo, 'Be lively then and gay' and its ritornello, and the violin obbligato to a chorus repeating the same words, are all formed by a ballad tune, 'Hey then, up go we'. This tune had lately appeared in a popular broadside to words beginning 'Down with the Whigs, we'll now grow wise'. Unfortunately, not even Purcell's ingenuity could make the tune work convincingly as a bass line.[21]

Shortly before Christmas John Playford died, aged 63. Purcell mourned him sincerely, not merely as an associate in getting his music published but as a friend too. His setting of Tate's pastoral elegy on Playford, 'Gentle shepherds', is genuinely poignant. It is also an imposing piece, over a hundred bars in length. Rather than include it in a songbook, Playford's son Henry issued it, rather grandly, as a separate item.[22]

Ecclesiastical extravagance

Early in the new year Evelyn, breathless with excitement, scribbled in his diary news of the latest sensation in London. He was evidently both impressed and scandalized. On the orders of the king, a Catholic chapel had been built in Whitehall Palace, and no expense had been spared:

I was to heare the Musique of the Italians in the new Chapel, now first of all opned at White-hall publiquely for the Popish Service: Nothing can be finer than the magnificent Marble work & Architecture at the End, where are 4 statues representing

---

[20] His name is noted above the solo in the fair-copy score, London, British Library, MS R.M. 20.h.8, f. 146v.
[21] The ode is in Purcell Society Edition, vol. 18 (2005), pp. 92–142.
[22] *A Pastoral Elegy on the Death of Mr. John Playford* (London, 1687); Purcell Society Edition, vol. 25 (1985), pp. 109–14.

st. Joh: st. Petre, st. Paule, & the Church, statues in white marble, the work of Mr. [Grinling] Gibbons, with all the carving & Pillars of exquisite art & greate cost: The history or Altar piece is the Salutation, the Volto [vault] in *fresca*, the Assumption of the blessed Virgin according to their Traditions[,] with our B: Saviour, & a world of figures, painted by *Verio*. The Thrones where the K. & Q: sits is very glorious in a Closset above just opposite to the Altar: Here we saw the Bishop in his Miter, & rich Copes, with 6 or 7: Jesuits & others in Rich Copes richly habited, often taking off, & putting on the Bishops Miter, who sate in a Chair with Armes pontificaly, was adored, & censed by 3 Jesuits in their Copes, then he went to the Altar & made divers Cringes [genuflections] there, censing the Images, & glorious Tabernacle placed upon the Altar . . . The Crosier (which was of silver) put into his hand, with a world of mysterious Ceremony[,] the Musique plaing & singing: & so I came away: not believing I should ever have lived to see such things in the K. of Englands palace, after it had pleas'd God to inlighten this nation; but our greate sinn, has (for the present) Eclips'd the Blessing, which I hope he will in mercy & his good time restore to its purity.[23]

Before the month was out Evelyn found a new matter for gossip and scandal. One of the singers was an Italian castrato – a phenomenon unheard of in England:

I heard the famous *Cifeccio* (Eunuch) sing, in the new popish chapell this afternoone, which was indeede very rare, & with greate skill: He came over from Rome, esteemed one of the best voices in *Italy*.[24]

Evelyn added a tart comment on the atmosphere ('much crowding, little devotion'), and from then on his disapproval seems to have kept him away from the new chapel – though he seized an opportunity to hear the same singer in a different context:

I heard the famous Singer the Eunuch *Cifacca*, esteemed the best in *Europe* & indeede his holding out [breath control] & delicate-nesse in extending & loosing a note with that incomparable softnesse, & sweetenesse was admirable: For the rest, I found him a meere wanton, effeminate child; very Coy, & prowdly conceited . . . He touch'd [played] the Harpsichord to his Voice

---

[23] Evelyn, 5 January 1687.
[24] Evelyn, 30 January 1687.

rarely well, & this was before a select number of some particular persons whom Mr. Pepys (Secretary of the Admiralty & a greate lover of Musick) invited to his house, where the meeting was, & this obtained by peculiar favour & much difficulty of the Singer, who much disdained to shew his talent to any but Princes.[25]

The new chapel was certainly costing a vast amount of money. A week after Evelyn's third visit to it, the king signed a warrant for establishment costs totalling more than £2000 a year. This sum was shortly doubled by the addition of six solo singers (only one of whom was English), an organist and nine 'Gregorians' (only three of them English), and nine instrumentalists.[26] All this seemed to bode ill for the English musicians of the Anglican chapel, which was still being maintained for the use of James's Protestant daughter Princess Anne. And Purcell must have looked particularly askance when an organ for the Popish chapel was commissioned from Renatus Harris. The specification does not survive, but it must have been a lavish one: the contract eventually cost nearly £1250 – five times what Purcell's friend Smith had been paid for the new instrument at St Katherine Cree.[27]

Domestic devotions and distractions

Like the previous year, 1687 might appear to have been relatively unproductive for Purcell, if we had to rely solely on the evidence of the official score-book of odes and anthems. Between the 1686 and 1687 odes he entered only two pieces – one of them, admittedly, by far the biggest of his symphony songs, *If ever I more riches did desire*. (Its text, ingeniously spliced together from two poems by Abraham Cowley, scorns ambition; perhaps Purcell was feeling despondent because the king obviously preferred foreign music above that of his own composers.) But the score-book does not tell the whole story. Possibly in response to official neglect of the Anglican chapel, Purcell was busying himself with music for domestic devotions. Before the year was out the fruits of his labours would be seen in print.

He had, in any case, more pressing worries than the situation at court. On 9 June his fourth son, another Henry, was baptized at St Margaret's, Westminster.[28] If the family had been feeling the pinch the previous autumn (and it may have been Frances's pregnancy then that had prompted Purcell to pursue the elusive Hodge), they would certainly be doing so

---

[25] Evelyn, 19 April 1687.
[26] Warrant dated 26 April 1687, establishment list dated 5 July 1687, both quoted in full in Zimmerman, *Purcell*, pp. 142, 143; *Cal. Tr. Books*, vol. 8: 1685–9, part iii, pp. 1326, 1441–2.
[27] J. Y. Akerman (ed.), *Moneys Received and Paid for Secret Services of Charles II and James II* (London: Camden Society, 1851), pp. 44, 169, 180, 186.
[28] St Margaret's, Westminster, Register of Baptisms 1681–1709 (unfoliated), entry dated 9 June.

now. The very next day after the baptism Purcell set about pursuing another debtor – this time the king, or at least his Treasury. Somehow or other, in the general sorting out of the royal finances back in the summer of 1685, Purcell's position as instrument keeper had been omitted from the establishment, and ever since then he had been doing this highly necessary work unpaid. Now he petitioned not only for the salary but also for over £20 in out-of-pocket expenses.[29] Eventually he was successful, but it was nine months before he saw a penny piece of the money. By that time, intriguingly, he had enlisted the help of a leading churchman, just as he had over Hodge. On this occasion he persuaded the Bishop of Durham to take up the case with the Treasury, and it was his intervention that finally prised the payment out of them – or most of it, for in the process Purcell's annual salary as instrument keeper was somehow reduced from £60 to £56.[30]

The summer brought a major event in music publishing. Grabu's *Albion and Albanius* was issued complete, in full score – the first opera to appear thus in England. (Locke's music for *Psyche* had appeared, together with that for *The Tempest*, without any other composer's contributions to either production.)[31] Grabu had financed the venture by subscription, with the announcement actually in the press at the moment the opera was taken off; evidently, intending purchasers were not deterred by the unfortunate timing – another indication, like the fact that Betterton continued giving commissions to Grabu, that it was political ill-luck, not musical incompetence, that sank the work.[32] Now the score was at last advertised in the press.[33] The thought of subscribing for one may have stuck in Purcell's craw, though he must have managed at least to borrow a copy.

In the autumn, while Purcell was busy with his next birthday ode for James II, his baby son Henry followed his three elder brothers to the grave, and was buried in the Abbey cloisters on 23 September.[34] Perhaps the sacred songs with which his father was also busy gave him some measure of comfort. Certainly the music of the ode, *Sound the trumpet!*

---

[29] *Cal. Tr. Books*, vol. 8: 1685–9, part iii, p. 1401 (10 June 1687), p. 1654 (12 December 1687), pp. 1763–4 (18 February 1688). The first of these entries is quoted in Zimmerman, *Purcell*, p. 144.
[30] *Cal. Tr. Books*, vol. 8: 1685–9, part iii, p. 1791 (5 March 1688); quoted in full in Zimmerman, *Purcell*, p. 155. Close examination of the figures reveals that the reduction resulted not from cheeseparing by Treasury officials but, curiously, from defective arithmetic on Purcell's own part.
[31] Locke, *The English Opera; or The Vocal Musick in Psyche, with the Instrumental Musick therein Intermix'd, to which is Adjoyned the Instrumental Musick in the Tempest* (London: the author, 1675).
[32] Grabu composed music for revivals in January 1687 of Beaumont and Fletcher's *The Maid's Tragedy* and in February 1688 of Massinger and Fletcher's *The Double Marriage* (*London Stage*, pp. 355, 362). *Albion and Albanius* was nevertheless dismissed by Dent (*Foundations*, p. 165) as a 'monument of stupidity'; this sealed the tomb of Grabu's reputation for the remainder of the twentieth century.
[33] *London Gazette*, 9–13 June 1687.
[34] WAR, Burials 1606–1706, f. 38.

beat the drum!, is unclouded, and also exceptionally elaborate.[35] Not content with having written his longest and grandest ode yet, Purcell decided at a late stage to add fully independent string parts to all the choruses, giving them a richness of sonority recalling *My heart is inditing*. Once again there is a showpiece solo for Gostling, at the end of which 'Pride and Discord headlong go / Down to the deep Abyss below' – their destination being represented, inevitably, by a bottom D, held for three bars: Purcell was not one to abandon a winning formula. But perhaps the finest movement in the work, and standing squarely at its midpoint, is a vast chaconne, nearly a hundred and thirty bars long and ceaselessly inventive: an unique feature in a royal ode. (We shall meet this magnificent movement again later, in very different surroundings.) One can only hope the king enjoyed the work, for it was to be the last offering he would receive from Purcell.

Political pressures

With the court back in London, there was trouble for the instrumentalists of the Anglican Chapel. A week after the birthday celebrations the Lord Chamberlain sent Staggins, the Master of the King's Music, a peremptory order:

> Whereas you have neglected to give Order to ye Violins to attend at ye Chappell at Whitehall where Her Royal Highnesse ye Princesse Ann of Denmarke is p^rsent. These are therefore to give notice to them that they give theire attendance there upon Sunday next & soe continue to doe soe as formerly they did.[36]

One wonders whether Purcell sympathized with the musicians or shared the princess's irritation at their laxity. He had composed no symphony anthems since the start of the reign. But he produced three in 1687, and it seems unlikely that they all belong to the last ten weeks of the year, after the order took effect, so he too may have been inconvenienced.

The Cecilian festival too had seemed to be an institution facing decline: in 1686 the ode had been set by a very minor figure, Isaac Blackwell. But in 1687 the event revived spectacularly. Politics doubtless took a hand, for the composer was a lifelong Catholic and the poet a recent convert to the faith. The ode, 'From harmony', is by Dryden. It describes an incandescent vision of the Creation and of the Last Judgment. At the beginning the music of the spheres brings order out of primordial chaos; at the end the last trumpet sounds; in between comes a vivid catalogue of musical instruments and their particular powers. The music was commissioned from Draghi. His setting, if perhaps over-long, is well crafted and

---

[35] Purcell Society Edition, vol. 18 (London, 2005), pp. 143–91.
[36] *RECM*, vol. 2, pp. 15–16 (21 October 1687).

imaginative – and richly scored, with choruses in five parts and accompaniments for recorders as well as strings.[37] But when he reached 'The trumpet's loud clangour excites us to arms', he startled his listeners by employing real trumpets. These instruments were, at the time, still almost exclusively ceremonial and military – used for sounding fanfares, and for signalling on the battlefield because their sound could cut through even its deafening noise. Hearing them indoors, in the Merchant Taylors' Hall, where the concert was held,[38] naturally made the audience sit up and take notice, and no one took more careful notice than Purcell. Draghi's actual treatment of the trumpets is disappointingly tentative and clumsy, but their potential was clear. Before long Purcell would exploit it fully, to triumphant effect.

Two days after the Cecilian celebrations Henry Playford initiated a new series to follow the final *Theater* volume. It was appetizingly entitled *The Banquet of Music*: 'a Collection of the Newest and Best Songs sung at Court, and at Publick Theatres. . . . Composed by several of the Best Masters. The Words by the Ingenious Wits of this Age'.[39] It contained six pieces by Purcell, including an extended symphony song with recorders, *How pleasant is this flowery plain*[40] – printed, as *Soft notes, and gently rais'd* had been two years previously, complete and in full score. And only the previous week the *London Gazette* had advertised yet another Playford songbook, though this one was very different in character. *Harmonia Sacra* offered a wide selection of devotional songs. The choice had been made by Purcell, who had also, Playford told his readers, edited the volume:

> the Words were penn'd by such Persons, as are, and have been, very Eminent both for Learning and Piety; and indeed, he that reads them as he ought, will soon find his Affections [emotions] warm'd, as with a Coal from the Altar, and feel the Breathings of Divine Love from every Line. As for the Musical Part, it was Compos'd by the most Skilful Masters of this Age; and though some of them are now dead, yet their Composures [compositions] have been review'd [edited] by Mr. *Henry Purcell*, whose tender Regard for the Reputation of those great Men made him careful that nothing should be published, which, through the negligence of Transcribers, might reflect upon their Memory. Here therefore the *Musical* and *Devout* cannot want Matter both to exercise their Skill, and heighten their Devotion.[41]

---

[37] Purcell Society Companion Series, vol. 3 (London, forthcoming).
[38] *London Gazette*, 21–4 November 1687.
[39] Ibid.
[40] Purcell Society Edition, vol. 27 (2007), pp. 28–40.
[41] Henry Playford (publ.), *Harmonia Sacra* (London, 1688), p. [iii]. The volume was advertised in the *London Gazette* dated 17–21 November 1687.

Harmonia Sacra includes no fewer than a dozen of Purcell's own sacred songs. Even the most modest of these, such as the tiny 'Thou wakeful shepherd' (*A Morning Hymn*), show Purcell at his most elevated and serious, and some of the larger ones, such as 'Now that the sun hath veiled his light' (*An Evening Hymn on a Ground*), are peerless examples of their kind.[42]

Purcell celebrated Christmas in style, with *Behold, I bring you glad tidings*, a new symphony anthem sung in Whitehall Chapel on Christmas Day.[43] It contains some fine music but is very uneven in invention. The opening symphony leads into a declamatory bass solo, evidently intended for Gostling and accompanied by the strings. This is a dignified and satisfying movement, but the ensuing dialogues between verse trio and full choir soon descend into note-spinning; even spatial separation in Whitehall Chapel can hardly have been enough to rescue them. All in all the piece, like the two other anthems Purcell had recently composed for the Chapel, *Praise the Lord, O my soul: O Lord my God* and *Thy way, O God, is holy*, has a slightly perfunctory air.[44] His interest in writing for the Chapel was on the wane.

By the time this anthem was first heard, however, Purcell must already have begun work on another, even if he did so reluctantly. The queen was pregnant, and the king had ordained a national thanksgiving for this prospect of an heir; a printed proclamation was issued on 23 December and reprinted in the next issue of the *London Gazette*.[45] It specified that on Sunday 15 January in London, and a fortnight later all over England, all Anglican churches should use a specified order of service: 'a solemn & particular office', John Evelyn called it, having attended at his local church. For the Chapel Royal Purcell produced *Blessed are they that fear the Lord*, a routine piece of journeyman work distinguished only by the inclusion, for obvious reasons, of two treble parts in the verse-group.[46] (For some reason the solos and ensembles in symphony anthems, whether by Purcell or by other composers, are nearly always for men's voices, with the boys singing only in the choruses.) The piece was completed in the nick of time, only three days before it was due to be performed.

Politically inspired though the thanksgiving was, the cleric who chose the words of the anthem resisted the temptation to edit. He probably judged that the text (Psalm 128) would be clearly understood as a call for loyalty to the king, whose policies were increasingly unpopular:

---

[42] Purcell Society Edition, vol. 30 (1965), contains all the devotional songs.
[43] Purcell Society Edition, vol. 28 (1959), pp. 1–27.
[44] Purcell Society Edition, vol. 17 (1996), pp. 187–209.
[45] *London Gazette*, 5–9 January 1687.
[46] Purcell Society Edition, vol. 28 (1959), pp. 42–59.

Thou shalt see Jerusalem in prosperity all thy life long.
O well is thee [repeated many times in Purcell's setting], and
    happy shalt thou be.
Yea, thou shalt see thy children's children: and peace upon Israel
O well is thee . . .

The royal propaganda machine was certainly hard at work. 30 January,
the day following the nationwide thanksgiving for the queen's pregnancy,
was the annual commemoration of the death – customarily described as
the martyrdom – of Charles I; the curate of Evelyn's church 'made a
florid Oration against the murder of that excellent Prince, with an exhort-
ation to Obedience'.[47] On 4 February the anniversary of the death of
Charles II was observed, and 6 February was celebrated, in the words of
the court diarist Narcissus Luttrell, as

a festival for joy of the king's comeing to the crown; there was
musick at the chappell, cannons discharged at the Tower, and at
night was a play at court.[48]

The play was probably Fletcher and Massinger's *The Double Marriage*,
which was revived that month. Significantly, the music for the revival was
composed not by Purcell but by the Catholic Grabu.[49]
    Another theatrical commission, however, did come Purcell's way that
spring, for Thomas D'Urfey's comedy *A Fool's Preferment*, licensed by
the censors on 21 May. It was his first substantial undertaking of this
kind since *Theodosius*, eight years before. As in that score there was no
instrumental music, but Purcell supplied eight songs, diverse in style
but uniform in their high musical quality, among them the rumbustious
'I'll sail upon the dog-star'.[50] The play was not a success, but Purcell's
music certainly was. The small publishing firm of Knight and Saunders
rushed out a slim volume devoted exclusively to the songs from the play
– the first of its kind ever issued in England.[51] This was not only a great
feather in Purcell's cap, but also a pointer to how his theatre music would
be exploited in future.

---

[47] Evelyn, 30 January 1688.
[48] Luttrell, vol. 1, p. 431.
[49] The tenacity of that ill-starred individual deserves admiration. Just as he had done after being
forced out of his post as Master of the King's Music, so after the misfortune that befell *Albion and
Albanius* he clung on in London for several years. By the end of 1686 he had even managed to
recover the arrears owing him from the reign of Charles II: a cool £225 (*RECM*, vol. 2, p. 211).
But eventually, in 1694, he left London, this time for good, his passport being issued for 4
December 1694 (*CSP Dom.*, January 1694–June 1695, p. 349).
[50] Purcell Society Edition, vol. 20 (1998), pp. 17–19.
[51] Henry Purcell, *New Songs Sung in The Fool's Preferment, or The Three Dukes of Dunstable*
(London, 1688).

His other songs continued to pour off the presses too. Four were included in the second volume of Playford's *The Banquet of Music*, advertised in early May; there were four more in the second volume of John Carr's *Vinculum Societatis: or, The Tie of Good Company*, which appeared later that month; and, in the second book of Carr's *Comes Amoris*, issued in January 1688 and aimed at rather coarser tastes, a short section with a separate title page, *A Small Collection of the Newest Catches*, included three of Purcell's latest catches – one of them among his lewdest.[52]

Confrontation

That same month the king took the step which would soon bring his reign to an ignominious end. Against advice, he issued a Declaration of Indulgence: in effect, this suspended the ban on Catholics from holding public office – the Test Act, which Charles II had reluctantly allowed to be introduced 15 years earlier. An order was given that the Declaration was to be read in all churches following the morning service on 20 May. Evelyn heard it at Whitehall Chapel, where one of the choirmen was obliged to read it. Purcell probably heard it there too, unless he did so instead at Westminster Abbey – which, Evelyn reported, was one of the few other churches in London where it actually was read.[53] In most it was ignored, for trouble was brewing. Two days earlier, seven prominent bishops had begged the king not to force them to obey the order. They were, they assured him, not anti-Catholic; they simply believed that the Declaration was legally invalid, because it had not been approved by Parliament. James flew into a rage. 'With threatning expressions', Evelyn tells us, he 'commanded them to obey him in reading of it at their perils; & so dismis'd them.'[54]

Purcell, like Evelyn, was no doubt deeply concerned as all this happened around him. But he had more immediate preoccupations. His daughter Frances was baptized in the Abbey on 30 May.[55] She would be the first of his children to survive into adulthood.

On the political front events moved rapidly. The Seven Bishops, unmoved by the king's bluster, refused to have the Declaration read in their dioceses. On 8 June they were thrown into the Tower, and Evelyn noted a wave of public sympathy:

> Wonderfull was the concerne of the people for them, infinite crowds of people on their knees, beging their blessing & praying for them as they past out of the Barge; along the Tower wharfe . . .[56]

---

[52] *Comes Amoris: or, The Companion of Love . . . The Second Book* (London, 1688)
[53] Evelyn, 20 May 1688.
[54] Evelyn, 18 May 1688.
[55] WAR, Baptisms 1607–1705, f. 10v. (Her date of birth is not recorded.)
[56] Evelyn, 8 June 1688.

Two days later the queen gave birth to a son – 'which will cost dispute', Evelyn noted gloomily.[57] He was right. The birth itself was widely doubted; a rumour spread that the proclaimed heir to James II was not his offspring at all, and had been smuggled into the palace in a warming-pan. But with all eyes on the fate of the Seven Bishops, public reaction to the arrival of the baby was muted. The king, nettled, ordered a public thanksgiving on the following Sunday, 17 June.[58] Like the earlier thanksgiving for the pregnancy, this one was to include an anthem, but neither Purcell nor Blow seems to have supplied one. As we shall see, the Anglican Chapel Royal was slipping out of the king's control, just as was the mood of the nation.

The thanksgiving duly took place, ending with bonfires and a firework display. Next day there was a concert on the river, given by the royal musicians. The event was noticed in *Public Occurrences*, a royal propaganda sheet:

> Mr. Abel, the celebrated Musician, and one of the Royal Band, entertained the public, and demonstrated his loyalty on the evening of 18th June 1688, by the performance of an aquatic concert. The barge prepared for this purpose was richly decorated, and illuminated by numerous torches. The music was composed expressly for the occasion by Signior Fede, Master of the Chapel Royal [*sic*: at this point Blow, if he bothered to read the piece, must have ground his teeth], and the performers, vocal and instrumental, amounted to one hundred and thirty, selected as the greatest proficients in the science. 'All ambitious,' says the author of *Public Occurrences*, 'hereby to express their loyalty and hearty joy for Her Majesty's safe deliverance, and birth of the Prince of Wales.' . . . Great numbers of barges and boats were assembled, and each having flambeaux on board, the scene was extremely brilliant and pleasing. The musick being ended, all the nobility and company that were upon the water gave three shouts to express their joy and satisfaction; and all the gentlemen of the musick went to Mr. Abel's house, which was nobly illuminated and honoured with the presence of a great many of the nobility; out of whose windows hung a fine machine full of lights, which drew hither a vast concourse of people. The entertainment lasted till three of the clock the next morning, the musick playing and the trumpets sounding all the while, the whole concluding with the health of their Majesties, the Prince of Wales, and all the Royal family.[59]

[57] Evelyn, 10 June 1688.
[58] Evelyn, 17 June 1688.
[59] Quoted in Edmund Sebastian Joseph van der Straeten, *The Romance of the Fiddle: The Origin of the Modern Virtuoso and the Adventures of His Ancestors* (London: Rebman, 1911), pp. 124–5. No copy of the original has been traced; this is unfortunate, given that Van der Straeten appears to be a little coy about the extent of his direct quotation from it.

The account does not relate how Abell's neighbours reacted to having trumpets sounding into the small hours, but presumably they were less than enthusiastic. So, no doubt, were many of the musicians involved. They had no choice but to take part in this overblown event. To make matters worse they were obliged to perform music which had been composed by one member of the vaunted popish chapel and was being directed by another.

Meanwhile, on 15 June, the bishops were put on trial at the High Court, charged with seditious libel upon the king. Once again there were popular demonstrations in their support, and it is clear that they also had the support of one significant faction at court. Four days into the trial, a new anthem by Blow was sung in Whitehall Chapel; the date is given in Gostling's own copy, and he is to be believed, for the anthem had obviously been written for him. It must have caused a sensation, for once not thanks to the soloist and his cavernous bottom notes but because of the words he sang:

O Lord, thou art my God: I will exalt thee. . . .
For thou hast been a strength to the poor: a strength to the needy
    in his distress.
A refuge from the storm: a shadow from the heat, when the blast
    of the terrible ones is as a great storm against the wall.
He shall bring down the noise of strangers: the branch of the
    terrible ones shall be brought low.

It is all too clear who was to be identified with the poor and the needy, and who with the terrible ones and the noisy strangers (foreigners, that is – a swipe at the Italian musicians of the popish chapel). And whoever compiled the text was confident of the outcome:

He will swallow up death in victory. . . .
And it shall be said in that day, Lo, this is our God: we have wait-
    ed for him, and he will save us: This is the Lord: we have waited
    for him, we will be glad and rejoice in his salvation.[60]

The spectacle of one government department briefing against another is a familiar one nowadays; but for the Chapel Royal to brief against the monarch was an event without parallel, before or since.

At the end of the month the jury delivered their verdict on the Seven Bishops to a courtroom packed with anxious citizens, Luttrell among them:

---

[60] Isaiah 25. 1, 4, 5, 8, 9; Blow's setting is in Texas Gostling MS (facsimile, ed. Franklin B. Zimmerman; Austin, TX: University of Texas Press, 1977), reverse end, pp. 130–4.

they found all the defendants Not guilty; at which there was a most mighty huzzah in the hall, which was very full of people; and all the way they came down people askt for their blessing on their knees; there was continued shoutings for ½ an hour, so that no business could be done; and they hist the [government] solicitor. And at night was mighty rejoyceing, in ringing of bells, discharging of gunns, lighting of candles, and bonefires in several places, tho forbid, and watchmen went about to take an account of such as made them: a joyfull deliverance to the church of England.[61]

The king's party, understandably jumpy about the outcome, had anticipated it by mustering the army on Hounslow Heath. Their displeasure at the events described by Luttrell will certainly have been compounded by the sentiments expressed in a second anthem by Blow, again with a prominent part for Gostling. In the singer's score-book it bears that same momentous date, 30 June 1688:

Blessed be the Lord my strength: who teacheth my hands to war, and my fingers to fight;
My hope, my fortress, my castle and deliverer: my defender, in whom I trust. . . .
Bow thy heavens, O Lord, and come down: touch the mountains, and they shall smoke.
Cast forth thy lightnings, and tear them: shoot out thine arrows, and consume them.
Take me out of the great waters: and from the hand of strange children. [Foreigners again!]
Whose mouth talketh of vanity: and whose right hand is a hand of iniquity.[62]

We do not know who, among the Anglican clerics of the Chapel, selected these texts; but the relish with which Blow set them is evident in his music. We do not know, either, how these two anthems were received; but their very existence tells its own tale of a fractured court.

It is tempting to link these astonishing events with Purcell's greatest anthem for the Chapel, *O sing unto the Lord*.[63] In Gostling's score-book the piece is placed immediately after Purcell's four other symphony anthems from 1687 and 1688; unfortunately the singer noted only the year of its composition, 1688, with no occasion identified. And its text, from Psalm

---

[61] Luttrell, vol. 1, p. 448 (30 June 1688).
[62] Psalm 144, vv. 1–8, 11; setting in Texas Gostling MS, reverse end, pp. 52–7.
[63] Purcell Society Edition, vol. 17 (1996), pp. 139–65.

96, has no obvious political overtones. But something extraordinary must have prompted Purcell to follow four workaday specimens with this imperishable masterpiece. It contains superb solo and ensemble numbers, including a wonderfully inventive ground-bass duet, 'The Lord is great', with a ritornello such as even Purcell rarely surpassed; it also, unlike many of his symphony anthems (especially the recent ones), makes generous provision for the full choir. In the concluding chorus, a pealing 'Alleluia', strings and voices weave an opulent tapestry of counterpoint, finishing with a virtuoso display of overlapping entries both direct and inverted. Alas, this splendid symphony anthem was to be the very last one that Purcell, or anyone else, composed for Whitehall Chapel.

A few days after the acquittal of the Seven Bishops, two of the four judges who had sat in the case were summarily dismissed: not even the judiciary was safe any longer. As for mere royal musicians – other than those of the popish chapel – James's disdainful attitude towards them was all too apparent. A few weeks later the Lord Chamberlain passed down an order that

> a number of his Majesty's musicians shall attend the Queen's Majesty's maids of honour to play whensoever they shall be sent to, at the houres of dancing, at such houres and such a number of them as they shall desire. And hereof the master of the musick and the musicians are to take notice that they observe this order.[64]

The order itself contains scant matter of offence: the royal violin band had been playing for balls (though admittedly only at court) ever since it was first set up in the previous century. But the hectoring tone of the last sentence will have done nothing to improve the mood of the players.

In mid-July the king, at once nervous and insensitive, again ordered his troops into camp at Hounslow, 'but the nation in high discontent', noted Evelyn darkly.[65] Two weeks later the court left Whitehall for Windsor: it was to be their last summer remove. Neither Purcell nor Blow was included among the unusually large contingent of musicians.[66] Purcell may have begun work on a birthday ode, but if he did, it was destined not to be completed, and no trace of it has survived.[67] Towards the end of

---

[64] *RECM*, vol. 2, p. 20 (19 August 1688), which twice misreads 'houres' as 'homes'. The original document is Kew, National Archives, LC 5/150 (Lord Chamberlain's Records), p. 192.
[65] Evelyn, 12 July 1688.
[66] Listed (for riding charges) in *RECM*, vol. 2, pp. 21–2.
[67] An ode fragment that I had identified as probably belonging to this date – Purcell Society Edition, vol. 18 (2005), pp. xviii–xx, 192–212 – now proves to have been composed for the birth of the Duke of Gloucester eight months later. See Bryan White, 'Music for "A brave livlylike boy": The Duke of Gloucester, Purcell and "The noise of foreign wars"', *Musical Times*, 148 (2007), pp. 75–83.

August reports began to arrive that William of Orange, the Protestant husband of James II's elder daughter Mary, was assembling an invasion force on Texel, the largest of the Frisian islands. At first James, paralysed with indecision, did nothing. At last, on 18 September, he hurried back to Whitehall, leaving the queen and most of the court at Windsor. The following day he went downriver in the royal barge, to inspect the state of naval preparedness at Chatham and Sheerness. The party was provisioned to stay for some days, but within hours James had to rush back to London, where panic had broken out on a rumour that the Dutch had already landed.

The queen, meanwhile, also returned to Whitehall. Four days later, in what must have been a decidedly strained atmosphere, a formal welcome ceremony was held, but there is no mention of music.[68] The following Sunday there were serious disturbances outside a popish chapel in the City; a week later these were repeated on a larger scale. After that things went rapidly downhill. By mid-October, with invasion expected daily, formal celebration of the king's birthday was out of the question; on the day itself even the customary artillery salute from the Tower was cancelled, presumably for fear of starting another panic, and a partial eclipse of the sun no doubt appeared to many as an ill portent.[69] On 5 November (an ominous date for the English crown) William's fleet, borne along the Channel by a favourable 'Protestant wind', landed at Torbay in Devon. From there he marched on London. The capital suffered a swift descent into anarchy. On 11 November, for instance, 'the rabble assembled in a tumultuous manner at St John's, Clerkenwell, the popish monastery, on a report of gridirons, spits, great cauldrons, &c. to destroy protestants',[70] and over the following weeks there were many other attacks on Catholic chapels. By mid-December James's regime had collapsed. Before Christmas, unexpectedly without bloodshed, he and his family fled to France, and William and Mary began negotiating the terms on which they would take the throne.

---

[68] Luttrell, vol. 1, p. 462 (22 September 1688); Evelyn, 22 September 1688.
[69] Evelyn, 14 October 1688.
[70] Luttrell, vol. 1, p. 474.

'Ambigue entertainments'

We routinely refer to *Dioclesian*, *King Arthur*, *The Fairy Queen*, and *The Indian Queen* as 'Purcell's operas'. But that is a gross oversimplification: all he did was write the music! In reality, these works are multimedia entertainments, with a separate cast of actors and actresses, and another of dancers, besides the singers – and there was an important contribution from the stage crew and the machinists, in the form of spectacular scene changes and special effects such as the flying chariot in which Delphia, the formidable Prophetess in *Dioclesian*, surveys the busy world beneath, and from which she launches some of her magical interventions in the doings of other characters. For Restoration audiences, the stage spectacle was as defining a feature of opera as the music.

What distinguishes dramatic opera from the West End (or Broadway) musical? The answer is that in dramatic opera the musical episodes rarely form part of the main plot, but are introduced ostensibly to entertain the characters on the stage. Musical numbers do occasionally impinge on the drama, but they are rarely essential to it. The operatic adaptation of *The Tempest*, for example, introduced a masque of devils whose sudden appearance strikes fear into Alonzo, Antonio, and Gonzalo, cast away on the enchanted island, and an echo song for Ferdinand and Ariel: neither of these items serves to advance the plot, any more than do the several inset songs that were retained from Shakespeare's original. In *Psyche* the musical and dramatic strands are much more closely woven together, but even here the most substantial musical passages – a celebration of sylvan peace at the beginning, a scene for Vulcan and the Cyclops hard at work adorning Cupid's palace, an invocation in the Temple of Mars, an extended song of furies and devils, and a final celebration, sung by Apollo and the gods, of the nuptials of Cupid and Psyche – are essentially decorative rather than dramatic. *King Arthur* adopts the *Psyche* model: a few of the musical numbers, such as 'Hither, this way' in Act II and 'Two daughters of this ancient stream' in Act IV, do something to move the action forward, but the big masque of the Cold Genius in Act III is introduced on a slender dramatic pretext (the attempt by the evil magician Osmond to seduce Emmeline by displaying his magical powers), while that of Britannia's Isle in Act V merely celebrates a dénouement already arrived at (Arthur's twofold victory, both over the Saxons and over the machinations of Osmond). In *Dioclesian*, *The Fairy Queen*, and *The Indian Queen* the music is simply grafted onto dramas which are functionally complete without it.[1]

The hybrid nature of dramatic opera has always been controversial. In the same issue of *The Gentleman's Journal* in which he first mentioned *The Fairy Queen*, Motteux seized the opportunity to publish an extended discussion of the art form:

> Other Nations bestow the name of Opera only on such Plays whereof every word is sung. But experience hath taught us that our English genius will not rellish that perpetual singing. I dare not accuse the language for being over-charged with Consonants, which may take off the beauty of the Recitative part, though in several other Countries I have seen their Opera's still Crowded every time, tho long and almost all Recitative. It is true that their Trio's, Chorus's, lively Songs and *Recits* with *Accompaniments* of Instruments, Symphony's, Machines, and excellent Dances make the rest be born with, and the one sets off the other: But our English Gentlemen, when their Ear is satisfied, are desirous to have their mind pleas'd, and Music and Dancing industriously intermix'd with Comedy or Tragedy: I have often observed that the Audience is no less attentive to some extraordinary Scenes of passion or mirth, than to what they call *Beaux Endroits*, or the most ravishing part of the Musical Performance. But had those Scenes, though never so well wrought up, been sung, they would have lost most of their beauty. All this however, doth not lessen the Power of Musick, for its Charms command our attention when used in their place, and the admirable Consorts [concerts] we have in *Charles-street* and *York buildings*; are an undeniable proof of it. But this shows that what is unnatural, as are Plays altogether sung, will soon make one uneasy, which Comedy or Tragedy can never do unless they be bad.[2]

This was special pleading, of course; it put a convenient gloss on an awkward fact. Nearly all English operas had been created by

---

[1] But see p. 168, below, for details of a gap in the plot-line of *The Indian Queen*, caused by careless cutting of the play text in order to accommodate the music.
[2] *Gent. J.*, January 1692, pp. 7–8.

the insertion of music into heavily cut spoken plays, the resulting hybrid entertainment being put on under the control of the straight-acting fraternity, in their own theatre. (There was no alternative to this, for the simple reason that England had no opera house; and the hostility of the actors towards Grabu had given due warning that they would not tolerate having their earnings jeopardized by all-sung entertainments.) But this line of development had left English dramatic opera vulnerable to critical attack on a point which Motteux blithely ignored, but on which Roger North shrewdly put his finger:

> there is a fatall objection to all these ambigue enter-
> teinements: they break unity, and distract the audience.
> Some come for the play and hate the musick, others
> come onely for the musick, and the drama is pennance
> to them, and scarce any are well reconciled to both. M^r
> Betterton (whose talent was speaking and not singing)
> was pleased to say, that 2 good dishes were better than
> one, which is a fond [foolish] mistake, for few care to see
> 2 at a time of equall choice.[3]

What was Purcell's view on this burning issue? Some have argued that the circumstances which obliged him to compose dramatic rather than all-sung opera constituted a great misfortune for English music.[4] But there is not a shred of evidence that he himself felt any frustration on this account; on the contrary, to the end of his life he seems to have accepted commissions for dramatic opera with relish. The all-sung *Dido and Aeneas* was a special case, and however great the results may appear in the context of the conventional operatic tradition, we need not imagine that Purcell hankered after writing more works of the same kind or chafed at the limitations of dramatic opera.

Nor need we regret that some of Purcell's greatest music graces what amounts to a mongrel theatrical genre.[5] What its detractors overlook – North among them – is the fact that in dramatic opera the climactic points of the spoken play and of the music do not coincide, and indeed by definition cannot: an apparent difficulty,

---

[3] North, p. 307.
[4] Dent, for instance, laments (*Foundations*, p. 230) that 'no great composer was ever so unfortunate in his surroundings'.
[5] The case for dramatic opera is persuasively argued in Richard Luckett, 'Exotick but Rational Entertainments: The English Dramatick Operas', in Marie Axton and Raymond Williams (eds), *English Drama: Forms and Development* (Cambridge: Cambridge University Press, 1977), pp. 132–41, and in Price, *Stage*, pp. 3–6.

but one which a skilled librettist or adaptor could turn to advantage. *King Arthur* thus offers the audience two affecting emotional high-points: in the spoken play, the restoration of Emmeline's sight in Act III; in the music, the masque conjured up by Merlin in celebration of Arthur's victory over the heathen Saxons and the evil Osmond, which crowns Act V with a succession of wonderful numbers culminating in 'Fairest Isle'. Intelligent modern productions, according a modicum of respect to the spoken text as well as the music, and also admitting the legitimate claim of stagecraft to its share of the limelight, could leave an audience as delighted and satisfied as Purcell's audiences were three hundred years ago – at least an audience that was prepared, unlike the one described by North, to give a fair hearing to music and words alike.

FOUR

'PRIDE AND WONDER OF THE AGE'[1]
(1689–1695)

'Turning times'

The Glorious Revolution of 1688 affected the musical life of London in all sorts of ways – some of them only temporary, others permanent; some predictable, others entirely unlooked for; some welcome, others quite the reverse. Its effects on Purcell were to be profound, radically changing the course of his professional life.

Public concert-giving was abruptly suspended on account of the crisis, and several weeks were to elapse before it began returning to normal. There were no Cecilian celebrations in November; possibly some unlucky poet and composer had been at work on an ode but, if they were, nothing is known of their efforts. And with the monarchy itself in abeyance there were, for the first time since the Restoration, no new year celebrations at court. But on 13 February 1689 William and Mary, signing a meticulously detailed agreement with Parliament, accepted the throne as joint monarchs, and the royal musicians, in feverish haste, set about preparing for the new reign.

The coronation was fixed for 11 April, only eight short weeks away: in that time a new order of service had to be carefully drawn up, not merely reversing the changes made in 1685 to accommodate the Catholic James but also, for the first time, devising suitable ceremonial for a queen regnant – ruling on equal terms with the king, instead of merely serving as a queen consort. Anthem texts, some traditional but some entirely new, had to be decided upon by the clergy. And only then could the musicians begin their own labours of composing, copying, and rehearsing the music for a

---

[1] 'Purcell! the Pride and Wonder of the Age / The Glory of the Temple, and the Stage'. From a dedicatory poem by Henry Hall, in Purcell, *Orpheus Britannicus*, Book I (London: Henry Playford, 1698), p. [x].

major state occasion. To make matters worse, less than three weeks after the coronation came the birthday of the new queen: an occasion which would henceforth be marked with the full-scale celebrations previously accorded only to the king – including the performance of an ode, newly penned by one of the court poets and set to music by a royal composer. This task now fell to Purcell: a perverse choice in the immediate circumstances, since as organist of Westminster Abbey he was also in overall charge of the music for the coronation service. This will have involved him in co-ordinating arrangements between the Abbey choir, the Chapel Royal, the Twenty-Four Violins, and the state trumpeters and drummers, scheduling rehearsals both in the Abbey and elsewhere, and – not least – composing what turned out to be the grandest of the nine anthems to be performed.

Luttrell, who was present in the Abbey, noted merely that the coronation was celebrated 'much in the matter the former was'; but in fact it was a good deal less elaborate. Henry Compton, Bishop of London, who drew up the order of service, stripped away many of the innovations introduced in 1685, in their place reinstating the Communion.[2] The music, too, was less lavish – perhaps in deference to the wishes of the new king, whose austere tastes had probably been made known. Fewer Gentlemen of the Chapel Royal took part, an economy clearly reflected in the modest vocal scoring of all the anthems. The introit, *I was glad*, was presumably sung once again in Purcell's full setting, though the text provided by Compton differed slightly from that for the 1685 service. At the Acclamation Compton made a more radical change, replacing the traditional *Let thy hand be strengthened* with a new anthem, *Blessed art thou, O land*; this has not survived, and its composer has not been identified. At the Anointing the choirs sang *Come, Holy Ghost* and *Zadok the priest* – probably the earlier settings by Turner and Lawes respectively, though again the texts of both anthems were slightly modified. After the Anointing came Blow's *Behold, O God our defender*: the opening was a reworking of his 1685 setting, with its five vocal parts reduced to four, but Blow introduced new musical material where the text had been changed to reflect the new king's martial prowess ('The adversaries of the Lord shall be broken to pieces: out of heaven shall he thunder upon them').[3] The putting on of the crowns was followed by the first of the two anthems with orchestra, Purcell's *Praise the Lord, O Jerusalem*.[4] This is laid out for only five voices, as against the eight

[2] Original drafts of the coronation order, though without the names of composers, survive in London, Heralds' College MS L.19 and Lambeth Palace MS 1077. The order is printed in John Wickham Legg, *Three Coronation Orders* (London: Henry Bradshaw Society, 1900), pp. 10–36, and L. G. Wickham Legg, *English Coronation Records* (London: Constable, 1901), pp. 317–42. The composers may have been named in an illustrated description of the coronation published shortly afterwards; unfortunately only a fragment of it survives (Oxford, Bodleian Library, Wood 276A, No. CV).
[3] *Musica Britannica*, vol. 7 (1953), pp. 51–3.
[4] Purcell Society Edition, vol. 17 (1996), pp. 166–86.

of *My heart is inditing*, and is only half as long, but the passages for full choir are cunningly scored so as to create rich sonorities, and at nearly two hundred and fifty bars it is hardly a slight piece: certainly not the 'short anthem' which Compton had hopefully prescribed. Finally, while the General Pardon was proclaimed, the King's Largesse scattered, and the homage of the Lords performed, the choirs sang Blow's symphony anthem *The Lord God is a sun and a shield*.[5] This too is only half the length of its 1685 counterpart, *God spake sometime in visions*, and is scored for four voices instead of eight, though it was probably quite long and ornate enough for the new king. For the Communion offertory Blow provided a tiny but eloquent anthem for four-part full choir, *Let my prayer come up*.[6]

If Purcell heaved a private sigh of relief when all this was over (and it seems to have gone off smoothly – at least there are no reports to the contrary), a week later he received a rude shock. It was

> ordered that Mr. Purcell the Organist to the Deane & Chapter of Westm^r. doe pay to the hand of Mr. John Nedham Receiver of the Colledge [of Westminster] All such money as was received by him for places in the Organ loft at the Coronačon of Kinge William & Queene Mary by or before Satturday next being the 20th day of this instant Aprill. And in default thereof his place is declared to be Null & void. And it is further ordered that his Stipend or Sallary due at our Lady Day last past be deteyned in the hands of the Treasurer untill further orders.[7]

It would be unthinkable nowadays for the Abbey organist to charge visitors for admission to the organ loft at a coronation service. In Purcell's day, though, it was part of a time-honoured system. Temporary seating galleries were erected in various parts of the church to accommodate paying spectators, and the cost of building them was met directly by various parties, including the choirmen, the choristers, the boarders and King's Scholars of Westminster School, and sundry Abbey employees – vergers, bellringers, gardener, cloister-porter, and so on – each group keeping a share of the proceeds and the balance going to Abbey funds. At the coronation of James II, however, no instructions were ever given for the Abbey's share to be paid over (the Catholic James had little interest in directing monies to an Anglican foundation). Now, in 1689, the Chapter were understandably anxious not to be deprived again: they successfully petitioned the new king and queen on the matter and, having secured their approval, issued an order just before the coronation that this time all

---

[5] *Musica Britannica*, vol. 79 (2002), pp. 163–79.
[6] *Musica Britannica*, vol. 7 (1953), p. 54.
[7] Westminster Abbey Chapter Minutes, 1683–1714, f. 25 (18 April 1689), deciphered by Sir Jack Westrup and printed in *Purcell*, p. 63.

the proceeds were to be pooled *before* each group was paid off. But no one seems to have informed either Purcell or Stephen Crespion, the precentor, who was collecting on behalf of the various Abbey employees – and, of course, the only coronation in their experience had been that of James II. Purcell, enjoying sole jurisdiction over his loft, had cleared nearly £80 after expenses – more than his annual salary as a royal musician – and Crespion, disposing of the proceeds from the nave, over £420.

On the face of it, this had been a simple oversight. The peremptory tone of the Chapter's order, though – not least the threat to withhold a salary payment that was already several weeks overdue – might suggest bad blood between the Dean of Westminster and his organist (something not unknown in more recent times). Sir John Hawkins (1719–89), admittedly writing nearly a century after the event, had no doubt about the rights and wrongs of the matter. Apparently quoting another and now lost version of the order, he observed that

> the penning of it is an evidence of great ignorance or malice, in that it describes him by the appellation of organ blower who was organist of their own church, and in truth the most excellent musician of his time.[8]

Conspiracy or cock-up? Despite Hawkins's dark surmise, it was almost certainly the latter. As can be seen from the wording of the order, Purcell was not referred to as a mere 'organ blower'. And in the event, having promptly paid over the money as demanded, he then received nearly half of it back, while of Crespion's £420, just over £360 was divided among those on whose behalf he had been operating, leaving £24 to be returned to him and about the same again as the institutional share.

One thing is certain: all this unpleasantness came at the worst possible time, for Purcell must have been frantically busy rehearsing (if indeed he was not still composing) the ode for the birthday of the new queen, which fell on 30 April, less than three weeks after the coronation. *Now does the glorious day appear* was his most imposing royal offering so far, richly scored for five-part strings – not the French scoring of *Albion and Albanius*, with one violin and three violas, but the Italianate orchestra of Draghi's Cecilian ode, with two viola parts as well as two violins.[9] What Purcell did not manage to secure, though, was the use of trumpets: he must have been itching to try them out, but had to make do instead with suggesting them by means of bold and arresting fanfare figures for the strings right at the beginning. He was obliged to wait another year before being able to employ real trumpets instead of pretend ones.

[8] Hawkins, vol. 2, p. 744.
[9] Purcell Society Edition, vol. 11 (1993), pp. 1–46.

Under the new regime, elaborate music at Whitehall Chapel fell into disfavour. William was not, perhaps, quite the philistine portrayed by some accounts: in 1699, for instance, a financial crisis in the royal household obliged him to make economies, but he maintained the musical establishment at full strength, and even contrived to carry out a long-cherished scheme of his late queen, that of creating for Blow a new post as Composer to the Chapel Royal.[10] But he had little personal interest in music other than that of military bands, and as a Calvinist he held strong views about its proper function in worship. On 23 February 1689 – well before the coronation, and only ten days after William and Mary had accepted the throne – the queen decreed that instruments were no longer to be used at services in Whitehall.[11] Only one more symphony anthem would be composed for the Chapel Royal: Purcell's *My song shall be alway of the lovingkindness of the Lord*, performed on 9 September 1690 to welcome the king home after the Siege of Limerick. Possibly it escaped the ban because the welcome ceremony took place not at Whitehall but at Windsor.

The following year the king made an intervention of his own, directing that

> the King's Chapell shall be all the year through kept both morning and evening with solemn music like a collegiate church.[12]

If this directive was intended to extinguish the pyrotechnics that were fashionable in solo anthems, it failed: those composed for the Chapel in the 1690s are every bit as florid as those of the late 1680s and, as Thomas Tudway noted,

> Symphonys, indeed, wth Instruments in y[e] Chappell, were laid aside; But they continu'd to make their Anthems wth all the Flourish, of interludes, & Retornellos, w[ch] are now perform'd, by y[e] Organ.[13]

All the same, the royal intervention marked the beginning of a sharp decline in the Chapel Royal – not only in the importance and rich scoring

---

[10] *Cheque Book*, p. 23. Rimbault indicates only the year; the order is actually superscribed 2 March 1700.

[11] Kew, National Archives, RG 8/110 (Registrar General's records), ff. 24–5v.

[12] *KM*, p. 407. This order was dated simply '1691' by Lafontaine in *KM*, and could not be traced at all by Ashbee (see *RECM*, vol. 2, p. 43). Its wording is remarkably close to that of an order issued, apparently in 1625, by Charles I, and quoted by Lafontaine on p. 60: 'Our express pleasure is that our Chappell be all the year through kept both morning and evening with solemne musicke like a collegiate church: unless it be at such times in the summer or other times when We are pleased to spare it' (*KM*, p. 60).

[13] London, British Library, Harl. MS 7338, f. 5.

of the music itself but also in the morale of the musicians and hence, inevitably, in standards of performance. By 1693 it would become necessary for the Subdean to remind the Gentlemen of their obligation to attend choir practices; but neither this admonition nor the threat of increased fines prevented the occurrence, within a matter of weeks, of 'a notorious neglect of the duty of the Chapel, at which the Queen was offended'. This time Subdean Battell warned the Gentlemen that any further 'scandalous omissions' of this kind might be punished with public reprimands or even with suspensions.[14] It was altogether a sorry tale of deterioration and decay; but Purcell had long before sensed the direction matters would take. Ever since the coronation he had devoted less and less of his time to the Chapel Royal, preferring to turn his energies elsewhere. Between the Revolution and his death he composed no more than four or five new anthems (as against some fifty between 1680 and 1688), leaving Blow to meet the needs of the Chapel.

Music for education

In the late spring of 1689 Purcell's name came before the public in two important collections of printed music: book 3 of *The Banquet of Music* and the second part of *Musick's Handmaid* were both advertised in May.[15] The first of these, like its predecessors and successors (in the end there were six books), was a collection of secular songs by eleven composers, among which Purcell's contribution, a catch and a short duet, was not particularly prominent. He made a much bigger showing in *Musick's Handmaid*, a book of teaching pieces for budding keyboard players. The title had originated in 1663, under the imprint of the enterprising John Playford; he and his son Henry had issued a revised edition, along with a second volume, in 1678. The 1689 edition included no fewer than eighteen pieces by Purcell, who had also edited the volume for publication. As a teacher himself Purcell was a shrewd judge of what was required, and the collection offers attractive and well-judged fare to learners of varying levels of ability.

It seems likely that his interests in education went beyond the purely practical. Also in 1689 he composed the ode *Celestial music*, a setting of a poem by an unnamed pupil (or possibly former pupil) at the school of Louis Maidwell in King Street, Westminster, a stone's throw from the Abbey.[16] The establishment was highly regarded and, in contrast to Westminster School, thoroughly progressive, with a curriculum that included mathematics and modern languages alongside Latin and Greek.

---

[14] *Cheque Book*, pp. 86–7 (entries dated 5 April and 21 August 1693).

[15] Term Catalogue, May 1689.

[16] Purcell noted at the head of the partly autograph score (London, British Library, MS R.M. 20.h.8, reverse end, ff. 125v–117) that the poem was 'by one of his [Maidwell's] scholars'; the term could mean alumnus as well as current pupil. The ode appears in Purcell Society Edition, vol. 1 (2008), pp. 1–34.

Nahum Tate, the librettist of *Dido and Aeneas* and a distinguished poet, praised the clarity of Maidwell's teaching even of grammar and the classics ('Unlike my Fate, by Pedants led astray', he adds ruefully):

> . . . thou in gen'rous Pity didst impart
> To weeping Youth this perfect Scheme of Art,
> Whose ready Method doubly eas'd their way,
> More short the Journey, and more bright the Day.
> Thy Art, like *Moses*, on the Mount appears,
> Shews at one View the Search of many years.
> So short and clear all thy Instructions lie,
> They teach the Mind, not load the Memory.
> Thy Tree performs for Boys more wonders now
> Than for the Heroe *Virgil*'s Golden Bough.[17]

And Maidwell himself was evidently regarded as something of an institution, to judge from the words of another contemporary poet, Charles Gildon:

> Thus far from Pleasure, Sir, or Grief,
> I fool away an Idle Life
> Till Mr. *Maidwell* cease to Teach.[18]

Yet the school had been founded only in 1687; so it may be that Purcell's ode – modestly scored for four soloists, four-part chorus, and strings – was a contribution to an early public-relations campaign. If so, it was a generous one. The new ode was performed at the school on 5 August. It borrows its opening symphony from *My heart is inditing*, one of Purcell's anthems for the coronation of James II, though this was doubtless done not to add dignity but merely to save effort; the symphony had, after all, been heard in public only once, and that on an occasion which most of its hearers will by 1689 have preferred to forget.

The year 1689 also saw another school performance of a Purcell work: the celebrated production of *Dido and Aeneas* at the girls' school in Chelsea run by the dancing master Josias Priest. (As we have already seen, this production, long believed to have been the premiere, was not even

---

[17] 'To Mr. L. Maidwell, *on* his New Grammar' and 'On the Translation of Eutropius, By Young Gentlemen, Educated by Mr. *L. Maidwell*', in Tate, *Poems Written on Several Occasions* (2nd edn, London: Tooke, 1684), pp. 167–8, 217–20. Maidwell's teaching of Latin grammar is praised in a second poem, attributed to Dryden, in Leeds University, Brotherton Collection, MS Lt 66, f. 1. For more details about Maidwell's establishment, see W. H. Godfrey, *London County Council Survey of London*, vol. 31 (London, 1963), pp. 177–9.
[18] In George Villiers, Duke of Buckingham, *Miscellany Poems upon Several Occasions . . .* (London: Peter Buck, 1692), p. 11.

the first time the work had been mounted at the school.)[19] It can safely be assumed that the music was arranged for high voices, just as *Venus and Adonis* had been in 1684, but the part of Aeneas, unlike that of Adonis in the earlier school show, may have been sung not by one of the girls but by a summer guest of the Priests': the poet Thomas D'Urfey, who obligingly wrote a topical spoken epilogue for the production, and who happened to possess a pleasant bass voice.[20]

Full orchestra

The autumn of 1689 brought a happy event for the Purcells: the baptism, on 6 September, of their son Edward, who unlike his brothers was to survive into adulthood. (He was himself to become a musician in a modest way, as organist of St Clement, Eastcheap, from 1711 until his death in 1740.) Coincidentally there occurred one of the crucial events in Purcell's professional life. Four years after the debacle of *Albion and Albanius*, the United Company at last plucked up the courage to commission another operatic entertainment. Playing safe, they settled for a time-honoured formula: the new piece would be a dramatic opera. It was adapted from a very old play, Massinger and Fletcher's *The Prophetess, or the History of Dioclesian*, dating from 1622, which was now to be tricked out with spectacular scenery and stage machines and adorned with lavish amounts of music. For the music the company turned not, as might have been expected, to Blow – England's senior composer – but to Purcell. It was a historic choice.[21]

The autumn coincidentally brought a second major commission from outside the court. The London Society of Yorkshiremen were planning a grand dinner to celebrate, *inter alia*, the involvement of prominent persons hailing from their county in events leading up to the Glorious Revolution; the centrepiece of the event was to be a splendid musical performance at Merchant Taylors' Hall. Thomas D'Urfey (no Yorkshireman he, but a Devonian) was for some reason commissioned to write a new ode for the occasion, and Purcell (a Londoner born and bred) to set it to music. Both of them responded with relish. D'Urfey, in the poetic equivalent of purple prose, hymned the achievements of Yorkshire worthies right back to the

---

[19] See pp. 81–2, above, and notes 77 and 78 on p. 81.

[20] P. H. Highfill, K. A. Burnim, and E. A. Langhans, *A Biographical Dictionary of Actors, Actresses, Musicians, Dancers, Managers, and Other Stage Personnel in London 1660–1800* (Carbondale: Southern Illinois University Press, 1973–), s.v. 'Durfey'. D'Urfey's stay with the Priests resulted in a comedy, *Love for Money; or, The Boarding-School*, produced in 1690 or early 1691: *London Stage*, pp. 392–3.

[21] It is possible, as Margaret Laurie has suggested to me in private correspondence, that Betterton – a canny operator – had commissioned Purcell's setting (replacing Banister's 1677 original) of the invocation scene in Charles Davenant's tragedy *Circe*, which was revived in October 1689, as a trial run for *Dioclesian*; Purcell's setting is lengthy and elaborate, and indeed Roger North (p. 353) refers to the play as an opera. See Purcell Society Edition, vol. 16 (2007), pp. xxiii, 104–31. Adams, *Purcell*, p. 295, posits a date around 1690. But the style of the music, especially the way in which the strings accompany the voices mainly by doubling them, seems to indicate an earlier date; a reprint of the play in 1685 implies a revival around that time.

11. *"Poet Stutter"* (see pp. 146–7): *portrait of Thomas D'Urfey, oil on canvas, by John van der Gucht.*

Emperor Constantine – a purely honorary citizen if ever there was one – while Purcell clothed the words in the opulent garb of the first English score for full baroque orchestra, with independent parts for trumpets, oboes, and recorders as well as the usual strings.

This was the first time he had ever written for trumpets. But unlike Draghi, in his brief and tentative pioneering effort of 1687, he displays consummate skill in their handling – giving them equal prominence with the violins in the overture, deploying them as obbligato instruments in one extended movement ('And now when the renown'd Nassau'), and exploiting their brilliance to the full in the thrilling final chorus ('Sound all!'). The woodwind, too, get their share of the spoils: the oboes in rattling militaristic dialogue with the strings ('The Pale and the Purple Rose') and the recorders in melting obbligato lines ('The bashful Thames'), while the strings come into their own in accompanying a haunting, almost hypnotic ground-bass air depicting a lunar eclipse ('Now when the glitt'ring Queen of Night'). In the rather modest spaces of Merchant Taylors' Hall – a room comparable in size to Stationers' Hall (see p. 43, above) – this magnificent score must have sounded nothing short of sensational. Publishing his poem nearly thirty years later, D'Urfey proudly described Purcell's setting as 'One of the finest compositions he ever made', adding 'and cost £100 the performing'.[22] If this information is correct it was certainly an impressive outlay.

But things did not go quite according to plan. The Yorkshire Feast was to be held on 14 February (a year and a day since William and Mary had accepted the throne), and was duly announced for that date in the *London Gazette*.[23] Then this intended celebration of high politics, and specifically of the various Yorkshiremen whose support for William of Orange had helped bring about the Revolution – an achievement trumpeted in D'Urfey's poem – was rudely disrupted by a more mundane political event, in the shape of a general election: Parliament was prorogued on 2 February, and four days later a proclamation was issued calling a new Parliament for 20 March. A second notice in the *London Gazette* announced the postponement of the dinner, and a third its rescheduling to 27 March.[24] And the lustre of the occasion may well have been dimmed by the outcome: the Whigs – among them several of the prominent Yorkshiremen who had been crucial participants in the ousting of James II in favour of the Dutch prince hailed by D'Urfey as "our Redeemer" – had been soundly beaten by the Tories.

The postponement had another unwelcome consequence, this time for Purcell himself. By the time the Yorkshire Feast was held, he must have been hard at work on the ode for the queen's birthday, less than five weeks later – and simultaneously in the middle of preparations for the new opera, if indeed he was not still busy composing it. He had also somehow to find the time to dash off a substantial score in response to another theatrical commission – an overture, a full set of act tunes and dances, and three songs, all for *Amphitryon*, a new comedy by Dryden planned to open in the Hall Theatre at the end of April, as part of the celebration of the queen's birthday.[25]

The birthday ode, *Arise, my Muse*, is a setting of another effusion from the pen of the prolific D'Urfey. Like Purcell's previous offering to the queen (and Blow's new year ode for 1690, *With cheerful hearts let all appear*, which had followed its example), it is laid out for strings in five parts. But on this occasion Purcell was able to call on the services of trumpeters and woodwind players too, and he set about employing this opulent orchestra to maximum effect. Just as in the Yorkshire Feast Song, the opening fanfares of the new birthday ode are real ones, and in the imitative second movement the trumpets again take an equal share with the strings – demanding of them an agility which few of their hearers could have imagined they might

[22] *Wit and Mirth: or Pills to Purge Melancholy* (5 vols, London: Tonson, 1719), vol. 1, pp. 114–16.

[23] *London Gazette*, 20–3 January 1690.

[24] *London Gazette*, 6–10 February, 20–4 March 1690.

[25] In the event *Amphitryon* was replaced by Crowne's *Sir Courtley Nice*, and its premiere was postponed until October: *London Stage*, pp. 381, 389. The music is in Purcell Society Edition, vol. 16 (2007), pp. 24–48.

12. *"The Bashfull Thames": part of the Yorkshire Feast Song,* Of old, when heroes thought it base, *in Purcell's composing score.*

possess. Later on come two substantial and sonorous choruses, 'Then sound your instruments and charm the earth' and 'Hail, gracious Gloriana', both crowned with brilliant trumpet parts, and the second of them paired with a ritornello that has independent parts for the oboes as well as for the trumpets – something Purcell had not attempted in the Yorkshire Feast Song. And the recorders supply a suitably mournful accompaniment to a countertenor solo depicting 'Eusebia drown'd in tears' (symbolizing the Church of England weeping at King William's departure for his continental wars, as a marginal note in the printed text of the poem explains). So far, so very impressive. But at this point Purcell, with too many competing projects on his hands, evidently ran out of time. He was obliged to truncate the work, leaving nearly a quarter of D'Urfey's text unset and hurriedly rounding things off with a chorus which does not even include trumpet parts.[26] How the queen reacted is not known – but she must have been aware of this desperate expedient, because D'Urfey's poem will already, as was customary, have been printed for the audience at the birthday concert.[27]

Purcell's discomfort at this turn of events will have been sharpened only two days later, when the king issued an order

> that the musicians be presently reduced to 24 and an instrument keeper, and that though there is provision made only for that number by the establishment, yet care will be taken for paying the rest for the time they have served.[28]

Among "the rest" was Purcell, harpsichordist in the Private Music, who was thus deprived of his annual salary of £40 in that capacity (though he remained a Gentleman of the Chapel Royal and keeper of the royal instruments). Thoroughly unwelcome as the retrenchment must have been – for all the rather stiff assurance that arrears would be duly paid – it confirmed the wisdom of his decision to turn to the theatre.

Dioclesian, when the curtain finally went up on it in late June, was worth all Purcell's embarrassment over the unfinished ode. The commissioning contract has not survived, but it is a fair guess that the original plan was for a work scored for strings like *The Tempest* and *Albion and Albanius*, perhaps with a dash of colour added, as it appears to have been in *Psyche*, by oboes and recorders; this would involve little extra cost, because players customarily doubled on both. (The published short score of *Psyche* also mentions kettledrums, though in only a single number – an expensive

---

[26] Purcell Society Edition, vol. 11 (1993), pp. 47–90.

[27] It was reprinted as early as 1698, in *Poems on Affairs of State* (London: n. publ., 1698, pp. 63–6.

[28] *Cal. Tr. Books*, vol. 9: 1689–92, part ii, p. 609 (2 May 1690). (The retrenchments were not directed solely against the musicians, but affected various functionaries in the royal household: ibid., p. 610.)

luxury.)[29] But Purcell had altogether more ambitious ideas, and it may well have been the splendours of the Yorkshire Feast Song that persuaded the theatre management to pay up for a full baroque orchestra. Evidently determined to efface any lingering recollections of Grabu's sonorous five-part string writing – the loss of the earlier commission to a foreigner no doubt still rankled – he produced a magnificently crafted score with separate parts for, and making sumptuous use of, trumpets, oboes, recorders, and even a bassoon. (Scores of the period do not normally distinguish the bassoon part from the general instrumental bass, but Purcell here pointedly provided a separate stave for it – highlighting his use of an instrument which, like the oboes, had strong French associations.) And all these dazzling colours were immediately paraded before the audience in the Second Music, even before the overture.[30]

The remainder of the score introduces novelties that no previous theatre composer had dared attempt, including a rousing solo air with obbligato trumpet part. Other numbers employ the same musical and theatrical devices that audiences had enjoyed in previous operas: an invocation scene, 'Great Diocles the boar has killed' (as in *Psyche*); a choreographic set-piece, the Dance of Fiends, with a soft slow introduction that breaks out into frenetic energy (very much like the Curtain Tune in *The Tempest*); a drinking song, 'Make room for the great god of wine', complete with musical glasses (*Psyche* again).[31] But there were innovations too, not least in terms of structure, as in the imposing chorus 'Let all rehearse', in which the repeated expression of Dioclesian's glory decreed by the words is deftly and economically symbolized by a varied *da capo* form. Purcell had also learnt a great deal from *Albion and Albanius*, even if he had shared in the general resentment at Grabu, and he was not above drawing on this source, most notably on the grand chaconne with which Grabu's second act ends. He unblushingly appropriated its structure and even its key, but went one better, writing a more succinct

---

[29] In *The English Opera* Locke designated the accompaniment of one chorus as 'Wind and Strung Instruments' and that of another as 'Kettle-Drums, Wind Instruments, Violins, &c'. (*Matthew Locke: Dramatic Music*, ed. Michael Tilmouth, *Musica Britannica*, vol. 51 (1986), Nos 15, 25). The wordbook (Thomas Shadwell, *Psyche: A Tragedy* (London: Herringman, 1675)) contains many more designations for specific instruments: 'A Symphony of Recorders and soft Musick' (Shadwell, p. 3; Tilmouth, No. 4); 'A short *Symphony* of Rustick Musick, representing the Cries and Notes of Birds' (Shadwell, p. 3; Tilmouth, No. 6); 'Flajolets, Violins, Cornets, Sackbuts, Hoaboys: All joyn in *Chorus*' (Shadwell, p. 4; Tilmouth, No. 9, bars 33–55); 'Hoboys and Rustick Musick' (Shadwell, p. 70; Tilmouth, No. 44, bars 24–40); 'Recorder, Organ and Harpsicals' (Shadwell, p. 68; Tilmouth, No. 40, bars 44–59); and 'Trumpets, Kettle Drums, Flutes, & Warlike Musick' (Shadwell, p. 69; Tilmouth, No. 43, bars 7–19). Much of what Shadwell specifies, however, is probably fanciful or aspirational rather than factual, and the editorial trumpet parts that Tilmouth provides in several movements are speculative. In his preface to *Psyche* Shadwell claimed to have 'chalked out the way to the Composer'; but no librettist ever presumed or attempted to guide Purcell's hand in this manner!
[30] Purcell Society Edition, vol. 9 (1900, rev. 1961).
[31] The passages in *Psyche* referred to are Nos 15 and 21 in Tilmouth's edition.

but also far grander and more inventive movement – and using it not at an intermediate point in the opera, as Grabu had done, but to supply a resounding ending to the final act. The movement was calculated to crown a breathtaking piece of stagecraft:

> While a Symphony is Playing, a Machine descends, so large, it fills all the Space, from the Frontispiece of the Stage, to the farther end of the House; and fixes it self by two Ladders of Clouds to the Floor. In it are Four several Stages, representing the Pallaces of two Gods, and two Goddesses: The first is the Pallace of *Flora*; the columns of red and white Marble, breaking through the Clouds; the Columns Fluted and Wreath'd about with all sorts of Flow'rage; the Pedestals and Flutings inrich'd with Gold. The Second is, The Pallace of the Goddess *Pomona*, the Columns of blue Marble, wound about with all kinds of Fruitage, and inrich'd with Gold as the other. The Third is, The Pallace of *Bacchus*, the Columns of green Marble, Wreath'd and Inrich'd with Gold, with Clusters of Grapes hanging round 'em. The last is the Pallace of the Sun; it is supported on either Side by Rows of *Terms*, the lower part white Marble, the upper part Gold. The whole Object is terminated with a glowing Cloud, on which is a Chair of State, all of Gold, the Sun breaking through the Cloud, and making a Glory about it: As this descends, there rises from under the Stage a pleasant Prospect of a Noble Garden, consisting of Fountains, and Orange Trees set in large Vases: the middle Walk leads to a Pallace at a great distance. At the same time Enters *Silvanus, Bacchus, Flora, Pomona, Gods* of the Rivers, *Fawns, Nymphs, Hero's, Heroines, Shepherds, Shepherdesses*, the *Graces*, and *Pleasures*, with the rest of their followers. The Dancers place themselves on every Stage in the Machine: the Singers range themselves about the Stage.[32]

There followed a deftly choreographed sequence of five song-and-dance scenes, one on the forestage and one on each of the four successive stages in the machine, ending on the rearmost one with a dance by two children, whose diminutive size combined with adult dress exaggerated the illusion of enormous depths of perspective within the confines of the theatre. Both the spectacular staging and the use made of it were inherited from the court masque: the printed wordbook describes the scenes as 'entries', using the time-honoured terminology of the masque, which traditionally

---

[32] *The Prophetess: or, The History of Dioclesian, written by Francis Beaumont and John Fletcher, with Alterations and Additions, After the Manner of an Opera* . . . (London: Tonson, 1690), pp. 67–8. For a full account of the techniques used in staging the work, see Muller and Muller, 'Purcell's *Dioclesian*'.

13. *The masque in* Dioclesian: *conjectural model of the Dorset Garden stage and scenery by Frans Muller, 1993, based on the stage directions in the printed word-book.*

ended with five such set-pieces. But no court masque had ever ended with anything like Purcell's great chaconne – over a hundred and thirty bars of endlessly resourceful music which brilliantly display all the instruments in the orchestra both in alternation and in combination with a vocal trio, leading to a short chorus for the whole company which sent the audience away with a catchy Purcell tune (and the sound of his trumpets) ringing in their ears.

This imposing finale, however, was only the culmination of a much grander musical plan, which disposed all the various forms and textures in the masque within a tightly controlled tonal scheme. Successive numbers in the masque trace an arc from C major, the home tonic, through C minor, C major again, A minor, D major and minor, and G minor and major, finally returning to C major for the chaconne. Such planning is a feature of all Purcell's longer works, including the royal odes and the biggest of the symphony anthems. That of the masque in *Dioclesian*, like that of *Dido and Aeneas*, was far in advance of anything his English predecessors had attempted, and although Grabu had made some effort to secure tonal variety in *Albion and Albanius*, Purcell's scheme is vastly more purposeful and better proportioned.

Dioclesian was a runaway success, instantly establishing Purcell as London's foremost composer for the theatre: in the words of John Downes the prompter, 'the Vocal and Instrumental Musick, done by Mr. *Purcel* . . . gratify'd the Expectation of Court and City; and got the

Author great Reputation'.[33] And there were further plaudits from an unexpected direction. Dryden had written the spoken prologue for *Dioclesian* – he was a friend of Betterton – and no doubt attended a performance and met the composer. In October, when he finally published *Amphitryon* (its planned opening in April having been postponed until the autumn, probably because the company were so busy rehearsing *Dioclesian*), he made handsome amends for his praise of Grabu in the preface to *Albion and Albanius* five years earlier:

> what has been wanting on my Part, has been abundantly supplyed by the Excellent Composition of Mr. *Purcell*, in whose Person we have at length found an *English-man*, equal with the best abroad. At least my Opinion of him has been such, since his happy and judicious Performances in the late Opera.[34]

The die was cast: Purcell was now commissioned to compose the music for all the new plays produced in the first three months of the new season. Just after *Amphitryon* came Elkanah Settle's *Distress'd Innocence* (eight instrumental numbers),[35] the anonymous and lost comedy *The Gordian Knot Unty'd* (eight more, though four of them were existing pieces either arranged or simply re-used),[36] and one other play which has remained unidentified. But there was more. The success of *Dioclesian* had emboldened the theatre company to mount another new opera the following summer, with Purcell the inevitable choice as composer.

Two other events in the autumn of 1690 demand mention. The king's birthday, 4 November, was celebrated as usual with an ode. *Welcome, thrice welcome this auspicious morn*, penned by Thomas Shadwell, now Poet Laureate, salutes the hero of the wars that had finally driven James II out of Ireland; unfortunately the music has not survived, and even the identity of the composer is unknown. On the 22nd of the same month the Cecilian festival, suspended amid the turmoil of the Glorious Revolution and remaining in abeyance the following year, was finally reinstated, with another ode written by the industrious Shadwell – this one, *O sacred Harmony*, set to music by Robert King, a successful and well-regarded minor composer of songs and domestic music.[37] The quality of his setting cannot be guessed at, for again not a note of it has survived; but its performance marked the resumption of an annual event which Purcell would, in due course, grace with an undisputed masterpiece.

---

[33] Downes, p. 42.
[34] Dryden, *Works*, vol. 15, p. 225.
[35] Purcell Society Edition, vol. 16 (2007), pp. 140–63.
[36] Purcell Society Edition, vol. 20 (1998), pp. 23–38.
[37] *The Complete Works of Thomas Shadwell*, ed. Montague Summers (London: Fortune Press, 1927), vol. 5, pp. 365–6, 367–8.

The end of 1690 and the early weeks of 1691 were a hectic time for the royal musicians. First there was the usual requirement for a new year ode; penned on this occasion by D'Urfey and set by Blow, *Behold, how all the stars give way* is chiefly concerned with celebrating King William's victories, actual and anticipated – likening him both to Caesar and to Alexander the Great (ludicrously extravagant as a panegyric to a warrior whose successes owed more to doggedness than to military talent).[38] Unfortunately the setting, like most of Blow's court odes after 1690, is lost. By the time it was heard, the court must already have been hard at work preparing for the king – accompanied by two-thirds of the Twenty-Four Violins, plus assorted oboists who were not members of the royal establishment – to travel to a congress at The Hague which aimed to co-ordinate action by English, Dutch, and German forces to curb the expansionist ambitions of Louis XIV. When they left in mid-January Purcell remained in London,[39] where he had quite enough to keep him busy, what with composing his new opera and seeing the score of its pred-ecessor through the press. Not content with having the music of *Dioclesian* eclipse that of *Albion and Albanius*, he had determined upon issuing a printed full score, just as Grabu had done. Its publication was announced in the *London Gazette* for 26 February to 2 March, and Purcell, in an 'Advertisement' printed at the end of the score, was at pains to explain why it had taken so long to appear:

> I employed two several Printers; but One of them falling into some trouble, and the Volume swelling to a Bulk beyond my expectation, have been the Occasions of this Delay. . . . I have, according to my Promise in the Proposals, been very carefull in the Examination of every Sheet, and hope the Whole will appear as Correct as any yet Extant. My desire to make it as cheap as possibly I cou'd to the Subscribers, prevail'd with me so far above the consideration of my own Interest, that I find, too late, the Subscription-money will scarcely amount to the Expence of completing this Edition.[40]

The apology, and the hopes expressed of accuracy, may be read as a sly dig at Grabu, who had taken two years to publish a score that is liberally sprinkled with errors. And the financial anxiety at which Purcell hints

---

[38] A printed copy of the poem, entitled *A Pindarick ODE ON NEW-YEAR'S DAY: Perform'd by Vocal and Instrumental MUSICK* . . . (London: Roper, 1691), survives in the Henry E. Huntington Library, San Marino, CA. I am grateful to Susan Collick for bringing it to my notice.
[39] See John Buttrey, 'Did Purcell go to Holland in 1691?', *Musical Times*, 110 (1969), pp. 929–31.
[40] Henry Purcell, *Vocal and Instrumental Musick of The Prophetess: or, The History of Dioclesian* (London: the author, 1691), p. [175].

should not be taken too literally either: the printed full score was the equivalent of what supermarkets nowadays term a loss-leader, and he had made a shrewd estimate of its likely value.

Arthurian magnificence

He was right. One of the first plays planned for the 1690–1 season, Thomas Southerne's new comedy *Sir Anthony Love*, had already brought him a commission – a fairly modest one, admittedly, for an overture and three vocal numbers.[41] But of course there was something altogether bigger to follow: the new opera. For its play and lyrics the United Company had turned to Dryden – who promptly dusted off the libretto of *King Arthur*, written seven years earlier for Grabu. How Purcell must have relished the irony! Of course, numerous changes had to be made for political reasons to allow an opera that had been written to celebrate the reign of Charles II to be produced in that of the king who had ousted his successor.[42] But there was a further problem: Dryden's lyrics, with varying line-lengths intended to accommodate Grabu's declamatory music, were ill-suited to the more expansive style of Purcell, and to his broad lyrical melodies, which demanded verse with greater regularity and symmetry. There must have been some lively exchanges of views between the young composer, who knew exactly what he wanted, and England's senior dramatist, understandably proud of what he had written and reluctant to make changes. It is much to Dryden's credit that he swallowed his pride and did what was demanded of him – and that he admitted as much in his preface to the published wordbook, which also comments ruefully on the changes he had been obliged to make for political reasons:

> not to offend the present Times . . . I have been oblig'd so much to alter the first Design, and take away so many Beauties from the Writing, that it is now no more what it was formerly, than the present Ship of the *Royal Sovereign*, after so often taking down, and altering, to the Vessel it was at the first Building. There is nothing better, than what I intended, but the Musick; which has since arriv'd to a greater Perfection in *England*, than ever formerly; especially passing through the Artful Hands of Mr. *Purcel*, who has Compos'd it with so great a Genius, that he has nothing to fear but an ignorant, ill-judging Audience. But the Numbers [metrical patterns] of Poetry and Vocal Musick, are sometimes so contrary, that in many places I have been obliged to cramp my Verses, and make them rugged to the Reader, that they may be

---

[41] *London Stage*, pp. 388–9; Purcell Society Edition, vol. 21 (forthcoming).
[42] See Andrew Pinnock, '*King Arthur* Expos'd: A Lesson in Anatomy', in Price, *Studies*, pp. 243–56.

harmonious to the Hearer: Of which I have no Reason to repent me, because these sorts of Entertainment are principally design'd for the Ear and Eye; and therefore in Reason my Art on this occasion, ought to be subservient to his.[43]

This generous tribute to Purcell's art bespeaks Dryden's ungrudging admiration for the results. But another factor also compelled his approval. As a Catholic he had forfeited his appointment as Poet Laureate in 1689 (he had converted to Rome following the succession to the throne of James II in 1685, and unlike many who had done so he refused to reconvert after the Revolution), and in consequence he was living somewhat precariously and in straitened circumstances. *King Arthur* scored a bigger success with the public even than *Dioclesian* had done – and Dryden will have been hoping for a share in the profits. He was not disappointed: *King Arthur* – alone among Purcell's operas – not merely covered its costs but, Downes noted approvingly, was 'very Gainful to the Company'.[44]

King Arthur, having been conceived as a work that carefully integrated the music into the spoken drama, differs markedly from *Dioclesian* and from all other dramatic operas, with the sole exception of *Psyche*. But Dryden, while no doubt admiring the latter, had evidently taken note of the rather piecemeal effect created by its numerous and mostly brief musical interpolations. In his own libretto he wisely concentrated much of the music he envisaged in extended episodes, and two in particular: the Frost Scene in Act III (summoned up by the evil magician Osmond with one stroke of his wand – cue a spectacular scene change – in an attempt to seduce Arthur's betrothed Emmeline), and the concluding masque of Britannia's Isle (conjured up by Merlin to celebrate Arthur's victory over his enemies). The setting of the Frost Scene probably borrowed its string *tremolandi* and shivering aspirations for the singers from a 'Chorus of People in Frozen Climes' in Lully's *Isis*, composed 14 years earlier – the two works were being linked as early as 1699 – though Purcell's intensity of harmony and expression were far beyond Lully's powers.[45] The scene became celebrated as 'the freezing piece of musick',[46] but many years

[43] Dryden, *Works*, vol. 16 (1996), p. 6.
[44] Downes, p. 42.
[45] Sawkins, *'Trembleurs'*, pp. 249–51; Curtis A. Price, '*King Arthur*', in Stanley Sadie (ed.), *The New Grove Dictionary of Opera* (4 vols, London: Macmillan, 1992), vol. 2, pp. 992–3; John Dennis, preface to John Eccles, *The Musical Entertainments in the Tragedy of Rinaldo and Armida* (London: Tonson, 1699), cited by Stephen E. Plank, '"And Now About the Cauldron Sing": Music and the Supernatural on the Restoration Stage', *Early Music*, 18 (1990), pp. 393–407. The distinctive notation of this instrumental and vocal effect – wavy lines over the parts – is found, as Sawkins observes, in other music of the period, by Italian as well as French composers. But Purcell's subsequent borrowing of another novel effect from Lully (see p. 147, below) makes it highly likely that the source of this one was indeed *Isis*.
[46] Thomas Tudway, quoted in full on p. 175, below.

later Roger North recalled it for a different reason – vividly describing the response its opening number elicited from one soloist:

> when Mrs Butler, in the person of Cupid, was to call up [the Cold] Genius, she had the liberty to turne her face to the scean, and her back to the theater. She was in no concerne for her face, but sang a *recitativo* ['What ho! thou Genius of this Isle'] of calling towards the place where [the] Genius was to rise, and performed it admirably, even beyond any thing I ever heard upon the English stage. And I could ascribe it to nothing so much as the liberty she had of concealing her face, which she could not endure should be so contorted as is necessary to sound well, before her gallants, or at least her envious sex.[47]

The mind boggles at the thought of an opera star nowadays choosing to turn her back on the audience rather than letting them see facial contortions! But it seems the sight of these was simply not acceptable in the Restoration theatre.

Elsewhere Purcell's score repeats several of the formulae that had proved successful in the past: an invocation scene; rousing martial music; and some meltingly beautiful melodic numbers, of which the last, 'Fairest Isle', is placed – with a sureness of touch any Broadway composer might envy – precisely at the emotional apex of the final act, sending the audience away with its soaring phrases etched on their memory. (There was an obvious marketing opportunity here, but no one at the United Company seems to have spotted it.) An echo chorus, 'Hither this way', gives a very old idea – borrowed from *The Tempest* and *Psyche* – a novel twist, with competing bands of good and evil spirits beckoning from either side of the stage. Purcell gave the scene an original form, too, and a highly effective one in dramatic terms, with modified repetitions of the spirits' music framing two extended solo airs sung by their respective leaders. For a final-act tableau depicting the Order of the Garter Purcell supplied the already obligatory trumpet air: 'Saint George' is sadly mangled by a later hand and only a muddled shadow of its original self, but was clearly intended as a stirring conclusion that would far outshine Grabu's music for a similar scene at the end of *Albion and Albanius*.

Yet despite all these riches there are signs that Purcell struggled to complete the score in time. The Grand Dance by the whole company, which rounds off the final-act masque, was evidently not finished (or

---

[47] North, pp. 217–18; see also Roger Savage, 'Calling up Genius: Purcell, Roger North, and Charlotte Butler', in Burden, *Performing Purcell*, pp. 213–31. For a full account of all the singers in the theatre company, see Olive Baldwin and Thelma Wilson, 'Purcell's Stage Singers', ibid., pp. 105–29.

perhaps not even started), and a makeshift had to be found. By great good fortune an imposing chaconne – the type of dance used at the same point in both *Dioclesian*, a year previously, and *The Fairy Queen*, a year later – lay buried in convenient obscurity in *Sound the trumpet! beat the drum!*, the by now forgotten 1687 welcome song for King James; this may well have been pressed into service despite not being in the same key as the preceding music. Although it does not appear in any of the manuscripts of *King Arthur* (a motley lot, with the last act in severe disarray), it must have been used at some point in the opera, for it was included with other numbers from it in *Ayres for the Theatre*, an anthology of instrumental numbers from Purcell's stage music published in 1697. Unfortunately no indication is given of where it fitted in; an eighteenth-century annotation in one copy identifies it as the First Music, but if that is correct it may, of course, have been in a much later and altered revival.[48]

Only days before the new opera opened, the queen's birthday had been celebrated with what had become customary splendour. Purcell's setting of the new ode, *Welcome, welcome, glorious morn*, is exhilarating as well as imposing: longer than his 1689 offering, half as long again as the unhappily truncated effort of 1690, and brilliantly scored for full orchestra, with the trumpets pealing out not only in the overture but also, very conspicuously indeed, in the concluding chorus (though, oddly, only in one short ritornello in between).[49] Purcell had made handsome amends to the queen for the previous year's fiasco, but it looks suspiciously as if, having misjudged his workload again, he had not dared to let the ode suffer this time – obliging him to cut corners in the opera instead.

He seems not to have been very busy during the summer, at least with new compositions, though of course his regular duties at Westminster Abbey and the Chapel Royal continued as normal. There was also an important family event to claim his time, when his younger sister Katherine, aged 29, was married in June.[50] But not far ahead was the new theatrical season, in the course of which he would furnish music for four or possibly five plays: no instrumental numbers, but a total of seven or eight songs. And the season had scarcely begun when Purcell took on what might appear a surprising commitment: giving lessons on the spinet to a young lady named Rhoda Cartwright, the daughter of a wealthy family who divided their time between a country estate in Northamptonshire and a more modest establishment just outside London, the manor of Barn Elms, across the Thames from Fulham. He continued teaching her at intervals (during their stays at Barn Elms) until the summer of 1693,

---

[48] The annotation appears in the copy belonging to the Royal College of Music, London.

[49] Purcell Society Edition, vol. 11 (1993), pp. 91–143.

[50] London, Guildhall Library, St Mary Magdalen, registers of marriages (typescript by W. H. Challen): 18 June 1691. (In fact, the marriage was solemnized on 20 June: see Zimmerman, *Purcell*, p. 200.)

being paid £2 a month.[51] It seems unlikely that he simply needed the money; more probably the Cartwrights were a potentially useful connection, though we know little about them. What we do know, however, is that in 1697 Purcell's widow, publishing the second volume of his trio sonatas, prefaced them with a graceful dedication to this former pupil, by then married as Lady Rhoda Cavendish.[52]

Instrumental innovations

November brought clear confirmation that the Cecilian festival had recovered its old vitality. The ode, *The glorious day is come* – a product, like the new year ode eleven months before, of the industrious partnership of D'Urfey and Blow – was not only on a grand scale, and scored for trumpets and woodwind as well as strings, but also featured an orchestral newcomer: kettledrums, which were immediately put under the spotlight in the opening symphony.[53] Purcell pricked up his ears, but several months would elapse before he had the opportunity to offer a riposte. (It seems unlikely that the kettledrums put in a second appearance in Blow's setting of the 1692 new year ode, *Be kind, great God of Time*: although most of it is lost, three movements have survived as separate fragments – one being the concluding chorus, which is in F major and accompanied by strings alone.[54] The poem, intriguingly, is by the Rev. Nicholas Brady.[55] Evidently he was well connected at court – probably through Nahum Tate[56] – which may explain how he had been able five years previously to enlist Purcell's help in appointing an organist for his church.)

The Cecilian festival also featured another instrumental novelty – not in the ode but in the table music accompanying the dinner that followed it. The exiled French poet Peter Motteux (1663–1718), proprietor of *The Gentleman's Journal*, described it in appreciative detail in the January 1692 issue. After outlining the background and general arrangements of the festival, and commenting approvingly on the ode, he goes on:

---

[51] See Michael Burden, '"He had the Honour to be Your Master": Lady Rhoda Cavendish's Music Lessons with Henry Purcell', *Music & Letters*, 76 (1995), pp. 532–9.
[52] The dedication is reprinted in full in the preface to the Purcell Society Edition of this set of sonatas – vol. 7 (1981).
[53] Modern edition by Maurice Bevan (London: Eulenburg, 1981).
[54] The fragments form the last three movements of the work: air, 'Oh when [originally 'But oh'], ye Pow'rs, when must his labours cease?', in Blow, *Amphion Anglicus*, pp. 83–5; air, 'Whilst he abroad does like the Sun display', and chorus, 'Ye great Defenders of the faith', in John Stafford Smith (ed.), *Musica Antiqua* (London: Preston, 1812), vol. 2, pp. 194–8.
[55] I am grateful to Susan Collick for bringing this item in the British Library to my notice. The poem was attributed to Brady by Donald Goddard Wing, in whose *Short-Title Catalogue of Books Printed in England . . . 1641–1700* (3 vols, New York: Columbia University Press, 1945–51; revised edn, New York: Modern Language Association of America, 1972–88) it forms item B4183.
[56] They worked together on a metrical psalter (*A New Version of the Psalms . . . Fitted to the Tunes Used in Churches* (London: Stationers' Company, 1696)).

This Feast is one of the genteelest in the world; there are no formalities nor gatherings like as at others, and the appearance there is always very splendid. Whilst the Company is at Table, the Hautbois [oboes] and Trumpets play successively. Mr. *Showers* [Shore, the Sergeant Trumpeter] hath taught the latter of late years to sound with all the softness imaginable, they played us some flat Tunes [tunes in minor keys], made by Mr. *Finger*, with a general applause, it being a thing formerly thought impossible upon an Instrument designed for a sharp [major] Key.[57]

So Purcell and Blow were not the only composers who had been exploring the technical capabilities of these battlefield instruments. The instrument that Shore had played on this occasion, however, and for which the Moravian expatriate Godfrey Finger (*c*.1660–1730) had written, was not a natural but a flat trumpet: one equipped with a slide like that of a trombone (except that, awkwardly, it extended backwards, over the player's shoulder), enabling it to play a complete chromatic scale. This, like the sound of the kettledrums, planted a seed in Purcell's imagination, though it was one that would take longer to bear fruit.

Motteux concluded with an appetizing titbit of news:

Now I speak of Music, I must tell you that we shall have speedily a New Opera, wherein something very surprising is promised us; Mr. *Purcel* who joins to the Delicacy and Beauty of the Italian way, the Graces and Gaiety of the French composes the Music, as he hath done for *The Prophetess*, and the last Opera called *King Arthur*, which hath been plaid several times the last Month.

Purcell, then, was at work on his third operatic commission in three years; Motteux's 'something very surprising' was *The Fairy Queen*. Based on a heavily cut and modernized version of Shakespeare's *A Midsummer Night's Dream*, it would indeed be surprising: not merely spectacular on stage but also by far Purcell's finest operatic score – and, many would say, his greatest work.[58]

In the first months of 1692, though, Purcell had something more mundane to occupy him than operatic composition: he and his family moved home, vacating their house in Bowling Alley East (before the quarter day, 25 March, when the rates fell due), and subsequently subletting it.[59] Their next known address is in nearby Marsham Street: this must have been a modern house, for the street itself was new, extending across the

[57] *Gent. J.*, January 1692, p. 7.
[58] Purcell Society Edition, vol. 12 (1901, rev. 1960).
[59] St Margaret's, Westminster, Parish Accounts, 1692, p. 80.

patch of marshy countryside that lay on the very edge of Westminster, between Market Street (now Horseferry Road) and Millbank.[60] For some unknown reason the Purcells are not listed as ratepayers in Marsham Street until 1694;[61] perhaps they spent the intervening couple of years living in the Abbey precincts, or perhaps their new home had not yet attracted the attention of the municipal valuers. But whether this was so or not, the removal must have been an unwelcome distraction from composing, and Purcell was facing a busy schedule. Just as in the two previous seasons, the queen's birthday coincided with final preparations for the first night of an opera. And in 1692 the theatre was again obliged to take second place, for the opera, first mentioned by Motteux in January, was repeatedly delayed. It was not to open until 2 May, a couple of days after the queen's birthday.[62]

For this, his fourth offering to Queen Mary, Purcell had been fortunate in the text, penned by Sir Charles Sedley, who was a court poet and wit though he held no formal royal appointment. Sedley had a colourful, not to say dubious reputation (he was notorious for having on one occasion preached a mock sermon while standing stark naked on the balcony of the Cock tavern in Covent Garden, before pelting the scandalized crowd that gathered with bottles of urine), but the poem he provided for Purcell to set is, as royal panegyrics go, unusually reflective in tone. Its obvious suitability for musical treatment that was intimate rather than bombastic must have appeared providential to Purcell. Turning aside from the line of development followed by his first three odes for the queen, each of which is grander and more opulent than its predecessor, he laid out the new piece, *Love's goddess sure was blind*, on a fairly modest scale, and scored it only for strings instead of using full orchestra.[63]

It contains some of the loveliest and most expressive music to be found among his court compositions, and three of its eight numbers invite particular comment. The solo air 'Long may she reign over this Isle', for treble – or perhaps soprano – has all the limpid directness of the popular melodies in Purcell's operas, suggesting that it may have been sung not by a Chapel Royal chorister but by a singer from the theatre (something which certainly happened in the birthday ode the following year). Another of the airs, 'May her blest example', famously employs as its bass line the ballad tune 'Cold and raw', which was, according to Sir John Hawkins, a favourite of the queen's:

---

[60] See map on p. 3, above.
[61] St Margaret's, Westminster, Overseers' Accounts, E307, p. 118.
[62] Luttrell, vol. 2, p. 435 (28 April 1692).
[63] Purcell Society Edition, vol. 24 (1998), pp. 1–49. In the old Purcell Society Edition (1926) its scoring includes recorders in one movement, but the source contains no such designation, and one of the two parts goes below the compass of the instrument.

The queen having a mind one afternoon to be entertained with music, sent to Mr. Gostling, . . . to Henry Purcell and Mrs. Arabella Hunt, who had a very fine voice, and an admirable hand on the lute, with a request to attend her; . . . Mr. Gostling and Mrs. Hunt sang several compositions of Purcell, who accompanied them on the harpsichord; at length the queen beginning to grow tired, asked Mrs. Hunt if she could not sing the old Scots ballad 'Cold and Raw', Mrs. Hunt answered yes, and sang it to her lute. Purcell was all the while sitting at the harpsichord unemployed, and not a little nettled at the queen's preference of a vulgar ballad to his music; but seeing her majesty delighted with this tune, he determined that she should hear it upon another occasion: and accordingly in the next birthday song, . . . he composed an air . . ., the bass whereof is the tune to Cold and Raw.[64]

This may be no more than the tittle-tattle of a later age, but one factor suggests otherwise. Before the countertenor solo begins, the melody is pointedly played right through by the continuo team alone – as if Purcell was afraid the queen might otherwise miss it![65] After this curious and ingenious number, and an agile duet for countertenors, the ode ends with a chorus in highly unusual mood, anticipating the mourning for the queen's eventual death: an all too prophetic literary fancy, reflected in music whose intensity is rare in royal command works, even those of Purcell.

A difficult birth

Work on *The Fairy Queen*, meanwhile, had not been progressing smoothly. The evidence is plain to see in the full score, which was being prepared by two theatre copyists to serve as the source of the instrumental parts.[66] Several numbers were originally either written in skeleton form or left blank, in particular the act tunes – which would obviously not need stage rehearsals – but other things too, including everything except the soprano and bass vocal parts in one sizeable number laid out for soloists, chorus, and orchestra. In most cases he went back (no doubt in the nick of time) and filled in what was missing, in handwriting marked by obvious signs of haste and using a different mix of ink – evidence which gives the game away. But increasingly often, in the later pages of the score,

[64] Hawkins, vol. 2, p. 564n.
[65] The only other ballad tune that Purcell borrowed in a royal ode, 'Hey then, up go we' in the 1686 ode *Ye tuneful Muses*, bars 136–97 (Purcell Society Edition, vol. 18 (2005), pp. 103–9), appears first as the bass line of an air, then as the obbligato violin part in a chorus, and finally as the bass line of a ritornello.
[66] London, Royal Academy of Music, MS 3. For more details see Wood and Pinnock, 'Fairy Queen', pp. 44–62.

there are blanks that were never filled: the continuo bass line of one song; the vocal bass part in a duet; the inner string parts in a dance movement; and three entire dances, left blank even though pages had been headed in readiness for them.[67] And the big Chaconne at the end was copied in a tremendous hurry (shades of *King Arthur*!), with numerous erasures and second thoughts, and some bars in the viola part left entirely blank. Presumably the performing material for these movements, if Purcell had managed to complete them, were hurriedly scribbled on loose sheets given separately to the singers and instrumentalists.

His need for haste must have been dire. But why, when the show had already been long delayed even since it was officially advertised? The answer lies in a collision – one of many in that turbulent period – between the theatre and the political establishment. A new tragedy by Dryden and Southerne, *Cleomenes, the Spartan Hero*, had been planned to precede the opening of the new opera; it too had been long postponed (it had been ready in December 1691), but had finally been announced in March.[68] It would have been acted on several nights over perhaps a couple of weeks, interspersed with revivals of other plays. But on 9 April, the eve of production, the new play was banned by the Lord Chamberlain on direct orders from the queen, who suspected it of political satire.[69] With a gap in the season looming, Purcell was obliged to put on an extra spurt. In the event, though, this proved unnecessary: by the middle of April *Cleomenes* had been hastily purged of the offending material and, as Motteux's *Gentleman's Journal* reported in May,

> since that time, the Innocence and Merit of the Play have rais'd it several eminent Advocates, who have prevailed to have it Acted, and you need not doubt but it has been with great Applause.[70]

The pressure on Purcell, nevertheless, had caused real disruption to the preparation of *The Fairy Queen*; and the resulting damage is apparent to this day.

Not that any of these problems troubled the opera's first audiences. They loved the piece, and with good reason. Its vocal highlights range from slapstick humour in the scene of the stammering Drunken Poet (almost certainly starring Thomas D'Urfey, whose nickname was Poet

---

[67] 'A Dance', at the end of Act I, 'A Dance for a Clown', near the end of Act III, and 'A Dance of the Four Seasons', at the conclusion of Act IV. (It is possible, of course, that a decision was taken to dispense with these numbers before Purcell had written the music, but the presence of headings in the manuscript suggests otherwise.)

[68] *Gent. J.*, March 1692, p. 9: 'after *Easter* we are to have a New *Opera*; and Mr *Dryden's Cleomenes* very shortly'.

[69] Luttrell, vol. 2, p. 413; *London Stage*, p. 408.

[70] *Gent. J.*, May 1692, p. 17. The wordbook of *Cleomenes* was finally advertised in the *London Gazette* for 2–5 May, and that for *The Fairy Queen* on 5–9 May.

Stutter) and the Haymakers' dialogue (with the comic John Pate in drag as an unlikely Mopsa) to such ravishing lyrical numbers as 'If love's a sweet passion'. As with *King Arthur*, the work unashamedly resorts to formulae that had previously met with success: an invocation scene, 'Hymen, appear!'; the by now expected trumpet air, 'Thus the gloomy world'; and even an echo number, 'May the God of Wit inspire', tracing its ancestry back to *The Tempest* and *Psyche*, but going one better by ending with an instrumental counterpart whose double echoes are scored not for strings but, ingeniously, for trumpets and oboes. The score is peppered with brilliantly imaginative dances – for fairies, of course, but also for savages dressed in green, for haymakers, for the followers of Night (this last an edgy double canon maintaining strict imitation between the two outside and between the two inside parts – a scheme blatantly purloined from the last movement of Locke's *Tempest* score). There is even a dance for six monkeys, and another for twenty-four Chinese men and women. And Purcell's orchestral writing is at its most sumptuous and inventive. The fully scored numbers are glorious, and complementing them are some exotic instrumental novelties. The Masque of Sleep in Act II features muted violins – their first use in England; this scoring, along with the entire plan of the masque and even the general drift of some of its lyrics, was unblushingly appropriated from a 1681 divertissement by Lully entitled *Le Triomphe de l'Amour*. (Purcell's music eclipses its model as completely as the Frost Scene in *King Arthur* had the one in *Isis*, but whereas that debt soon came to light, more than three hundred years were to pass before anyone noticed these further borrowings.)[71] There is an eloquent obbligato part for a single oboe in The Plaint (though sadly, when it was first published after Purcell's death, what is surely an error in the first volume of *Orpheus Britannicus* assigned it to the violin). In the Act IV Masque of the Four Seasons, summoned up on the thinnest of pretexts (Oberon's birthday, an occurrence not so much as mentioned by Shakespeare!), Purcell, on the equally thin pretext of Oberon's royalty, saluted him with those royal instruments, trumpets and drums – opening the entire masque, arrestingly, with the first kettledrum solo in orchestral history. The masque also embodies perhaps the most vaultingly ambitious of all Purcell's large-scale formal plans: a vast *da capo* structure in which a chorus addressed to the sun god Phoebus, and accompanied by full orchestra, opens and closes a sequence of contrasting solo airs, one for each season.

Modern-day audiences have taken this music to their hearts as much as did its first hearers.[72] But no modern audience has seen the work staged as spectacularly as in 1692. One device of stagecraft in particular was used

[71] See Tuppen, *French Influence*, pp. 345–7.
[72] Purcell Society Edition, vol. 12 (1903, rev. 1968).

to create an illusion of magic: the use, in the fairy roles, of child actors – the same visual trick used for the final entry in the masque in *Dioclesian*.[73] Just as with that work and *King Arthur*, Purcell's music for *The Fairy Queen* was only part of the story – as Downes implied in his memoirs:

> This in Ornaments was superior to the other Two; especially in Cloaths, for all the Singers and Dancers, Scenes, Machines and Decorations, all most profusely set off; and excellently perform'd, chiefly the Instrumental and Vocal part Compos'd by the said Mr. *Purcel*, and Dances by Mr. *Priest*. The Court and the town were wonderfully satisfy'd with it; but the Expences in setting it out being so great, the Company got very little by it.[74]

The United Company poured £3000 into staging the new opera – between a third and a half of its annual working budget, and equivalent in purchasing power to over half a million pounds today.[75] Where did all the money go? We have to take Downes's word about the splendid costumes, of which not even an illustration survives, but clearly some of the stage effects described in the printed wordbook will not have come cheap:

> *The Scene changes to a great Wood; a long row of large Trees on each side: a River in the middle: two rows of lesser Trees of a different kind just on the side of the River, which meet in the middle, and make so many Arches: two great Dragons make a Bridge over the River; their Bodies form two Arches, through which two Swans are seen in the river at a great distance. . . . While a Symphany's playing, the two Swans come Swimming on through the Arches to the bank of the River, as if they would Land; there turn themselves into* Fairies, *and Dance; at the same time the Bridge vanishes, and the Trees that were Arch'd, raise themselves upright.*

(Act III)

> *The Scene changes to a Garden of Fountains. A Sonata plays while the Sun rises, it appears red through the Mist, as it ascends it dissipates the Vapours, and is seen in its full Lustre; then the Scene is perfectly discovered, the Fountains enrich'd with gilding, and adorn'd with Statues: the View is terminated by a Walk of Cypress Trees which lead to a delightful Bower. Before the Trees stand rows of Marble Columns, which support many Walks which rise by Stairs to the top of the House; the*

---

[73] See Michael Burden, 'Casting Issues in the Original Production of Purcell's Opera "The Fairy-Queen"', *Music & Letters*, 84 (2003), pp. 596–607.

[74] Downes, pp. 42–3.

[75] The expenditure is reported by Luttrell, vol. 2, p. 435 (28 April 1692), and its relation to the company budget in Milhous, 'Finances', pp. 567–92.

*Stairs are adorn'd with Figures on Pedestals, and Rails; and Balasters
on each side of 'em. Near the top, vast Quantities of Water break out of
the Hills, and fall in mighty Cascade's to the bottom of the Scene, to feed
the Fountains which are on each side. In the middle of the Stage is
a very large Fountain, where the Water rises about twelve Foot.*

(Act IV)

*While the Scene is darken'd, a single Entry is danced; Then a
Symphony is play'd; after that the Scene is suddainly Illuminated, and
discovers a transparent Prospect of a Chinese Garden, the Architecture,
the Trees, the Plants, the Fruit, the Birds, the Beasts, quite different from
what we have in this part of the World. It is terminated by an Arch,
through which is seen other Arches with close Arbors, and a row of Trees
to the end of the View. Over it is a hanging Garden, which rises by several ascents to the top of the House; it is bounded on either side with
pleasant Bowers, various Trees, and numbers of strange Birds flying in
the Air[;] on the Top of a Platform is a Fountain, throwing up Water,
which falls into a large Basin.*

(Act V)[76]

Despite such extravagances, Downes does not claim that the United
Company made a loss on *The Fairy Queen*. The opera ran for at least a
dozen consecutive performances, and on opera nights double ticket
prices were customary.[77] There was also one subsequent revival, though
it will have been expensive to prepare. But whether or not the
investment was recouped, the opera was to prove costly in more than
money. The lavish initial outlay on it fuelled an already simmering row
which would, as we shall see later, eventually destroy the company.[78]
Purcell made a novel effort to maximize his own returns: he had the ten
most popular songs in *The Fairy Queen* printed, and copies were sold in the
theatre from the opening night onwards, along with the comic
Haymakers' scene issued as a separate item.[79] Strikingly, these slim book-
lets represent two of only three published appearances of Purcell's music
in the entire year, apart from single songs in *The Gentleman's Journal* and,
worryingly, pirate editions. The latter were increasingly numerous, and

---

[76] *The Fairy-Queen: An Opera Represented at the Queen's-Theatre* . . . (London: Tonson, 1692),
pp. 29–30, 40, 48–9.
[77] *Gent. J.* (May 1692, licensed on 14 May)·states that the opera 'continues to be represented
daily'. The initial run may therefore have been longer. Certainly the piece was performed as late
as 13 June (see John Harold Wilson, 'More Theatre Notes from the Newdigate Newsletters',
Theatre Notebook, 16 (1962), p. 59), though by then a new play, John Crowne's tragicomedy
Regulus, had opened (*London Stage*, p. 409).
[78] Milhous, 'Finances', concludes (p. 570) that *The Fairy Queen* 'probably broke even'. But she also
notes that 'in a nutshell, assured profits from plays guaranteed the sums ventured on opera'.
[79] *Some Select Songs as They Are Sung in the Fairy Queen* (London: the author, 1692).

one of them, bundling up 'the best and newest songs' in *Dioclesian* and *King Arthur*, appeared just before the *Select Songs . . . in the Fairy Queen*, no doubt to Purcell's displeasure.[80] But even pirate editions, though they brought him no direct financial benefit, were of some value to him. The wide circulation of his popular numbers stimulated demand for revivals of his operas, which in turn sold more copies of the songs, and raised expectations that he would receive new commissions and write more hit songs: a kind of virtuous circle. Purcell thus became the first composer in England of a type taken for granted nowadays: one whose music was promoted commercially – even though not, in his case, by means of a systematic and co-ordinated campaign by a single publisher.

Triumph and tragedy

The following concert and theatrical season brought what had become the usual string of commissions for Purcell; most of the five or six plays involved only songs, though for one of them, Dryden and Lee's tragedy *Oedipus*, he provided an extended and powerful invocation scene, whose still centre is the ground-bass song 'Music for a while' (a familiar and just-ly celebrated piece whose context is much less well known). But the cash-strapped company had no new operatic project to bring forward. As if by way of compensation, the commission for the Cecilian ode in November went to Purcell, and he proceeded to excel himself. The poem, like that of the new year ode for 1692, was commissioned from Nicholas Brady, whose literary efforts mark him as little better than a poetaster, and the unfortunate Purcell found himself presented with something vastly inferior to the inspiring text Dryden had written for Draghi five years earlier. But this did not in the least cramp his imagination, fired as it was by the subject matter of music itself. Limping lines such as

> Hark! hark! each tree its silence breaks,
> The box and fir to talk begin!
> This in the sprightly violin,
> That in the flute distinctly speaks

might have elicited dross from a lesser composer, but Purcell contrived, miraculously, to garb the entire poem in cloth of gold – even deftly circumventing its major structural flaw: the fact that the last three of its six verses are all devoted to describing, at tedious length, the supremacy of the organ above all other instruments.[81]

---

[80] *Philomela, or The Vocal Musitian: Being a Collection of the Best and Newest Songs, Especially Those in the Two Operas 'The Prophetess' and 'King Arthur' Written by Mr Dryden, and Set to Musick by Mr. Henry Purcell . . .* (London, 1692; entered in the Term Catalogue for Trinity).
[81] Purcell Society Edition, vol. 8 (1978).

The performance of *Hail! bright Cecilia*, in Stationers' Hall, must have sounded every bit as impressive as the Yorkshire Feast Song had done, and its reception was rapturous: the entire work – lasting more than fifty minutes – was encored, as Motteux reported:

> The . . . Ode was admirably set to Music by Mr. *Henry Purcell*, and performed twice with universal applause, particularly the second Stanza, which was sung with incredible Graces by Mr. *Purcell* himself.[82]

This report spawned a stubbornly enduring myth. The stanza to which Motteux refers, ''Tis Nature's voice', is a countertenor solo, and it is, as he says, profusely ornamented. But it was not – as he might appear to be stating – sung by the composer. Purcell's place in the Chapel Royal was not as a countertenor but as a bass (and, as one of the three organists, he probably did not do much singing anyway). What Motteux meant was 'incredible graces *written* by Mr Henry Purcell himself', as distinct from ornaments added, as was customary, by the singer. And indeed the ornaments are all notated meticulously in the autograph score – which contains a second misleading piece of evidence seeming to confirm the myth, for the singer is identified in a jotted annotation as 'Mr P.'. But this was almost certainly the countertenor John Pate, whom we have already met, cross-dressed as Mopsa in *The Fairy Queen*.[83]

Only a couple of weeks after this Cecilian triumph came a theatrical tragedy – not a thespian one but a real event: the talented young playwright and singing actor William Mountfort was killed in a brawl. Hours earlier an unsuccessful attempt had been made to abduct one of Mountfort's colleagues, the singing actress Anne Bracegirdle, by a theatregoer, a young military captain named Richard Hill, whose advances she had spurned. Hill wrongly suspected her of having done so because she preferred Mountfort and, encountering him by chance, stabbed him to death.[84]

Theatrical London was appalled. Mountfort was popular and widely respected: Colley Cibber, the leading actor-manager of the next generation, praised him as having been 'in Tragedy . . . the most affecting lover within my Memory', adding that 'in Comedy, his Spirit shone the brighter for being polish'd with Decency'.[85] Purcell must have known him fairly

[82] *Gent. J.*, November 1692, p. 18. The same issue also reprints the poem in its entirety (pp. 19–20) – anonymously, by request of the author.
[83] The assertion that Purcell himself sang ''Tis Nature's voice' is repeated – no doubt through the same misunderstanding of Motteux's report – in a pirate edition of the solo, issued by an unnamed publisher in 1693.
[84] Albert S. Borgman, *The Life and Death of William Mountfort* (Cambridge, MA: Harvard University Press, 1935), pp. 123–210.
[85] Cibber, *Apology*, pp. 74–5.

well, for he had variously co-written or acted in most of the plays for which Purcell had composed the music, singing in several of them. At his funeral in St Clement Danes, which was attended by a thousand mourners including many theatregoers, Purcell himself is said to have directed the anthem, which was sung by a contingent from the Chapel Royal: a quite exceptional gesture of respect for the dead man from royalty itself.[86]

Mountfort was scarcely in his grave when another leading actor, the comedian Anthony Leigh, died suddenly – of grief, it was suggested.[87] This twofold loss to the United Company, sustained in successive weeks, brought theatrical life in the capital to the brink of collapse, as Motteux lamented:

> We are like to be without new Plays this month and next; the death of Mr. *Mountfort*, and that of Mr. *Leigh* soon after him, being partly the cause of this delay.[88]

Purcell would have felt the privation as much as anyone: quite apart from any ties of professional respect for, or friendship with, the two actors, he had been commissioned to supply at least half a dozen plays with music, for which payment would now be delayed. In addition, there was an abrupt cessation of music at court, other than that in Chapel. On 2 January 1693, the day after the performance of Tate and Blow's new ode (entitled, with painful irony, *The happy, happy year is born*), official mourning began for the Electress of Bavaria, the wife of an important ally in King William's wars, who had died young.[89]

It was not until February that the theatrical season was resumed. Among the first productions was a revival on the 16th of the month of *The Fairy Queen*, with a mortal queen and her maids of honour among the audience. (It was long believed that this presented the work in an extensively revised version.[90] But close examination of the surviving materials of the work, manuscript and printed, reveals that only a single new song was added – a common ploy for tempting the audience back to see a revival.)[91] The next few weeks brought two new comedies, both with

---

[86] Cibber, *Apology*, p. 128, recalls that Queen Mary admired Mountfort's acting – hence, perhaps, the participation of such distinguished musicians. Luttrell (vol. 2, p. 641, 15 December 1692), states merely that 'some of the choristers at Whitehall and kings organist were there, and sung an anthem'; Purcell's connection with Mountfort and the theatre makes it likely that he himself, rather than either of the other organists of the Chapel Royal, played the organ. A later but probably reliable source, the anonymous preface to *Six Plays Written by Mr. Mountfort* (2 vols, London: Tonson, Strahan, and Mears, 1720) makes specific mention (p. x) of 'Mr. *Purcell* performing the Funeral Anthem'.

[87] Ibid.

[88] *Gent. J.*, December 1692, p. 15.

[89] Evelyn, 2 January 1693.

[90] See, for instance, Laurie, *Stage Works*, vol. 1, pp. 102–21; Price, *Stage*, pp. 320–54.

[91] Wood and Pinnock, '*Fairy Queen*', pp. 44–62.

music by Purcell: Southerne's *The Maid's Last Prayer*, for which he produced a couple of songs and one extended duet, and Congreve's *The Old
Bachelor*, which required a full suite of nine instrumental numbers, one
solo song, and another, shorter duet.[92]

Purcell, left at something of a loose end for several weeks, seems to have
made good use of his time. First, he was prevailed upon by his friend and
copyist John Walter, organist of Eton College, to take on an organ pupil,
a talented ex-chorister named John Weldon, who was himself destined
to become a theatre composer of distinction; the lessons continued until
the following year, when Weldon, by then 18 years old, was appointed
organist of New College, Oxford.[93] Meanwhile, Purcell composed for the
queen's birthday in April the longest and most elaborate of all his royal
odes. *Celebrate this festival* sets a poem by Tate, who had recently, on the
death of Shadwell, been appointed Poet Laureate. Scored for full baroque
orchestra, though with only a single trumpet, it consists of no fewer than
16 numbers, totalling almost a thousand bars of music including
repeats.[94] Only two of his occasional works are longer, or grander: the
Yorkshire Feast Song and *Hail! bright Cecilia*. (Somewhat surprisingly, he
borrowed the opening symphony of the latter in the new ode; perhaps he
had found himself under pressure again as the theatrical season resumed.)
The work includes some striking novelties: not one but two numbers
with an obbligato trumpet part for Shore – a successful formula import-
ed from the operas. The rousing air 'While for a righteous cause he arms',
saluting the king's personal involvement in the continental wars and
deriding the non-combatant Louis XIV ('Let guilty monarchs shun the
field'), was sung, as an annotation in the score tells us, by the Chapel bass
Leonard Woodson. But the florid and brilliant "Tis sacred: bid the
trumpet cease', for soprano, was composed for Mrs Ayliff,[95] who had also
been borrowed from the theatre, and for whom Purcell also provided
something thoroughly apt to her background: the solo 'Kindly treat
Maria's day', repeated as the final chorus, is in his best show-stopping
style. Another solo number, the ingenious ground-bass air 'Crown the
altar', is for a new or at least an unfamiliar type of voice, which the score
explicitly designates *'high countratenor'* – the falsettist John Howell,
who had joined the Chapel Royal in 1691. The performance formed the
centrepiece of a celebration which, Luttrell informs us, spanned two
days because the queen's birthday fell on the Sabbath:

---

[92] Purcell Society Edition, vol. 20 (1998), pp. 76–88; vol. 21 (forthcoming).
[93] Eton College Audit Books, 1692–3, 1693, 1694; quoted in full in Zimmerman, *Purcell*,
p. 237.
[94] Purcell Society Edition, vol. 24 (1998), pp. 50–123.
[95] Mrs Ayliff, or Aliff (*fl.* 1692–6), whose first name is unknown, was Purcell's leading soprano;
more than a dozen of his songs were published as having been sung by her.

Sunday last, being the queens birth day, the guns were discharged at the Tower as usuall; and the next day the nobility congratulated her majestie thereon [when the ode will have been sung]; and at night was a great ball at court.[96]

An occurrence some three weeks later shows the royal music in a less happy light, when an administrative bungle made at the beginning of the reign of William and Mary came to a head: a petition of 'their Majesties' vocal musick' complained that

[because] the vocal and instrumental music were joined in the late reigns of King Charles and King James, with an allowance of 40l. *per annum* each, and they were sworn in indifferently [without any distinction being made] and directed to be paid to Lady Day 1690, since which the instrumental only had been paid.[97]

This entry in the Treasury papers is endorsed 'To be respited till the establishment is altered'. The wording is ambiguous, but appears to direct that the arrears be paid only pending further entrenchments – an unwelcome prospect. It also appears to refer solely to the singers in the Private Music, for those in the Chapel Royal were not affected; but three months later came a petition from Nicholas Staggins, the Master of the Music, who had also gone unpaid since the Revolution.[98] It was all a bitter reminder of the administrative incompetence and procrastination from which the royal musicians had suffered ever since the Restoration.

Meanwhile the theatrical season continued – though one conspicuous element was missing. In May, when in each of the three previous years a new Purcell opera had opened, the audience was obliged to content itself with a revival of *Dioclesian* (probably freshened up, as was customary, with a couple of new songs).[99]

The summer saw the publication of the second volume of Henry Playford's *Harmonia Sacra*, which included eight devotional songs by

[96] Luttrell, vol. 3, p. 87 (2 May 1693).
[97] 24 May 1693: *Cal. Tr. Papers*, p. 295.
[98] 17 August 1693: ibid., p. 311. (Staggins was fortunate in being owed only £200 – and in managing to get it paid. Around the same date the widow of Charles II's personal physician petitioned, unsuccessfully, for arrears amounting to £4400: ibid., p. 312.)
[99] *London Stage*, p. 421. Two new songs by Purcell apparently composed for the revival, 'When first I saw the bright Aurelia's eyes' and 'Since from my dear Astrea's sight', were first published in *Gent. J.*, December 1693, pp. 421–8; since the opera is not known to have been revived during the autumn, it seems likely that these were first heard in May. (One new song, 'Let us dance, let us sing', had already been added, for a revival in the 1690–1 season.) But by a curious coincidence another setting of 'Since from my dear Astrea's sight', by Samuel Akeroyde, appeared in *Gent. J.* for August 1693, pp. 277–81 – though no link with *Dioclesian* is claimed for it. *London Stage* appears to be in error, placing it and a second, anonymous song in the June issue of *Gent. J.*, and making the unsupported statement that both were composed for the revival; no anonymous song is to be found in *Gent. J.* for any month in 1693.

Purcell – among them some very substantial pieces for up to three voices. Motteux's enthusiastic notice of the volume makes it clear that, just as in the theatre, Purcell's name sufficed as a selling point:

> A Music Book, intituled *Harmonia Sacra*, will shortly be printed for Mr. *Playford*. I need not say anything more to recommend it to you, than that you will find in it many of Mr. *Henry Purcell's* admirable Composures. As they charm all men, they are universally extoll'd, and even those who know him no otherwise than by his Notes, are fond of expressing their Sense of his Merit.[100]

This claim sounds suspiciously like mere puffery, but Playford, as if to rebut any such suspicion, printed in the volume itself a poem by Thomas Brown addressed *'To his unknown Friend, Mr.* Henry Purcell, *upon his Excellent Compositions in the First and Second Books of* HARMONIA SACRA'. Whether Brown actually knew Purcell or not, he was familiar enough with the music to offer some shrewd comments on its worth:

> Not Italy, *the Mother of each Art*
> *Did e'er a Juster, Happier Son impart.*
> *In thy Performance we with Wonder find*
> Bassani's *Genius to* Corelli's *joyn'd.*
> *Sweetness combined with Majesty, prepares*
> *To raise Devotion with Inspiring Airs* [melodies].
>
> *Thus I unknown my Gratitude express,*
> *And conscious Gratitude could pay no less.*
> *This Tribute from each* British Muse *is due,*
> *Our whole Poetic Tribe's oblig'd to you.*
> *For where the Author's scanty Words have fail'd,*
> *Your happier Graces,* Purcell, *have prevail'd.*
> *And surely none but you with equal Ease*
> *Could add to* David [when setting verses from the Psalms], *and make* Durfy *please.*[101]

Pageantry, pupils, plays

The tumultuous reception accorded to *Hail! bright Cecilia* must have made the Cecilian commission for 1693 appear something of a poisoned chalice, but Finger, to whom the task fell, seems to have risen to the challenge. There is no record of the first performance, but the piece was

---

[100] *Gent. J.*, June 1693, p. 196.
[101] *Harmonia Sacra . . . The Second Book* (London: H. Playford, 1693), p. [v]. Brown's poem was reprinted in *Gent. J.*, June 1693, pp. 196–7.

soon afterwards repeated – not once but twice, on 11 January and 1 February, on both occasions in York Buildings. In between, on 25 January, came a revival of *Hail! bright Cecilia*, at a concert in the same venue advertised in the *London Gazette* as being 'for the entertainment of His Highness Prince Lewis of Baden'.[102] For such an event the Chapel Royal and the Twenty-Four Violins would normally have been turned out in full, but it is impossible to imagine how such numbers, together with at least four woodwind players, two trumpeters, and a kettledrummer, could have squeezed into the small concert room at York Buildings while leaving space for an audience of any size. Even so, the succession of three such large-scale performances speaks volumes for London's burgeoning concert life.

The new year had already been celebrated with the ode *Sound, sound the trumpet* by Motteux, set by Blow. The music is lost save for two solo vocal numbers which were published, but from the poem – indeed from the title alone – one can make a guess at style and scoring, both of which presumably reflected the fact that the king was still pursuing his long and dogged campaign against Louis XIV.[103]

Eight days later another new ode, *Great Parent, hail!*, received its premiere; this time it was the work of Tate and Purcell, and it was given not in London but in Dublin, where Trinity College was celebrating its centenary. That of its founding had occurred, inconveniently, while William III was still waging war in Ireland upon the followers of the deposed James II; but by 1694 the institution was able to commemorate in safety the passing of 100 years since its first students had matriculated. The occasion, according to one eyewitness, followed a predictable pattern:

> In the Afternoon, there was several Orations in Latin spoke by the Scholars, in praise of Queen *Elizabeth*, and the succeeding Princes: and an Ode made by Mr. *Tate* (the Poet Laureat) who was bred up in this College . . . After this *Ode* had been sung by the Principal Gentlemen of the Kingdom, there was a very diverting speech.[104]

This glittering academic occasion, however, must in purely musical terms have been a decidedly subfusc affair in comparison with the Yorkshire

---

[102] *London Gazette*, 11–15 January, 22–5 January, 1–5 February 1694.
[103] 'The sullen year is past', in Blow's *Amphion Anglicus* (London: the author, 1700), pp. 66–7, is headed 'Perform'd before the Queen', as if to imply that the gruff king was not present. But in *Gent. J.*, January and February 1694, 'He leaves, he slights his precious rest' (pp. 29–32) is headed 'Sung before their Majesties', and the complete poem (pp. 5–7) is described by Motteux as having been 'perform'd on New-Years-Day before Their Majesties'. Luttrell does not mention the event, but refers in several entries to the king's presence in or around London throughout January (vol. 3, pp. 250, 251, 254, 255, 260, 261).
[104] John Dunton, *The Dublin Scuffle . . . Also Some Account of His Conversation in Ireland* (London: the author, 1699), pp. 414–16.

Feast, the 1692 Cecilian festival, or the queen's birthday in most recent years: Purcell was unable to call on trumpets or even oboes, and was obliged to confine his scoring to strings, plus a couple of recorders (presumably local players who could not reliably manage double-reed instruments as well); he made shift to suggest the absent trumpets with fanfare figures given to the strings at suitable points.[105] Despite the importance of the centenary for Ireland, and that of the institution – a royal foundation – for the monarchy, all eyes in London were turned nervously in the opposite direction: across the English Channel towards Flanders, after a disastrous season's campaigning by the English army in 1693, and with battle soon to be rejoined.

It may be presumed that Tate had been officially commanded, as Poet Laureate, to write the ode text, which begins by setting the scene and welcoming Queen Mary (addressed as 'Awful Matron' – an unhappy turn of phrase for modern readers).[106] On a literary level the verses are even less distinguished than most such effusions, but they do offer a sweeping survey of the history of the college, evoking in turn its foundation under Queen Elizabeth ('Blest Eliza' rather than 'Gloriana', which sobriquet the royal poets had now appropriated for Mary herself); those who had succeeded Elizabeth on the throne, and hence as patrons of the institution, especially William and Mary; the Duke of Ormonde, a brave royalist soldier, Lieutenant-General of Ireland and for many years Chancellor of Trinity; and finally King William once more ('a second Ormond' on account of his military prowess).

There are martial references again, though fewer, in Tate's poem *Come, ye Sons of Art, away*, which was to be the last birthday ode Purcell was to set for the queen.[107] This splendid music is too well known nowadays to need description here; yet it narrowly escaped the fate of Blow's new year ode, for it survives only (save again for a couple of movements which were published) in a thoroughly unreliable copy dating from 70 years later. The copyist, one Robert Pindar, was careless over details, as the two published numbers make painfully clear, but he also had the deplorable habit of 'improving' Purcell's music to suit the tastes of his own period – in particular, adding to the scoring: the second trumpet part throughout the ode, the use of strings as well as oboes in the prelude to the opening solo, the oboe parts in the ensuing chorus, the recorder parts in the ritornello following the countertenor air 'Strike the viol', the string accompaniment to the bass air 'The day that such a blessing gave', and the kettledrum part in the closing chorus have all been called into

---

[105] Purcell Society Edition, vol. 1 (2008), pp. 102–41.
[106] Despite the fact that Tate's poem directly addresses her at this point, there is no evidence that Queen Mary actually attended the ceremony.
[107] Purcell Society Edition, vol. 24 (1997), pp. 124–90.

question.[108] Even worse, the symphony that Pindar copied at the beginning may not belong to the ode at all, for it also appears in *The Indian Queen*, Purcell's last dramatic opera, composed the following year. That fact by itself proves nothing; but in the same manuscript as *Come, ye Sons of Art, away* Pindar also copied the Yorkshire Feast Song, and there he certainly replaced the opening symphony with a movement from the same opera, the Trumpet Overture. (Worryingly, this substitution was not made to fill in for something of which he had no copy, for he duly included the original symphony at its repeat in the middle of the work!) We are fortunate enough to have Purcell's own draft copy of the Yorkshire Feast Song, but unless the autograph score of the 1694 ode turns up – unlikely at this late date – musicologists will still be arguing over its details, like those of *Dido and Aeneas*, in another hundred years.

In the early months of the year Purcell had accepted another pupil: not, this time, a budding professional high-flyer like John Weldon, but, like Rhoda Cartwright, the daughter of a wealthy family. The Howards, of Ashtead Manor in Surrey, paid Purcell a little over £2 a month for their daughter Katherine's harpsichord lessons. This fee – about the same as he had charged the Cartwrights – was hefty compared with the £5 per half-year he was earning from teaching Weldon, but money is unlikely to have been his reason for taking the girl on. He also taught her mother, Arabella, who was the fourth wife of Sir Robert Howard (1626–98), a prominent playwright and poet, brother-in-law of Dryden and one of his early collaborators, and an influential member of the court circle. It was probably through Dryden that Purcell had first come into contact with the Howards; certainly his professional path and that of Sir Robert were to cross, with important results, in the last months of Purcell's life.

Even if Purcell took on Katherine out of self-interest, he was by no means indifferent to the actual techniques of teaching. It was in this same year of 1694 that Playford published a revised edition of his *Brief Introduction to the Skill of Music*; the reviser of book 3, *The Art of Descant, or Composing Music in Parts*, was Purcell. He writes with admirable clarity about the basic rules of harmony and counterpoint, the proper treatment of dissonances, and the Italian style, with its frequent reliance on contrapuntal movement in thirds ('this is the smoothest, and carries more Air and Form in it, and I'm sure 'tis the constant Practise of the *Italians* in all their Musick, either Vocal or Instrumental, which I presume ought to be a Guide to us'). He also expresses frank admiration for music by his old teacher Blow, declaring that his canonic setting of 'Glory be to the Father' (from the Service in G major) 'is enough to recommend him for one of the greatest Masters in the World'. But his own illustrations of what he

---

[108] See Rebecca Herissone, 'Robert Pindar, Thomas Busby, and the Mysterious Scoring of Purcell's "Come ye Sons of Art" ', *Music & Letters*, 88 (2007), pp. 1–48.

describes as 'fugueing' – invertible counterpoint, as we would term it – show such dazzling proficiency at inversion, augmentation, and retrograde motion, all using variants of one subject, that they raise a suspicion that dazzlement was indeed at least part of the intended effect. So does his throwaway remark that composing ground-bass movements is 'a very easie thing to do, and requires but little Judgment'.[109]

Such vaunting by Purcell of his technical mastery, however, seems to have been confined to print (and to his compositions!). One of the few glimpses we have of him at work as a performing musician shows the opposite side of the coin; the occasion is unknown, but it may well have occurred during 1694, for it concerns an exceptionally talented theatre treble, Jemmy Bowen, who rose to stardom the following spring:

> He, when practising a Song set by Mr PURCELL, some of the Music told him to grace and run a Division in such a place. *O let him alone,* said Mr Purcell; *he will grace it more naturally than you, or I, can teach him.* ——— In short, an Actor, like a Poet, *Nascitur, non fit* [is born, not made].[110]

(There may be a subtext here: Purcell not merely intervening out of kindly concern for the confidence of the lad, but also keeping *instrumentalists* – the seventeenth-century meaning of 'the music' – in their place when they presumed to teach a *singer* how to do his job!)

Spanish practices

The 1693–4 theatrical season ran with a smoothness that must have been welcome after the turbulence of the preceding year. It brought the usual string of commissions for Purcell to compose music for plays. Some of these, including the tragicomedy *Love Triumphant*, Dryden's last full-length play, required no more than one or two songs, but for Congreve's sparkling new comedy *The Double Dealer*, which opened in late November 1693, he provided a full set of instrumental numbers too.[111] It was a chancy business every time, for although Purcell's own reputation was bankable, his music inevitably sank or swam with the play. *The Double Dealer* was not well received at first, though it gained acceptance later, but even Dryden's name offered no guarantee of success: when *Love Triumphant* opened in January 1694 it was promptly 'damn'd by the universal cry of the town', and Purcell's music (plus a contribution from

---

[109] *Introduction to the Skill of Musick* (12th edn, '*Corrected and Amended by Mr.* Henry Purcell', London: H. Playford, 1694), pp. 115, 141, 144; cf. Rebecca Herissone, *Music Theory in Seventeenth-Century England* (Oxford: Oxford University Press, 2000), p. 203.
[110] Anthony Aston, *A Brief Supplement to Colley Cibber, Esq; His Lives of the Late Famous Actors and Actresses* (London: the author, [1747]).
[111] Purcell Society Edition, vol. 20 (1998), pp. 74–5; vol. 16 (2007), pp. 236–58.

John Eccles, a house composer with the United Company) went down with it.

For a second year running the United Company had planned no new opera – making do with another revival of *Dioclesian*, also in January (this time without even the sweetener of a new song or two). But no fewer than six other new plays produced that season featured music commissioned from Purcell, and three of them in particular – all, unusually, sharing a single literary source – offered the audience generous helpings of music. The plot of John Crowne's comedy *The Married Beau* was borrowed (probably with the help of Motteux as translator) from an episode in Cervantes's *Don Quixote*; Purcell provided nine instrumental movements, among them a fleet-footed overture and a splendid hornpipe on a ground bass, and one song, with another supplied by Eccles.[112] The play proved a hit: opening at the end of April, it had been 'already acted many times' by mid-May.[113] D'Urfey, meanwhile, had adapted a second Cervantes episode: *The Comical History of Don Quixote* was staged in mid-May 1694 – only two or three weeks after the curtain had gone up on *The Married Beau*.[114] Although the script calls for several pieces of instrumental music, only the vocal numbers, which were published within weeks, have survived, and Purcell was not responsible for all of them, sharing the honours with Eccles. But the four pieces that Purcell did contribute (alongside three by Eccles) are all substantial – in particular 'With this sacred charming wand', a quasi-operatic scene over three hundred bars long including repeats, and scored for three voices and strings, and the extended and passionate love song 'Let the dreadful engines', falling into no fewer than eight sections in contrasting time signatures.[115] The songs were hurried into print, appearing on 14 June.[116]

It is possible that Crowne and D'Urfey had both drawn on Cervantes by coincidence. But it seems likelier that Crowne's success had given D'Urfey his cue. The fact that his *Don Quixote* opened only two or three weeks after *The Married Beau* appears astonishing by modern standards, but the United Company could move fast when profits beckoned. *The Comical History* was such a success that D'Urfey cobbled together a sequel, predictably entitled *The Comical History . . . Part the Second*, which followed its predecessor a mere two or three weeks later. Once again Purcell shared the vocal music, this time not only with Eccles but also with two minor composers, Simon Pack and the prolific Anon.; once again the instrumental music is lost. Purcell's three numbers include a lengthy

---

[112] Purcell Society Edition, vol. 20 (1998), pp. 96–116. Eccles's song is preserved in Oxford, Bodleian Library, MS Mus.Sch. C.95, f. 102.

[113] *London Stage*, p. 434; *Gent. J.*, May 1694, p. 134.

[114] *London Stage*, p. 435.

[115] Purcell Society Edition, vol. 16 (2007), pp. 164–204.

[116] Advertised in *London Gazette*, 11–14 June 1694.

comic dialogue and a rousing twofold air with trumpet obbligato, begun in common time by St George (countertenor) and continued in triple metre by the Genius of England (soprano) – recalling, no doubt intentionally, another stage hit three years earlier![117] The sequel proved as successful as the original. Motteux reported:

> The first part of Mr D'Urfy's *Don Quixote* was so well received, that we have had a second Part of that Comical History acted lately, which doubtless must be thought as entertaining as the first; since in this hot season it could bring such a numerous Audience.[118]

This second success prompted D'Urfey to return the next season for a third draught at this Castilian spring. Meanwhile the songs were rushed through the press, being on sale by early July; the play itself was still running in late July, well after the date when the theatre would normally have closed for the summer.[119]

Dated just a week after the *London Gazette* had announced the publication of the songs comes a private document, relating to an entirely different area of Purcell's busy professional life:

> 20 July 1694.

> Ordered that an Agreem^t made by Mr. Stephen Crispian [sic] Chanter and Mr Purcell Organist of the Collegiate Church of Westm^r for and on the behalfe of the Deane & Chapter of Westm^r with Mr Bernard [Smith] Organ Maker for the amending & altering & new Makinge of the Organ belonginge to the said Collegiate Church in such a manner as the said Stephen Crespian & Henry Purcell shall direct, and that the said Mr Smyth shall have the sum of £200 for the pformance thereof to be paid as shall be agreed.[120]

The contract, signed by Smith with Crespion, Purcell, and John Needham as witnesses, laid on Purcell and Crespion the responsibility for approving the work before Smith might receive the final payment, which was to be made on 28 November 1695. The rebuild was extensive, including the addition of four new stops. Crespion, who was not an organist, is unlikely to have taken a hand in specifying or supervising the work, but

---

[117] Purcell Society Edition, vol. 16 (2007), pp. 205–26.
[118] *Gent. J.*, June 1694, p. 170. The issue seems to have been published towards the end of the month.
[119] *London Gazette*, 5–9 July (*Songs*) and 19–23 July 1693 (performances).
[120] Westminster Abbey Chapter Minutes, 1693–4, f. 47v.

Purcell will certainly have been busy doing so – having no inkling that by the time the new organ was finished he would, far from presiding at it, be lying in his grave just beside it.

A heavenly host

The Cecilian festival proved to be one of the highlights of the 1694–5 season – curiously, it might appear, since of the ode not even the title has survived.[121] But what stole the show was a new setting of the Te Deum and Jubilate, sung in St Bride's Church, Fleet Street, at the choral service which traditionally preceded the concert. The music, by Purcell, was not in the deeply conservative style expected of liturgical music but instead in that of the most up-to-date and flamboyant of verse anthems; and unlike any previous setting of the English liturgy it had an orchestral accompaniment, scored not merely for strings but also for trumpets – their very first use in English church music of any kind.[122] The work caused a sensation. Thomas Tudway was enraptured:

> there is in this Te Deum, such a glorious representation, of ye Heavenly Choirs, of Cherubins & Seraphins, falling down before ye Throne & singing Holy, Holy, Holy &c as hath not been Equall'd, by any Foreigner, or Other . . . He brings in ye treble voices, or Choristers, singing, To thee Cherubins, & Seraphins, continually do cry; and then ye Great Organ, Trumpets, the Choirs, & at least thirty or forty instruments besides, all Joine, in most excellent Harmony & Accord . . . This most beautifull & sublime Representation, I dare challenge all ye Orators, Poets, Painters &c of any Age whatsoever, to form so lively an Idea, of Choirs of Angels singing, & paying their Adorations.[123]

(Although Tudway was probably unaware of it, there seems to have been a scramble to get the work ready for performance. The autograph score has disappeared, but we do have the fair copy used for preparing the vocal and orchestral parts.[124] Most unusually, instead of being the work of one copyist it involved two, both of them reliable veterans: John Walter and William Isaack, taking turns of a few pages – perhaps relieving each other when writer's cramp threatened.)

The work was repeated before the king and queen on Sunday 9 December; as with the performance of *Hail! bright Cecilia* in York

---

[121] A duet by 'Mr Pickett' (presumably Francis Pigott), 'The Consort of the sprinkling Lute', published in *Thesaurus Musicus* . . . *The Fourth Book* (London: Hudgebut, 1695), pp. 30–3, and 'sung at St. Celia's Feast', may be part of it.

[122] Purcell Society Edition, vol. 23 (1923), pp. 90–131.

[123] London, British Library, Harl. MS 7342, f. 12v.

[124] Stanford University, California, MS MLM #850.

Buildings, one wonders how all the performers managed to squeeze into Whitehall Chapel. The king had returned from Flanders on 11 November, to be greeted with what had become a rarity: a new anthem by Purcell – though one that is well below his best. *The way of God is an undefiled way* is scored only for three solo voices, chorus and organ – no instruments – but it runs to over two hundred bars of music which is extremely intricate in places, with flamboyant roulades highlighting martial elements in the text: 'It is God that girdeth me with *strength* of war', 'teacheth my hands to *fight*', 'mine arm shall *break* ev'n a bow of steel' (plus, with a careless lack of discrimination that is unusual in Purcell, 'un*to* the battle').[125] The feelings of the unmusical king as he heard such passages, and subsequently some of the equally florid ones in the Te Deum and Jubilate, may be imagined; worse, four days after being welcomed home with the anthem he had also been obliged to endure Tate and Staggins's birthday ode *Spring, where are thy flow'ry treasures?*, whose performance had been postponed from his actual birthday, 4 November, on account of his absence.[126]

A theatrical rift

The theatrical season, meanwhile, had started unusually slowly for Purcell. He composed a richly comical dialogue between two quarrelling wives – eventually forced into reconciliation by their irritated husbands – for Ravenscroft's *The Canterbury Guests*. But that was the only new play put on before Christmas, and it was acted by the junior players only. Trouble was brewing in the United Company.

For several years internal tensions had been growing. In 1690 a disreputable former lawyer, Christopher Rich, had bought up the company, and his abrasive managerial style, coupled with financial pressures, caused increasing friction between the proprietors (whose possession of a royal patent allowed them to run the two London theatres as a monopoly) and the principal actors. His response to the expenses of mounting operatic productions – an attempt to cut the actors' salaries – was particularly insensitive, and the way he set about it characteristically unscrupulous. Colley Cibber, a very junior member of the company at the time, watched the sorry saga unfold:

> Though the Success of the *Prophetess*, and King *Arthur* (two dramatic Opera's, in which the Patentees had embark'd all their Hopes) was, in Appearance, very great, yet their whole Receipts did not so far balance their Expence, as to keep them out of a

---

[125] Purcell Society Edition, vol. 32 (1962), pp. 58–70. In the Texas Gostling MS the anthem is subscribed 'November ye 11th 1694 King William then returnd from Flanders'.
[126] Luttrell, vol. 3, p. 400 (15 November 1694).

large Debt, which it was publickly known was, about this time, contracted, and which found work for the Court of Chancery for about twenty Years following, till one side of the Cause grew weary. But this was not all that was wrong; every Branch of the Theatrical Trade had been sacrific'd, to the necessary fitting out those tall Ships of Burthen [merchant ships – i.e. the dramatic operas], that were to bring home the Indies. Plays of course were neglected, Actors held cheap, and slightly dress'd, while Singers, and Dancers were better paid, and embroider'd. These Measures, of course, created Murmurings, on one side, and ill Humour and Contempt on the other. When it became necessary therefore to lessen the Charge, a Resolution was taken to begin with the Sallaries of the Actors.[127]

The management first targeted the principal actors, including Betterton, and also began offering their most popular roles to younger players: a particularly crass misjudgment, this, which also alienated the audience. By the autumn of 1694 the actors were close to open revolt, though as long as the royal patent prohibited unlicensed performances they were powerless.

Rich and his party, casting around for supporters at court, hit on the idea of proffering a sweetener to Sir Robert Howard by proposing an 'operatic' revival of the tragedy The Indian Queen, on which he and Dryden had collaborated some 30 years earlier – a play both melodramatic and invitingly exotic – and of turning Betterton's flank by paying him £50 to create and direct the adaptation. The ploy failed: relationships had deteriorated too far. At the beginning of December Betterton and his followers presented a petition to the Lord Chamberlain seeking redress of their grievances. After the Patentees had responded on 10 December, the contending factions were called to a meeting a week later at the house of Sir Robert Howard. They were unable to agree terms and, to the dismay of the Patentees, Howard subsequently sided with the rebel faction.[128]

Solemn music

At this point fate made a cruel intervention. On 19 December Queen Mary, at home in Kensington Palace with a bad cold, noticed a rash on her arms and shoulders: the deadly symptoms of smallpox, of which an epidemic had begun to sweep the city. Eight days later she was dead, at the age of only 32.

---

[127] Cibber, Apology, p. 105. As an actor, of course, Cibber had an axe to grind. His complaints do not quite tally with Downes's approving remarks about the takings from King Arthur (p. 139, above) and his noncommittal comments about The Fairy Queen (p. 148).
[128] Nicoll, Restoration Drama, pp. 368–79; R. W. Lowe, Thomas Betterton (London: Kegan Paul, Trench, Trübner, 1891), p. 143.

In the aftermath, private heartbreak and public grief collided head-on. Mary had not wanted an elaborate funeral – had, indeed, specifically forbidden one in her will. The king, initially set on respecting her wishes, was obliged to bow to a public demand for a state funeral whose magnificence would reflect how universally she had been loved. In the event, the grandeur of her obsequies bid fair to eclipse that of the coronation of the joint monarchs.

From 21 February the queen's embalmed body lay in state at Whitehall, where thousands filed past it to pay their respects. On 5 March, in bitter weather, her coffin was carried in a horse-drawn hearse to Westminster Abbey, passing between rails sheathed in black along the entire way, which was lined with guardsmen and thronged with members of the public. The funeral procession was headed by three hundred old and poor women, each with her train carried by a page; then came the royal heralds, the horse guards, leading members of the government, the Lords and the Commons, the Lord Mayor and aldermen of London, the queen's ladies-in-waiting, and the gentlemen and boys of the Chapel Royal, who sang as they went (though we do not know what). There was also an oboe band, playing marches composed by two supernumerary royal musicians, Paisible and Tollett, and a consort of four slide trumpets, sounding Purcell's funeral march – awe-inspiring in its sombre simplicity – all in time to a solemn and ancient tattoo played on military drums.[129]

In the Abbey the choir, together with the full Chapel Royal, sang the funeral sentences in the dignified polyphonic setting by Thomas Morley (1557/8–1602), which dated from the beginning of the century and had become a time-honoured feature of state funerals.[130] There was, however, one problem: Morley's setting of the sentence beginning 'Thou knowest, Lord, the secrets of our hearts' had been lost during the Commonwealth years. (Copies of the music had never been widely circulated, and indeed it was not until well into the eighteenth century that a set of vocal parts of the missing sentence came to light.) Accordingly Purcell, who as Abbey organist was in charge of the music at the funeral, composed a new setting. Its harmonic intensity is peculiarly his own, but otherwise it fits perfectly with the antique language of Morley's music. The listening Thomas Tudway was moved more deeply even than he had been at the Cecilian festival three months earlier:

[129] For a full account of the marches and the choral music performed on the occasion, see Wood, 'First Performance'; all the music is assembled in Purcell, Morley, Paisible, Tollett, *Funeral Music for Queen Mary*, ed. Bruce Wood (London: Novello, 1996).
[130] It was still in use as late as 1852, at the funeral of the Duke of Wellington: John E. Uhler, 'Thomas Morley and the First Music for the English Burial Service', *Renaissance News*, 9 (1956), pp. 144–6.

14. *Queen Mary's funeral procession, showing the marching instrumentalists: engraving by L. Scherm, 1695.*

15. *Queen Mary's catafalque in Westminster Abbey, designed by Christopher Wren.*

I appeal to all y^t were present, as well such as understand Music, as those y^t did not, whither, they ever heard any thing, so rapturously fine, & solemn, & so Heavenly in ye Operation, wch drew tears from all: & yet a plain, Naturall Composition[,] wch shews ye pow'r of Music, when tis rightly fitted, & Adapted to devotional purposes.[131]

At the interment itself, as the officers of the queen's household broke their staves of office and flung them, with their keys, into the grave, the four slide trumpeters played Purcell's remaining contribution to the music, the austere polyphonic Canzona, full of ululating repeated notes.

The music for the funeral constitutes Purcell's public memorial to his sovereign and patroness. A more private expression of grief is to be found in two settings of pastoral elegies: the first, *Incassum, Lesbia*, for a single voice, the other, *O dive custos*, a duet.[132] The poems are conventional pastoral elegies, but there is nothing routine about the music, which is wonderfully eloquent in its expression of grief. The use of Latin texts might easily have prompted Purcell to ape a mainstream Italian style, but the music's combination of powerful declamatory writing, limpid melody, contrapuntal mastery, and potent harmonic expressiveness is utterly personal. Both pieces were published, together with Blow's solo setting of the first elegy in an English translation, *No, Lesbia, no*, around the end of April 1695 – quite possibly to mark the anniversary of the late queen's birth.[133]

An operatic waif

Meanwhile the feud in the theatre company was being played out behind the scenes, even though the theatres themselves were closed for three months' mourning. In February the Patentees made offers to Betterton, who contemptuously turned them down. Early in March the Lord Chamberlain tabled compromise proposals, which the management accepted on the 19th, but it was too late: the rebellious actors, by now confident of securing a patent of their own, formed a breakaway company to reopen the long-disused theatre in Lincoln's Inn Fields. They got their way, and their patent, only six days later, and opened for business on 30 April – ironically, the late queen's birthday.[134]

The split was disastrous for the rump of the company who had stayed with Rich. Betterton had taken with him the cream of the acting fraternity, and his new company opened with what proved a smash hit: Congreve's new comedy *Love for Love*, brilliantly acted, which had an

---

[131] London, British Library, Harl. MS 7340, f. 3.
[132] Purcell Society Edition, vol. 25 (1985), pp. 206–12; vol. 22 (2007), pp. 85–93.
[133] *Three Elegies upon the Much Lamented Loss of Our Late Most Gracious Queen Mary* (London: H. Playford, 1695).
[134] Nicoll, *Restoration Drama*, p. 361.

extraordinary run of thirteen performances in front of an audience so well disposed towards the breakaways, the playwright Charles Gildon observed, that 'before a Word was spoke, each Actor was clapt for a considerable Time'.[135] What was worse, the Patentees' remaining actors, junior though most of them were, seized their chance to demand – and secure – a doubling of their salaries, to £4 a week. Worse still, Betterton, the seasoned opera director whose record stretched back to *The Tempest* in 1674, had reneged on the agreement he had made to adapt *The Indian Queen* as the first new opera the United Company had planned since *The Fairy Queen*.[136] The Patentees were now obliged to make shift to do so, deprived of Betterton's skills, with an inexperienced cast, and having themselves just suffered a self-inflicted public relations disaster.

But Purcell stayed with them. Why he did so is a mystery – unless he simply chose to remain at the theatre that could stage operas – but his name still had its magic: sufficient, as Gildon acknowledged in his memoirs 15 years later, to sustain the efforts of 'a Company of raw young Actors, against the best and most favour'd of that Time'.[137] With his name now desperately needed to keep the ship afloat, Purcell received a string of new commissions – most or all of them, probably, after the rift: songs for one new play and for three revivals, act tunes for another revival, at least one substantial masque for a further revival (the depleted company was all too obviously reduced to scraping the barrel), and, above all, the opera.

The adaptation of *The Indian Queen* was a clumsy piece of work: a bungling abridger somehow managed to cut out an important event in the first act (Queen Zempoalla's vow to the God of Vengeance) to which reference is made at several points subsequently.[138] And Purcell's score is – at least, compared with its three mighty predecessors – a poor waif of a work: richly inventive, but only modestly scored, and devoid of the grand set-pieces which *The Fairy Queen* in particular had so liberally provided. It contains a bare hour of music, less than half as much as *The Fairy Queen*. It was evidently written in a great hurry, even to the point of borrowing one

---

[135] Downes, pp. 43–4; Gildon, *Poets*, p. 22.

[136] The Patentees had indignantly complained of this on 10 December, in their response to Betterton's petition: Public Record Office LC 7/3, quoted in Allardyce Nicoll, *A History of English Drama*, vol. 1 (4th edn, Cambridge: Cambridge University Press, 1952), p. 376, and in Judith Milhous, *Thomas Betterton and the Management of Lincoln's Inn Fields, 1695–1708* (Carbondale: Southern Illinois University Press, 1979), p. 240.

[137] Charles Gildon, *The Life of Mr Thomas Betterton* (London: Gosling, 1710), p. 167.

[138] See Andrew Pinnock, 'Play into Opera: Purcell's *The Indian Queen*', *Early Music*, 18 (1990), pp. 3–21; Purcell Society Edition, vol. 19 (1994). Laurie, *Stage Works*, vol. 1, pp. 122–3, observes that the adaptation may have been made by Betterton, and completed before the company split – a conclusion shared by Price, *Stage*, pp. 126–31, and by Robert Hume, 'Opera in London, 1695–1706', in Shirley Strum Kenny (ed.), *British Theatre and the Other Arts, 1660–1800* (Washington, DC: Folger Shakespeare Library, 1984), pp. 67–91, at pp. 70–1. But the Patentees' complaint of Betterton's dereliction (see above, and note 136), and the clumsiness of the adaptation, suggest otherwise.

number from that work. And the distribution of the score is very odd, with just one song in Act IV, and in Act V only a sacrifice scene, less than a hundred bars long, where a terminal masque on a substantial scale would also have been expected. It looks suspiciously as if Purcell had yet again run out of time. At some point – perhaps after his death – his brother Daniel filled the gap in the final act with a Masque of Hymen (a somewhat incongruous celebration, on a stage by then littered with bodies).

The new opera probably opened in June 1695, though the date is not quite certain.[139] But it was evidently a success, enjoying many performances over the next few years.[140] More immediately, nine of the vocal numbers were promptly issued in a pirate edition – either Purcell or the struggling theatre company had missed a chance – with a preface addressed to the composer:

SIR,

HAving had the good Fortune to meet with the Score or Original Draught of your Incomparable Essay of Musick compos'd for the Play, call'd The Indian Queen. *It soon appear'd that we had found a Jewel of very great Value; on which account we were unwilling that so rich a Treasure should any longer lie bury'd in Oblivion; and that the Common-wealth of Musick should be depriv'd of so considerable a Benefit. Indeed we well knew your innate Modesty to be such, as not to be easily prevail'd upon to set forth any thing in Print, much less to Patronize your own Works, although in some respects Inimitable. But in regard that (the Press being now open) any one might print an imperfect Copy of these admirable Songs, or publish them in the nature of a Common Ballad, We were so much the more emboldened to make this Attempt, even without acquainting you with our Design; not doubting but your accustomed Candor and Generosity will induce you to pardon this Presumption: As for our parts, if you shall think fit to condescend so far, we shall always endeavour to approve our selves,*

Your Obedient Servants,

J. May,
J. Hudgebutt.[141]

---

[139] Jonathan Keates, *Purcell: A Biography* (London: Chatto & Windus, 1995), p. 272, speculates that the opera may have been put on after Purcell's death, but that seems unlikely in view of the preface to the pirate edition of songs from the opera, quoted below. Margaret Laurie and Andrew Pinnock, in Purcell Society Edition, vol. 19 (1994), pp. xii–xiii, argue convincingly for June, pointing out that two of the songs appeared in *The Self-Instructor for the Violin*, book 1, advertised in *The London Gazette* for 15–18 July.

[140] Gildon, *Poets*, p. 75.

[141] *The Songs in the Indian Queen* (London: Hudgebut and May, 1695), p. [ii].

Purcell must have fumed as he read this: he ought to have shared the profits from publication, as with the songs in *The Fairy Queen* and *Don Quixote*. But in the absence of an effective copyright law he was powerless against these insolent thieves.

If Purcell was indeed struggling to finish *The Indian Queen*, that trusty old standby, the 1674 operatic version of *The Tempest*, may well have been hurried onto the stage in its place. At all events it was certainly revived before the end of the season, with Purcell supplying a single new song, 'Dear pretty youth' – though that will have been enough for the theatre to flaunt his name on the playbill.[142] It was probably also in the early summer that Shakespeare's *Timon of Athens* was revived, in Shadwell's adaptation dating from 1678. The original music, including a masque in Act II (where Shadwell had moved it from Act I), was probably by Grabu, but the play now returned to the stage with a new masque by Purcell – though the text is considerably altered, with that for three of the nine movements probably written two years previously for use in a different context.[143] At different points, variously in this and in subsequent revivals, the play also seems to have picked up other music: an overture by Purcell, a ground-bass Curtain Tune attributed to him, and a set of eight instrumental numbers probably by Paisible, and presumably intended as the first and second music and the four act tunes. All this suggests hasty work first time around, just as with *The Indian Queen*, and it may well be that Purcell was feeling the strain, for in May his brother Daniel, possibly in response to a call for help, had resigned as organist of Magdalen College, Oxford, and moved to London, becoming organist of St Andrew's, Holborn.[144]

Two other plays had also helped keep Purcell exceptionally busy in the spring and summer of 1695. On 25 March, before the breakaway company had been able to open, the Patentees attempted to wrong-foot them with a revival of the 1677 tragedy *Abdelazer*, by that renowned early feminist Aphra Behn.[145] Purcell furnished the piece with a particularly fine set of nine instrumental numbers (including the Rondeau whose opening has gone round the world in Britten's *Young Person's Guide to the Orchestra*), together with one song.[146] Unfortunately the play sank without trace[147] – taking Purcell's music with it until well into the twentieth

---

[142] It was long believed that Purcell provided the entire score, which is still published under his name; but Margaret Laurie, in 'Did Purcell Set *The Tempest*?', *Proceedings of the Royal Musical Association*, 90 (1963–4), pp. 43–57, proved otherwise. His solitary contribution was published in July 1695, in the same volume as the two songs from *The Indian Queen* (see note 139, above).
[143] Purcell Society Edition, vol. 2 (1994), p. ix.
[144] Documented in Zimmerman, *Purcell*, pp. 290–1.
[145] *London Stage*, pp. 443–4. The accepted wisdom is that the revival opened on 1 April, but Margaret Laurie has shown (Purcell Society Edition, vol. 16 (2007), p. xxxviii, n. 5) that it was a week earlier.
[146] Purcell Society Edition, vol. 16 (2007), pp. 1–23.
[147] Cibber, *Apology*, p. 195.

century. The date of two further revivals is uncertain: either or both of them may belong to the autumn. D'Urfey's *The Virtuous Wife*, like *Abdelazer*, received a full set of instrumental numbers, while Shadwell's tragicomedy *The Libertine* elicited a striking score consisting of just three substantial pieces, all for voices and instruments.[148] The second of these, a supernatural conjuration scene, is eerily introduced by the late queen's funeral march – arranged, doubtless in the interests of economy, for just two trumpets, with undesignated tenor and bass parts that were probably played on viola or tenor oboe and bass violin or bassoon. Even in this mangled version the music, with the funeral still fresh in the public memory, will have lost little of its power.

The theatre had scarcely closed for the summer before Purcell had a new royal duty to discharge. On 24 July the birthday of the six-year-old Duke of Gloucester, the sickly and deformed son of Prince George and Princess Anne who embodied the hopes of England for a Protestant succession to the throne, was celebrated with an ode, *Who can from joy refrain?* Despite his pitiful disabilities (to encourage him to walk unaided, his father used to whip him), the little boy had a passion for all things military, enthusiastically drilling a private regiment of urchins armed with wooden swords. This martial hobby is celebrated with distasteful relish in the ode text which, perhaps fortunately, is anonymous:

> Sound the trumpet, beat the warlike drums:
> The Prince will be with laurels crown'd
> Before his manhood comes

(though in fact his manhood never did come, for he died five years later). Purcell's response was at best lukewarm; the result is a sad codicil to his rich legacy of royal odes.[149]

'Cut down like a flower'

Five further productions with music by Purcell were to reach the stage, though the number of commissions he held for the 1695–6 season is anyone's guess. In October *Bonduca*, a hasty adaptation of a blatantly nationalistic tragedy by John Fletcher, opened at Drury Lane, with a very substantial score by Purcell: tripartite overture, six act tunes and dances, and eight vocal numbers – five of them, forming a lengthy sacrifice scene, with orchestra. (Two numbers, 'Britons, strike home' and 'To arms, your ensigns straight display', were destined to become as popular, and as emblematic of British imperialism, as in a later age did 'Land of hope and glory' set to Elgar's great melody). For Part III of *The Comical History of*

---

[148] Purcell Society Edition, vol. 21 (forthcoming); vol. 20 (1998), pp. 48–73.
[149] Purcell Society Edition, vol. 4 (1990).

Don Quixote, which followed in November, he provided only a single song with continuo, 'From rosy bowers', though it is one of the greatest of all his vocal numbers for the stage.

But he was already ill with some unidentified malady. All kinds of speculative diagnoses have been made, including tuberculosis, poisoning by drinking a contaminated cup of chocolate, and pneumonia contracted through being locked out by his wife after an evening's carousing (an old chestnut, for which there is not a shred of evidence). He had fallen sick soon after setting an obscure but obviously allegorical text, 'Lovely Albina's come ashore', which was published as 'the last song the author set before his sickness'.[150] The song is obviously linked to King William's continental wars, but its exact subject remains obscure – frustratingly so, for knowing what event it describes would help us date the onset of Purcell's fatal illness. 'From rosy bowers' was identified on publication as 'the last song that Mr Purcell set, it being in his sickness' – something of which, nevertheless, this magnificent number shows not the smallest sign.[151] But that is no surprise: his illness was not recognized as being anything serious, even by his family, until 21 November, when it suddenly became clear that he was on his deathbed.

Events now moved swiftly. A will was drawn up with frantic haste – as may be judged from the untidy scrawl of the notary – and Purcell signed it with a hand so shaky that his signature is nearly illegible.[152] He died the same day.

His passing was untimely in a double sense: he was only 36 years old, and he had died on the very eve of the Cecilian festival which he had founded a dozen years before. The celebration – with an orchestral setting of the Te Deum and Jubilate composed by Blow in flattering imitation of that by Purcell, and a grand ode by Peter Motteux, *Great choir of heav'n, attend!*, also set by Blow – must have been a muted affair indeed.[153]

Five days after his death Purcell was buried in the north aisle of Westminster Abbey, near the newly rebuilt organ which he had never been able to try over as the builder's contract had required. Lady Howard commissioned a handsome marble tablet, which still marks the spot. The epitaph it bears is as simple as it is moving: 'He is gone to that blessed place where only [i.e. where alone] his harmony can be exceeded.' Equally simple and equally affecting are the words of an unnamed journalist reporting his death in *The Post Boy*: 'He is much lamented, being a very great Master of Musick.'[154] But perhaps the most striking tribute of

[150] Purcell Society Edition, vol. 25 (1985), pp. 218–20; *Orpheus Britannicus*, book 1 (London: H. Playford, 1698), pp. 133–4.
[151] Purcell Society Edition, vol. 16 (2007), pp. 227–35; *Orpheus Britannicus*, book 1, pp. 90–4.
[152] Facsimile in Zimmerman, *Purcell*, facing p. 254.
[153] Blow's setting of the Te Deum and Jubilate is preserved in London, British Library, Add. MS 31457, ff. 45–74v, and that of the ode in London, Guildhall Library, MS G.Mus. 451, pp. 1–62.
[154] *The Post Boy*, 26–8 November 1695.

all came jointly from the Abbey authorities and from the court, and it reflected the reality that Purcell was the first English composer ever to become a public figure. A London newspaper, the *Flying Post*, reported in graphic terms:

> Mr Henry *Pursel* one of the most Celebrated *Masters* of the Science of Musick in the Kingdom, and scarce inferiour to any in Europe, dying on Thursday last; the Dean of Westminster knowing the great worth of the deceased, forthwith summoned a Chapter, and unanimously Resolved that he shall be interred in the Abbey, with all the Funeral Solemnity they are capable to perform for him, granting his Widow the choice of the ground to Reposite his Corps free from any charge . . . and this Evening he will be interred, the whole Chapter Assisting with their Vestments; together with all the Lovers of that Noble Science, with the united Choyres of that and the Chappel Royal, when the Dirges composed by the Deceased for her late Majesty of Ever Blessed Memory, will be played by Trumpets and other Musick.[155]

All this pomp amounted, in everything but name, to something that few composers anywhere in the world have ever been accorded: a state funeral.

In terms of his posthumous reputation Purcell was fortunate to die when he did. His early death did nothing to diminish his renown: on the contrary, the lack of any composer of remotely comparable stature, at least in the theatrical realm, meant that his music did not, as so often happens with composers nowadays, fall out of fashion immediately after his death. The theatre itself, though, was in crisis, with neither the Patentees nor the breakaway company able to mount operatic productions to match those of the glory days; increasingly faded revivals of Purcell's operas continued for years (except for *The Fairy Queen*, whose score was lost around the time of his death),[156] but in new works by lesser composers the dramatic-opera concept itself was progressively cheapened, eventually creating a market opportunity for Handel and Italian opera. The royal music, including the Chapel Royal, was entering a long spiral of decline; the Chapel would never recover its pre-eminence, and all the rest was doomed to eventual extinction. Some of Purcell's music, too, was to suffer early eclipse – and not merely royal odes and political anthems, which he himself would probably have regarded as ephemera. A collection of his songs published in 1698 (with a grateful preface by his widow Frances,

---

[155] *The Flying Post*, 23–6 November 1695.
[156] The tale of its loss in 1695 and dramatic rediscovery in 1900 is briefly told in Purcell Society Edition, vol. 12 (forthcoming, 2009); the original editor of the volume, John Shedlock, stumbled across the manuscript in the library of the Royal Academy of Music.

dedicating it to Lady Howard)[157] was entitled, and thereby styled him, Britain's Orpheus (*Orpheus Britannicus*); it was so successful that a second volume was published four years later – and many of his songs have never been out of print since (just as some of his anthems have never been out of the cathedral repertoire). But if his countrymen cherished Orpheus's voice, they were not so receptive towards his lyre: in 1699 his widow recalled all copies of his printed music from the booksellers and began to distribute it herself, offering both the set of trio sonatas which she had issued in 1697 and the 1683 set for the knock-down price of only 8s. 6d. the pair – half the original price of the 1683 set on its own. Even so, at the time of her own death in 1706, copies of both sets remained unsold.

Changes in musical taste inevitably affected various aspects of Purcell's posthumous reputation, but his name retained much of its magic for later generations.[158] Nearly a hundred years after his death a lawyer and amateur musician named Benjamin Goodison projected a complete edition of his works – the first ever attempted for any composer.[159] By the standards of his day Goodison was a surprisingly capable editor, and between 1788 and 1790 he managed to issue on subscription nearly a dozen scores, including three operas and three odes, before the enterprise lapsed (whether for lack of support or on Goodison's death is not clear). Almost another century passed – during which collected editions of several leading continental composers were begun, and some of them completed – before the task was begun afresh, with the foundation of the Purcell Society by some of the leading English musicians of the age. Between 1878 and 1926 the society issued, again on subscription, scholarly editions of some three-quarters of Purcell's output, before financial pressures forced the abandonment of the project. The revival of the society by Edward Dent in 1950 prompted a scathing comment by Ralph Vaughan Williams (editor of two of the 26 volumes that had made it into print) concerning

> the devotion of a few experts who gave their scanty leisure to the work, and were entirely neglected by the State . . . Meantime, Austria, Germany, Italy and France have all produced at the public expense complete and critical editions, not only of their great masters, but also of their lesser lights. In this country we have too long allowed one of the greatest geniuses of music to languish unwept, unhonoured and almost unsung.[160]

---

[157] Reprinted in Michael Burden, *Purcell Remembered* (London: Faber and Faber, 1995), pp. 117–18.
[158] For a fuller account see Andrew Pinnock, 'The Purcell Phenomenon', in Burden, *Companion*, pp. 3–17.
[159] See Alec Hyatt King, 'Benjamin Goodison's Complete Edition of Purcell', *Monthly Musical Record*, 81 (1951), pp. 81–9.
[160] Foreword to *Eight Concerts of Henry Purcell's Music: Commemorative Book of Programmes, Notes and Texts* (London: Arts Council of Great Britain, 1951), p. 7.

The edition was at last completed in 1965. Since then the society has been steadily engaged – to this day without receiving a penny of public funding – initially on the revision of earlier volumes, more recently on replacing them with completely new editions which embody information and sources unknown to previous editors, and which conform to the highest standards of modern scholarship. An increasingly important part of the society's future work will be securing the production of performing material.

Perhaps the last word, though, should offer the perspective not of two centuries' intermittent scholarship but of professional acquaintance and lifelong friendship. Many years after Purcell's death Thomas Tudway recalled him in a letter to his son:

> I knew him perfectly well; he had a most commendable ambition of exceeding every one of his time, and he succeeded in it without contradiction, there being none in England, nor anywhere else that I know of, that could come into competition with him for compositions of all kinds. Towards the latter end of his life he was prevailed with to compose for the English stage; there was nothing that ever had appeared in England like the representations he made of all kinds, whether for pomp or solemnity; in his grand chorus, &c., or that exquisite piece called the freezing piece of musick [the Frost Scene in *King Arthur*]; in representing a mad couple, or country swains making love, or indeed any other kind of musick whatever. But these are trifles in comparison with the solemn pieces he made for the church, in which I will name but one, and that is his Te Deum. &c., with instruments, a composition for skill and invention beyond what was ever attempted in England before his time.[161]

Tudway, though claiming to know Purcell 'perfectly well', was not a personal friend. But that honour could legitimately be claimed by Henry Hall, from whose dedicatory poem for the first volume of *Orpheus Britannicus* (printed there beneath the artless heading 'To the Memory of my Dear Friend') a few lines were quoted in the first chapter of this book. Hall's final stanza begins with an affecting sentiment, and ends with a memorable one:

> Hail! and for ever hail Harmonious Shade!
> I lov'd thee Living, and admire thee dead. . . .
>
> *Sometimes a HERO in an Age appears,*
> *But scarce a PURCELL in a Thousand Years.*[162]

---

[161] Quoted in Hawkins, vol. 2, p. 795 (and at several other points). The letter is now missing.
[162] *Orpheus Britannicus*, book 1 (London: H. Playford, 1698), p. vi.

Bibliography

SOURCES CITED MORE THAN ONCE, IN ABBREVIATED FORM

Adams, *Purcell*	Adams, Martin, *Henry Purcell: The Origins and Development of His Musical Style* (Cambridge: Cambridge University Press, 1995)
Baker, *Chronicle*	Baker, Richard, *A Chronicle of the Kings of England* (London, 4th edn, 1665)
Boswell, *Stage*	Boswell, Eleanor, *The Restoration Court Stage* (Cambridge, MA: Harvard University Press, 1932)
Burden, *Companion*	Burden, Michael (ed.), *The Purcell Companion* (London: Faber and Faber, 1995)
Burden, *Performing Purcell*	Burden, Michael (ed.), *Performing the Music of Henry Purcell* (Oxford: Oxford University Press, 1996)
Cal. Tr. Books	Shaw, William A. (ed.), *Calendar of Treasury Books* 1660–67 (etc.) (London: HMSO, 1904–)
Cal. Tr. Papers	Redington, Joseph (ed.), *Calendar of Treasury Papers*, vol. 1: 1556/7–1696 (London: Longman, Green, Reader and Dyer, 1868)
Cheque Book	Rimbault, Edward F. (ed.), *The Old Cheque-Book or Book of Remembrance of the Chapel Royal* (London: Camden Society, 1872; photographic reprint, New York: Johnson, 1966)
Cibber, *Apology*	Cibber, Colley, *An Apology for the Life of Colley Cibber*, ed. B. R. S. Fone (Ann Arbor: University of Michigan Press, 1968)
CSP Dom.	Green, Mary A. E. (ed.); F. H. Blackburne Daniell (ed.); W. J. Hardy (ed.): *Calendar of State Papers, Domestic Series*, 1660–61 (etc.) (London, 1860 (etc.))
Dent, *Foundations*	Dent, Edward, *Foundations of English Opera* (Cambridge: Cambridge University Press, 1928)
Downes	Downes, John, *Roscius Anglicanus, or an Historical Review of the Stage* (London: Henry Playford, 1708)
Dryden, *Works*	*The Works of John Dryden* (various editors; Berkeley, Los Angeles, and London: University of California Press, 1956–2000)
Duffy, *Purcell*	Duffy, Maureen, *Henry Purcell* (London: Fourth Estate, 1994)
Ebsworth, *Ballads*	Ebsworth, J. Woodfall (ed.), *The Roxburghe Ballads*, vol. 5 (Hertford: Ballad Society, 1885)
Evelyn	Beer, E. S. de (ed.), *The Diary of John Evelyn* (6 vols, Oxford: Clarendon Press, 1955)
Falkus, *Charles II*	Falkus, Christopher, *The Life and Times of Charles II* (London: Weidenfeld and Nicolson, 1972)
Gent. J.	Motteux, Peter (ed.), *The Gentleman's Journal* (London: Richard Baldwin, 1692–4)
Gildon, *Poets*	Gildon, Charles, *The Lives and Characters of the English Dramatick Poets* (London: Tho. Leigh and William Turner, [1699])

Hawkins	Hawkins, Sir John, *A General History of the Science and Practice of Music* (5 vols, London: T. Payne & Son, 1776; rev. in 2 vols, 1875, facsimile, Graz: Akademische Druck- und Verlagsantalt, 1969)
HMC Rutland	*Historical Manuscripts Commission, Twelfth Report*, Appendix: *Rutland MSS.*, part 5, vol. 2 (London: Public Record Office, 1889)
Hodges, *Loimologia*	Hodges, Nathaniel, *Loimologia; or, An Historical Account of the Plague in London in 1665* (London: E. Bell and J. Osborn, 1720)
Holman, *Fiddlers*	Holman, Peter, *Four and Twenty Fiddlers: The Violin at the English Court, 1540–1690* (Oxford: Oxford University Press, 1993)
Holman, *Purcell*	Holman, Peter, *Henry Purcell* (Oxford: Oxford University Press, 1994)
KM	Lafontaine, Henry Cart de, *The King's Musick* (London: Novello, [1909])
Laurie, *Stage Works*	Laurie, Alison Margaret, *Purcell's Stage Works* (Ph.D. diss., 2 vols, University of Cambridge, 1962)
London Stage	Lennep, William van (ed.), *The London Stage 1660–1800*, part 1: *1660–1700* (Carbondale: Southern Illinois University Press, 1965)
Luttrell	Luttrell, Narcissus, *A Brief Historical Relation of State Affairs from September 1678 to April 1714* (5 vols, Oxford: Oxford University Press, 1857)
Milhous, 'Finances'	Milhous, Judith, 'Opera Finances in London, 1674–1738', *Journal of the American Musicological Society*, 37 (1984), pp. 567–92
Muller and Muller, 'Purcell's *Dioclesian*'	Muller, Julia, and Frans Muller, 'Purcell's *Dioclesian* on the Dorset Garden Stage', in Burden, *Performing Purcell*, pp. 232–42
Nicoll, *Restoration Drama*	Nicoll, Allardyce, *A History of Restoration Drama 1660–1700* (Cambridge: Cambridge University Press, 1923)
North	Wilson, John (ed.), *Roger North on Music* (London: Novello, 1959)
Oxford DNB	Matthew, H. C. G., and Brian Harrison (eds.), *Oxford Dictionary of National Biography* (60 vols, Oxford: Oxford University Press, 2004)
Pepys	Latham, Robert, and William Matthews (eds), *The Diary of Samuel Pepys* (11 vols, London: Bell, 1970)
Price, *Stage*	Price, Curtis A., *Henry Purcell and the London Stage* (Cambridge: Cambridge University Press, 1984)
Price, *Studies*	Price, Curtis A. (ed.), *Purcell Studies* (Cambridge: Cambridge University Press, 1995)
RECM	Ashbee, Andrew (ed.), *Records of English Court Music*, vol. 1 (1660–85); vol. 2 (1685–1714) (Snodland, Kent: Andrew Ashbee, 1986, 1987)
Sawkins, 'Trembleurs'	Sawkins, Lionel, '*Trembleurs* and Cold People: How Should They Shiver?', in Burden, *Performing Purcell*, pp. 243–64

Shay and Thompson, *Manuscripts*	Shay, Robert, and Robert Thompson, *Purcell Manuscripts: The Principal Musical Sources* (Cambridge: Cambridge University Press, 2000)
Term Catalogue	Clavel, Robert (ed.), *A Catalogue of Books Printed in England since . . . 1666, to the End of Michaelmas Term, 1695* (London: Robert Clavel, 1696; facsimile, Farnborough, Hants: Gregg, 1965)
Tuppen, *French Influence*	Tuppen, Sandra, *'Equal with the best abroad': French Influence on English Theatre Music 1660–1685* (Ph.D. diss., 2 vols, University of Wales, 1997)
WAM	Westminster Abbey Muniments
WAR	Westminster Abbey Registers
Westrup, *Purcell*	Westrup, Jack, *Purcell* (London: Dent, 1937)
White, *Grabu*	White, Bryan Douglas, *Louis Grabu and his Opera 'Albion and Albanius'* (Ph.D. diss., 2 vols, University of Wales, 1999)
Wood, 'First Performance'	Wood, Bruce, 'The First Performance of Purcell's Funeral Music for Queen Mary', in Burden, *Performing Purcell*, pp. 61–81
Wood and Pinnock, 'Fairy Queen'	Wood, Bruce, and Andrew Pinnock, 'The Fairy Queen: A Fresh Look at the Issues', *Early Music*, 21 (1993), pp. 44–62
Works	Accounts of His Majesty's Office of Works (National Archives, Kew)
Zimmerman, *Purcell*	Zimmerman, Franklin B., *Henry Purcell 1659–1695* (London: Macmillan, 1967)

SOURCES CITED ONLY ONCE, IN FULL

Adams, Martin, 'Purcell's *Laudate Ceciliam*: An Essay in Stylistic Experimentation', in Gerald Gillen and Harry White (eds), *Musicology in Ireland*, Irish Musical Studies, 1 (Dublin: Irish Academic Press, 1990), pp. 227–47

——, 'Purcell, Blow and the English Court Ode', in Price, *Studies*, pp. 172–91

Akerman, J. Y. (ed.), *Moneys Received and Paid for Secret Services of Charles II and James II* (London: Camden Society, 1851)

Aston, Anthony, *A Brief Supplement to Colley Cibber, Esq; His Lives of the Late Famous Actors and Actresses* (London: the author, [1747])

Aubrey, John, *Brief Lives*, ed. Oliver Lawson Dick (London: Secker and Warburg, 1949)

Baldwin, Olive, and Thelma Wilson, 'Purcell's Stage Singers', in Burden, *Performing Purcell*, pp. 105–29

Borgman, Albert S., *The Life and Death of William Mountfort* (Cambridge, MA: Harvard University Press, 1935)

Burden, Michael, *Purcell Remembered* (London: Faber and Faber, 1995)

——, '"He had the Honour to be Your Master": Lady Rhoda Cavendish's Music Lessons with Henry Purcell', *Music & Letters*, 76 (1995), pp. 532–9

——, 'Casting Issues in the Original Production of Purcell's Opera 'The Fairy-Queen'', *Music & Letters*, 84 (2003), pp. 596–607

Burney, Charles, *A General History of Music*, vol. 2 (London: the author, 1782)

Buttrey, John, 'Did Purcell go to Holland in 1691?', *Musical Times*, 110 (1969), pp. 929–31

——, 'New Light on Robert Cambert in London, and His *Ballet en Musique*', *Early Music*, 23 (1995), pp. 198–220

Chamberlayne, Edward, *Angliæ Notitia*, 12th edn (London: J. Martin, 1679); 14th edn (London: R. Littlebury, R. Scott, and G. Wells, 1682)

Danchin, Pierre, 'The Foundation of the Royal Academy of Music in 1674 and Pierre Perrin's *Ariane*', *Theatre Survey*, 25 (1984), pp. 55–67

Dunton, John, *The Dublin Scuffle . . . Also Some Account of his Conversation in Ireland* (London: the author, 1699)

D'Urfey, Thomas, *Wit and Mirth: or Pills to Purge Melancholy* (5 vols, London: Tonson, 1719)

Edmond, Mary, 'Davenant, William', *Oxford DNB*

Gaskell, Philip, *A New Introduction to Bibliography* (Oxford: Clarendon Press, 1972)

Gildon, Charles, *The Life of Mr Thomas Betterton* (London: Gosling, 1710)

Harley, John, *Music in Purcell's London: The Social Background* (London: Dobson, 1968)

Harris, Anthony, *Night's Black Agents: Witchcraft and Magic in Seventeenth-Century English Drama* (Manchester: Manchester University Press, 1980)

Herissone, Rebecca, *Music Theory in Seventeenth-Century England* (Oxford: Oxford University Press, 2000)

——, 'Robert Pindar, Thomas Busby, and the Mysterious Scoring of Purcell's "Come ye Sons of Art"', *Music & Letters*, 88 (2007), pp. 1–48

Highfill, P. H., K. A. Burnim, and E. A. Langhans, *A Biographical Dictionary of Actors, Actresses, Musicians, Dancers, Managers, and Other Stage Personnel in London 1660–1800* (Carbondale: Southern Illinois University Press, 1973–)

Holman, Peter, '*Valentinian*, Rochester and Louis Grabu', in John Caldwell, Edward Olleson, and Susan Wollenberg (eds), *The Well Enchanting Skill: Music, Poetry, and Drama in the Culture of the Renaissance* (Oxford: Oxford University Press, 1990), pp. 127–41

——, 'Grabu, Luis', *Grove Music Online*, ed. L. Macy (accessed 20 May 2008), <http://www.grovemusic.com>

Holst, Imogen, 'Purcell's Librettist, Nahum Tate', in Imogen Holst (ed.), *Henry Purcell, 1659–1695: Essays on His Music* (London: Oxford University Press, 1959), pp. 35–41

Howarth, R. G. (ed.), *Letters and the Second Diary of Samuel Pepys* (London: Dent, 1932)

Hume, Robert, 'Opera in London, 1695–1706', in Shirley Strum Kenny (ed.), *British Theatre and the Other Arts, 1660–1800* (Washington, DC: Folger Shakespeare Library, 1984), pp. 67–91

Husk, William Henry, *An Account of the Musical Celebrations on St Cecilia's Day in the Sixteenth, Seventeenth and Eighteenth Centuries* (London: Bell and Daldy, 1857)

[Hyde, Ralph (ed.)], *Find Your Way round Early Georgian London* (CD-ROM, Guildford: Motco Enterprises, 2003)

Keates, Jonathan, *Purcell: A Biography* (London: Chatto & Windus, 1995)

King, Alec Hyatt, 'Benjamin Goodison's Complete Edition of Purcell', *Monthly Musical Record*, 81 (1951), pp. 81–9

Langhans, Edward A., 'A Conjectural Reconstruction of the Dorset Garden Theatre', *Theatre Survey*, 13 (1972), pp. 74–93

Lasocki, David, 'Professional Recorder Playing in England 1500–1740, II: 1640–1740', *Early Music*, 10 (1982), pp. 183–91

Laurie, Margaret, 'Did Purcell Set *The Tempest*?', *Proceedings of the Royal Musical Association*, 90 (1963–4), pp. 43–57

Legg, John Wickham, *Three Coronation Orders* (London: Henry Bradshaw Society, 1900)

Legg, L. G. Wickham, *English Coronation Records* (London: Constable, 1901)

Locke, Matthew, *The Present Practice of Musick Vindicated* (London: N. Brooke and John Playford, 1673)

———, *The English Opera; or The Vocal Musick in Psyche, with the Instrumental Musick therein Intermix'd, to which is Adjoyned the Instrumental Musick in the Tempest* (London: the author, 1675)

Lowe, R. W., *Thomas Betterton* (London: Kegan Paul, Trench, Trübner, 1891)

Luckett, Richard, 'Exotick but Rational Entertainments: The English Dramatick Operas', in Marie Axton and Raymond Williams (eds), *English Drama: Forms and Development* (Cambridge: Cambridge University Press, 1977), pp. 132–41

Mace, Thomas, *Musick's Monument* (London: the author, 1676)

Marly, Diana de, 'The Architect of Dorset Garden Theatre', *Theatre Notebook*, 29 (1975), pp. 119–24

Martin, G. H., 'Baker, Richard', *Oxford DNB*

Milhous, Judith, *Thomas Betterton and the Management of Lincoln's Inn Fields, 1695–1708* (Carbondale: Southern Illinois University Press, 1979)

[Mountfort, William], *Six Plays Written by Mr. Mountfort* (2 vols, London: Tonson, Strahan, and Mears, 1720)

Nicoll, Allardyce, *A History of English Drama*, vol. 1 (4th edn, Cambridge: Cambridge University Press, 1952)

Pinnock, Andrew, '*King Arthur* Expos'd: A Lesson in Anatomy', in Price, *Studies*, pp. 243–56

———, 'Play into Opera: Purcell's *The Indian Queen*', *Early Music*, 18 (1990), pp. 3–21

———, 'The Purcell Phenomenon', in Burden, *Companion*, pp. 3–17

———, '"From Rosy Bowers": Coming to Purcell the Bibliographical Way', in Michael Burden (ed.), *Henry Purcell's Operas: The Complete Texts* (Oxford: Oxford University Press, 2000), pp. 31–93

——— and Bruce Wood, 'A Mangled Chime: The Accidental Death of the Opera Libretto in Civil War England', *Early Music*, 36 (2008), pp. 265–84

Plank, Stephen E., '"And Now About the Cauldron Sing": Music and the Supernatural on the Restoration Stage', *Early Music*, 18 (1990), pp. 393–407

Playford, John, *Introduction to the Skill of Musick* (12th edn, London, 1694)

Poems on Affairs of State (London: n. publ., 1698)

Porter, Stephen, *The Great Plague* (Stroud: Sutton, 1999)

Price, Curtis, *Music in the Restoration Theatre: With a Catalogue of Instrumental Music in the Plays 1665–1713* (Ann Arbor, MI: UMI Research Press, 1979)

———, '*King Arthur*', in Stanley Sadie (ed.), *The New Grove Dictionary of Opera* (4 vols, London: Macmillan, 1992), vol. 2, pp. 992–3

——— and Irena Cholij, 'Dido's Bass Sorceress', *Musical Times*, 127 (1989), pp. 615–18

[Purcell, Henry], *Eight Concerts of Henry Purcell's Music: Commemorative Book of Programmes, Notes and Texts* (London: Arts Council of Great Britain, 1951)

Radice, Mark A., 'Theater Architecture at the Time of Purcell and Its Influence on His "Dramatick Operas" ', *Musical Quarterly*, 74 (1990), pp. 98–130

——, 'Sites for Music in Purcell's Dorset Garden Theatre', *Musical Quarterly*, 81 (1997), pp. 430–48

Rohrer, Kathleen, *'The Energy of English Words': a Linguistic Approach to Henry Purcell's Methods of Setting Texts* (PhD diss., Princeton University, 1980)

Sandford, Francis, *Genealogical History of the Kings and Queens of England* (London: Nicholson, 1707)

——, *The History of the Coronation of . . . James II, King of England, . . . and of . . . Queen Mary* (London: Newcomb, 1687)

Savage, Roger, 'Calling up Genius: Purcell, Roger North, and Charlotte Butler', in Burden, *Performing Purcell*, pp. 213–31

Scott, Hugh Arthur, 'London's First Concert Room', *Music & Letters*, 18 (1937), pp. 379–90

Smith, John Stafford (ed.), *Musica Antiqua* (2 vols, London: Preston, 1812)

Spink, Ian, *English Song: Dowland to Purcell* (London: Batsford, 1974)

——, *Henry Lawes, Cavalier Songwriter* (Oxford: Oxford University Press, 2000)

——, 'Purcell's Odes: Propaganda and Panegyric', in Price, *Studies*, pp. 145–71

Spring, John R., 'Platforms and Picture Frames: A Conjectural Reconstruction of the Duke of York's Theatre, Dorset Garden, 1669–1709', *Theatre Notebook*, 31 (1977), pp. 6–19

——, 'The Dorset Garden Theatre: Playhouse or Opera House?', *Theatre Notebook*, 34 (1980), pp. 60–9

Straeten, Edmund Sebastian Joseph van der, *The Romance of the Fiddle: The Origin of the Modern Virtuoso and the Adventures of His Ancestors* (London: Rebman, 1911)

Summers, Montague (ed.), *The Complete Works of Thomas Shadwell* (5 vols, London: Fortune Press, 1927)

Tate, Nahum, *Poems Written on Several Occasions* (2nd edn, London: Tooke, 1684)

Tilmouth, Michael, 'A Calendar of References to Music in Newspapers Published in London and the Provinces, 1660–1719', *RMA Research Chronicle*, 1 (1961)

Uhler, John E., 'Thomas Morley and the First Music for the English Burial Service', *Renaissance News*, 9/3 (1956), pp. 144–6

Villiers, George, Duke of Buckingham, *Miscellany Poems upon Several Occasions . . .* (London: Peter Buck, 1692)

Visser, Colin, 'French Opera and the Making of Dorset Garden Theatre', *Theatre Research International*, 6 (1981), pp. 163–71

Walkling, Andrew, 'Masque and Politics at the Restoration Court: John Crowne's *Calisto*', *Early Music*, 24 (1996), pp. 27–62

[Ward, Edward], *A Compleat and Humorous Account of All the Remarkable Clubs and Societies in the Cities of London and Westminster* (7th edn, London: J. Wren, 1756)

Westminster Abbey Chapter Minutes 1683–1714

White, Bryan, 'Music for "A brave livlylike boy": The Duke of Gloucester, Purcell and "The noise of foreign wars" ', *Musical Times*, 148 (2007), pp. 75–83

Wilson, John Harold, 'More Theatre Notes from the Newdigate Newsletters', *Theatre Notebook*, 16 (1962), p. 59

Wing, Donald Goddard, *Short-Title Catalogue of Books Printed in England . . . 1641–1700* (3 vols, New York: Columbia University Press, 1945–51; revised edn, New York: Modern Language Association of America, 1972–88)

Winn, James Anderson, *John Dryden and His World* (New Haven and London: Yale University Press, 1987)

———, 'Heroic Song: A Proposal for a Revised History of English Theatre and Opera, 1656–1711', *Eighteenth-Century Studies*, 30 (1997), pp. 113–37

———, ' "A Versifying Maid of Honour": Anne Finch and the Libretto for *Venus and Adonis*', *Review of English Studies*, 59 (2008), pp. 67–85

Wood, Bruce, 'A Coronation Anthem – Lost and Found', *Musical Times*, 118 (1977), pp. 466–8

———, 'Purcell's Odes: A Re-appraisal', in Burden, *Companion*, pp. 200–53

———, and Andrew Pinnock, ' "Unscarr'd by turning times"? The Dating of Purcell's *Dido and Aeneas*', *Early Music*, 20 (1992), pp. 373–90

Zaslaw, Neal, 'The Enigma of the Haute-Contre', *Musical Times*, 115 (1974), pp. 939–41

SCORES, WORDBOOKS, SONGBOOKS, AND INSTRUMENTAL TUTORS

Barnard, John (compiler), *The First Book of Selected Church Musick* (London: Griffin, 1641)

Blow, John, *Amphion Anglicus* (London: the author, 1700)

Carr, John (publ.), *Comes Amoris: or, The Companion of Love . . . The Second Book* (London, 1688)

———, *Vinculum Societatis: or, The Tie of Good Company*, book 2 (London, 1688)

Davenant, William, *The Siege of Rhodes* (London: Herringman, 1656)

Eccles, John, *The Musical Entertainments in the Tragedy of Rinaldo and Armida* (London: Tonson, 1699)

The Fairy-Queen: An Opera Represented at the Queen's-Theatre . . . (London: Tonson, 1692)

Hudgebut, John (publ.), *Thesaurus Musicus . . . The Fourth Book* (London, 1695)

Philomela, or The Vocal Musitian: Being a Collection of the Best and Newest Songs; Especially Those in the Two Operas 'The Prophetess' and 'King Arthur' Written by Mr Dryden: and Set to Musick by Mr. Henry Purcell . . . (London, 1692)

Playford, Henry (publ.), *The Banquet of Music*, book 1 (London, 1687); book 2 (1688); book 3 (1689)

———, *Harmonia Sacra*, book 1 (London, 1688); book 2 (1693)

———, *Musick's Handmaid*, book 2 (London, 1689)

———, *The Theater of Music*, book 4 (London, 1686)

———, *Wit and Mirth: or Pills to Purge Melancholy . . . The Second Part* (London, 1700)

——— and John Carr (publ.), *The Theater of Music*, book 3 (London, 1686)

Playford, John (publ.), *Choice Ayres and Songs*, book 1 (London, 1679); book 3 (1681); book 5 (1684)

———, *The Theater of Music*, book 2 (London, 1685)

The Prophetess: or, The History of Dioclesian, written by Francis Beaumont *and* John Fletcher, *with Alterations and Additions, After the Manner of an Opera . . .* (London: Tonson, 1690)

Purcell, Henry, *Sonatas of Three Parts* (London: J. Playford and Carr, 1683)

————, *A Musical Entertainment Perform'd on November XXII. 1683* . . . (London: J. Playford and Carr, 1684)

Purcell, Henry, *A Pastoral Elegy on the Death of Mr. John Playford* (London: H. Playford, 1687)

————, *New Songs Sung in The Fool's Preferment, or the Three Dukes of Dunstable* (London: Knight and Saunders, 1688)

————, *Vocal and Instrumental Musick of The Prophetess: or, The History of Dioclesian* (London: the author, 1691)

————, *Some Select Songs as They Are Sung in the Fairy Queen* (London: the author, 1692)

————, *The Dialogue in the last Opera, call'd the Fairy Queen* (London: n. publ., c.1692)

————, *The Songs in the Indian Queen* (London: Hudgebut and May, 1695)

————, *Orpheus Britannicus*, book 1 (London: H. Playford, 1698)

————, and John Blow, *Three Elegies upon the Much Lamented Loss of our Late Most Gracious Queen Mary* (London: H. Playford, 1695)

Songs set by Signior Pietro Reggio (London: n. publ., 1680)

Shadwell, Thomas, *Psyche: A Tragedy* (London: Herringman, 1675)

The Tempest, or the Enchanted Island (London: Herringman, 1674; facsimile edn, London: Cornmarket Press, 1969)

SCHOLARLY EDITIONS OF MUSIC

Blow, John, *The glorious day is come*, ed. Maurice Bevan (London: Eulenburg, 1981)

Four Hundred Songs & Dances from the Stuart Masque, ed. Andrew J. Sabol (Providence, RI: Brown University Press, 1978; enlarged 2nd edn, 1982)

Musica Britannica (various editors; London: Stainer & Bell, 1951–)

Purcell, Henry, *A Purcell Anthology: 12 Anthems*, ed. Bruce Wood (Oxford: Oxford University Press, 1995)

Purcell, Henry, Thomas Morley, James Paisible, and Thomas Tollett, *Funeral Music for Queen Mary*, ed. Bruce Wood (London: Novello, 1996)

Purcell Society Edition (various editors; London and Sevenoaks: Novello, 1878–2007; London: Stainer & Bell, 2007–)

Purcell Society Edition, Companion Series (various editors; London: Stainer & Bell, 2007–)

MANUSCRIPT FACSIMILE

The Gostling Manuscript (foreword by Franklin B. Zimmerman) (Austin, TX: University of Texas Press, 1977)

Index

PURCELL, HENRY (*cont.*)